THE FRIEND OF THE FAMILY

THE COLLECTED EDITION OF FYODOR DOSTOEVSKY

Translated from the Russian by CONSTANCE GARNETT

THE BROTHERS KARAMAZOV
THE IDIOT
THE POSSESSED
CRIME AND PUNISHMENT
THE HOUSE OF THE DEAD
THE INSULTED AND INJURED
A RAW YOUTH
THE ETERNAL HUSBAND AND OTHER STORIES
THE GAMBLER AND OTHER STORIES
WHITE NIGHTS AND OTHER STORIES
AN HONEST THIEF AND OTHER STORIES
THE FRIEND OF THE FAMILY

FYODOR DOSTOEVSKY

•

THE
FRIEND OF
THE FAMILY

*Translated from
the Russian by*
CONSTANCE GARNETT

HEINEMANN : LONDON

William Heinemann Ltd
15 Queen Street, Mayfair, London W1X 8BE

LONDON MELBOURNE TORONTO
JOHANNESBURG AUCKLAND

First published 1920
New impression 1949
Reprinted 1951, 1961, 1969, 1974

434 20403 X

Printed Offset Litho and bound in Great Britain
by Cox & Wyman Ltd
London, Fakenham and Reading

CONTENTS

PART I

CHAPTER I

INTRODUCTION

WHEN my uncle, Colonel Yegor Ilyitch Rostanev, left the army, he settled down in Stepantchikovo, which came to him by inheritance, and went on steadily living in it, as though he had been all his life a regular country gentleman who had never left his estates. There are natures that are perfectly satisfied with everyone and can get used to everything; such was precisely the disposition of the retired colonel. It is hard to imagine a man more peaceable and ready to agree to anything. If by some caprice he had been gravely asked to carry some one for a couple of miles on his shoulders he would perhaps have done so. He was so good-natured that he was sometimes ready to give away everything at the first asking, and to share almost his last shirt with anyone who coveted it. He was of heroic proportions; tall and well made, with ruddy cheeks, with teeth white as ivory, with a long brown moustache, with a loud ringing voice, and with a frank hearty laugh; he spoke rapidly and jerkily. He was at the time of my story about forty and had spent his life, almost from his sixteenth year, in the Hussars. He had married very young and was passionately fond of his wife; but she died, leaving in his heart a noble memory that nothing could efface.

When he inherited Stepantchikovo, which increased his fortune to six hundred serfs, he left the army, and, as I have said already, settled in the country together with his children, Ilyusha, a boy of eight, whose birth had cost his mother's life, and Sashenka, a girl of fifteen, who had been brought up at a boarding-school in Moscow. But my uncle's house soon became a regular Noah's Ark. This was how it happened.

Just at the time when he came into the property and retired from the army, his mother, who had, sixteen years before, married a certain General Krahotkin, was left a widow. At the time of her second marriage my uncle was only a cornet, and yet he, too, was thinking of getting married. His mother had for a long time refused her blessing, had shed bitter tears, had reproached him with egoism, with ingratitude, with disrespect. She had proved to him that his estates, amounting to only two hundred and fifty serfs, were, as it was, barely sufficient for the maintenance of his family (that is, for the maintenance of his mamma, with all her retinue of toadies, pug-dogs, Pomeranians, Chinese cats and so on). And, in the midst of these reproaches, protests and shrill upbraidings, she all at once quite unexpectedly got married herself before her son, though she was forty-two years of age. Even in this, however, she found an excuse for blaming my poor uncle, declaring that she was getting married solely to secure in her old age the refuge denied her by the undutiful egoist, her son, who was contemplating the unpardonable insolence of making a home of his own.

I never could find out what really induced a man apparently so reasonable as the deceased General Krahotkin to marry a widow of forty-two. It must be supposed that he suspected she had money. Other people thought that he only wanted a nurse, as he had already had a foretaste of the swarm of diseases which assailed him in his old age. One thing is certain, the general never had the faintest respect for his wife at any time during his married life, and he ridiculed her sarcastically at every favourable opportunity. He was a strange person. Half educated and extremely shrewd, he had a lively contempt for all and everyone; he had no principles of any sort; laughed at everything and everybody, and in his old age, through the infirmities that were the consequence of his irregular and immoral life, he became spiteful, irritable and merciless. He had been a successful officer; yet he had been forced, through "an unpleasant incident", to resign his commission, losing his pension and only just escaping prosecution. This had completely soured his temper. Left almost without means, with no fortune but a hundred ruined serfs, he folded his hands and never during the remaining twelve years of his life troubled himself to inquire what he was living on and who was supporting him. At the same time he insisted on having all the comforts of life, kept his carriage and refused to curtail his expenses. Soon after his marriage he lost the use of his legs and spent the last ten years of his life in an invalid chair wheeled about by two seven-foot flunkeys, who never heard anything from him but abuse of the most varied kind. The carriage, the flunkeys and the invalid chair were paid for by the undutiful son, who sent his mother his last farthing, mortgaged and re-mortgaged his estate, denied himself necessaries, and incurred debts almost impossible for him to pay in his circumstances at the time; and yet the charge of being an egoist and an undutiful son was persistently laid at his door. But my uncle's character was such that at last he quite believed himself that he was an egoist, and therefore, to punish himself and to avoid being an egoist, he kept sending them more and more money. His mother stood in awe of her husband; but what pleased her most was that he was a general, and that through him she was "Madame la Générale"

She had her own apartments in the house, where, during the whole period of her husband's semi-existence, she queened it in a society made up of toadies, lapdogs, and the gossips of the town. She was an important person in her little town. Gossip, invitations to stand godmother at christenings and to give the bride away at weddings, a halfpenny rubber, and the respect shown her in all sorts of ways as the wife of a general fully made up to her for the drawbacks of her home life. All the magpies of the town came to her with their reports, the first place everywhere was always hers—in fact, she got out of her position all she could get out of it. The general did not meddle in all that; but before people he laughed mercilessly at his wife, asked himself, for instance, such questions as why he had married "such a dowdy", and nobody dared contradict him. Little by little all his acquaintances left him, and at the same time society was essential to him; he loved chatting, arguing; he liked to have a listener always sitting beside him. He was a free-thinker and atheist of the old school, and so liked to hold forth on lofty subjects.

But the listeners of the town of N—— had no partiality for lofty subjects, and they became fewer and fewer. They tried to get up a game of whist in the household; but as a rule the game ended in outbreaks on the part of the general, which so terrified his wife and her companions that they put up candles before the ikons, had a service sung, divined the future with beans and with cards, distributed rolls among the prisoners, and looked forward in a tremor to the after-dinner hour when they would have to take a hand at whist again and at every mistake to endure shouts, screams, oaths and almost blows. The general did not stand on ceremony with anybody when something was not to his taste; he screamed like a peasant woman, swore like a coachman, sometimes tore up the cards, threw them about the floor, drove away his partners, and even shed tears of anger and vexation—and for no more than a

3

knave's having been played instead of a nine. At last, as his eyesight was failing, they had to get him a reader; it was then that Foma Fomitch Opiskin appeared on the scene.

I must confess I announce this new personage with a certain solemnity. There is no denying that he is one of the principal characters in my story. How far he has a claim on the attention of the reader I will not explain; the reader can answer that question more suitably and more readily himself.

Foma Fomitch entered General Krahotkin's household as a paid companion—neither more nor less. Where he turned up from is shrouded in the mists of obscurity. I have, however, made special researches and have found out something of the past circumstances of this remarkable man. He was said in the first place to have been sometime and somewhere in the government service, and somewhere or other to have suffered, I need hardly say, "for a good cause". It was said, too, that at some time he had been engaged in literary pursuits in Moscow. There is nothing surprising in that; Foma Fomitch's crass ignorance would, of course, be no hindrance to him in a literary career. But all that is known for certain is that he did not succeed in anything, and that at last he was forced to enter the general's service in the capacity of reader and martyr. There was no ignominy which he had not to endure in return for eating the general's bread. It is true that in later years, when on the general's death he found himself a person of importance and consequence, he more than once assured us all that his consenting to be treated as a buffoon was an act of magnanimous self-sacrifice on the altar of friendship; that the general had been his benefactor; that the deceased had been a great man misunderstood, who only to him, Foma, had confided the inmost secrets of his soul; that in fact, if he, Foma, had actually at the general's urgent desire played the part of various wild beasts and posed in grotesque attitudes, this had been solely in order to entertain and distract a suffering friend shattered by disease. But Foma Fomitch's assurances and explanations on this score can only be accepted with considerable hesitation; and yet this same Foma Fomitch, even at the time when he was a buffoon, was playing a very different part in the ladies' apartments of the general's house. How he managed this, it is difficult for anyone not a specialist in such matters to conceive. The general's lady cherished a sort of mysterious reverence for him—why? There is no telling. By degrees he acquired over the whole feminine half of the general's household a marvellous

4

influence, to some extent comparable to the influence exercised by the Ivan Yakovlevitches and such-like seers and prophets, who are visited in madhouses by certain ladies who devote themselves to the study of their ravings. He read aloud to them works of spiritual edification; held forth with eloquent tears on the Christian virtues; told stories of his life and his heroic doings; went to mass, and even to matins; at times foretold the future; had a peculiar faculty for interpreting dreams, and was a great hand at throwing blame on his neighbours. The general had a notion of what was going on in the back rooms, and tyrannised over his dependent more mercilessly than ever. But Foma's martyrdom only increased his prestige in the eyes of Madame la Générale and the other females of the household.

At last everything was transformed. The general died. His death was rather original. The former free-thinker and atheist became terror-stricken beyond all belief. He shed tears, repented, had ikons put up, sent for priests. Services were sung, and extreme unction was administered. The poor fellow screamed that he did not want to die, and even asked Foma Fomitch's forgiveness with tears. This latter circumstance was an asset of some value to Foma Fomitch later on. Just before the parting of the general's soul from the general's body, however, the following incident took place. The daughter of Madame la Générale by her first marriage, my maiden aunt, Praskovya Ilyinitchna, who always lived in the general's house, and was one of his favourite victims, quite indispensable to him during the ten years that he was bedridden, always at his beck and call, and with her meek and simple-hearted mildness the one person who could satisfy him, went up to his bedside shedding bitter tears, and would have smoothed the pillow under the head of the sufferer; but the sufferer still had strength to clutch at her hair and pull it violently three times, almost foaming at the mouth with spite. Ten minutes later he died. They had sent word to the colonel, though Madame la Générale had declared that she did not want to see him and would sooner die than set eyes on him at such a moment. There was a magnificent funeral at the expense, of course, of the undutiful son on whom the widowed mother did not wish to set her eyes.

In the ruined property of Knyazevka, which belonged to several different owners and in which the general had his hundred serfs, there stands a mausoleum of white marble, diversified with laudatory inscriptions to the glory of the intellect, talents, nobility of soul, orders of merit and rank of the deceased. Foma Fomitch took a prominent part in the composition of these eulogies. Madame la Générale persisted for a long time in keeping up her dignity and refusing to forgive her disobedient son. Sobbing and making a great outcry, surrounded by her crowd of toadies and pug-dogs, she kept declaring that she would sooner live on dry bread and I need hardly say "soak it in her tears", that she would sooner go stick in hand to beg alms under the windows than yield to the request of her "disobedient" son that she should come and live with him at Stepantchikovo, and that she would never, never set foot within his house! As a rule the word foot in this connection is uttered with peculiar effect by ladies. Madame la Générale's utterance of the word was masterly, artistic. . . . In short, the amount of eloquence that was expended was incredible. It must be observed that at the very time of these shrill protests they were by degrees packing up to move to Stepantchikovo. The colonel knocked up all his horses driving almost every day thirty miles from Stepantchikovo to the town, and it was not till a fortnight after the general's funeral that he received permission to appear before the eyes of his aggrieved parent. Foma Fomitch was employed as go-between. During the whole of that fortnight he was reproaching the disobedient son and putting him to shame for his "inhuman" conduct, reducing him to genuine tears, almost to despair. It is from this time that the incomprehensible, inhumanly despotic domination of Foma Fomitch over my poor uncle dates. Foma perceived the kind of man he had to deal with, and felt at once that his days of playing the buffoon were over, and that in the wilds even Foma might pass for a nobleman. And he certainly made up for lost time.

"What will you feel like," said Foma, "if your own mother, the authoress, so to speak, of your days, should take a stick and, leaning on it with trembling hands wasted with hunger, should actually begin to beg for alms under people's windows? Would it not be monstrous, considering her rank as a general's lady and the virtues of her character? What would you feel like if she should suddenly come, by mistake, of course—but you know it might happen—and should stretch out her hand under your windows, while you, her own son, are perhaps at that very moment nestling in a feather bed, and . . . in fact, in luxury? It's awful, awful! But what is most awful of all— allow me to speak candidly, Colonel—what is most awful of all is the fact that you are standing before me now like an unfeeling post, with your mouth open and your eyes blinking, so that it is a positive disgrace, while you ought to be ready at the mere thought of such a thing to tear your hair out by the roots and to shed streams—what am I saying?—rivers, lakes, seas, oceans of tears. . . ."

In short, Foma in his excessive warmth grew almost incoherent. But such was the invariable outcome of his eloquence. It ended, of course, in Madame la Générale together with her female dependents and lapdogs, with Foma Fomitch and with Mademoiselle Perepelitsyn, her chief favourite, at last honouring Stepantchikovo by her presence. She said that she would merely make the *experiment* of living at her son's till she had tested his dutifulness. You can imagine the colonel's position while his dutifulness was being tested! At first, as a widow recently bereaved, Madame la Générale thought it her duty two or three times a week to be overcome by despair at the thought of her general, never to return; and punctually on each occasion the colonel for some unknown reason came in for a wigging. Sometimes, especially if visitors were present, Madame la Générale would send for her grandchildren, little Ilyusha and fifteen-year-old Sashenka, and making them sit down beside her would fix upon them a prolonged, melancholy, anguished gaze, as upon children ruined in the hands of *such a father;* she would heave deep, painful sighs, and finally melt into mute mysterious tears, for at least a full hour. Woe betide the colonel if he failed to grasp the significance of those tears! And, poor fellow, he hardly ever succeeded in grasping their significance, and in the simplicity of his heart almost always put in an appearance at such tearful moments, and whether he liked it or not came in for a severe heckling. But his filial respect in no way decreased and reached at last an extreme limit. In short, both Madame la Générale and Foma Fomitch were fully conscious that the storm which had for so many years menaced them in the presence of General Krahotkin had passed away and would never return. Madame la Générale used at times to fall on her sofa in a swoon. A great fuss and commotion arose. The colonel was crushed, and trembled like a leaf.

"Cruel son!" Madame la Générale would shriek as she came to. "You have lacerated my inmost being . . . *mes entrailles, mes entrailles!*"

"But how have I lacerated your inmost being, mamma?" the colonel would protest timidly.

7

"You have lacerated it, lacerated it! He justifies himself, too. He is rude. Cruel son! I am dying! . . ."

The colonel was, of course, annihilated. But it somehow happened that Madame la Générale always revived again. Half an hour later he would be taking someone by the button-hole and saying—

"Oh, well, my dear fellow, you see she is a *grande dame*, the wife of a general. She is the kindest-hearted old lady; she is accustomed to all this refined . . . She is on a different level from a blockhead like me! Now she is angry with me. No doubt I am to blame. My dear fellow, I don't know yet what I've done, but no doubt it's my fault. . . ."

It would happen that Mademoiselle Perepelitsyn, an old maid in a shawl, with no eyebrows, with little rapacious eyes, with lips thin as a thread, with hands washed in cucumber water, and with a spite against the whole universe, would feel it her duty to read the colonel a lecture.

"It's all through your being undutiful, sir; it's all through your being an egoist, sir; through your wounding your mamma, sir—she's not used to such treatment. She's a general's lady, and you are only a colonel, sir."

"That is Mademoiselle Perepelitsyn, my dear fellow," the colonel would observe to his listener; "an excellent lady, she stands up for my mother like a rock! A very rare person! You mustn't imagine that she is in a menial position; she is the daughter of a major herself! Yes, indeed."

But, of course, this was only the prelude. The great lady who could carry out such a variety of performances in her turn trembled like a mouse in the presence of her former dependent. Foma Fomitch had completely bewitched her. She could not make enough of him and she saw with his eyes and heard with his ears. A cousin of mine, also a retired hussar, a man still young, though he had been an incredible spendthrift, told me bluntly and simply that it was his firm conviction, after staying for a time at my uncle's, that Madame la Générale was on terms of improper intimacy with Foma Fomitch. I need hardly say that at the time I rejected this supposition with indignation as too coarse and simple. No, it was something different, and that something different I cannot explain without first explaining to the reader the character of Foma Fomitch as I understood it later.

Imagine the most insignificant, the most cowardly creature, an outcast from society, of no service to anyone, utterly use-

8

less, utterly disgusting, but incredibly vain, though entirely destitute of any talent by which he might have justified his morbidly sensitive vanity. I hasten to add that Foma Fomitch was the incarnation of unbounded vanity, but that at the same time it was a special kind of vanity—that is, the vanity found in a complete nonentity, and, as is usual in such cases, a vanity mortified and oppressed by grievous failures in the past; a vanity that has begun rankling long, long ago, and ever since has given off envy and venom, at every encounter, at every success of anyone else. I need hardly say that all this was seasoned with the most unseemly touchiness, the most insane suspiciousness. It may be asked, how is one to account for such vanity? How does it arise, in spite of complete insignificance, in pitiful creatures who are forced by their social position to know their place? How answer such a question? Who knows, perhaps, there are exceptions, of whom my hero is one? He certainly is an exception to the rule, as will be explained later. But allow me to ask: are you certain that those who are completely resigned to be your buffoons, your parasites and your toadies, and consider it an honour and a happiness to be so, are you certain that they are quite devoid of vanity and envy? What of the slander and backbiting and tale-bearing and mysterious whisperings in back corners, somewhere aside and at your table? Who knows, perhaps, in some of these degraded victims of fate, your fools and buffoons, vanity far from being dispelled by humiliation is even aggravated by that very humiliation, by being a fool and buffoon, by eating the bread of dependence and being for ever forced to submission and self-suppression? Who knows, maybe, this ugly exaggerated vanity is only a false fundamentally depraved sense of personal dignity, first outraged, perhaps, in childhood by oppression, poverty, filth, spat upon, perhaps, in the person of the future outcast's parents before his eyes? But I have said that Foma Fomitch was also an exception to the general rule; that is true. He had at one time been a literary man slighted and unrecognised, and literature is capable of ruining men very different from Foma Fomitch—I mean, of course, when it is not crowned with success. I don't know, but it may be assumed that Foma Fomitch had been unsuccessful before entering on a literary career; possibly in some other calling, too, he had received more kicks than halfpence, or possibly something worse. About that, however, I cannot say; but I made inquiries later on, and I know for certain that Foma Fomitch composed,

9

at some time in Moscow, a romance very much like those that were published every year by dozens in the 'thirties, after the style of *The Deliverance of Moscow, The Chieftains of the Tempest, Sons of Love, or the Russians in* 1104—novels which in their day afforded an agreeable butt for the wit of Baron Brambeus. That was, of course, long ago; but the serpent of literary vanity sometimes leaves a deep and incurable sting, especially in insignificant and dull-witted persons. Foma Fomitch had been disappointed from his first step in a literary career, and it was then that he was finally enrolled in the vast army of the disappointed, from which all the crazy saints, hermits and wandering pilgrims come later on. I think that his monstrous boastfulness, his thirst for praise and distinction, for admiration and homage, dates from the same period. Even when he was a buffoon he got together a group of idiots to do homage to him. Somewhere and somehow to stand first, to be an oracle, to swagger and give himself airs—that was his most urgent craving! As others did not praise him he began to praise himself. I have myself in my uncle's house at Stepantchikovo heard Foma's sayings after he had become the absolute monarch and oracle of the household. "I am not in my proper place among you," he would say sometimes with mysterious impressiveness. "I am not in my proper place here. I will look round, I will settle you all, I will show you, I will direct you, and then good-bye; to Moscow to edit a review! Thirty thousand people will assemble every month to hear my lectures. My name will be famous at last, and then—woe to my enemies."

But while waiting to become famous the genius insisted upon immediate recognition in substantial form. It is always pleasant to receive payment in advance, and in this case it was particularly so. I know that he seriously assured my uncle that some great work lay before him, Foma, in the future—a work for which he had been summoned into the world, and to the accomplishment of this work he was urged by some sort of person with wings, who visited him at night, or something of that kind. This great work was to write a book full of profound wisdom in the soul-saving line, which would set the whole world agog and stagger all Russia. And when all Russia was staggered, he, Foma, disdaining glory, would retire into a monastery, and in the catacombs of Kiev would pray day and night for the happiness of the Fatherland. All this imposed upon my uncle.

Well, now imagine what this Foma, who had been all his life oppressed and crushed, perhaps actually beaten too, who was vain and secretly lascivious, who had been disappointed in his literary ambitions, who had played the buffoon for a crust of bread, who was at heart a despot in spite of all his previous abjectness and impotence, who was a braggart, and insolent when successful, might become when he suddenly found himself in the haven he had reached after so many ups and downs, honoured and glorified, humoured and flattered, thanks to a patroness who was an idiot and a patron who was imposed upon and ready to agree to anything. I must, of course, explain my uncle's character more fully, or Foma Fomitch's success cannot be understood. But for the moment I will say that Foma was a complete illustration of the saying, "Let him sit down to the table and he will put his feet on it." He paid us out for his past! A base soul escaping from oppression becomes an oppressor. Foma had been oppressed, and he had at once a craving to oppress others; he had been the victim of whims and caprices and now he imposed his own whims and caprices on others. He had been the butt of others, and now he surrounded himself with creatures whom he could turn into derision. His boasting was ridiculous; the airs he gave himself were incredible; nothing was good enough for him; his tyranny was beyond all bounds, and it reached such a pitch that simple-hearted people who had not witnessed his manœuvres, but only heard queer stories about him, looked upon all this as a miracle, as the work of the devil, crossed themselves and spat.

I was speaking of my uncle. Without explaining his remarkable character (I repeat) it is, of course, impossible to understand Foma Fomitch's insolent domination in another man's house; it is impossible to understand the metamorphosis of the cringing dependent into the great man. Besides being kind-hearted in the extreme, my uncle was a man of the most refined delicacy in spite of a somewhat rough exterior, of the greatest generosity and of proved courage. I boldly say of "courage"; nothing could have prevented him from fulfilling an obligation, from doing his duty—in such cases no obstacle would have dismayed him. His soul was as pure as a child's. He was a perfect child at forty, open-hearted in the extreme, always good-humoured, imagining everybody an angel, blaming himself for other people's shortcomings, and exaggerating the good qualities of others, even pre-supposing them where they could not possibly exist. He was one of those very generous and pure-hearted men who are positively ashamed to assume any harm of another, are always in haste to endow their neighbours with every virtue, rejoice at other people's success, and in that way always live in an ideal world, and when anything goes wrong always blame themselves first. To sacrifice themselves in the interests of others is their natural vocation. Some people would have called him cowardly, weak-willed and feeble. Of course he was weak, and indeed he was of too soft a disposition; but it was not from lack of will, but from the fear of wounding, of behaving cruelly, from excess of respect for others and for mankind in general. He was, however, weak-willed and cowardly only when nothing was at stake but his own interests, which he completely disregarded, and for this he was continually an object of derision, and often with the very people for whom he was sacrificing his own advantage. He never believed, however, that he had enemies; he had them, indeed, but he somehow failed to observe them. He dreaded fuss and disturbance in the house like fire, and immediately gave way to anyone and submitted to anything. He gave in through a sort of shy good nature, from a sort of shy delicacy. "So be it," he would say, quickly brushing aside all reproaches for his indulgence and weakness; "so be it . . . that everyone may be happy and contented!" I need hardly say that he was ready to submit to every honourable influence. What is more, an adroit rogue might have gained complete control over him, and even have lured him on to do wrong, of course misrepresenting the wrong action as a right one. My uncle very readily put faith in other people, and was often far from right in doing so. When, after many sufferings, he brought himself at last to believe that the man who deceived him was dishonest, he always blamed himself first—and sometimes blamed himself only. Now imagine, suddenly queening it in his quiet home, a capricious, doting, idiot woman—inseparable from another idiot, her idol—a woman who had only feared her general, and was now afraid of nothing, and impelled by a craving to make up to herself for what she had suffered in the past; and this idiot woman my uncle thought it his duty to revere, simply because she was his mother. They began with proving to my uncle at once that he was coarse, impatient, ignorant and selfish to the utmost degree. The remarkable thing is that the idiotic old lady herself believed in what she professed. And I believe that Foma Fomitch did also, at least to some extent. They persuaded my uncle, too, that Foma had been sent from heaven

by Divine Providence for the salvation of his soul and the sub-
duing of his unbridled passions; that he was haughty, proud of
his wealth, and quite capable of reproaching Foma Fomitch
for eating his bread. My poor uncle was very soon convinced
of the depth of his degradation, was ready to tear his hair and
to beg forgiveness. . . .

"It's all my own fault, brother," he would say sometimes to
one of the people he used to talk to. "It's all my fault! One
ought to be doubly delicate with a man who is under obligations
to one. . . . I mean that I . . . Under obligations, indeed!
I am talking nonsense again! He is not under obligations to
me at all: on the contrary, it is I who am under an obligation to
him for living with me! And here I have reproached him for
eating my bread! . . . Not that I did reproach him, but it
seems I made some slip of the tongue—I often do make such
slips. . . . And, after all, the man has suffered, he has done
great things; for ten years in spite of insulting treatment he was
tending his sick friend! And then his learning. . . . He's a
writer! A highly educated man! A very lofty character; in
short . . ."

The conception of the highly educated and unfortunate Foma
ignominiously treated by the cruel and capricious general rent
my uncle's heart with compassion and indignation. All Foma's
peculiarities, all his ignoble doings my uncle at once ascribed to
his sufferings, the humiliations he had endured in the past, and
the bitterness left by them. . . . He at once decided in his soft
and generous heart that one could not be so exacting with a man
who had suffered as with an ordinary person; that one must not
only forgive him, but more than that, one must, by gentle treatment, heal his wounds, restore him and reconcile him with
humanity. Setting this object before him he was completely
fired by it, and lost all power of perceiving that his new friend
was a lascivious and capricious animal, an egoist, a sluggard, a
lazy drone—and nothing more. He put implicit faith in Foma's
genius and learning. I forgot to mention that my uncle had
the most naïve and disinterested reverence for the words
"learning" and "literature", though he had himself never
studied anything. This was one of his chief and most guileless
peculiarities.

"He is writing," he would whisper, walking on tiptoe,
though he was two rooms away from Foma's study. "I don't
know precisely what he is writing," he added, with a proud and
mysterious air, "but no doubt he is brewing something,

brother. . . . I mean in the best sense, of course; it would be clear to some people, but to you and me, brother, it would be just a jumble that . . . I fancy he is writing of productive forces of some sort—he said so himself. I suppose that has something to do with politics. Yes, his name will be famous! Then we shall be famous through him. He told me that himself, brother. . . ."

I know for a fact that my uncle was forced by Foma's orders to shave off his beautiful fair whiskers. Foma considered that these whiskers made my uncle look like a Frenchman, and that wearing them showed a lack of patriotism. Little by little Foma began meddling in the management of the estate, and giving sage counsels on the subject. These sage counsels were terrible. The peasants soon saw the position and understood who was their real master, and scratched their heads uneasily. Later on I overheard Foma talking to the peasants; I must confess I listened. Foma had told us before that he was fond of talking to intelligent Russian peasants. So one day he went to the threshing floor: after talking to the peasants about the farm-work, though he could not tell oats from wheat, after sweetly dwelling on the sacred obligations of the peasant to his master, after touching lightly on electricity and the division of labour, subjects of which I need hardly say he knew nothing, after explaining to his listeners how the earth went round the sun, and being at last quite touched by his own eloquence—he began talking about the ministers. I understood. Pushkin used to tell a story of a father who impressed upon his little boy of four that he, his papa, was so brave "that the Tsar loves Papa. . . ." So evidently this papa needed this listener of four years old! And the peasants always listened to Foma Fomitch with cringing respect.

"And did you get a large salary from royalty, little father?" a grey-headed old man called Arhip Korotky asked suddenly from the crowd of peasants, with the evident intention of being flattering; but the question struck Foma Fomitch as familiar, and he could not endure familiarity.

"And what business is that of yours, you lout?" he answered, looking contemptuously at the poor peasant. "Why are you thrusting forward your pug-face? Do you want me to spit in it?"

Foma Fomitch always talked in that tone to the "intelligent Russian peasant".

"You are our father," another peasant interposed; "you

14

know we are ignorant people. You may be a major or a colonel or even your Excellency, we don't know how we ought to speak to you."

"You lout!" repeated Foma Fomitch, mollified however. "There are salaries and salaries, you blockhead! One will get nothing, though he is a general—because he does nothing to deserve it, he is of no service to the Tsar. But I got twenty thousand when I was serving in the Ministry, and I did not take it, I served for the honour of it. I had plenty of money of my own. I gave my salary to the cause of public enlightenment, and to aid those whose homes have been burnt in Kazan."

"I say! So it was you who rebuilt Kazan, little father?" the amazed peasant went on.

The peasants wondered at Foma Fomitch as a rule.

"Oh, well, I had my share in it," Foma answered, with a show of reluctance, as though vexed with himself for deigning to converse on *such* a subject with *such* a person.

His conversations with my uncle were of a different stamp.

"What were you in the past?" Foma would say, for instance, lolling after an ample dinner in an easy-chair, while a servant stood behind him brandishing a fresh lime branch to keep off the flies. "What were you like before I came? But now I have dropped into your soul a spark of that heavenly fire which is glowing there now. Did I drop a spark of heavenly fire into your soul or not? Answer. Did I drop a spark or did I not?"

Foma Fomitch, indeed, could not himself have said why he asked such a question. But my uncle's silence and confusion at once spurred him on. He who had been so patient and down-trodden in the past now exploded like gunpowder at the slightest provocation. My uncle's silence seemed to him insulting, and he now insisted on an answer.

"Answer: is the spark glowing in you or not?"

My uncle hesitated, shrank into himself, and did not know what line to take.

"Allow me to observe that I am waiting," said Foma in an aggrieved voice.

"*Mais, répondez donc*, Yegorushka," put in Madame la Générale, shrugging her shoulders.

"I am asking you, is that spark burning within you or not?" Foma repeated condescendingly, taking a sweetmeat out of a bonbon box, which always stood on a table before him by Madame la Générale's orders.

"I really don't know, Foma," my uncle answered at last with despair in his eyes. "Something of the sort, no doubt. . . . You really had better not ask or I am sure to say something wrong. . . ."

"Oh, very well! So you look upon me as so insignificant as not to deserve an answer—that's what you meant to say. But so be it; let me be a nonentity."

"Oh, no, Foma, God bless you! Why, when did I imply that?"

"Yes, that's just what you did mean to say."

"I swear I didn't."

"Oh, very well, then, I lie. So then you charge me with trying to pick a quarrel on purpose; it's another insult added to all the past, but I will put up with this, too. . . ."

"*Mais, mon fils!*" cried Madame la Générale in alarm.

"Foma Fomitch! Mamma!" exclaimed my uncle in despair. "Upon my word it's not my fault. Perhaps I may have let slip such a thing without knowing it. . . . You mustn't mind me, Foma; I am stupid, you know; I feel I am stupid myself; I feel there is something amiss with me. . . . I know, Foma, I know! You need not say anything," he went on, waving his hand. "I have lived forty years, and until now, until I knew you, I thought I was all right . . . like everyone else. And I didn't notice before that I was as sinful as a goat, an egoist of the worst description, and I've done such a lot of mischief that it is a wonder the world puts up with me."

"Yes, you certainly are an egoist," observed Foma, with conviction.

"Well, I realise myself that I am an egoist now! Yes, that's the end of it! I'll correct myself and be better!"

"God grant you may!" concluded Foma Fomitch, and sighing piously he got up from his arm-chair to go to his room for an after-dinner nap. Foma Fomitch always dozed after dinner.

To conclude this chapter, may I be allowed to say something about my personal relations with my uncle, and to explain how I came to be face to face with Foma Fomitch, and with no thought or suspicion suddenly found myself in a vortex of the most important incidents that had ever happened in the blessed village of Stepantchikovo? With this I intend to conclude my introduction and to proceed straight with my story.

In my childhood, when I was left an orphan and alone in the world, my uncle took the place of a father to me; educated me at his expense, and did for me more than many a father does

16

for his own child. From the first day he took me into his house I grew warmly attached to him. I was ten years old at the time, and I remember that we got on capitally, and thoroughly understood each other. We spun tops together, and together stole her cap from a very disagreeable old lady, who was a relation of both of us. I promptly tied the cap to the tail of a paper kite and sent it flying to the clouds. Many years afterwards I saw something of my uncle for a short time in Petersburg, where I was finishing my studies at his expense. During that time I became attached to him with all the warmth of youth: something generous, mild, truthful, light-hearted and naïve to the utmost degree struck me in his character and attracted everyone. When I left the university I spent some time in Petersburg with nothing to do for the time, and, as is often the case with callow youths, was convinced that in a very short time I should do much that was very interesting and even great. I did not want to leave Petersburg. I wrote to my uncle at rather rare intervals and only when I wanted money, which he never refused me. Meanwhile, I heard from a house serf of my uncle's, who came to Petersburg on some business or other, that marvellous things were taking place at Stepantchikovo. These first rumours interested and surprised me. I began writing to my uncle more regularly. He always answered me somewhat obscurely and strangely, and in every letter seemed trying to talk of nothing but learned subjects, expressing great expectations of me in the future in a literary and scientific line, and pride in my future achievements. At last, after a rather long silence, I received a surprising letter from him, utterly unlike all his previous letters. It was full of such strange hints, such rambling and contradictory statements that at first I could make nothing of it. All that one could see was that the writer was in great perturbation. One thing was clear in the letter: my uncle gravely, earnestly, almost imploringly urged me as soon as possible to marry his former ward, the daughter of a very poor provincial government clerk, called Yezhevikin. This girl had received an excellent education at a school in Moscow at my uncle's expense, and was now the governess of his children. He wrote that she was unhappy, that I might make her happy, that I should, in fact, be doing a noble action. He appealed to the generosity of my heart, and promised to give her a dowry. Of the dowry, however, he spoke somewhat mysteriously, timidly, and he concluded the letter by beseeching me to keep all this a dead secret. This letter made such an impression on me that my head began to go round. And, indeed, what raw young man would not have been affected by such a proposition, if only on its romantic side? Besides, I had heard that this young governess was extremely pretty. Yet I did not know what to decide, though I wrote to my uncle that I would set off for Stepantchikovo immediately. My uncle had sent me the money for the journey with the letter. Nevertheless, I lingered another three weeks in Petersburg, hesitating and somewhat uneasy.

All at once I happened to meet an old comrade of my uncle's, who had stayed at Stepantchikovo on his way back from the Caucasus to Petersburg. He was an elderly and judicious person, an inveterate bachelor. He told me with indignation about Foma Fomitch, and thereupon informed me of one circumstance of which I had no idea till then: namely, that Foma Fomitch and Madame la Générale had taken up a notion, and were set upon the idea of marrying my uncle to a very strange lady, not in her first youth and scarcely more than half-witted, with an extraordinary history, and almost half a million of dowry; that Madame la Générale had nearly succeeded in convincing this lady that they were relations, and so alluring her into the house; that my uncle, of course, was in despair, but would probably end by marrying the half million of dowry; and that, finally, these two wiseacres, Madame la Générale and Foma Fomitch, were making a terrible onslaught on the poor defenceless governess, and were doing their utmost to turn her out of the house, apparently afraid that my uncle might fall in love with her, or perhaps knowing that he was already in love with her. These last words impressed me. However, to all my further questions as to whether my uncle really was or was not in love with her, my informant either could not or would not give me an exact answer, and indeed he told his whole story briefly, as it were reluctantly, and noticeably avoided detailed explanations. I thought it over; the news was so strangely contradictory of my uncle's letter and his proposition! . . . But it was useless to delay. I decided to go to Stepantchikovo, hoping not only to comfort my uncle and bring him to reason, but even to save him; that is, if possible, to turn Foma out, to prevent the hateful marriage with the old maid, and finally—as I had come to the conclusion that my uncle's love was only a spiteful invention of Foma's—to rejoice the unhappy but of course interesting young lady by the offer of my hand, and so on and so on. By degrees I so worked myself up that, being young and having nothing to do, I passed from hesitation to the opposite extreme; I began burning with the desire to perform all sorts of great and wonderful deeds as quickly as possible. I even fancied that I was displaying extraordinary generosity by nobly sacrificing myself to secure the happiness of a charming and innocent creature; in fact, I remember that I was exceedingly well satisfied with myself during the whole of my journey. It was July, the sun was shining brightly, all around me stretched a vast expanse of fields full of unripe corn. . . . I had so long sat bottled up in Petersburg that I felt as though I were only now looking at God's world!

CHAPTER II

MR. BAHTCHEYEV

I WAS approaching my destination. Driving through the little town of B——, from which I had only eight miles farther to Stepantchikovo, I was obliged to stop at the blacksmith's near the town gate, as the tyre of the front wheel of my chaise broke. To repair it in some way well enough to stand the remaining eight miles was a job that should not take very long, and so I made up my mind not to go elsewhere, but to remain at the blacksmith's while he set it right. As I got out of the chaise I saw a stout gentleman who, like me, had been compelled to stop to have his carriage repaired. He had been standing a whole hour in the insufferable heat, shouting and swearing, and with fretful impatience urging on the blacksmiths who were busy about his fine carriage. At first sight this angry gentleman struck me as extremely peevish. He was about five-and-forty, of middle height, very stout, and pockmarked; his stoutness, his double chin and his puffy, pendant cheeks testified to the blissful existence of a landowner. There was something feminine about his whole figure which at once caught the eye. He was dressed in loose, comfortable, neat clothes which were, however, quite unfashionable.

I cannot imagine why he was annoyed with me, since he saw me for the first time in his life, and had not yet spoken a single word to me. I noticed the fact from the extraordinarily furious looks he turned upon me as soon as I got out of the carriage. Yet I felt a great inclination to make his acquaintance. From the chatter of his servants, I gathered that he had just come from Stepantchikovo, from my uncle's, and so it was an opportunity for making full inquiries about many things. I was just taking off my cap and trying as agreeably as possible to observe how unpleasant these delays on the road sometimes were; but the fat gentleman, as it were reluctantly, scanned me from head to boots with a displeased and ill-humoured stare, muttered something to himself and turned heavily his full back view to me. This aspect of his person, however interesting to the observer, held out no hopes of agreeable conversation.

"Grishka! Don't grumble to yourself! I'll thrash you! . . ." he shouted suddenly to his valet, as though he had not heard what I said about delays on the journey.

This Grishka was a grey-headed, old-fashioned servant dressed in a long-skirted coat and wearing very long grey whiskers. Judging from certain signs, he too was in a very bad humour, and was grumbling morosely to himself. An explanation immediately followed between the master and the servant.

"You'll thrash me! Bawl a little louder!" muttered Grishka, as though to himself, but so loudly that everybody heard it; and with indignation he turned away to adjust something in the carriage.

"What? What did you say? 'Bawl a little louder. . . .' So you are pleased to be impudent!" shouted the fat man, turning purple.

"What on earth are you nagging at me for? One can't say a word!"

"Why nag at you? Do you hear that? He grumbles at me and I am not to nag at him!"

"Why, what should I grumble at?"

"What should you grumble at . . . you're grumbling, right enough! I know what you are grumbling about; my having come away from the dinner—that's what it is."

"What's that to me! You can have no dinner at all for all I care. I am not grumbling at you; I simply said a word to the blacksmiths."

"The blacksmiths. . . . Why grumble at the blacksmiths?"

"I did not grumble at them, I grumbled at the carriage."

"And why grumble at the carriage?"

"What did it break down for? It mustn't do it again."

"The carriage. . . . No, you are grumbling at me, and not at the carriage. It's his own fault and he swears at other people!"

"Why on earth do you keep on at me, sir? Leave off, please!"

"Why have you been sitting like an owl all the way, not saying a word to me, eh? You are ready enough to talk at other times!"

"A fly was buzzing round my mouth, that's why I didn't talk and sat like an owl. Why, am I to tell you fairy tales, or what? Take Malanya the storyteller with you if you are fond of fairy tales."

The fat man opened his mouth to reply, but apparently could think of nothing and held his peace. The servant, proud of his skill in argument and his influence over his master displayed before witnesses, turned to the workmen with redoubled dignity and began showing them something.

My efforts to make acquaintance were fruitless, and my own awkwardness did not help matters. I was assisted, however, by an unexpected incident. A sleepy, unwashed and unkempt countenance suddenly peeped out of the window of a closed carriage which had stood from time immemorial without wheels in the blacksmith's yard, daily though vainly expecting to be repaired. At the appearance of this countenance there was a general outburst of laughter from the workmen. The joke was that the man peeping out of the dismantled carriage was locked in and could not get out. Having fallen asleep in it drunk, he was now vainly begging for freedom; at last he began begging someone to run for his tool. All this immensely entertained the spectators.

There are persons who derive peculiar delight and entertainment from strange things. The antics of a drunken peasant, a man stumbling and falling down in the street, a wrangle between two women and other such incidents arouse at times in some people the most good-humoured and unaccountable delight. The fat gentleman belonged precisely to that class. Little by little his countenance from being sullen and menacing began to look pleased and good-humoured, and at last brightened up completely.

"Why, that's Vassilyev, isn't it?" he asked with interest. "How did he get here?"

"Yes, it is Vassilyev, sir!" was shouted on all sides.

"He's been on the spree, sir," added one of the workmen, a tall, lean, elderly man with a pedantically severe expression of face, who seemed disposed to take the lead; "he's been on the spree, sir. It's three days since he left his master, and he's lying hidden here; he's come and planted himself upon us! Here he is asking for a chisel. Why, what do you want a chisel for now, you addle-pate? He wants to pawn his last tool."

"Ech, Arhipushka! Money's like a bird, it flies up and flies away again! Let me out, for God's sake," Vassilyev entreated in a thin cracked voice, poking his head out of the carriage.

"You stay where you are, you idol; you are lucky to be there!" Arhip answered sternly. "You have been drunk since the day before yesterday; you were hauled out of the street at daybreak this morning. You must thank God we hid you, we told Matvey Ilyitch that you were ill, that you had a convenient attack of colic."

There was a second burst of laughter.

"But where is the chisel?"

"Why, our Zuey has got it! How he keeps on about it! A drinking man, if ever there was one, Stepan Alexyevitch."

"He-he-he! Ah, the scoundrel! So that's how you work in the town; you pawn your tools!" wheezed the fat man, spluttering with glee, quite pleased and suddenly becoming extraordinarily good-humoured. "And yet it would be hard to find such a carpenter even in Moscow, but this is how he always recommends himself, the ruffian," he added, quite unexpectedly turning to me. "Let him out, Arhip, perhaps he wants something."

The gentleman was obeyed. The nail with which they had fastened up the carriage door, chiefly in order to amuse themselves at Vassilyev's expense when he should wake up, was taken out, and Vassilyev made his appearance in the light of day, muddy, dishevelled and ragged. He blinked at the sunshine, sneezed and gave a lurch; and then putting up his hand to screen his eyes, he looked round.

"What a lot of people, what a lot of people," he said, shaking his head, "and all, seemingly, so . . . ober," he drawled, with a sort of mournful pensiveness as though reproaching himself. "Well, good-morning, brothers, good-day."

Again there was a burst of laughter.

"Good-morning! Why, see how much of the day is gone, you heedless fellow!"

"Go it, old man!"

"As we say, have your fling, if it don't last long."

"He-he-he! he has a ready tongue!" cried the fat man,

rolling with laughter and again glancing genially at me. "Aren't you ashamed, Vassilyev?"

"It's sorrow drives me to it! Stepan Alexyevitch, sir, it's sorrow," Vassilyev answered gravely, with a wave of his hand, evidently glad of another opportunity to mention his sorrow.

"What sorrow, you booby?"

"A trouble such as was never heard of before. We are being made over to Foma Fomitch."

"Whom? When?" cried the fat man, all of a flutter.

I, too, took a step forward; quite unexpectedly, the question concerned me too.

"Why, all the people of Kapitonovko. Our master, the colonel—God give him health—wants to give up all our Kapitonovko, his property, to Foma Fomitch. Full seventy souls he is handing over to him. 'It's for you, Foma,' says he. 'Here, now, you've nothing of your own, one may say; you are not much of a landowner; all you have to keep you are two smelts in Lake Ladoga—that's all the serfs your father left you. For your parent,'" Vassilyev went on, with a sort of spiteful satisfaction, putting touches of venom into his story in all that related to Foma Fomitch—"'for your parent was a gentleman of ancient lineage, though from no one knows where, and no one knows who he was; he too, like you, lived with the gentry, was allowed to be in the kitchen as a charity. But now when I make over Kapitonovko to you, you will be a landowner too, and a gentleman of ancient lineage, and will have serfs of your own. You can lie on the stove and be idle as a gentleman. . . .'"

But Stepan Alexyevitch was no longer listening. The effect produced on him by Vassilyev's half-drunken story was extraordinary. The fat man was so angry that he turned positively purple; his double chin was quivering, his little eyes grew bloodshot. I thought he would have a stroke on the spot.

"That's the last straw!" he said, gasping. "That low brute, Foma, the parasite, a landowner! Tfoo! Go to perdition! Damn it all! Hey, you make haste and finish! Home!"

"Allow me to ask you," I said, stepping forward uncertainly, "you were pleased to mention the name of Foma Fomitch just now; I believe his surname, if I am not mistaken, is Opiskin. Well, you see, I should like . . . in short, I have a special reason for being interested in that personage, and I should be very glad to know, on my own account, how far one may believe the words of this good man that his master,

Yegor Ilyitch Rostanev, means to make Foma Fomitch a present of one of his villages. That interests me extremely, and I . . ."

"Allow me to ask you," the fat man broke in, "on what grounds are you interested in that personage, as you style him; though to my mind 'that damned low brute' is what he ought to be called, and not a personage. A fine sort of personage, the scurvy knave! He's a simple disgrace, not a personage!"

I explained that so far I was in complete ignorance in regard to this person, but that Yegor Ilyitch Rostanev was my uncle, and that I myself was Sergey Alexandrovitch So-and-so.

"The learned gentleman? My dear fellow! they are expecting you impatiently," cried the fat man, genuinely delighted. "Why, I have just come from them myself, from Stepantchikovo; I went away from dinner, I got up from the pudding, I couldn't sit it out with Foma! I quarrelled with them all there on account of that damned Foma. . . . Here's a meeting! You must excuse me, my dear fellow. I am Stepan Alexyevitch Bahtcheyev, and I remember you that high. . . . Well, who would have thought it! . . . But allow me."

And the fat man advanced to kiss me.

After the first minutes of excitement, I at once proceeded to question him: the opportunity was an excellent one.

"But who is this Foma?" I asked. "How is it he has gained the upper hand of the whole house? Why don't they kick him out of the yard? I must confess . . ."

"Kick him out? You must be mad. Why, Yegor Ilyitch tiptoes before him! Why, once Foma laid it down that Thursday was Wednesday, and so everyone in the house counted Thursday Wednesday. 'I won't have it Thursday, let it be Wednesday!' So there were two Wednesdays in one week. Do you suppose I am making it up? I am not exaggerating the least little bit. Why, my dear fellow, it's simply beyond all belief."

"I have heard that, but I must confess . . ."

"I confess and I confess! The way the man keeps on! What is there to confess? No, you had better ask me what sort of jungle I have come out of. The mother of Yegor Ilyitch, I mean of the colonel, though a very worthy lady and a general's widow too, in my opinion is in her dotage; why, that damned Foma is the very apple of her eye. She is the cause of it all; it was she brought him into the house. He has talked her

24

silly, she hasn't a word to say for herself now, though she is
called her Excellency—she skipped into marriage with General
Krahotkin at fifty! As for Yegor Ilyitch's sister, Praskovya
Ilyinitchna, who is an old maid of forty, I don't care to speak
of her. It's oh dear, and oh my, and cackling like a hen. I am
sick of her—bless her! The only thing about her is that she is
of the female sex; and so I must respect her for no cause or
reason, simply because she is of the female sex! Tfoo! It's
not the thing for me to speak of her, she's your aunt. Alexandra
Yegorovna, the colonel's daughter, though she is only a little
girl—just in her sixteenth year—to my thinking is the cleverest
of the lot; she doesn't respect Foma; it was fun to see her.
A sweet young lady, and that's the fact! And why should she
respect him? Why, Foma was a buffoon waiting on the late
General Krahotkin. Why, he used to imitate all sorts of beasts
to entertain the general! And it seems that in old days Jack
was the man; but nowadays Jack is the master, and now the
colonel, your uncle, treats this retired buffoon as though he
were his own father. He has set him up in a frame, the rascal,
and bows down at the feet of the man who is sponging upon
him. Tfoo!"

"Poverty is not a vice, however . . . and I must confess
. . . allow me to ask you, is he handsome, clever?"

"Foma? A perfect picture!" answered Bahtcheyev, with
an extraordinary quiver of spite in his voice. (My questions
seemed to irritate him, and he began to look at me suspiciously.)
"A perfect picture! Do you hear, good people: he makes him
out a beauty! Why, he is like a lot of brute beasts in one, if
you want to know the whole truth, my good man. Though that
wouldn't matter if he had wit; if only he had wit, the rogue—
why, then I would be ready to do violence to my feelings and
agree, maybe, for the sake of wit; but, you see, there's no trace
of wit about him whatever! He has cast a spell on them all;
he is a regular alchemist! Tfoo! I am tired of talking. One
ought to curse them and say no more about it. You have
upset me with your talk, my good sir! Hey, you! Are you
ready or not?"

"Raven still wants shoeing," Grishka answered gloomily.

"Raven. I'll let you have a raven! . . . Yes, sir, I could
tell you a story that would simply make you gape with wonder,
so that you would stay with your mouth open till the Second
Coming. Why, I used to feel a respect for him myself. Would
you believe it? I confess it with shame, I frankly confess it,

25

I was a fool. Why, he took me in too. He's a know-all He knows the ins and outs of everything, he's studied all the sciences. He gave me some drops; you see, my good sir, I am a sick man, a poor creature. You may not believe it, but I am an invalid. And those drops of his almost turned me inside out. You just keep quiet and listen; go yourself and you will be amazed. Why, he will make the colonel shed tears of blood; the colonel will shed tears of blood through him, but then it will be too late. You know, the whole neighbourhood all around has dropped his acquaintance owing to this accursed Foma. No one can come to the place without being insulted by him. I don't count; even officials of high rank he doesn't spare. He lectures every one. He sets up for a teacher of morality, the scoundrel. 'I am a wise man,' says he; 'I am cleverer than all of you, you must listen to no one but me, I am a learned man.' Well, what of it? Because he is learned, must he persecute people who are not? . . . And when he begins in his learned language, he goes hammering on ta-ta-ta! Ta-ta-ta! I'll tell you his tongue is such a one to wag that if you cut it off and throw it on the dungheap it will go on wagging there till a crow picks it up. He is as conceited and puffed out as a mouse in a sack of grain. He is trying to climb so high that he will overreach himself. Why, here, for instance, he has taken it into his head to teach the house serfs French. You can believe it or not, as you like. It will be a benefit to him, he says. To a lout, to a servant! Tfoo! A shameless fellow, damn him, that is what he is. What does a clodhopper want with French, I ask you? And indeed what do the likes of us want with French? For gallivanting with young ladies in the mazurka or dancing attendance on other men's wives? Profligacy, that's what it is, I tell you! But to my thinking, when one has drunk a bottle of vodka one can talk in any language. So that is all the respect I have for your French language! I dare say you can chatter away in French: Ta-ta-ta, the tabby has married the tom," Bahtcheyev said, looking at me in scornful indignation. "Are you a learned man, my good sir—eh? Have you gone in for some learned line?"

"Well . . . I am somewhat interested . . ."

"I suppose you have studied all the sciences, too?"

"Quite so, that is, no . . . I must own I am more interested now in observing . . . I have been staying in Petersburg, but now I am hurrying to my uncle's."

"And who is the attraction at your uncle's? You had better have stayed where you were, since you had somewhere to stay. No, my good sir, I can tell you, you won't make much way by being learned, and no uncle will be of any use to you; you'll get caught in a trap! Why, I got quite thin, staying twenty-four hours with them. Would you believe that I got thin, staying with them? No, I see you don't believe it. Oh, well, you needn't believe it if you don't want to, bless you."

"No, really I quite believe it, only I still don't understand," I answered, more and more bewildered.

"I believe it, but I don't believe you! You learned gentlemen are all fond of cutting capers! All you care about is hopping about on one leg and showing off! I am not fond of learned people, my good sir; they give me the spleen! I have come across your Petersburgers—a worthless lot! They are all Freemasons; they spread infidelity in all directions; they are afraid of a drop of vodka, as though it would bite them—Tfoo! You have put me out of temper, sir, and I don't want to tell you anything! After all, I have not been engaged to tell you stories, and I am tired of talking. One doesn't pitch into everybody, sir, and indeed it's a sin to do it. . . . Only your learned gentleman at your uncle's has driven the footman Vidoplyasov almost out of his wits. Vidoplyasov has gone crazy all through Foma Fomitch. . . ."

"As for that fellow Vidoplyasov," put in Grishka, who had till then been following the conversation with severe decorum, "I'd give him a flogging. If I came across him, I'd thrash the German nonsense out of him. I'd give him more than you could get into two hundred."

"Be quiet!" shouted his master. "Hold your tongue; no one's talking to you."

"Vidoplyasov," I said, utterly nonplussed and not knowing what to say. "Vidoplyasov, what a queer name!"

"Why is it queer? There you are again. Ugh, you learned gentlemen, you learned gentlemen!"

I lost patience.

"Excuse me," I said, "but why are you so cross with me? What have I done? I must own I have been listening to you for half an hour, and I still don't know what it is all about. . . ."

"What are you offended about, sir?" answered the fat man. "There is no need for you to take offence! I am speaking to you for your good. You mustn't mind my being such a

27

grumbler and shouting at my servant just now. Though he is the most natural rascal, my Grishka, I like him for it, the scoundrel. A feeling heart has been the ruin of me—I tell you frankly; and Foma is to blame for it all. He'll be the ruin of me, I'll take my oath of that. Here, thanks to him, I have been baking in the sun for two hours. I should have liked to have gone to the priest's while these fools were dawdling about over their job. The priest here is a very nice fellow. But he has so upset me, Foma has, that it has even put me off seeing the priest. What a set they all are! There isn't a decent tavern here. I tell you they are all scoundrels, every one of them. And it would be a different thing if he were some great man in the service," Bahtcheyev went on, going back again to Foma Fomitch, whom he seemed unable to shake off, "it would be pardonable perhaps for a man of rank; but as it is he has no rank at all; I know for a fact that he hasn't. He says he has suffered in the cause of justice in the year forty something that never was, so we have to bow down to him for that! If the least thing is not to his liking—up he jumps and begins squealing: 'They are insulting me, they are insulting my poverty, they have no respect for me.' You daren't sit down to table without Foma, and yet he keeps them waiting. 'I have been slighted,' he'd say; 'I am a poor wanderer, black bread is good enough for me.' As soon as they sit down he turns up, our fiddle strikes up again, 'Why did you sit down to table without me? So no respect is shown me in anything.' In fact your soul is not your own. I held my peace for a long time, sir, he imagined that I was going to fawn upon him, like a lapdog on its hind legs begging; 'Here, boy, here's a bit, eat it up.' No, my lad, you run in the shafts, while I sit in the cart. I served in the same regiment with Yegor Ilyitch, you know; I took my discharge with the rank of a Junker, while he came to his estate last year, a retired colonel. I said to him, 'Aïe, you will be your own undoing, don't be too soft with Foma! You'll regret it.' 'No,' he would say, 'he is a most excellent person' (meaning Foma), 'he is a friend to me; he is teaching me a higher standard of life.' Well, thought I, there is no fighting against a higher standard; if he has set out to teach a higher standard of life, then it is all up. What do you suppose he made a to-do about to-day? To-morrow is the day of Elijah the Prophet" (Mr. Bahtcheyev crossed himself), "the patron saint of your uncle's son Ilyusha. I was thinking to spend the day with them and to dine there, and had ordered a plaything from Petersburg, a German on springs, kissing the hand of his betrothed, while she wiped away a tear with her handkerchief—a magnificent thing! (I shan't give it now, no, thank you; it's lying there in my carriage and the German's nose is smashed off; I am taking it back.) Yegor Ilyitch himself would not have been disinclined to enjoy himself and be festive on such a day, but Foma won't have it. As much as to say: 'Why are you beginning to make such a fuss over Ilyusha? So now you are taking no notice of me.' Eh? What do you say to a goose like that? He is jealous of a boy of eight over his nameday! 'Look here,' he says, 'it is my nameday too.' But you know it will be St. Ilya's, not St. Foma's. 'No,' he says, 'that is my nameday too!' I looked on and put up with it. And what do you think? Now they are walking about on tiptoe, whispering, uncertain what to do—to reckon Ilya's day as the nameday or not, to congratulate him or not. If they don't congratulate him he may be offended, if they do he may take it for scoffing. Tfoo, what a plague! We sat down to dinner. . . . But are you listening, my good sir?"

"Most certainly I am; I am listening with peculiar gratification, in fact, because through you I have now learned . . . and . . . I must say . . ."

"To be sure, with peculiar gratification! I know your peculiar gratification. . . . You are not jeering at me, talking about your gratification?"

"Upon my word, how could I be jeering? On the contrary. And indeed you express yourself with such originality that I am tempted to note down your words."

"What's that, sir, noting down?" asked Mr. Bahtcheyev, looking at me with suspicion and speaking with some alarm.

"Though perhaps I shall not note them down. . . . I didn't mean anything."

"No doubt you are trying to flatter me?"

"Flatter you, what do you mean?" I asked with surprise.

"Why, yes. Here you are flattering me now; I am telling you everything like a fool, and later on you will go and write a sketch of me somewhere."

I made haste at once to assure Mr. Bahtcheyev that I was not that sort of person, but he still looked at me suspiciously.

"Not that sort of person! Who can tell what you are? Perhaps better still. Foma there threatened to write an account of me and to send it to be published."

"Allow me to ask," I interrupted, partly from a desire to

change the conversation. "Is it true that my uncle wants to get married?"

"What if he does? That would not matter. Get married if you have a mind to, that's no harm; but something else is. . . ." added Mr. Bahtcheyev meditatively. "H'm! that question, my good sir, I cannot answer fully. There are a lot of females mixed up in the business now, like flies in jam; and you know there is no making out which wants to be married. And as a friend I don't mind telling you, sir, I don't like woman! It's only talk that she is a human being, but in reality she is simply a disgrace and a danger to the soul's salvation. But that your uncle is in love like a Siberian cat, that I can tell you for a fact. I'll say no more about that now, sir, you will see for yourself; but what's bad is that the business drags on. If you are going to get married, get married; but he is afraid to tell Foma and afraid to tell the old lady, she will be squealing all over the place and begin kicking up a rumpus. She takes Foma's part: 'Foma Fomitch will be hurt,' she'd say, 'if a new mistress comes into the house, for then he won't be able to stay two hours in it.' The bride will chuck him out by the scruff of his neck, if she is not a fool, and in one way or another will make such an upset that he won't be able to find a place anywhere in the neighbourhood. So now he is at his pranks, and he and the mamma are trying to foist a queer sort of bride on him. . . . But why did you interrupt me, sir? I wanted to tell you what was most important, and you interrupted me! I am older than you are, and it is not the right thing to interrupt an old man."

I apologised.

"You needn't apologise! I wanted to put before you, as a learned man, how he insulted me to-day. Come, tell me what you think of it, if you are a good-hearted man. We sat down to dinner; well, he fairly bit my head off at dinner, I can tell you! I saw from the very beginning; he sat there as cross as two sticks, as though nothing were to his liking. He'd have been glad to drown me in a spoonful of water, the viper! He is a man of such vanity that his skin's not big enough for him. So he took it into his head to pick a quarrel with me, to teach me a higher standard. Asked me to tell him why I was so fat! The man kept pestering me, why was I fat and not thin? What do you think of that question? Tell me, my good sir. Do you see anything witty in it? I answered him very reasonably: 'That's as God has ordained, Foma Fomitch. One man's fat and one man's thin; and no mortal can go against the decrees of Divine Providence.' That was sensible, wasn't it? What do you say? 'No,' said he; 'you have five hundred serfs, you live at your ease and do nothing for your country; you ought to be in the service, but you sit at home and play your concertina'—and it is true when I am depressed I am fond of playing on the concertina. I answered very reasonably again: 'How should I go into the service, Foma Fomitch? What uniform could I pinch my corpulence into? If I pinched myself in and put on a uniform, and sneezed unwarily—all the buttons would fly off, and what's more, maybe before my superiors, and, God forbid! they might take it for a practical joke, and what then?' Well, tell me, what was there funny in that? But there, there was such a roar at my expense, such a ha-ha-ha and he-he-he. . . . The fact is he has no sense of decency, I tell you, and he even thought fit to slander me in the French dialect: 'cochon,' he called me. Well I know what cochon means. 'Ah, you damned philosopher,' I thought. 'Do you suppose I'm going to give in to you?' I bore it as long as I could, but I couldn't stand it. I got up from the table, and before all the honourable company I blurted out in his face: 'I have done you an injustice, Foma Fomitch, my kind benefactor.' I said, 'I thought that you were a well-bred man, and you turn out to be just as great a hog as any one of us.' I said that and I left the table, left the pudding—they were just handing the pudding round. 'Bother you and your pudding!' I thought. . . ."

"Excuse me," I said, listening to Mr. Bahtcheyev's whole story; "I am ready, of course, to agree with you completely. The point is, that so far I know nothing positive. . . . But I have got ideas of my own on the subject, you see."

"What ideas, my good sir?" Mr. Bahtcheyev asked mistrustfully.

"You see," I began, hesitating a little, "it is perhaps not the moment, but I am ready to tell it. This is what I think: perhaps we are both mistaken about Foma Fomitch, perhaps under these oddities lies hidden a peculiar, perhaps a gifted nature, who knows? Perhaps it is a nature that has been wounded, crushed by sufferings, avenging itself, so to speak, on all humanity. I have heard that in the past he was something like a buffoon; perhaps that humiliated him, mortified him, overwhelmed him. . . . Do you understand: a man of noble nature . . . perception . . . and to play the part of a

31

buffoon! . . . And so he has become mistrustful of all mankind and . . . and perhaps if he could be reconciled to humanity . . . that is, to his fellows, perhaps he would turn out a rare nature, perhaps even a very remarkable one and . . . and . . . you know there must be something in the man. There is a reason, of course, for everyone doing homage to him."

I was conscious myself that I was maundering horribly. I might have been forgiven in consideration of my youth. But Mr. Bahtcheyev did not forgive me. He looked gravely and sternly into my face and suddenly turned crimson as a turkey cock.

"Do you mean that Foma's a remarkable man?" he asked abruptly.

"Listen, I scarcely myself believe a word of what I said just now. It was merely by way of a guess. . . ."

"Allow me, sir, to be so inquisitive as to ask: have you studied philosophy?"

"In what sense?" I asked in perplexity.

"No, in no particular sense; you answer me straight out, apart from any sense, sir: have you studied philosophy or not?"

"I must own I am intending to study it, but . . ."

"There it is!" shouted Mr. Bahtcheyev, giving full rein to his indignation. "Before you opened your mouth, sir, I guessed that you were a philosopher! There is no deceiving me! No, thank you! I can scent out a philosopher two miles off! You can go and kiss your Foma Fomitch. A remarkable man, indeed! Tfoo! confound it all! I thought you were a man of good intentions too, while you . . . Here!" he shouted to the coachman, who had already clambered on the box of the carriage, which by now had been put in order. "Home!"

With difficulty I succeeded somehow in soothing him; somehow or other he was mollified at last; but it was a long time before he could bring himself to lay aside his wrath and look on me with favour. Meantime he got into the carriage, assisted by Grishka and Arhip, the man who had reproved Vassilyev.

"Allow me to ask you," I said, going up to the carriage. "Are you never coming again to my uncle's?"

"To your uncle's? Curse the fellow who has told you that! Do you think that I am a consistent man, that I shall keep it up? That's just my trouble, that I am not a man, but a rag.

32

Before a week's past, I shall fly round there again. And why? There it is, I don't know myself why, but I shall go; I shall fight with Foma again. That's just my trouble, sir! The Lord has sent that Foma to chastise me for my sins. I have as much will as an old woman, there is no consistency in me, I am a first-class coward, my good sir. . . ."

We parted friends, however; he even invited me to dine with him.

"You come, sir, you come, we will dine together; I have got some vodka brought on foot from Kiev, and my cook has been in Paris. He serves such fricassees, he makes such pasties, that you can only lick your fingers and bow down to him, the rascal. A man of culture! Only it is a long time since I thrashed him, he is getting spoilt with me. . . . It is a good thing you reminded me. . . . Do come. I'd invite you to come to-day, only somehow I am out of sorts, down in the mouth—in fact, quite knocked up. I am a sick man, you know, a poor creature. Maybe you won't believe it. . . . Well, good-bye, sir, it is time for me to set sail. And your little trap yonder is ready. And tell Foma he had better not come across me; I should give him such a sentimental greeting that he . . ."

But his last words were out of hearing; the carriage, drawn by four strong horses, vanished in clouds of dust. My chaise too was ready; I got into it and we at once drove through the little town. "Of course this gentleman is exaggerating," I thought; "he is too angry and cannot be impartial. But, again, all that he said about uncle was very remarkable. So that makes two people in the same story, that uncle is in love with that young lady. . . . H'm! Shall I get married or not?" This time I meditated in earnest.

CHAPTER III

MY UNCLE

I MUST own I was actually a little daunted. My romantic dreams suddenly seemed to me extremely queer, even rather stupid as soon as I reached Stepantchikovo. That was about five o'clock in the afternoon. The road ran by the manor house. I saw again after long absence the immense garden in which some happy days of my childhood had been passed, and which I had often seen afterwards in my dreams, in the dormitories of the various schools which undertook my education. I jumped out of the carriage and walked across the garden to the house. I very much wanted to arrive unannounced, to inquire for my uncle, to fetch him out and to talk to him first of all. And so I did. Passing down the avenue of lime trees hundreds of years old, I went up on to the veranda, from which one passed by a glass door into the inner rooms. The veranda was surrounded by flower-beds and adorned with pots of expensive flowers. Here I met one of the natives, old Gavrila, who had at one time looked after me and was now the honoured valet of my uncle. The old fellow was wearing spectacles, and was holding in his hand a manuscript book which he was reading with great attention. I had seen him three years before in Petersburg, where he had come with my uncle, and so he recognised me at once. With exclamations of joy he fell to kissing my hand, and as he did so the spectacles fell off his nose on to the floor. Such devotion on the part of the old man touched me very much. But disturbed by my recent conversation with Mr. Bahtcheyev, I looked first at the suspicious manuscript book which had been in Gavrila's hands.

"What's this, Gavrila? Surely they have not begun teaching you French too?" I asked the old man.

"They are teaching me in my old age, like a starling, sir," Gavrila answered mournfully.

"Does Foma himself teach you?"

"Yes, sir; a very clever man he must be."

"Not a doubt that he is clever! Does he teach you by conversations?"

"By a copy-book, sir."

"Is that what you have in your hands? Ah! French words in Russian letters, a sharp dodge! You give in to such a block-head, such an arrant fool, aren't you ashamed, Gavrila?" I cried, instantly forgetting my lofty theories about Foma Fomitch for which I had caught it so hotly from Mr. Bahtcheyev.

"How can he be a fool, sir?" answered the old man, "if he manages our betters as he does."

"H'm, perhaps you are right, Gavrila," I muttered, pulled up by this remark. "Take me to my uncle."

"My falcon! But I can't show myself, I dare not, I have begun to be afraid even of him. I sit here in my misery and step behind the flower-beds when he is pleased to come out."

"But why are you afraid?"

34

"I didn't know my lesson this morning. Foma Fomitch made me go down on my knees, but I didn't stay on my knees. I am too old, Sergey Alexandrovitch, for them to play such tricks with me. The master was pleased to be vexed at my disobeying Foma Fomitch, 'he takes trouble about your education, old grey-beard,' said he; 'he wants to teach you the pronunciation.' So here I am walking to and fro repeating the vocabulary. Foma Fomitch promised to examine me again this evening."

It seemed to me that there was something obscure about this.

"There must be something connected with French," I thought, "which the old man cannot explain."

"One question, Gavrila: what sort of man is he? Good-looking, tall?"

"Foma Fomitch? No, sir, he's an ugly little scrub of a man."

"H'm! Wait a bit, Gavrila, perhaps it can be all set right; in fact I can promise you it certainly will be set right. But . . . where is my uncle?"

"He is behind the stables seeing some peasants. The old men have come from Kapitonovko to pay their respects to him. They had heard that they were being made over to Foma Fomitch. They want to beg not to be."

"But why behind the stables?"

"They are frightened, sir. . . ."

I did, in fact, find my uncle behind the stables. There he was, standing before a group of peasants who were bowing down to the ground and earnestly entreating him. Uncle was explaining something to them with warmth. I went up and called to him. He turned round and we rushed into each other's arms.

He was extremely glad to see me; his delight was almost ecstatic. He hugged me, pressed my hands, as though his own son had returned to him after escaping some mortal danger, as though by my arrival I had rescued him from some mortal danger and brought with me the solution of all his perplexities, as well as joy and lifelong happiness for him and all whom he loved. Uncle would not have consented to be happy alone. After the first outburst of delight, he got into such a fuss that at last he was quite flustered and bewildered. He showered questions upon me, wanted to take me at once to see his family. We were just going, but my uncle turned back, wishing to

35

present me first to the peasants of Kapitonovko. Then, I remember, he suddenly began talking, apropos of I don't know what, of some Mr. Korovkin, a remarkable man whom he had met three days before, on the high road, and whom he was very impatiently expecting to pay him a visit. Then he dropped Mr. Korovkin too and spoke of something else. I looked at him with enjoyment. Answering his hurried questions, I told him that I did not want to go into the service, but to continue my studies. As soon as the subject of study was broached, my uncle at once knitted his brows and assumed an extraordinarily solemn air. Learning that of late I had been engaged on mineralogy, he raised his head and looked about him proudly, as though he had himself, alone and unaided, discovered the whole of that science and written all that was published about it. I have mentioned already that he cherished the most disinterested reverence for the word "science", the more disinterested that he himself had no scientific knowledge whatever.

"Ah, my boy, there are people in the world who know everything," he said to me once, his eyes sparkling with enthusiasm. "One sits among them, listens, and one knows one understands nothing of it all, and yet one loves it. And why? Because it is in the cause of reform, of enlightenment, of the general welfare! That I do understand. Here I now travel by train, and my Ilyusha, perhaps, may fly through the air. . . . And then trade, manufactures—those channels, so to say . . . that is, I mean, turn it which way you will, it's of service. . . . It is of service, isn't it?"

But to return to our meeting.

"But wait a bit, wait a bit, my dear," he began, speaking rapidly and rubbing his hands, "you will see a man! A rare man, I tell you, a learned man, a man of science; 'he will survive his century.' It's a good saying, isn't it, 'will survive his century'? Foma explained it to me. . . . Wait a little, I will introduce you to him."

"Are you speaking of Foma Fomitch, uncle?"

"No, no, my dear, I was speaking of Korovkin, though Foma too, he too . . . but I am simply talking of Korovkin just now," he added, for some unknown reason turning crimson, and seeming embarrassed as soon as Foma's name was mentioned.

"What sciences is he studying, uncle?"

"Science, my boy, science, science in general. I can't tell you which exactly, I only know that it is science. How he

36

speaks about railways! And, you know," my uncle added in a half whisper, screwing up his right eye significantly, "just a little of the free-thinker. I noticed it, especially when he was speaking of marriage and the family . . . it's a pity I did not understand much of it myself (there was no time), I would have told you all about it in detail. And he is a man of the noblest qualities, too! I have invited him to visit me, I am expecting him from hour to hour."

Meanwhile the peasants were gazing at me with round eyes and open mouths as though at some marvel.

"Listen, uncle," I interrupted him; "I believe I am hindering the peasants. No doubt they have come about something urgent. What do they want? I must own I suspect something, and I should be very glad to hear. . . ."

Uncle suddenly seemed nervous and flustered.

"Oh, yes! I had forgotten. Here, you see . . . what is one to do with them? They have got a notion—and I should very much like to know who first started it—they have got a notion, that I am giving them away together with the whole of Kapitonovko—do you remember Kapitonovko? We used to drive out there in the evenings with dear Katya—the whole of Kapitonovko with the sixty-eight souls in it to Foma Fomitch. 'We don't want to leave you,' they say, and that is all about it."

"So it is not true, uncle, you are not giving him Kapitonovko," I cried, almost rapturously.

"I never thought of it, it never entered my head! And from whom did you hear it? Once one drops a word, it is all over the place, And why do they so dislike Foma? Wait a little, Sergey, I will introduce you to him," he added, glancing at me timidly, as though he were aware in me, too, of hostility towards Foma Fomitch. "He is a wonderful man, my boy."

"We want no one but you, no one!" the peasants suddenly wailed in chorus. "You are our father, we are your children!"

"Listen, uncle," I said. "I have not seen Foma Fomitch yet, but . . . you see . . . I have heard something. I must confess that I met Mr. Bahtcheyev to-day. However, I have my own idea on that subject. Anyway, uncle, finish with the peasants and let them go, and let us talk by ourselves without witnesses. I must own, that's what I have come for. . . ."

"To be sure, to be sure," my uncle assented; "to be sure. We'll dismiss the peasants and then we can have a talk, you know, a friendly, affectionate, thorough talk. Come," he went on, speaking rapidly and addressing the peasants, "you can go

37

now, my friends. And for the future come to me whenever there is need; straight to me, and come at any time."

"You are our father, we are your children! Do not give us to Foma Fomitch for our undoing! All we, poor people, are beseeching you!" the peasants shouted once more.

"See what fools! But I am not giving you away, I tell you."

"Or he'll never leave off teaching us, your honour. He does nothing but teach the fellows here, so they say."

"Why, you don't mean to say he is teaching you French?" I cried, almost in alarm.

"No, sir, so far God has had mercy on us!" answered one of the peasants, probably a great talker, a red-haired man with a huge bald patch on the back of his head, with a long, scanty, wedge-shaped beard, which moved as he talked as though it were a separate individual. "No, sir, so far God has had mercy on us."

"But what does he teach you?"

"Well, your honour, what he teaches us, in a manner of speaking, is buying a gold casket to keep a brass farthing in."

"How do you mean, a brass farthing?"

"Seryozha, you are mistaken, it's a slander!" cried my uncle, turning crimson and looking terribly embarrassed. "The fools have misunderstood what was said to them. He merely . . . there was nothing about a brass farthing. There is no need for you to understand everything, and shout at the top of your voice," my uncle continued, addressing the peasant reproachfully. "One wants to do you good and you don't understand, and make an uproar!"

"Upon my word, uncle, teaching them French?"

"That's for the sake of pronunciation, Seryozha, simply for the pronunciation," said my uncle in an imploring voice. "He said himself that it was for the sake of the pronunciation. . . . Besides, something special happened in connection with this, which you know nothing about and so you cannot judge. You must investigate first and then blame. . . . It is easy to find fault!"

"But what are you about?" I shouted, turning impetuously to the peasants again. "You ought to speak straight out. You should say, 'This won't do, Foma Fomitch, this is how it ought to be!' You have got a tongue, haven't you?"

"Where is the mouse who will bell the cat, your honour? 'I am teaching you, clodhoppers, cleanliness and order,' he says. 'Why is your shirt not clean?' Why, one is always in a sweat, that's why it isn't clean! One can't change every day. Cleanliness won't save you and dirt won't kill you."

"And look here, the other day he came to the threshing floor," began another peasant, a tall lean fellow all in patches and wearing wretched bark shoes, apparently one of those men who are always discontented about something and always have some vicious venomous word ready in reserve. Till then he had been hidden behind the backs of the other peasants, had been listening in gloomy silence, and had kept all the time on his face an ambiguous, bitterly subtle smile. "He came to the threshing floor. 'Do you know,' he said, 'how many miles it is to the sun?' 'Why, who can tell? Such learning is not for us but for the gentry.' 'No,' says he; 'you are a fool, a lout, you don't understand what is good for you; but I,' said he, 'am an astronomer! I know all God's planets.'"

"Well, and did he tell you how many miles it is to the sun?" my uncle put in, suddenly reviving and winking gaily at me, as though to say, "See what's coming!"

"Yes, he did tell us how many," the peasant answered reluctantly, not expecting such a question.

"Well, how many did he say, how many exactly?"

"Your honour must know best, we live in darkness."

"Oh, I know, my boy, but do you remember?"

"Why, he said it would be so many hundreds or thousands, it was a big number, he said. More than you could carry in three cartloads."

"Try and remember, brother! I dare say you thought it would be about a mile, that you could reach up to it with your hand. No, my boy; you see, the earth is like a round ball, do you understand?" my uncle went on, describing a sphere in the air with his hands.

The peasant smiled bitterly.

"Yes, like a ball, it hangs in the air of itself and moves round the sun. And the sun stands still, it only seems to you that it moves. There's a queer thing! And the man who discovered this was Captain Cook, a navigator . . . devil only knows who did discover it," he added in a half whisper, turning to me. "I know nothing about it myself, my boy. . . . Do you know how far it is to the sun?"

"I do, uncle," I answered, looking with surprise at all this scene. "But this is what I think: of course ignorance means slovenliness; but on the other hand . . . to teach peasants astronomy . . ."

39

"Just so, just so, slovenliness," my uncle assented, delighted with my expression, which struck him as extremely apt. "A noble thought! Slovenliness precisely! That is what I have always said . . . that is, I never said so, but I felt it. Do you hear?" he cried to the peasants. "Ignorance is as bad as slovenliness, it's as bad as dirt. That's why Foma wanted to teach you. He wanted to teach you something good—that was all right. That's as good as serving one's country—it's as good as any official rank. So you see what science is! Well, that's enough, that's enough, my friends. Go, in God's name; and I am glad, glad. . . . Don't worry yourselves, I won't forsake you."

"Protect us, father!"

"Let us breathe freely!"

And the peasants plumped down at his feet.

"Come, come, that's nonsense. Bow down to God and your Tsar, and not to me. . . . Come, go along, behave well, be deserving . . . and all that. You know," he said, turning suddenly to me as soon as the peasants had gone away, and beaming with pleasure, "the peasant loves a kind word, and a little present would do no harm. Shall I give them something, eh? What do you think? In honour of your arrival. . . . Shall I or not?"

"But you are a kind of Frol Silin, uncle, a benevolent person, I see."

"Oh, one can't help it, my boy, one can't help it; that's nothing. I have been meaning to give them a present for a long time," he said, as though excusing himself. "And as for your thinking it funny of me to give the peasants a lesson in science, I simply did that, my boy, in delight at seeing you, Seryozha. I simply wanted the peasants to hear how many miles it was to the sun and gape in wonder. It's amusing to see them gape, my dear. . . . One seems to rejoice over them. Only, my boy, don't speak in the drawing-room of my having had an interview with the peasants, you know. I met them behind the stables on purpose that we should not be seen. It was impossible to have it there, my boy: it is a delicate business, and indeed they came in secret themselves. I did it more for their sake. . . ."

"Well, here I have come, uncle," I began, changing the conversation and anxious to get to the chief point as quickly as possible. "I must own your letter so surprised me that I . . ."

"My dear, not a word of that," my uncle interrupted, as

though in alarm, positively dropping his voice. "Afterwards, afterwards, all that shall be explained. I have, perhaps, acted wrongly towards you, very wrongly, perhaps. . . ."

"Acted wrongly towards me, uncle?"

"Afterwards, afterwards, my dear, afterwards! It shall all be explained. But what a fine fellow you have grown! My dear boy! How eager I have been to see you! I wanted to pour out my heart, so to speak . . . you are clever, you are my only hope . . . you and Korovkin. I must mention to you that they are all angry with you here. Mind, be careful, don't be rash."

"Angry with me?" I asked, looking at uncle in wonder, unable to understand how I could have angered people with whom I was as yet unacquainted. "Angry with me?"

"Yes, with you, my boy. It can't be helped! Foma Fomitch is a little . . . and . . . well . . . mother following his example. Be careful, respectful, don't contradict. The great thing is to be respectful. . . ."

"To Foma Fomitch, do you mean, uncle?"

"It can't be helped, my dear; you see, I don't defend him. Certainly he has his faults, perhaps, and especially just now, at this particular moment. . . . Ah, Seryozha, dear, how it all worries me. And if only it could be settled comfortably, if only we could all be satisfied and happy! . . . But who has not faults? We are not perfect ourselves, are we?"

"Upon my word, uncle! Consider what he is doing. . . ."

"Oh, my dear! It's all trivial nonsense, nothing more! Here, for instance, let me tell you, he is angry with me, and what for, do you suppose? . . . Though perhaps it's my own fault. . . . I'd better tell you afterwards. . . ."

"But, do you know, uncle, I have formed an idea of my own about it," I interrupted, in haste to give expression to my theory. Indeed, we both seemed nervous and hurried. "In the first place, he has been a buffoon; that has mortified him, rankled, outraged his ideal; and that has made his character embittered, morbid, resentful, so to say, against all humanity. . . . But if one could reconcile him with mankind, if one could bring him back to himself . . ."

"Just so, just so," cried my uncle, delighted; "that's just it. A generous idea! And in fact it would be shameful, ungenerous of us to blame him! Just so! . . . Oh, my dear, you understand me; you have brought me comfort! If only things could be set straight, somehow! Do you know, I am afraid to show

41

myself. Here you have come, and I shall certainly catch it from them!"

"Uncle, if that is how it is . . ." I began, disconcerted by this confession.

"No-no-no! For nothing in the world," he cried, clutching my hands. "You are my guest and I wish it!"

"Uncle, tell me at once," I began insistently, "why did you send for me? What do you expect of me, and, above all, in what way have you been to blame towards me?"

"My dear, don't ask. Afterwards, afterwards; all that shall be explained afterwards. I have been very much to blame, perhaps, but I wanted to act like an honest man, and . . . and . . . you shall marry her! You will marry her, if there is one grain of gentlemanly feeling in you," he added, flushing all over with some sudden feeling and warmly and enthusiastically pressing my hand. "But enough, not another word, you will soon see for yourself. It will depend on you. . . . The great thing is that you should be liked, that you should make a good impression. Above all—don't be nervous."

"Come, listen, uncle. Whom have you got there? I must own I have been so little in society, that . . ."

"That you are rather frightened," put in my uncle, smiling. "Oh, that's no matter. Cheer up, they are all our own people! The great thing is to be bold and not afraid. I keep feeling anxious about you. Whom have we got there, you ask? Yes, who is there. . . . In the first place, my mother," he began hurriedly. "Do you remember mamma or not? The most kind-hearted, generous woman, no airs about her—that one can say; a little of the old school, perhaps, but that's all to the good. To be sure she sometimes takes fancies into her head, you know, will say one thing and another; she is vexed with me now, but it is my own fault, I know it is my own fault. And the fact is —you know she is what is called a *grande dame,* a general's lady . . . her husband was a most excellent man. To begin with, he was a general, a most cultivated man; he left no property, but he was covered with wounds—he was deserving of respect, in fact. Then there's Miss Perepelitsyn; well, she . . . I don't know . . . of late she has been rather . . . her character is so . . . but one mustn't find fault with everyone. There, never mind her . . . you mustn't imagine she is in a menial position, she's a major's daughter herself, my boy, she is mother's confidante and favourite, my dear! Then there is my sister Praskovya Ilyinitchna. Well, there is no need to say much about her, she is simple and good-natured, a bit fussy, but what a heart! The heart is the great thing. Though she is middle-aged, yet, do you know, I really believe that queer fellow Bahtcheyev is making up to her. He wants to make a match of it. But mind you don't say a word, it is a secret! Well, and who else is there? I won't tell you about the children, you will see for yourself. It's Ilyusha's nameday to-morrow. . . . Why there, I was almost forgetting, we have had staying with us for the last month Ivan, Ivanitch Mizintchikov, your second cousin, I believe; yes, of course, he is your second cousin! He has lately given up his commission; he was a lieutenant in the Hussars; still a young man. A noble soul! But, you know, he has got through his money. I really can't think how he managed to get rid of it. Though indeed he had next to nothing, but anyway he got through it and ran into debt. . . . Now he is staying with me. I didn't know him at all till lately; he came and introduced himself. He is a dear fellow, good-humoured, quiet and respectful. No one gets a word out of him. He is always silent. Foma calls him in jest the 'silent stranger'—he doesn't mind; he isn't vexed. Foma's satisfied, he says Ivan's not very bright. And Ivan never contradicts him, but always falls in with everything he says. H'm! he seems so crushed . . . but there, God bless him, you will see for yourself. There are guests from the town, Pavel Semyonitch Obnoskin and his mother; he's young but a man of superior mind, something mature, steadfast, you know . . . only I don't know how to express it; and what's more, of the highest principles; strict morals. And lastly there is staying with us, you know, a lady called Tatyana Ivanovna; she, too, may be a distant relation. You don't know her. She is not quite young, that one must own, but . . . she is not without attractions: she is rich enough to buy Stepantchikovo twice over, she has only lately come into her money, and has had a wretched time of it till now. Please, Seryozha, my boy, be careful; she is such a nervous invalid . . . something phantasmagorial in her character, you know. Well, you are a gentleman, you will understand; she has had troubles, you know, one has to be doubly careful with a person who has had troubles! But you mustn't imagine anything, you know. Of course she has her weaknesses; sometimes she is in such a hurry, she speaks so fast, that she says the wrong thing. Not that she lies, don't imagine that . . . it all comes, my boy, from a pure and noble heart, so to say. I mean, even if she

43

does say something false, it's simply from excess of noble-heartedness, so to say—do you understand?''

I fancied that my uncle was horribly confused.

"Listen, uncle,'' I began, "I am so fond of you . . . forgive the direct question: are you going to marry someone here or not?''

"Why, from whom did you hear that?'' he answered, blushing like a child. "You see, my dear . . . I'll tell you all about it; in the first place, I am not going to get married. Mamma, my sister to some extent, and most of all Foma Fomitch, whom mamma worships—and with good reason, with good reason, he has done a great deal for her—they all want me to marry that same Tatyana Ivanovna, as a sensible step for the benefit of all. Of course they desire nothing but my good—I understand that, of course; but nothing will induce me to marry—I have made up my mind about that. In spite of that I have not succeeded in giving them a decided answer, I have not said yes, or no. It always happens like that with me, my boy. They thought that I had consented and are insisting that to-morrow, in honour of the festive occasion, I should declare myself . . . and so there is such a flutter in preparation for to-morrow that I really don't know what line to take! And besides, Foma Fomitch, I don't know why, is vexed with me, and mamma is too. I must say, my boy, I have simply been reckoning on you and on Korovkin. . . . I wanted to pour out my troubles, so to say. . . .''

"But how can Korovkin be of any use in this matter, uncle?''

"He will help, he will help, my dear—he is a wonderful man; in short, a man of learning! I build upon him as on a rock; a man who would conquer anything! How he speaks of domestic happiness! I must own I have been reckoning on you too; I thought you might bring them to reason. Consider and judge . . . granted that I have been to blame, really to blame—I understand all that—I am not without feeling. But all the same I might be forgiven some day! Then how well we should get on together! Oh, my boy, how my Sashenka has grown up, she'll be thinking of getting married directly! What a fine boy my Ilyusha has become! To-morrow is his nameday. But I am afraid for my Sashenka—that's the trouble.''

"Uncle! Where is my portmanteau? I will change my things and make my appearance in a minute, and then . . .''

"In the upper room, my boy, in the upper room. I gave

44

orders beforehand that as soon as you arrived you should be taken straight up there, so that no one should see you. Yes, yes, change your things! That's capital, capital, first-rate. And meanwhile I will prepare them all a little. Well, good luck to us! You know, my boy, we must be diplomatic. One is forced to become a Talleyrand. But there, never mind. They are drinking tea there now. We have tea early. Foma Fomitch likes to have his tea as soon as he wakes up; it is better, you know. Well, I'll go in, then, and you make haste and follow me, don't leave me alone; it will be awkward for me, my boy, alone. . . . But, stay! I have another favour to ask of you: don't cry out at me in there as you did out here just now—will you? If you want to make some criticism you can make it afterwards here when we are alone; till then hold yourself in and wait! You see, I have put my foot in it already with them. They are annoyed with me . . ."

"I say, uncle, from all that I have seen and heard it seems to me that you . . ."

"That I am as soft as butter, eh? Don't mind speaking out!" he interrupted me quite unexpectedly. "There is no help for it, my boy. I know it myself. Well, so you will come? Come as quick as you can, please!"

Going upstairs, I hurriedly opened my portmanteau, remembering my uncle's instructions to come down as soon as possible. As I was dressing, I realised that I had so far learned scarcely anything I wanted to know, though I had been talking to my uncle for a full hour. That struck me. Only one thing was pretty clear to me: my uncle was still set upon my getting married; consequently, all rumours to the opposite, that is, that my uncle was in love with the same lady himself, were wide of the mark. I remember that I was much agitated. Among other things the thought occurred to me that by my coming, and by my silence, I had almost made a promise, given my word, bound myself for ever. "It is easy," I thought, "it is easy to say a word which will bind one, hand and foot, for ever. And I have not yet seen my proposed bride!" And again: why this antagonism towards me on the part of the whole family? Why were they bound to take a hostile attitude to my coming as my uncle said they did? And what a strange part my uncle was playing here in his own house! What was the cause of his secretiveness? Why these worries and alarms? I must own that it all struck me suddenly as something quite senseless; and my romantic and heroic dreams took flight completely at the first contact with reality. Only now, after my conversation with my uncle, I suddenly realised all the incongruity and eccentricity of his proposition, and felt that no one but my uncle would have been capable of making such a proposal and in such circumstances. I realised, too, that I was something not unlike a fool for galloping here full speed at his first word, in high delight at his suggestion. I was dressing hurriedly, absorbed in my agitating doubts, so that I did not at first notice the man who was waiting on me.

"Will your honour wear the Adelaïda-coloured tie or the one with the little checks on it?" the man asked suddenly, addressing me with exceptionally mawkish obsequiousness.

I glanced at him, and it seemed to me that he, too, was worthy of attention. He was a man still young, for a flunkey well dressed, quite as well as many a provincial dandy. The brown coat, the white breeches, the straw-coloured waistcoat, the patent-leather boots and the pink tie had evidently been selected with intention. All this was bound at once to attract attention to the young dandy's refined taste. The watch-chain was undoubtedly displayed with the same object. He was pale, even greenish in fact, and had a long hooked nose, thin and remarkably white, as though it were made of china. The smile on his thin lips expressed melancholy, a refined melancholy, however. His large prominent eyes, which looked as though made of glass, had an extraordinarily stupid expression, and yet there was a gleam of refinement in them. His thin soft ears were stuffed up with cotton-wool—also a refinement. His long, scanty, flaxen hair was curled and pomaded. His hands were white, clean, and might have been washed in rose-water; his fingers ended in extremely long dandified pink nails. All this indicated a spoilt and idle fop. He lisped and mispronounced the letter "r" in fashionable style, raised and dropped his eyes, sighed and gave himself incredibly affected airs. He smelt of scent. He was short, feeble and flabby-looking, and moved about with knees and haunches bent, probably thinking this the height of refinement—in fact he was saturated with refinement, subtlety and an extraordinary sense of his own dignity. This last characteristic displeased me, I don't know why, and moved me to wrath.

"So that tie is Adelaïda colour?" I asked, looking severely at the young valet.

"Yes, Adelaïda," he answered, with undisturbed refinement.

"And is there an Agrafena colour?"

"No, sir, there cannot be such a colour."

"Why not?"

"Agrafena is not a polite name, sir."

"Not polite! Why not?"

"Why, Adelaïda, we all know, is a foreign name anyway, a ladylike name, but any low peasant woman can be called Agrafena."

"Are you out of your mind?"

"No, sir, I am in my right mind, sir. Of course you are free to call me any sort of name, but many generals and even some counts in Moscow and Petersburg have been pleased with my conversation, sir."

"And what's your name?"

"Vidoplyasov."

"Ah, so you are Vidoplyasov?"

"Just so, sir."

"Well, wait a bit, my lad, and I will make your acquaintance."

"It is something like Bedlam here," I thought to myself as I went downstairs.

CHAPTER IV

AT TEA

TEA was being served in the room that gave on to the veranda where I had that afternoon met Gavrila. I was much perturbed by my uncle's mysterious warnings in regard to the reception awaiting me. Youth is sometimes excessively vain, and youthful vanity is almost always cowardly. And so it was extremely unpleasant for me when, immediately going in at the door and seeing the whole party round the tea-table, I stumbled over a rug, staggered and, recovering my balance, flew unexpectedly into the middle of the room. As overwhelmed with confusion as though I had at one stroke lost my career, my honour and my good name, I stood without moving, turning as red as a crab and looking with a senseless stare at the company. I mention this incident, in itself so trivial, only because of the effect it had on my state of mind during the whole of that day, and consequently my attitude to

47

some of the personages of my story. I tried to bow, did not fully succeed, turned redder than ever, flew up to my uncle and clutched at his hand.

"How do you do, uncle," I gasped out breathlessly, intending to say something quite different and much cleverer, but to my own surprise I said nothing but, "how do you do."

"Glad to see you, glad to see you, my boy," answered my uncle, distressed on my account. "You know, we have met already. Don't be nervous, please," he added in a whisper, "it's a thing that may happen to anyone, and worse still, one sometimes falls flat! . . . And now, mother, let me introduce to you: this is our young man; he is a little overcome at the moment, but I am sure you will like him. My nephew, Sergey Alexandrovitch," he added, addressing the company.

But before going on with my story, allow me, gentle reader, to introduce to you by name the company in which I suddenly found myself. This is essential to the orderly sequence of my narrative.

The party consisted of several ladies and two men besides my uncle and me. Foma Fomitch, whom I was so eager to see, and who—even then I felt it—was absolute monarch in the house, was not there; he was conspicuous by his absence, and seemed to have taken with him all brightness from the room. They all looked gloomy and worried. One could not help noticing it from the first glance; embarrassed and upset as I was at the moment, I yet discerned that my uncle, for instance, was almost as upset as I was, though he was doing his utmost to conceal his anxiety under a show of ease. Something was lying like a heavy weight on his heart. One of the two gentlemen in the room was a young man about five-and-twenty, who turned out to be the Obnoskin my uncle had spoken of that afternoon, praising his intelligence and high principles. I did not take to this gentleman at all, everything about him savoured of vulgar chic; his dress, in spite of its chic, was shabby and common; his face looked, somehow, shabby too. His thin flaxen moustaches like a beetle's whiskers, and his unsuccessful wisps of beard, were evidently intended to show that he was a man of independent character and perhaps advanced ideas. He was continually screwing up his eyes, smiling with an affectation of malice; he threw himself into attitudes on his chair, and repeatedly stared at me through his eyeglass; but when I turned to him, he immediately dropped his eyeglass and seemed overcome with alarm. The other gentleman was young too, being about twenty-eight. He was my cousin, Mizintchikov. He certainly was extremely silent. He did not utter a single word at tea, and did not laugh when everyone else laughed; but I saw in him no sign of that "crushed" condition my uncle had detected; on the contrary, the look in his light brown eyes expressed resoluteness and a certain decision of character. Mizintchikov was dark and rather good-looking, with black hair; he was very correctly dressed— at my uncle's expense, as I learned later. Of the ladies the one I noticed first of all from her spiteful anæmic face was Miss Perepelitsyn. She was sitting near Madame la Générale— of whom I will give a special account later—not beside her, but deferentially a little behind; she was continually bending down and whispering something into the ear of her patroness. Two or three elderly lady companions were sitting absolutely mute in a row by the window, gazing open-eyed at Madame la Générale and waiting respectfully for their tea. My attention was attracted also by a fat, absolutely redundant lady, of about fifty, dressed very tastelessly and gaudily, wearing rouge, I believe, though she had hardly any teeth except blackened and broken stumps; this fact did not, however, prevent her from mincing, screwing up her eyes, dressing in the height of fashion and almost making eyes. She was hung round with chains, and like Monsieur Obnoskin was continually turning her lorgnette on me. This was his mother. Praskovya Ilyinitchna, my meek aunt, was pouring out the tea. She obviously would have liked to embrace me after our long separation, and of course to have shed a few tears on the occasion, but she did not dare. Everything here was, it seemed, under rigorous control. Near her was sitting a very pretty black-eyed girl of fifteen, who looked at me intently with childish curiosity—my cousin Sashenka. Finally, and perhaps most conspicuous of all, was a very strange lady, dressed richly and extremely youthfully, though she was far from being in her first youth and must have been at least five-and-thirty. Her face was very thin, pale, and withered, but extremely animated; a bright colour was constantly appearing in her pale cheeks, almost at every movement, at every flicker of feeling; she was in continual excitement, twisting and turning in her chair, and seemed unable to sit still for a minute. She kept looking at me with a kind of greedy curiosity, and was continually bending down to whisper something into the ear of Sashenka, or of her neighbour on the other side, and

49

immediately afterwards laughing in the most childish and simple-hearted way. But to my surprise her eccentricities seemed to pass unnoticed by the others, as though they had all agreed to pay no attention to them. I guessed that this was Tatyana Ivanovna, the lady in whom, to use my uncle's expression, "there was something phantasmagorial", whom they were trying to force upon him as a bride, and whose favour almost everyone in the house was trying to court for the sake of her money. But I liked her eyes, blue and mild; and though there were already crow's-feet round the eyes, their expression was so simple-hearted, so merry and good-humoured, that it was particularly pleasant to meet them. Of Tatyana Ivanovna, one of the real "heroines" of my story, I shall speak more in detail later; her history was very remarkable. Five minutes after my entrance, a very pretty boy, my cousin Ilyusha, ran in from the garden, with his pockets full of knuckle-bones and a top in his hand. He was followed by a graceful young girl, rather pale and weary-looking, but very pretty. She scanned the company with a searching, mistrustful, and even timid glance, looked intently at me, and sat down by Tatyana Ivanovna. I remember that I could not suppress a throb at my heart; I guessed that this was the governess. . . . I remember, too, that on her entrance my uncle stole a swift glance at me and flushed crimson, then he bent down, caught up Ilyusha in his arms, and brought him up to me to be kissed. I noticed, too, that Madame Obnoskin first stared at my uncle and then with a sarcastic smile turned her lorgnette on the governess. My uncle was very much confused and, not knowing what to do, was on the point of calling to Sashenka to introduce her to me; but the girl merely rose from her seat and in silence, with grave dignity, dropped me a curtsy. I liked her doing this, however, for it suited her. At the same instant my kindly aunt, Praskovya Ilyinitchna, could hold out no longer and, abandoning the tea-tray, dashed up to embrace me; but before I had time to say a couple of words to her I heard the shrill voice of Miss Perepelitsyn hissing out that Praskovya Ilyinitchna seemed to have forgotten Madame la Générale. "Madame has asked for her tea, and you do not pour it out, and she is waiting." And Praskovya Ilyinitchna, leaving me, flew back in all haste to her duties. Madame la Générale, the most important person of the party, in whose presence all the others were on their best behaviour, was a lean spiteful old woman, dressed in mourning—spiteful, however, chiefly from old age and from the loss of her mental faculties which had never been over-brilliant); even in the past, she had been a nonsensical creature. Her rank as a general's wife had made her even stupider and more arrogant. When she was in a bad humour the house became a perfect hell. She had two ways of displaying her ill humour. The first was a silent method, when the old lady would not open her lips for days together, but maintained an obstinate silence and pushed away or even sometimes flung on the floor everything that was put before her. The other method was the exact opposite— garrulous. This would begin, as a rule, by my grandmother's— for she was my grandmother, of course—being plunged into a state of extreme despondency, and expecting the end of the world and the failure of all her undertakings, foreseeing poverty and every possible trouble in the future, being carried away by her own presentiments, reckoning on her fingers the calamities that were coming, and reaching a climax of enthusiasm and intense excitement over the enumeration. It always appeared, of course, that she had foreseen all this long before, and had said nothing only because she was forced to be silent "in this house". But if only she had been treated with respect, if only they had cared to listen to her earlier, then, etc., etc. In all this, the flock of lady companions and Miss Perepelitsyn promptly followed suit, and finally it was solemnly ratified by Foma Fomitch. At the minute when I was presented to her she was in a horrible rage, and apparently it was taking the silent form, the most terrible. Everyone was watching her with apprehension. Only Tatyana Ivanovna, who was completely unconscious of it all, was in the best of spirits. My uncle purposely with a certain solemnity led me up to my grand-mother; but the latter, making a wry face, pushed away her cup ill-humouredly.

"Is this that *vol-ti-geur?*" she drawled through her teeth, addressing Miss Perepelitsyn.

This foolish question completely disconcerted me. I don't understand why she called me a *voltigeur*. But such questions were easy enough to her. Miss Perepelitsyn bent down and whispered something in her ear, but the old lady waved her off angrily. I remained standing with my mouth open and looked inquiringly at my uncle. They all looked at one another and Obnoskin even grinned, which I did not like at all.

"She sometimes talks at random, my boy," my uncle, a little

51

disconcerted himself, whispered in my ear; "but it means nothing, it's just her goodness of heart. The heart is what one must look at."

"Yes, the heart, the heart," Tatyana Ivanovna's bell-like voice rang out. She had not taken her eyes off me all this time, and seemed as though she could not sit still in her chair. I suppose the word "heart", uttered in a whisper, had reached her ear.

But she did not go on, though she was evidently longing to express herself. Whether she was overcome with confusion or some other feeling, she suddenly subsided into silence, flushed extremely red, turned quickly to the governess and whispered something in her ear, and suddenly putting her handkerchief before her mouth and sinking back in her chair, began giggling as though she were in hysterics. I looked at them all in extreme amazement; but to my surprise, everyone was particularly grave and looked as though nothing exceptional had happened. I realised, of course, the kind of person Tatyana Ivanovna was. At last I was handed tea, and I recovered myself a little. I don't know why, but I suddenly felt that it was my duty to begin a polite conversation with the ladies.

"It was true what you told me, uncle," I began, "when you warned me that I might be a little abashed. I openly confess— why conceal it?" I went on, addressing Madame Obnoskin with a deprecating smile, "that I have hitherto had hardly any experience of ladies' society. And just now when I made my entry so unsuccessfully, it seemed to me that my position in the middle of the room was very ridiculous and made me look rather a simpleton, didn't it? Have you read *The Simpleton?*" I added, feeling more and more lost, blushing at my ingratiating candour, and glaring at Monsieur Obnoskin, who was still looking me up and down with a grin on his face.

"Just so, just so, just so!" my uncle cried suddenly with extreme animation, genuinely delighted that the conversation had been set going somehow and that I had recovered myself. "That's no great matter, my boy, your talking of the likelihood of your being abashed. Well, you have been, and that's the end of it. But when I first made my debut, I actually told a lie, my boy, would you believe that? Yes, really, Anfisa Petrovna, I assure you, it's worth hearing. Just after I had become a Junker, I went to Moscow, and presented myself to a very important lady with a letter of introduction;

that is, she was a very haughty woman, but in reality very good-natured, in spite of what they said. I went in—I was shown up. The drawing-room was full of people, chiefly swells. I made my bow and sat down. At the second word, she asked me: 'Have you estates in the country?' And I hadn't got as much as a hen—what was I to answer? I felt crushed to the earth. Everyone was looking at me (I was only a young Junker!). Why not say: no, I have nothing; and that would have been the right thing because it was the truth. But I couldn't face it! 'Yes,' I said, 'a hundred and seventeen serfs.' And why did I stick on that seventeen? If one must tell a lie, it is better to tell it with a round number, isn't it? A minute later, through my letter of introduction, it appeared that I was as poor as a church mouse, and I had told a lie into the bargain! . . . Well, there was no help for it. I took myself off as fast as I could, and never set foot in the place again. In those days I had nothing, you know. All I have got now is three hundred serfs from Uncle Afanasy Matveyitch, and two hundred serfs with Kapitonovko, which came to me earlier from my grandmother Akulina Panfilovna, a total of more than five hundred serfs. That's capital! But from that day I gave up lying and don't tell lies now."

"Well, I shouldn't have given it up, if I were you. There is no knowing what may happen," observed Obnoskin, smiling ironically.

"To be sure, that's true! Goodness knows what may happen," my uncle assented good-naturedly.

Obnoskin burst into loud laughter, throwing himself back in his chair; his mother smiled; Miss Perepelitsyn sniggered in a particularly disgusting way; Tatyana Ivanovna giggled too, without knowing why, and even clapped her hands; in fact, I saw distinctly that my uncle counted for nothing in his own house. Sashenka's eyes flashed angrily, and she looked steadily at Obnoskin. The governess flushed and looked down. My uncle was surprised.

"What is it? What's happened?" he repeated, looking round at us all in perplexity.

All this time my cousin Mizintchikov was sitting a little way off, saying nothing and not even smiling when everyone laughed. He drank tea zealously, gazed philosophically at the whole company, and several times as though in an access of unbearable boredom broke into whistling, probably a habit of his, but pulled himself up in time. Obnoskin, who had jeered at my uncle and had attempted to attack me, seemed not to dare to glance at Mizintchikov; I noticed that. I noticed, too, that my silent cousin looked frequently at me and with evident curiosity, as though he was trying to make up his mind what sort of person I was.

"I am certain," Madame Obnoskin minced suddenly, "I am perfectly certain Monsieur Serge—that is your name, I believe? —that at home, in Petersburg, you were not greatly devoted to the ladies. I know that there are many, a great many young men nowadays in Petersburg who shun the society of ladies altogether. But in my opinion they are all free-thinkers. Nothing would induce me to regard it as anything but unpardonable free-thinking. And I must say it surprises me, young man, it surprises me, simply surprises me! . . ."

"I have not been into society at all," I answered with extraordinary animation. "But that . . . I imagine at least . . . is of no consequence. I have lived, that is I have generally had lodgings . . . but that is no matter, I assure you. I shall be known one day; but hitherto I have always stayed at home. . . ."

"He is engaged in learned pursuits," observed my uncle, drawing himself up with dignity.

"Oh, uncle, still talking of your learned pursuits! . . . Only fancy," I went on with an extraordinary free and easy air, smirking affably, and again addressing Madame Obnoskin, "my beloved uncle is so devoted to learning that he has unearthed somewhere on the high road a marvellous practical philosopher, a Mr. Korovkin; and his first words to me after all these years of separation were that he was expecting this phenomenal prodigy with the most acute, one may say, impatience . . . from love of learning, of course. . . ."

And I sniggered, hoping to provoke a general laugh at my facetiousness.

"Who is that? Of whom is he talking?" Madame la Générale jerked out sharply, addressing Miss Perepelitsyn.

"Yegor Ilyitch has been inviting visitors, learned gentlemen; he drives along the high road collecting them," the lady hissed out.

My uncle was completely dumbfounded.

"Oh, yes! I had forgotten," he cried, turning upon me a glance that expressed reproach. "I am expecting Korovkin. A man of learning, a man who will survive his century. . . ."

He broke off and relapsed into silence. Madame la Générale

54

waved her arm, and this time so successfully that she knocked over a cup, which flew off the table and was smashed. General excitement followed.

"She always does that when she is angry; she throws things on the floor," my uncle whispered in confusion. "But she only does it when she is angry. . . . Don't stare, my boy, don't take any notice, look the other way. . . . What made you speak of Korovkin? . . ."

But I was looking away already; at that moment I met the eyes of the governess, and it seemed to me that in their expression there was something reproachful, even contemptuous; a flush of indignation glowed upon her pale cheeks. I understood the look in her face, and guessed that by my mean and disgusting desire to make my uncle ridiculous in order to make myself a little less so, I had not gained much in that young lady's estimation. I cannot express how ashamed I felt!

"I must go on about Petersburg with you," Anfisa Petrovna gushed again, when the commotion caused by the breaking of the cup had subsided. "I recall with such enjoyment, I may say, our life in that charming city. . . . We were very intimately acquainted with a family—do you remember, Pavel, General Polovitsin. . . . Oh, what a fascinating, fas-ci-na-ting creature his wife was! You know that aristocratic distinction, *beau monde!* . . . Tell me, you have most likely met her? . . . I must own I have been looking forward to your being here with impatience; I have been hoping to hear a great deal, a very great deal about our friends in Petersburg. . . ."

"I am very sorry that I cannot . . . excuse me. . . . As I have said already, I have rarely been into society, and I don't know General Polovitsin; I have never even heard of him," I answered impatiently, my affability being suddenly succeeded by a mood of extreme annoyance and irritability.

"He is studying mineralogy," my incorrigible uncle put in with pride. "Is that investigating all sorts of stones, mineralogy, my boy?"

"Yes, uncle, stones. . . ."

"H'm. . . . There are a great many sciences and they are all of use! And do you know, my boy, to tell you the truth, I did not know what mineralogy meant! It's all Greek to me. In other things I am so-so, but at learned subjects I am stupid —I frankly confess it!"

55

"You frankly confess!" Obnoskin caught him up with a snigger.

"Papa!" cried Sashenka, looking reproachfully at her father.

"What is it, darling? Oh, dear, I keep interrupting you, Anfisa Petrovna," my uncle caught himself up suddenly, not understanding Sashenka's exclamation. "Please forgive me."

"Oh, don't distress yourself," Anfisa Petrovna answered with a sour smile. "Though I have said everything already to your nephew, and will finish perhaps, Monsieur Serge—that is right, isn't it?—by telling you that you really must reform. I believe that the sciences, the arts . . . sculpture, for instance . . . all those lofty ideas, in fact, have their fas-cin-na-ting side, but they do not take the place of ladies! . . . Women, women would form you, young man, and so to do without them is impossible, young man, impossible, im-poss-ible!"

"Impossible, impossible," Tatyana Ivanovna's rather shrill voice rang out again. "Listen," she began, speaking with a sort of childish haste and flushing crimson, of course, "listen, I want to ask you something. . . ."

"Pray do," I answered, looking at her attentively.

"I wanted to ask you whether you have come to stay long or not?"

"I really don't know, that's as my affairs . . ."

"Affairs! What sort of affairs can he have? Oh, the mad fellow! . . ."

And Tatyana Ivanovna, blushing perfectly crimson and hiding behind her fan, bent down to the governess and at once began whispering something to her. Then she suddenly laughed and clapped her hands.

"Stay! stay!" she cried, breaking away from her confidante and again addressing me in a great hurry as though afraid I were going away. "Listen, do you know what I am going to tell you? You are awfully, awfully like a young man, a fas-ci-na-ting young man! Sashenka, Nastenka, do you remember? He is awfully like that madman—do you remember, Sashenka? We were out driving when we met him . . . on horseback in a white waistcoat . . . he put up his eyeglass at me, too, the shameless fellow! Do you remember, I hid myself in my veil, too, but I couldn't resist putting my head out of the carriage window and shouting to him: 'You shameless fellow!' and then I threw my bunch of flowers on the road? . . . Do you remember, Nastenka?"

And the lady, half crazy over eligible young men, hid her

56

face in her hands, all excitement; then suddenly leaped up from her seat, darted to the window, snatched a rose from a bowl, threw it on the floor near me and ran out of the room. She was gone in a flash! This time a certain embarrassment was apparent, though Madame la Générale was again completely unmoved. Anfisa Petrovna, for instance, showed no surprise, but seemed suddenly a little troubled and looked with anxiety at her son; the young ladies blushed, while Pavel Obnoskin, with a look of vexation which at the time I did not understand, got up from his chair and went to the window. My uncle was beginning to make signs to me, but at that instant another person walked into the room and drew the attention of all.

"Ah, here is Yevgraf Larionitch! Talk of angels!" cried my uncle, genuinely delighted. "Well, brother, have you come from the town?"

"Queer set of creatures! They seem to have been collected here on purpose!" I thought to myself, not yet understanding fully what was passing before my eyes, and not suspecting either that I was probably adding another to the collection of queer creatures by appearing among them.

CHAPTER V

YEZHEVIKIN

THERE walked or rather squeezed himself into the room (though the doors were very wide ones) a little figure which even in the doorway began wriggling, bowing and smirking, looking with extraordinary curiosity at all the persons present. It was a little pockmarked old man with quick and furtive eyes, with a bald patch at the top of his head and another at the back, with a look of undefined subtle mockery on his rather thick lips. He was wearing a very shabby dress-coat which looked as though it were second-hand. One button was hanging by a thread; two or three were completely missing. His high boots full of holes, and his greasy cap, were in keeping with his pitiful attire; he had a very dirty check pocket-handkerchief in his hand, with which he wiped the sweat from his brow and temples. I noticed that the governess blushed slightly and looked rapidly at me. I fancied, too, that there was something proud and challenging in this glance.

"Straight from the town, benefactor! Straight from there, my kind protector! I will tell you everything, only first let me pay my respects," said the old man. And he made straight for Madame la Générale, but stopped half-way and again addressed my uncle.

"You know my leading characteristic, benefactor—a sly rogue, a regular sly rogue! You know that as soon as I walk in I make for the chief person of the house, I turn my toes in her direction first of all, so as from the first step to win favour and protection. A sly rogue, my good sir, a sly rogue, benefactor. Allow me, my dear lady, allow me, your Excellency, to kiss your dress, or I might sully with my lips your hand of gold, of general's rank."

Madame la Générale to my surprise gave him her hand to kiss rather graciously.

"And my respects to you, our beauty," he went on, "Miss Perepelitsyn. There is no help for it, Madam, I am a sly rogue. As long ago as 1841 it was settled that I was a rogue, when I was dismissed from the service just at the time when Valentin Ignatyevitch Tihontsev became 'your honour'. He was made an assessor; he was made an assessor and I was made a rogue. And, you know, I am so open by nature that I make no secret of it. It can't be helped. I have tried living honestly, I have tried it, but now I must try something else. Alexandra Yegorovna, our little apple in syrup," he went on, going round the table and making his way up to Sashenka, "let me kiss your dress; there is a smell of apples and all sorts of nice things about you, young lady. Our respects to the hero of the day; I have brought you a bow and arrow, my little sir. I was a whole morning making it, my lads helped me; we will shoot with it presently. And when you grow up you will be an officer and cut off a Turk's head. Tatyana Ivanovna . . . but oh, she is not here, my benefactress! Or I would have kissed her dress too. Praskovya Ilyinitchna, my kindest friend, I can't get near you or I would kiss your foot as well as your hand, so there! Anfisa Petrovna, I protest my profound respect for you. I prayed for you only to-day, benefactress, on my knees with tears I prayed for you and for your son also that God might send him honours of all sorts—and talents too, talents especially! And by the way, our humblest duty to Ivan Ivanitch Mizintchikov. May God send you all that you desire for yourself, for you will never make out, sir, what you do want for yourself: such a silent gentleman. . . . Good-day,

Nastya! All my small fry send their love to you, they talk of you every day. And now a deep bow to my host. I come from the town, your honour, straight off from the town. And this, no doubt, is your nephew who is being trained in a learned faculty? My humble duty, sir; let me have your hand."

There was laughter. One could see that the old man played the part of an amateur clown. His arrival livened the party up. Many did not even understand his sarcasms, and yet he had made slight digs at them all. Only the governess, whom to my surprise he called simply Nastya, blushed and frowned. I was pulling back my hand, but I believe that was just what the horrid old man wanted.

"But I only asked to shake it, sir, if you will allow me; not to kiss it. And you thought I meant to kiss it? No, my dear sir, for the time being I will only shake it. I suppose you took me for the clown of the establishment, kind sir?" he said, looking at me mockingly.

"N—o, no, really, I . . ."

"To be sure, sir! If I am a fool, then someone else here is one too. Treat me with respect; I am not such a rogue yet as you imagine. Though maybe I am a clown too. I am a slave, my wife is a slave, and so there is nothing for it but flattery. That's how it is! You get something by it anyway, if only to make sop for the children. Sugar, scatter as much sugar as you can in everything, that will make things more wholesome for you. I tell you this in secret, sir; maybe you will have need of it. Fortune has been hard on me, that is why I am a clown."

"He-he-he! The old man is a comical fellow! He always makes us laugh!" piped Anfisa Petrovna.

"My dear madam and benefactress, a fool has a better time of it in this world! If I had only known that, I would have enlisted among the fools in early childhood, and I dare say by now I might have been a wise man. But as it is, I wanted to be a clever man at first, so now I am a fool in my old age."

"Tell me, please," interposed Obnoskin (he probably was not pleased by the remark about *talents*), lolling in a particularly free and easy way in his arm-chair and staring at the old man through his eyeglass as though at an insect, "tell me, please . . . I always forget your surname . . . what the deuce is it? . . ."

"Oh, my dear sir! Why, my surname, if it please you, is Yezhevikin; but what does that matter? Here I have been sitting without a job these nine years, I just go on living in

59

accordance with the laws of nature. And my children, my children are simply a family of Holmskys. As the proverb goes, 'The rich man has calves, the poor man has kids.' "

"Oh, yes . . . calves . . . but that's beside the point. Come, listen, I have been wanting to ask you a long time: why is it that when you come in, you look back at once? It's very funny."

"Why do I look back? Why, I am always fancying, sir, that someone behind me wants to slap me on the back and squash me like a fly. That is why I look round. I have become a monomaniac, sir."

Again there was laughter. The governess got up from her seat as though she would go away, but sank back in her chair again. There was a look of pain and suffering on her face in spite of the colour that flooded her cheeks.

"You know who it is, my boy?" my uncle whispered. "It's *her* father, you know!"

I stared at my uncle open-eyed. The name of Yezhevikin had completely slipped out of my mind. I had been playing the hero, had been dreaming all the journey of my proposed bride, had been building magnificent plans for her benefit, and had utterly forgotten her name, or rather had taken no notice of it from the first.

"What, her father?" I answered, also in a whisper. "Why, I thought she was an orphan."

"It's her father, my boy, her father. And do you know, a most honest, a most honourable man and he does not even drink, but only plays at being a fool; fearfully poor, my boy, eight children! They live on Nastya's salary. He was turned out of the service through his tongue. He comes here every week. He is such a proud fellow—nothing will induce him to take help. I have offered it, many times I have offered it—he won't take it. An embittered man."

"Well, Yevgraf Larionitch, what news have you?" uncle asked, and slapped him warmly on the shoulder, noticing that the suspicious old man was already listening to our conversation.

"What news, benefactor? Valentin Ignatyitch made a statement about Trishin's case yesterday. The flour under his charge turned out to be short weight. It is that Trishin, madam, who looks at you and puffs like a samovar. Perhaps you graciously remember him? So Valentin Ignatyitch writes of Trishin: 'If,' said he, 'the often-mentioned Trishin could not guard his own niece's honour—she eloped with an officer last year—

'how,' said he, 'should he take care of government property?'
He stuck that into his report, by God, I am not lying.''

"Fie! What stories you tell!" cried Anfisa Petrovna.

"Just so, just so, just so! You've overshot the mark, friend
Yevgraf," my uncle chimed in. "*Aïe!* your tongue will be your
ruin. You are a straightforward man, honourable and upright,
I can say that, but you have a venomous tongue! And I can't
understand how it is you can't get on with them. They seem
good-natured people, simple . . ."

"Kind friend and benefactor! But it's just the simple man
that I am afraid of," cried the old man with peculiar fervour.

I liked the answer. I went rapidly up to Yezhevikin and
warmly pressed his hand. The truth is, I wanted in some way
to protest against the general tone and to show my sympathy
for the old man openly. And perhaps, who knows? perhaps I
wanted to raise myself in the opinion of Nastasya Yevgrafovna!
But my movement led to no good.

"Allow me to ask you," I said, blushing and flustered as
usual, "have you heard of the Jesuits?"

"No, my good sir, I haven't; well, maybe something . . .
though how should we! But why?"

"Oh . . . I meant to tell you something apropos. . . . But
remind me some other time. But now let me assure you, I
understand you and . . . know how to appreciate . . ."

And utterly confused, I gripped his hand again.

"Certainly, I will remind you, sir, certainly. I will write it
in golden letters. If you will allow me, I'll tie a knot in my
handkerchief."

And he actually looked for a dry corner in his dirty, snuffy
handkerchief, and tied a knot in it.

"Yevgraf Larionitch, take your tea," said Praskovya
Ilyinitchna.

"Immediately, my beautiful lady; immediately, my princess,
I mean, not my lady! That's in return for your tea. I met
Stepan Alexyevitch Bahtcheyev on the road, madam. He was
so festive that I didn't know what to make of it! I began to
wonder whether he wasn't going to get married. Flatter away,
flatter away!" he said in a half whisper, winking at me and
screwing up his eyes as he carried his cup by me. "And how
is it that my benefactor, my chief one, Foma Fomitch, is not to
be seen? Isn't he coming to tea?"

My uncle started as though he had been stung, and glanced
timidly at his mother.

"I really don't know," he answered uncertainly, with a strange perturbation. "We sent for him, but he . . . I don't know really, perhaps he is indisposed. I have already sent Vidoplyasov and . . . Perhaps I ought to go myself, though?"

"I went in to him myself just now," Yezhevikin brought out mysteriously.

"Is it possible!" cried out my uncle in alarm. "Well, how was it?"

"I went in to him, first of all, I paid him my respects. His honour said he should drink his tea in solitude, and then added that a crust of dry bread would be enough for him, yes."

These words seemed to strike absolute terror into my uncle.

"But you should have explained to him, Yevgraf Larionitch; you should have told him," my uncle said at last, looking at the old man with distress and reproach.

"I did, I did."

"Well?"

"For a long time he did not deign to answer me. He was sitting over some mathematical problem, he was working out something; one could see it was a brain-racking problem. He drew the breeches of Pythagoras, while I was there, I saw him myself. I repeated it three times, only at the fourth he raised his head and seemed to see me for the first time. 'I am not coming,' he said; 'a *learned* gentleman has arrived here now, so I should be out of place beside a luminary like that!' He made use of that expression 'beside a luminary'."

And the horrid old man stole a sly glance at me.

"That is just what I expected," cried my uncle, clasping his hands. "That's how I thought it would be. He says that about you, Sergey, that you are a 'learned gentleman'. Well, what's to be done now?"

"I must confess, uncle," I answered with dignity, shrugging my shoulders, "it seems to me such an absurd refusal that it is not worth noticing, and I really wonder at your being troubled by it. . . ."

"Oh, my boy, you know nothing about it!" he cried, with a vigorous wave of his hand.

"It's no use grieving now, sir," Miss Perepelitsyn put in suddenly, "since all the wicked causes of it have come from you in the first place, Yegor Ilyitch. If you take off your head you don't weep for your hair. You should have listened to your mamma, sir, and you would have had no cause for tears now."

"Why, how am I to blame, Anna Nilovna? Have some fear of God!" said my uncle in an imploring voice, as though begging for an explanation.

"I do fear God, Yegor Ilyitch; but it all comes from your being an egoist, sir, and not loving your mother," Miss Perepelitsyn answered with dignity. "Why didn't you respect her wishes in the first place? She is your mother, sir. And I am not likely to tell you a lie, sir. I am a major's daughter myself, and not just anybody, sir."

It seemed to me that Miss Perepelitsyn had intervened in the conversation with the sole object of informing us all, and me in particular as a new-comer, that she was a major's daughter and not just anybody.

"It's because he ill-treats his own mother," Madame la Générale herself brought out at last in a menacing voice.

"Mamma, have mercy on us! How am I ill-treating you?"

"It is because you are a black-hearted egoist, Yegorushka," Madame la Générale went on, growing more and more animated.

"Mamma, mamma! in what way am I a black-hearted egoist?" cried my uncle, almost in despair. "For five days, for five whole days you have been angry with me and will not speak to me. And what for? what for? Let them judge me, let the whole world judge me! But let them hear my defence too. I have long kept silent, mamma, you would not hear me; let these people hear me now. Anfisa Petrovna! Pavel Semyonitch, generous Pavel Semyonitch! Sergey, my dear! You are an outsider, you are, so to speak, a spectator. You can judge impartially. . . ."

"Calm yourself, Yegor Ilyitch, calm yourself," cried Anfisa Petrovna, "don't kill your mamma."

"I am not killing my mamma, Anfisa Petrovna; but here I lay bare my heart, you can strike at it!" my uncle went on, worked up to the utmost pitch as people of weak character sometimes are when they are driven out of all patience, though their heat is like the fire of burning straws. "I want to say, Anfisa Petrovna, that I am not ill-treating any one. I start with saying that Foma Fomitch is the noblest and the most honourable of men, and a man of superior qualities too, but . . . but he has been unjust to me in this case."

"H'm!" grunted Obnoskin, as though he wanted to irritate my uncle still more.

"Pavel Semyonitch, noble-hearted Pavel Semyonitch! Can you really think that I am, so to speak, an unfeeling stone?

Why, I see, I understand—with tears in my heart, I may say I understand—that all this misunderstanding comes from the excess of *his* affection for me. But, say what you like, he really is unjust in this case. I will tell you all about it. I want to tell the whole story, Anfisa Petrovna, clearly and in full detail, that you may see from what the thing started, and whether mamma is right in being angry with me for not satisfying Foma Fomitch. And you listen too, Seryozha," he added, addressing me, which he did, indeed, during the rest of his story, as though he were afraid of his other listeners and doubtful of their sympathy; "you, too, listen and decide whether I am right or wrong. You will see what the whole business arose from. A week ago—yes, not more than a week—my old chief, General Rusapetov, was passing through our town with his wife and stepdaughter, and broke the journey there. I was overwhelmed. I hastened to seize the opportunity, I flew over, presented myself and invited them to dinner. He promised to come if it were possible. He is a very fine man, I assure you; he is conspicuous for his virtues and is a man of the highest rank into the bargain! He has been a benefactor to his stepdaughter; he married an orphan girl to an admirable young man (now a lawyer at Malinova; still a young man, but with, one may say, an all-round education); in short, he is a general of generals. Well, of course there was a tremendous fuss and bustle in the house—cooks, fricassees—I sent for an orchestra. I was delighted, of course, and looked festive; Foma Fomitch did not like my being delighted and looking festive! He sat down to the table—I remember, too, he was handed his favourite jelly and cream—he sat on and on without saying a word, then all at once jumped up. 'I am being insulted, insulted!' 'But why, in what way are you being insulted, Foma Fomitch?' 'You despise me now,' he said; 'you are taken up with generals now, you think more of generals now than of me.' Well, of course I am making a long story short, so to say, I am only giving you the pith of it; but if only you knew what he said besides . . . in a word, he stirred me to my inmost depths. What was I to do? I was depressed by it, of course; it was a blow to me, I may say. I went about like a cock drenched with rain. The festive day arrived. The general sent to say he couldn't come, he apologised—so he was not coming. I went to Foma. 'Come, Foma,' I said, 'set your mind at rest, he is not coming.' And would you believe it, he wouldn't forgive me, and that was the end of it. 'I have

64

been insulted,' he said, 'and that is all about it!' I said this and that. 'No,' he said. 'You can go to your generals; you think more of generals than of me, you have broken our bonds of friendship,' he said. Of course, my dear. I understand what he was angry over, I am not a block, I am not a sheep, I am not a perfect post. It was, of course, from the excess of his affection for me, from jealousy—he says that himself—he is jealous of the general on my account, he is afraid of losing my affection, he is testing me, he wants to see how much I am ready to sacrifice for him. 'No,' he said, 'I am just as good as the general for you, I am myself "your Excellency" for you! I will be reconciled to you when you prove your respect for me.' 'In what way am I to prove my respect for you, Foma Fomitch?' 'Call me for a whole day "your Excellency", says he, 'then you will prove your respect.' I felt as though I were dropping from the clouds; you can picture my amazement. 'That will serve you,' said he, 'as a lesson not to be in ecstasies at the sight of generals when there are other people, perhaps, superior to all your generals.' Well, at that point I lost patience, I confess it! I confess it openly. 'Foma Fomitch,' I said, 'is such a thing possible? Can I take it upon myself to do it? Can I, have I the right to promote you to be a general? Think who it is bestows the rank of a general. How can I address you as, "your Excellency"? Why, it is infringing the decrees of Providence! Why, the general is an honour to his country; the general has faced the enemy, he has shed his blood on the field of honour. How am I to call you "your Excellency"?' He would not give way, there was no doing anything. 'Whatever you want, Foma,' I said, 'I will do anything for you. Here you told me to shave off my whiskers because they were not patriotic enough—I shaved them off; I frowned, but I did shave them. What is more, I will do anything you like, only do give up the rank of a general!' 'No,' said he, 'I won't be reconciled till you call me "your Excellency"; that,' said he, 'will be good for your moral character, it will humble your spirit!' said he. And so now for a week, a whole week, he won't speak to me; he is cross to everyone that comes; he heard about you, that you were learned—that was my fault; I got warm and said too much—so he said he would not set foot in the house if you came into it. 'So I am not learned enough for you now,' said he. So there will be trouble when he hears now about Korovkin! Come now, please, tell me in what way have I been to blame? Was

65

I to take on myself to call him 'your Excellency'? Why, it is impossible to live in such a position! What did he drive poor Bahtcheyev away from the table to-day for? Supposing Bahtcheyev is not a great astronomer, why I am not a great astronomer, and you are not a great astronomer. . . . Why is it? Why is it?"

"Because you are envious, Yegorushka," mumbled Madame la Générale again.

"Mamma," cried my uncle in despair, "you will drive me out of my mind! . . . Those are not your words, you are repeating what others say, mamma! I am, in fact, made out a stone, a block, a lamp-post and not your son."

"I heard, uncle," I interposed, utterly amazed by his story—"I heard from Bahtcheyev, I don't know whether it was true or not—that Foma Fomitch was jealous of Ilyusha's nameday, and declares that to-morrow is his nameday too. I must own that this characteristic touch so astounded me that I . . ."

"His birthday, my dear, his birthday!" my uncle interrupted me, speaking rapidly. "He only made a mistake in the word, but he is right; to-morrow is his birthday. Truth, my boy, before everything. . . ."

"It's not his birthday at all!" cried Sashenka.

"Not his birthday!" cried my uncle, in a fluster.

"It's not his birthday, papa. You simply say what isn't true to deceive yourself and to satisfy Foma Fomitch. His birthday was in March. Don't you remember, too, we went on a pilgrimage to the monastery just before, and he wouldn't let anyone sit in peace in the carriage? He kept crying out that the cushion was *crushing* his side, and pinching us; he pinched auntie twice in his ill humour. 'I am fond of camellias,' he said, 'for I have the taste of the most refined society, and you grudge picking me any from the conservatory.' And all day long he sulked and grizzled and would not talk to us. . . ."

I fancy that if a bomb had fallen in the middle of the room it would not have astounded and alarmed them all as much as this open mutiny—and of whom?—of a little girl who was not even permitted to speak aloud in her grandmother's presence. Madame la Générale, dumb with amazement and fury, rose from her seat, stood erect and stared at her insolent grandchild, unable to believe her eyes. My uncle was paralysed with horror.

"She is allowed to do just as she likes, she wants to be the death of her grandmother!" cried Miss Perepelitsyn.

66

"Sasha, Sasha, think what you are saying! What's the matter with you, Sasha?" cried my uncle, rushing from one to the other, from his mother to Sashenka to stop her.

"I won't hold my tongue, papa!" cried Sashenka, leaping up from her chair with flashing eyes and stamping with her feet. "I won't hold my tongue! We have all suffered too long from Foma Fomitch, from your nasty, horrid Foma Fomitch! Foma Fomitch will be the ruin of us all, for people keep on telling him that he is so clever, generous, noble, learned, a mix-up of all the virtues, a sort of potpourri, and like an idiot Foma Fomitch believes it all. So many nice things are offered to him that anyone else would be ashamed; but Foma Fomitch gobbles up all that is put before him and asks for more. You'll see, he will be the ruin of us all, and it's all papa's fault! Horrid, horrid Foma Fomitch! I speak straight out, I am not afraid of anyone! He is stupid, ill-tempered, dirty, ungentle-manly, cruel-hearted, a bully, a mischief-maker, a liar. . . . Oh, I'd turn him out of the house this minute, I would, but papa adores him, papa is crazy over him!"

"Oh!" shrieked her grandmother, and she fell in a swoon on the sofa.

"Agafya Timofyevna, my angel," cried Anfisa Petrovna, "take my smelling-salts! Water, make haste, water!"

"Water, water!" shouted my uncle. "Mamma, mamma, calm yourself! I beg you on my knees to calm yourself! . . ."

"You ought to be kept on bread and water and shut up in a dark room . . . you're a murderess!" Miss Perepelitsyn, shaking with spite, hissed at Sashenka.

"I will be kept on bread and water, I am not afraid of anything!" cried Sashenka, moved to frenzy in her turn. "I will defend papa because he can't defend himself. Who is he, who is your Foma Fomitch compared with papa? He eats papa's bread and insults papa, the ungrateful creature. I would tear him to pieces, your Foma Fomitch! I'd challenge him to a duel and shoot him on the spot with two pistols! . . ."

"Sasha, Sasha," cried my uncle in despair. "Another word and I am ruined, hopelessly ruined."

"Papa," cried Sashenka, flinging herself headlong at her father, dissolving into tears and hugging him in her arms, "papa, how can you ruin yourself like this, you so kind, and good, and merry and clever? How can you give in to that horrid ungrateful man, be his plaything and let him turn you into ridicule? Papa, my precious papa! . . ."

She burst into sobs, covered her face with her hands and ran out of the room.

A fearful hubbub followed. Madame la Générale lay in a swoon. My uncle was kneeling beside her kissing her hands. Miss Perepelitsyn was wriggling about them and casting spiteful but triumphant glances at us. Anfisa Petrovna was moistening the old lady's temples and applying her smelling-salts. Praskovya Ilyinitchna was shedding tears and trembling, Yezhevikin was looking for a corner to seek refuge in, while the governess stood pale and completely overwhelmed with terror. Mizintchikov was the only one who remained unchanged. He got up, went to the window and began looking out of it, resolutely declining to pay attention to the scene around him.

All at once Madame la Générale sat up, drew herself up and scanned me with a menacing eye.

"Go away!" she shouted, stamping her foot at me.

I must confess that this I had not in the least expected.

"Go away! Go out of the house! What has he come for? Don't let me see a trace of him!"

"Mamma, mamma, what do you mean? Why, this is Seryozha," my uncle muttered, shaking all over with terror. "Why, he has come to pay us a visit, mamma."

"What Seryozha? Nonsense. I won't hear a word. Go away! It's Korovkin. I am convinced it is Korovkin. My presentiments never deceive me. He has come to turn Foma Fomitch out; he has been sent for with that very object. I have a presentiment in my heart. . . . Go away, you scoundrel!"

"Uncle, if this is how it is," I said, spluttering with honest indignation, "then excuse me, I'll . . ." And I reached after my hat.

"Sergey, Sergey, what are you about? . . . Well, this really is. . . . Mamma, this is Seryozha! . . . Sergey, upon my word!" he cried, racing after me and trying to take away my hat. "You are my visitor; you'll stay, I wish it! She doesn't mean it," he went on in a whisper; "she only goes on like this when she is angry. . . . You only keep out of her sight just at first . . . keep out of the way and it will all pass over. She will forgive you, I assure you! She is good-natured, only she works herself up. You hear she takes you for Korovkin, but afterwards she will forgive you, I assure you. . . . What do you want?" he cried to Gavrila, who came into the room trembling with fear.

68

Gavrila came in not alone; with him was a very pretty peasant boy of sixteen who had been taken as a house serf on account of his good looks, as I heard afterwards. His name was Falaley. He was wearing a peculiar costume, a red silk shirt with embroidery at the neck and a belt of gold braid, full black velveteen breeches, and goatskin boots turned over with red. This costume was designed by Madame la Générale herself. The boy was sobbing bitterly, and tears rolled one after another from his big blue eyes.

"What's this now?" cried my uncle. "What has happened? Speak, you ruffian!"

"Foma Fomitch told us to come here; he is coming after us himself," answered the despondent Gavrila. "Me for an examination, while he . . ."

"He?"

"He has been dancing, sir," answered Gavrila in a tearful voice.

"Dancing!" cried my uncle in horror.

"Dancing," blubbered Falaley with a sob.

"The Komarinsky!"

"Yes, the Kom-a-rin-sky."

"And Foma Fomitch found him?"

"Ye-es, he found me."

"You'll be the death of me!" cried my uncle. "I am done for!" And he clutched his head in both hands.

"Foma Fomitch!" Vidoplyasov announced, entering the room.

The door opened, and Foma Fomitch in his own person stood facing the perplexed company.

CHAPTER VI

OF THE WHITE BULL AND THE KOMARINSKY PEASANT

BEFORE I have the honour of presenting the reader with Foma Fomitch in person, I think it is absolutely essential to say a few words about Falaley and to explain what there was terrible in the fact of his dancing the Komarinsky and Foma Fomitch's finding him engaged in that light-hearted diversion. Falaley was a house serf boy, an orphan from the cradle, and a godson of my uncle's late wife. My uncle was very fond of him. That fact alone was quite sufficient to make Foma

Fomitch, after he had settled at Stepantchikovo and gained complete domination over my uncle, take a dislike to the latter's favourite, Falaley. But Madame la Générale took a particular fancy to the boy, who, in spite of Foma Fomitch's wrath, remained upstairs in attendance on the family. Madame la Générale herself insisted upon it, and Foma gave way, storing up the injury—he looked on everything as an injury—in his heart and revenging it on every favourable occasion on my uncle, who was in no way responsible. Falaley was wonderfully good-looking. He had a girlish face, the face of a beautiful peasant girl. Madame la Générale petted and spoiled him, prized him as though he were a rare and pretty toy, and there was no saying which she loved best, her little curly black dog Ami or Falaley. We have already referred to his costume, which was her idea. The young ladies gave him pomatum, and it was the duty of the barber Kuzma to curl his hair on holidays. This boy was a strange creature. He could not be called a perfect idiot or imbecile, but he was so naïve, so truthful and simple-hearted, that he might sometimes be certainly taken for a fool. If he had a dream, he would go at once to tell it to his master or mistress. He joined in the conversation of the gentle-folk without caring whether he was interrupting them. He would tell them things quite impossible to tell gentlefolks. He would dissolve into the most genuine tears when his mistress fell into a swoon or when his master was too severely scolded. He sympathised with every sort of distress. He would some-times go up to Madame la Générale, kiss her hands, and beg her not to be cross—and the old lady would magnanimously forgive him these audacities. He was sensitive in the extreme, kind-hearted, as free from malice as a lamb and as gay as a happy child. They gave him dainties from the dinner-table.

He always stood behind Madame la Générale's chair and was awfully fond of sugar. When he was given a lump of sugar he would nibble at it with his strong milk-white teeth, and a gleam of indescribable pleasure shone in his merry blue eyes and all over his pretty little face.

For a long time Foma Fomitch raged; but reflecting at last that he would get nothing by anger, he suddenly made up his mind to be Falaley's benefactor. After first pitching into my uncle for doing nothing for the education of the house serfs, he determined at once to set about training the poor boy in morals, good manners and French.

"What!" he would say in defence of his absurd idea (an idea

not confined to Foma Fomitch, as the writer of these lines can testify), "what! he is always upstairs waiting on his mistress; one day, forgetting that he does not know French, she will say to him, for instance: "Donnay mooah mon mooshooar'—he ought to be equal to the occasion and able to do his duty even then!'"

But it appeared not only that it was impossible to teach Falaley French, but that the cook Andron, the boy's uncle, who had disinterestedly tried to teach him to read Russian, had long ago given it up in despair and put the alphabet away on the shelf. Falaley was so dull at book-learning that he could understand absolutely nothing. Moreover, this led to further trouble. The house serfs began calling Falaley, in derision, a Frenchman, and old Gavrila, my uncle's valet, openly ventured to deny the usefulness of learning French. This reached Foma Fomitch's ears and, bursting with wrath, he made his opponent, Gavrila, himself learn French as a punishment. This was the origin of the whole business of teaching the servants French which so exasperated Mr. Bahtcheyev. It was still worse in regard to manners. Foma was absolutely unable to train Falaley to suit his ideas, and in spite of his prohibition, the boy would go in to tell him his dreams in the morning, which Foma Fomitch considered extremely ill-mannered and familiar. But Falaley obstinately remained Falaley. My uncle was, of course, the first to suffer for all this.

"Do you know, do you know what he has done to-day?" Foma would exclaim, selecting a moment when all were gathered together in order to produce a greater sensation. "Do you know what your systematic spoiling is coming to? To-day he gobbled up a piece of pie given him at the table; and do you know what he said of it? Come here, come here, silly fool; come here, idiot; come here, red face. . . ."

Falaley would come up weeping and rubbing his eyes with both hands.

"What did you say when you greedily ate up your pie? Repeat it before everyone!"

Falaley would dissolve in bitter tears and make no answer.

"Then I'll speak for you, if that's how it is. You said, slapping yourself on your stuffed and vulgar stomach: 'I've gobbled up the pie as Martin did the soap!' Upon my word, Colonel, can expressions like that be used in educated society, still more in aristocratic society? Did you say it or not? Speak!"

"I di-id . . ." Falaley would assent, sobbing.

"Well, then, tell me now, does Martin eat soap? Where have you seen a Martin who eats soap? Tell me, give me an idea of this phenomenal Martin!"

Silence.

"I am asking you," Foma would persist, "who is this Martin? I want to see him, I want to make his acquaintance. Well, what is he? A registry clerk, an astronomer, a provincial, a poet, an army captain, a serving man—he must have been something. Answer!"

"A ser-er-ving ma-an," Falaley would answer at last, still weeping.

"Whose? Who is his master?"

But Falaley was utterly unable to say who was his master. It would end, of course, in Foma Fomitch's rushing out of the room in a passion, crying out that he had been insulted; Madame la Générale would show symptoms of an attack, while my uncle would curse the hour of his birth, beg everybody's pardon, and for the rest of the day walk about on tiptoe in his own rooms.

As ill-luck would have it, on the day after the trouble over Martin and the soap, Falaley, who had succeeded in completely forgetting about Martin and all his woes of the previous day, informed Foma Fomitch as he took in his tea in the morning that he had had a dream about a white bull. This was the last straw! Foma Fomitch was moved to indescribable indignation, he promptly summoned my uncle and began upbraiding him for the vulgarity of the dream dreamed by his Faleley. This time severe steps were taken: Falaley was punished, he had to kneel down in the corner. He was sternly forbidden to dream of such coarse rustic subjects.

"What I am angry at," said Foma, "apart from the fact that he really ought not to dare to think of blurting out his dreams to me, especially a dream of a white bull—apart from that—you must agree, Colonel—what is the white bull but a proof of coarseness, ignorance and loutishness in your unkempt Falaley? As the thoughts are, so will the dreams be. Did I not tell you before that you would never make anything of him, and that he ought not to remain upstairs waiting upon the family? You will never, never develop that senseless peasant soul into anything lofty or poetical. Can't you manage," he went on, addressing Falaley, "can't you manage to dream of something elegant, refined, genteel, some scene from good society, such

72

as gentlemen playing cards or ladies walking in a lovely garden?"

Falaley promised he would be sure to dream next night of gentlemen or ladies walking in a lovely garden.

As he went to bed, Falaley prayed tearfully on the subject and wondered for a long time what he could do so as not to dream of the accursed white bull. But deceitful are the hopes of man. On waking up next morning, he remembered with horror that he had again been dreaming all night of the hateful white bull, and had not dreamed of even one lady walking in a lovely garden. This time the consequences were singular. Foma Fomitch positively declared that he did not believe in the possibility of such a coincidence, the possibility of such a repetition of a dream, and that Falaley was prompted to say this by someone of the household, perhaps even by the colonel himself on purpose to annoy Foma Fomitch. There was no end of an uproar, tears and reproaches. Madame la Générale was taken ill towards the evening, the whole household wore a dejected air. There was still a faint hope that the following, that is the third, night Falaley would be sure to have some dream of refined society. What was the universal indignation when for a whole week, every blessed night, Falaley went on dreaming of the white bull and nothing but the white bull. It was no use even to think of refined society.

But the most interesting point was that Falaley was utterly incapable of thinking of lying, of simply saying that he had dreamed not of the white bull, but of a carriage, for instance, full of ladies and Foma Fomitch. This was all the more strange since lying indeed would not have been so very sinful in so extreme a case. But Falaley was so truthful that he positively could not tell a lie even if he wanted to. It was, indeed, not even suggested to him by anyone. They all knew that he would betray himself at the first moment, and Foma Fomitch would immediately detect him in lying. What was to be done? My uncle's position was becoming intolerable. Falaley was absolutely incorrigible. The poor boy was positively growing thinner from worry.

The housekeeper Malanya declared that he was bewitched, and sprinkled him with magic water. She was assisted in this compassionate and salutary operation by the tender-hearted Praskovya Ilyinitchna, but even that was no use. Nothing was of use!

"The deuce take the damned thing!" Falaley said. "The

same dream every night! Every evening I pray, 'Don't let me dream of the white bull, don't let me dream of the white bull!' and there it is, there it is, the damned beast facing me, huge, with horns and such thick lips, oo-oo-oo!"

My uncle was in despair, but luckily Foma Fomitch seemed all at once to have forgotten about the white bull. Of course no one believed that Foma Fomitch could forget a circumstance so important. Everyone assumed with terror that he was keeping the white bull in reserve, and would bring it out on the first suitable occasion. It appeared later on that Foma Fomitch had no thoughts to spare for the white bull at that moment. He had other business in hand, other cares. Other plans were maturing in his beneficent and fertile brain. That is why he let Falaley breathe in peace, and everyone else too had a respite. The boy grew gay again, and even began to forget what had happened; even the white bull began to visit him less and less frequently, though it still at times reminded him of its fantastic existence. In fact, everything would have gone well if there had been no such thing as the Komarinsky.

It must be noted that Falaley was an excellent dancer. Dancing was his chief accomplishment, even something like his vocation. He danced with vigour, with inexhaustible gaiety, and he was particularly fond of dancing the Komarinsky Peasant. Not that he was so much attracted by the frivolous and in any case inexplicable steps of that volatile peasant—no, he liked dancing the Komarinsky solely because to hear the Komarinsky and not dance to the tune was utterly beyond him. Sometimes in the evenings two or three of the footmen, the coachmen, the gardener who played the fiddle, and even some of the ladies of the servants' hall would gather together in a circle in some back yard as far away as possible from Foma Fomitch. Music and dances would begin, and finally the Komarinsky would triumphantly come into its own. The orchestra consisted of two balalaikas, a guitar, a fiddle, and a tambourine, with which the postilion Mityushka was a capital hand. Falaley's condition was worth watching at such times: he would dance to complete oblivion of himself, to utter exhaustion, encouraged by the shouts and laughter of his audience. He would squeal, shout, laugh, clap his hands. He danced as though carried away by some intangible outside force with which he could not cope, and he struggled persistently to keep up with the continually increasing pace of the reckless tune as he tapped on the ground with his heels. These were

74

minutes of real delight to him; and everything would have gone happily and merrily if rumours of the Komarinsky had not at last reached Foma Fomitch.

Foma Fomitch was petrified, and sent at once for the colonel.

"There is only one thing I wish to learn from you," Foma began, "have you positively sworn to be the ruin of that luckless idiot or not? In the first case I will stand aside at once; if not, then I . . ."

"But what is the matter? What has happened?" cried my uncle, alarmed.

"You ask what has happened? Do you know that he is dancing the Komarinsky?"

"Well . . . well, what of it?"

"Well, what of it!" shrieked Foma. "And you say that—you, their master, standing in a sense in the place of their father! But have you then a true idea of what the Komarinsky is? Do you know that that song describes a debauched peasant, attempting in a state of drunkenness the most immoral action? Do you know what sacrilege it is that vicious Little Russian is committing? He is trampling upon the most precious bonds and, so to say, stamping them under his big loutish boots, accustomed to tread only the floor of the village inn. And do you realise that you have wounded my moral feelings by your answer? Do you realise that you have insulted me personally by your answer? Do you understand that or not?"

"But, Foma; why, it's only a song, Foma. . . ."

"You say only a song! And you are not ashamed that you own to me that you know that song—you, a member of honourable society, the father of honourable, innocent children and a colonel into the bargain! Only a song! But I am certain that the song is drawn from real life. Only a song! But what decent man can without a blush of shame admit that he knows that song, that he has ever heard that song? What man could?"

"Well, but, you see, you know it yourself, Foma, since you ask about it," my disconcerted uncle answered in the simplicity of his heart.

"What, I know it, I . . . I? You have insulted me," Foma Fomitch cried at once, leaping up from his chair and spluttering with fury.

He had never expected such a crushing answer.

I will not undertake to describe the wrath of Foma Fomitch. The colonel was ignominiously driven from the presence of the guardian of morality for the ill manners and tactlessness of his reply. But from that hour Foma Fomitch vowed to catch Falaley in the act of dancing the Komarinsky. In the evening, when everyone supposed he was busy at work, he stole out into the garden, went the round of the kitchen garden, and threaded his way into the hemp patch, from which there was a view in the distance of the back yard in which the dances took place. He stalked poor Falaley as a sportsman stalks a bird, picturing with relish the wigging he would, if he succeeded, give the whole household and the colonel in particular. His unwearying efforts were at last crowned with success. He had come upon the Komarinsky! It will be understood now why my uncle tore his hair when he saw Falaley weeping and heard Vidoplyasov announce Foma Fomitch, who so unexpectedly and at such a moment of perturbation was standing before us in person.

CHAPTER VII

FOMA FOMITCH

I SCRUTINISED this gentleman with intense curiosity. Gavrila had been right in saying that he was an ugly little man. Foma was short, with light eyebrows and eyelashes and grizzled hair, with a hooked nose, and with little wrinkles all over his face. On his chin there was a big wart. He was about fifty. He came in softly with measured steps, with his eyes cast down. But yet the most insolent self-confidence was expressed in his face, and in the whole of his pedantic figure. To my astonishment, he made his appearance in a dressing-gown—of a foreign cut it is true, but still a dressing-gown—and he wore slippers too. The collar of his shirt unadorned by any cravat was a lay-down one *à l'enfant;* this gave Foma Fomitch an extremely foolish look. He went up to an empty arm-chair, moved it to the table, and sat down in it without saying a word to anyone. All the hubbub, all the excitement that had been raging a minute before, vanished instantaneously. There was such a hush that one could have heard a pin drop. Madame la Générale became as meek as a lamb. The cringing infatuation of this poor imbecile for Foma Fomitch was apparent now.

She fixed her eyes upon her idol as though gloating over the sight of him. Miss Perepelitsyn rubbed her hands with a simper, and poor Praskovya Ilyinitchna was visibly trembling with alarm. My uncle began bustling about at once.

"Tea, tea, sister! Only plenty of sugar in it, sister; Foma Fomitch likes plenty of sugar in his tea after his nap. You do like plenty of sugar, don't you, Foma?"

"I don't care for any tea just now!" Foma pronounced deliberately and with dignity, waving him off with a careworn air. "You always keep on about plenty of sugar."

These words and Foma's entrance, so incredibly ludicrous in its pedantic dignity, interested me extremely. I was curious to find out to what point, to what disregard of decency the insolence of this upstart little gentleman would go.

"Foma," cried my uncle. "Let me introduce my nephew Sergey Alexandrovitch! He has just arrived."

Foma Fomitch looked him up and down.

"I am surprised that you always seem to take pleasure in systematically interrupting me, Colonel," he said after a significant silence, taking absolutely no notice of me. "One talks to you of something serious, and you . . . *discourse* . . . of goodness knows what. . . . Have you seen Falaley?"

"I have, Foma. . . ."

"Ah, you have seen him. Well, I will show you him again though you have seen him; you can admire your handiwork . . . in a moral sense. Come here, you idiot! come here, you Dutch-faced fool! Well, come along! Don't be afraid!"

Falaley went up to him with his mouth open, sobbing and gulping back his tears. Foma Fomitch looked at him with relish.

"I called him a Dutch-faced fool with intention, Pavel Semyonitch," he observed, lolling at his ease in his low chair and turning slightly towards Obnoskin, who was sitting next him. "And speaking generally, you know, I see no necessity for softening my expressions in any case. The truth should be the truth. And however you cover up filth it will still remain filth. Why trouble to soften it? It's deceiving oneself and others. Only a silly worldly numskull can feel the need of such senseless conventions. Tell me—I submit it to your judgment— do you find anything lovely in that face? I mean, of course, anything noble, lovely, exalted, not just vulgar red cheeks."

Foma Fomitch spoke quietly, evenly, and with a kind of majestic nonchalance.

"Anything lovely in him?" answered Obnoskin, with insolent carelessness. "I think that he is simply a good piece of roast beef—and nothing else."

"Went up to the looking-glass and looked into it to-day," Foma continued, pompously omitting the pronoun *I*. "I am far from considering myself a beauty, but I could not help coming to the conclusion that there is something in these grey eyes which distinguished me from any Falaley. There is thought, there is life, there is intelligence in these eyes. It is not myself I am praising. I am speaking generally of our class. Now what do you think, can there be a scrap, a grain of soul in that living beefsteak? Yes, indeed, take note, Pavel Semyonitch, how these people, utterly devoid of thought and ideal, and living by meat alone, always have revoltingly fresh complexions, coarsely and stupidly fresh! Would you like to know the level of his intellectual faculties. Hey, you image! Come nearer, let us admire you. Why are you gaping? Do you want to swallow a whale? Are you handsome? Answer, are you handsome?"

"I a-am!" answered Falaley, with smothered sobs.

Obnoskin roared with laughter. I felt that I was beginning to tremble with anger.

"Do you hear?" Foma went on, turning to Obnoskin in triumph. "Would you like to hear something more? I have come to put him through an examination. You see, Pavel Semyonitch, there are people who are desirous of corrupting and ruining this poor idiot. Perhaps I am too severe in my judgment, perhaps I am mistaken; but I speak from love of humanity. He was just now dancing the most improper of dances. That is of no concern to anyone here. But now hear for yourself. . . . Answer: what were you doing just now? Answer, answer immediately—do you hear?"

"I was da-ancing," said Falaley, mastering his sobs.

"What were you dancing? What dance? Speak!"

"The Komarinsky. . . ."

"The Komarinsky! And who was that Komarinsky? What was the Komarinsky? Do you suppose I can understand anything from that answer? Come, give us an idea. Who was your Komarinsky?"

"A pea-easant. . . ."

"A peasant, only a peasant! I am surprised! A remarkable peasant, then! Then was it some celebrated peasant, if poems and dances are made about him? Come, answer!"

Foma could not exist without tormenting people, he played with his victim like a cat with a mouse; but Falaley remained mute, whimpering and unable to understand the question.

"Answer," Foma persisted. "You are asked what sort of peasant was it? Speak! . . . Was he a seignorial peasant, a crown peasant, free, bond, industrial? There are ever so many sorts of peasants. . . ."

"In-dus-tri-al. . . ."

"Ah, industrial! Do you hear, Pavel Semyonitch? A new historical fact: the Komarinsky peasant was industrial. H'm. . . . Well, what did that industrial peasant do? For what exploits is he celebrated in song . . . and dance?"

The question was a delicate one, and since it was put to Falaley, a risky one too.

"Come . . . Though . . ." Obnoskin began, glancing towards his mamma, who was beginning to wriggle on the sofa in a peculiar way.

But what was to be done? Foma Fomitch's whims were respected as law.

"Upon my word, uncle, if you don't suppress that fool he'll . . . you see what he is working up to—Falaley will blurt out some nonsense, I assure you . . ." I whispered to my uncle, who was utterly distracted and did not know what line to take.

"You had really better, Foma . . ." he began. "Here, I want to introduce to you, Foma, my nephew, a young man who is studying mineralogy."

"I beg you, Colonel, not to interrupt me with your mineralogy, a subject of which, as far as I am aware, you know nothing, and *others* perhaps little more. I am not a baby. He will answer me that this peasant, instead of working for the welfare of his family, has been drinking till he is tipsy, has sold his coat for drink, and is running about the street in an inebriated condition. That is, as is well known, the subject of the poem that sings the praises of drink. Don't be uneasy, he knows *now* what he has to answer. Come, answer: what did that peasant do? Come, I have prompted you, I have put the words into your mouth. What I want is to hear it from you yourself, what he did, for what he was famous, how he gained the immortal glory of being sung by the troubadours. Well?"

The luckless Falaley looked round him in misery and, not knowing what to say, opened and shut his mouth like a carp hauled out of the water on to the sand.

"I am ashamed to sa-ay!" he bellowed at last in utter despair.

"Ah, ashamed to say!" bellowed Foma in triumph. "See, that's the answer I have wrung out of him, Colonel! Ashamed to say, but not ashamed to do. That's the morality which you have sown, which has sprung up and which you are now . . . watering; but it is useless to waste words! Go to the kitchen now, Falaley. I'll say nothing to you now, out of regard for my audience, but to-day, to-day you will be severely and rigorously punished. If not, if this time they put you before me, you may stay here and entertain your betters with the Komarinsky while I will leave this house to-day! That's enough. I have spoken, you can go!"

"Come, I think you really are severe . . ." mumbled Obnoskin.

"Just so, just so, just so," my uncle began crying out, but he broke off and subsided. Foma looked gloomily askance at him.

"I wonder, Pavel Semyonitch," he went on, "what all our contemporary writers, poets, learned men and thinkers are about. How is it they pay no attention to what songs are being sung by the Russian people and to what songs they are dancing? What have the Pushkins, the Lermontovs, the Borozdins been about all this time? I wonder at them. The people dance the Komarinsky, the apotheosis of drunkenness, while they sing of forget-me-nots! Why don't they write poems of a more moral tone for popular use, why don't they fling aside their forget-me-nots? It's a social question. Let them depict a peasant, but a peasant made genteel, so to say, a villager and not a peasant; let them paint me the village sage in his simplicity, maybe even in his bark shoes—I don't object even to that—but brimming over with the virtues which—I make bold to say—some over-lauded Alexander of Macedon may envy. I know Russia and Russia knows me, that is why I say this. Let them portray that peasant, weighed down maybe with a family and grey hair, in a stuffy hut, hungry, too, maybe, but contented; not repining, but blessing his poverty, and indifferent to the rich man's gold. Let the rich man at last with softened heart bring him his gold; let, indeed, in this the virtues of the peasant be united with the virtues of his master, perhaps a grand gentleman. The villager and the grand gentleman so widely sparated in social grade are made one at last in virtue—that is an exalted thought! But what

80

do we see? On one side forget-me-nots, and on the other the peasant dashing out of the pothouse and running about the street in a dishevelled condition! What is there poetic in that? Tell me, pray, what is there to admire in that? Where is the wit? Where is the grace? Where is the morality? I am amazed at it!"

"I am ready to pay you a hundred roubles for such words," said Yezhevikin, with an enthusiastic air. "And you know the bald devil will try and get it out of me," he whispered on the sly. "Flatter away, flatter away!"

"H'm, yes . . . you've put that very well," Obnoskin pronounced.

"Exactly so, exactly so," cried my uncle, who had been listening with the deepest attention and looking at me with triumph. "What a subject has come up!" he whispered, rubbing his hands. "A topic of many aspects, dash it all! Foma Fomitch, here is my nephew," he added, in the overflow of his feelings. "He is engaged in literary pursuits too, let me introduce him."

As before, Foma Fomitch paid not the slightest attention to my uncle's introduction.

"For God's sake, don't introduce me any more! I entreat you in earnest," I whispered to my uncle, with a resolute air.

"Ivan Ivanitch!" Foma began, suddenly addressing Mizintchikov and looking intently at him, "we have just been talking. What is your opinion?"

"Mine? You are asking me?" Mizintchikov responded in surprise, looking as though he had only just woken up.

"Yes, you. I am asking you because I value the opinion of really clever people, and not the problematic wiseacres who are only clever because they are being continually introduced as clever people, as learned people, and are sometimes sent for expressly to be made a show of or something of the sort."

This thrust was aimed directly at me. And yet there was no doubt that though Foma Fomitch took no notice whatever of me, he had begun this whole conversation concerning literature entirely for my benefit, to dazzle, to annihilate, to crush at the first step the clever and learned young man from Petersburg. I at any rate had no doubt of it.

"If you want to know my opinion, I . . . I agree with your opinion," answered Mizintchikov listlessly and reluctantly.

"You always agree with me! It's positively wearisome,"

replied Foma. "I tell you frankly, Pavel Semyonitch," he went on, after a brief silence again addressing Obnoskin, "if I respect the immortal Karamzin it is not for his history, not for *Marfa Posadnitsa,* not for *Old and New Russia,* but just for having written *Frol Silin;* it is a noble epic! It is a purely national product, and will live for ages and ages! a most lofty epic!"

"Just so, just so! a lofty *epoch!* Frol Silin, a benevolent man! I remember, I have read it. He bought the freedom of two girls, too, and then looked towards heaven and wept. A very lofty trait," my uncle chimed in, beaming with satisfaction.

My poor uncle! he never could resist taking part in an *intellectual* conversation. Foma gave a malicious smile, but he remained silent.

"They write very interestingly, though, even now," Anfisa Petrovna intervened discreetly. *"The Mysteries of Brussels,* for instance."

"I should not say so," observed Foma, as it were regretfully. "I was lately reading one of the poems . . . not up to much! 'Forget-me-nots'. Of contemporary writers, if you will, the one I like best of all is 'Scribbler', a light pen!"

" 'Scribbler'!" cried Anfisa Petrovna. "Is that the man who writes letters in the magazines? Ah, how enchanting it is, what playing with words!"

"Precisely, playing with words; he, so to speak, plays with his pen. An extraordinary lightness of style."

"Yes, but he is a pedant!" Obnoskin observed carelessly.

"Yes, a pedant he is, I don't dispute it; but a charming pedant, a graceful pedant! Of course, not one of his ideas would stand serious criticism, but one is carried away by his lightness! A babbler, I agree, but a charming babbler, a graceful babbler. Do you remember, for instance, in one of his articles he mentions that he has his own estates?"

"Estates!" my uncle caught up. "That's good! In what province?"

Foma stopped, looking fixedly at my uncle, and went on in the same tone:

"Tell me in the name of common sense, of what interest is it to me, the reader, to know that he has his own estates? If he has—I congratulate him on it! But how charmingly, how jestingly, it is described! He sparkles with wit, he splashes with wit, he boils over? He is a Narzan of wit! Yes, that is the way to write! I fancy I should write just like that, if I were to consent to write for magazines. . . ."

"Perhaps you would do even better," Yezhevikin observed respectfully.

"There is positively something musical in the language," my uncle put in.

Foma Fomitch lost patience at last.

"Colonel," he said, "is it not possible to ask you—with all conceivable delicacy of course—not to interfere with us, but to allow us to finish our conversation in peace. You cannot offer an opinion in our conversation! You cannot. Don't disturb our agreeable literary chat. Look after your land, drink your tea, but . . . leave literature alone. It will lose nothing by it, I assure you—I assure you!"

This was surpassing the utmost limit of impudence! I did not know what to think.

"Why, you yourself, Foma, said it was musical," my uncle brought out in confusion and distress.

"Quite so, but I spoke with a knowledge of the subject, I spoke appropriately; while you . . ."

"To be sure, but we spoke with intellect," put in Yezhevikin, wriggling round Foma Fomitch. "We have just a little intelligence, though we may have to borrow some; just enough to run a couple of government departments and we might manage a third, if need be—that's all we can boast of!"

"So it seems I have been talking nonsense again," said my uncle in conclusion, and he smiled his good-natured smile.

"You admit it, anyway," observed Foma.

"It's all right, it's all right, Foma, I am not angry. I know that you pull me up like a friend, like a relation, like a brother. I have myself allowed you to do it, begged you to, indeed. It's a good thing. It's for my benefit. I thank you for it and will profit by it."

My patience was exhausted. All that I had hitherto heard about Foma Fomitch had seemed to me somewhat exaggerated. Now when I saw it all for myself, my astonishment was beyond all bounds. I could not believe my senses; I could not understand such impudence, such insolent domineering on one side and such voluntary slavery, such credulous good nature on the other. Though, indeed, my uncle himself was confused by such impudence. That was evident . . . I was burning with desire to come to grips with Foma, to do battle with him, to be rude to him in some way, in as startling a fashion as possible —and then let come what may! This idea excited me. I looked for an opportunity, and completely ruined the brim of my hat while I waited for it. But the opportunity did not present itself. Foma absolutely refused to notice me.

"You are right, perfectly right, Foma," my uncle went on, doing his utmost to recover himself, and to smoothe over the unpleasantness of what had been said before. "What you say is true, Foma. I thank you for it. One must know the subject before one discusses it. I am sorry! It is not the first time I have been in the same predicament. Only fancy, Sergey, on one occasion I was an examiner . . . you laugh! But there it is! I really was an examiner, and that was all about it. I was invited to an institution, to be present at an examination, and they set me down together with the examiners, as a sign of respect, there was an empty seat. So, I will own to you, I was frightened, I was positively alarmed, I do not know a single science. What was I to do? I thought that in another minute they would drag me myself to the black board! Well, what then? Nothing happened, it went off all right, I even asked questions myself; who was Noah? On the whole they answered splendidly; then we had lunch and toasted enlightenment in champagne. It was a fine school!"

Foma Fomitch and Obnoskin burst into roars of laughter.

"Indeed, I laughed myself afterwards," cried my uncle, laughing in a most good-natured way and delighted that general cheerfulness was restored. "Yes, Foma, here goes! I will amuse you all by telling you how I put my foot in it once. . . . Only fancy, Sergey, we were staying at Krasnogorsk . . ."

"Allow me to inquire, Colonel, will you be long in telling your story?" Foma interposed.

"Oh, Foma! Why, it is the most delightful story, enough to make one split with laughter; you only listen, it is good, it really is good. I'll tell you how I put my foot in it."

"I always listen with pleasure to your stories when they are of that sort," Obnoskin pronounced, yawning.

"There is no help for it, we must listen," Foma decided.

"But upon my word it is good, Foma, it really is. I want to tell you how I put my foot into it on one occasion, Anfisa Petrovna. You listen too, Sergey, it is an edifying story indeed. We were staying at Krasnogorsk," my uncle began, beaming with pleasure, talking with nervous haste, and falling into innumerable parentheses as he always did when he was beginning

84

to tell some story for the pleasure of his audience. "As soon as we arrived, the same evening we went to the theatre. There was a first-rate actress, Kuropatkina; she afterwards ran away with the cavalry captain Zvyerkov and did not finish the play she was acting: so they let down the curtain. . . . This Zvyerkov was a beast, both for drinking and playing cards, and not that he was a drunkard, but simply ready to join his comrades at festive moments. But when he did get really drunk then he forgot everything, where he lived, in what country, and what his name was. Absolutely everything, in fact: but he was a very fine fellow really. . . . Well, I was sitting in the theatre. In the interval I got up, and I ran across a comrade called Kornouhov. . . . A unique fellow, I assure you. We had not see each other for six years, it is true. Well, he had stayed in the company and was covered with crosses. I have heard lately—he's an actual civil councillor; he transferred to the civil service and worked his way up to a high grade. . . . Well, of course, we were delighted. One thing and another. In the box next to us were three ladies; the one on the left was the ugliest woman in the world. . . . Afterwards I found out that she was a splendid woman, the mother of a family, and the happiness of her husband. . . . Well, so I like a fool blurt out to Kornouhov: 'I say, old man, can you tell me who that scarecrow is?' 'Who do you mean?' 'Why, that one.' 'That's my cousin.' Tfoo, the devil! judge of my position! To put myself right: 'Not that one,' I said. 'What eyes you've got! I mean the one who is sitting there, who is that?' 'That's my sister.' Tfoo, plague take it all! And his sister, as luck would have it, was a regular rosebud, a sweet little thing; dressed up like anything—brooches, gloves, bracelets, in fact a perfect cherub. Afterwards she married a very fine fellow called Pyhtin; she eloped with him, it was a runaway match; but now it is all right, and they are very well off; their parents are only too delighted! Well, so I cried out, 'Oh, no!' not knowing how to get out of it, 'not that one, the one in the middle, who is she?' 'In the middle? Well, my boy, that's my wife.' . . . And she, between ourselves, was a perfect sugarplum. I felt that I could have eaten her up at one mouthful, I was so delighted with her. . . . 'Well,' I said, 'have you ever seen a fool? Here is one facing you, and here's his head; cut it off, don't spare it!' He laughed. Afterwards he introduced them to me and must have told them, the rascal. They were in fits of laughter over something! And I must say I never spent an evening more merrily. So you see, Foma, old man, how one can put one's foot in it! Ha-ha-ha-ha!''

But it was no use my poor uncle laughing; in vain he looked round the company with his kind and good-humoured eyes; a dead silence was the response that greeted his light-hearted story. Foma Fomitch sat in gloomy dumbness and all the others followed his example; only Obnoskin gave a faint smile, foreseeing the baiting my uncle would get. My uncle was embarrassed and flushed crimson. This was what Foma desired.

"Have you finished?" he asked at last, turning with dignity to the embarrassed story-teller.

"Yes, Foma."

"And are you satisfied?"

"How do you mean, satisfied?" asked my poor uncle miserably.

"Are you happier now? Are you pleased at having broken up the pleasant literary conversation of your friends by interrupting them and so satisfying your petty vanity?"

"Oh, come, Foma, I wanted to amuse you all, and you . . ."

"Amuse!" cried Foma, suddenly becoming extraordinarily heated; "but you are only able to depress us, not amuse us. Amuse! but do you know that your story was almost immoral! I say nothing of its impropriety, that is self-evident. . . . You informed us just now with rare coarseness of feeling that you laughed at innocence, at an honourable lady, simply because she had not the honour to please you, and you wanted to make us, *us* laugh, that is applaud you, that is applaud a coarse and improper action, and all because you are the master of this house! You can do as you like, Colonel, you can seek out toadies, flatterers, sycophants, you can even send for them from distant parts and so increase your retinue to the detriment of straightforwardness and frank nobility of soul, but never will Foma Opiskin be your toady, your flatterer, your sycophant! I can assure you of that, if of anything. . . ."

"Oh, Foma! You misunderstand me, Foma."

"No, Colonel; I have seen through you for a long time, I know you through and through. You are devoured by boundless vanity. You have pretensions to an incomparable keenness of wit, and forget that wit is blunted by pretension. You . . ."

"Oh, stop, Foma, for God's sake! Have some shame, if only before people!"

"It's sad, you know, to see all this, Colonel, and it's im-

86

possible to be silent when one sees it. I am poor, I am living at the expense of your mother. It may be expected, perhaps, that I should flatter you by my silence, and I don't care for any milksop to take me for your toady! Possibly when I came into this room just now I intentionally accentuated my truthful candour, was forced to be intentionally rude, just because you yourself put me into such a position. You are too haughty with me, Colonel, I may be taken for your slave, your toady. Your pleasure is to humiliate me before *strangers*, while I am really your equal—your equal in every respect. Perhaps *I* am doing you a favour in living with you, and not *you* doing me one. I am insulted, so I am forced to sing my own praises—that's natural! I cannot help speaking, I must speak, I am bound at once to protest, and that is why I tell you straight out that you are phenomenally envious. You see, for instance, someone in a simple friendly conversation unconsciously reveals his knowledge, his reading, his taste, and so you are annoyed, you can't sit still. 'Let me display my knowledge and my taste,' you think! And what taste have you, if you will allow me to ask? You know as much about art—if you will excuse my saying so, Colonel—as a bull about beef! That's harsh and rude, I admit; anyway it is straightforward and just. You won't hear that from your flatterers, Colonel."

"Oh, Foma! . . ."

"It is 'Oh, Foma,' to be sure. The truth is not a feather bed, it seems. Very well, then, we will speak later about this, but now let me entertain the company a little. You can't be the only one to distinguish yourself all the time. Pavel Semyonitch, have you seen this sea monster in human form? I have been observing him for a long time. Look well at him; why, he would like to devour me whole, at one gulp."

He was speaking of Gavrila. The old servant was standing at the door, and certainly was looking on with distress at the scolding of his master.

"I want to entertain you, too, with a performance, Pavel Semyonitch. Come here, you scarecrow, come here! Condescend to approach us a little nearer, Gavrila Ignatitch! Here you see, Pavel Semyonitch, is Gavrila; as a punishment for rudeness he is studying the French dialect. Like Orpheus, I soften the manners of these parts not only with songs but with the French dialect. Come, Mossoo Frenchy—he can't bear to be called Mossoo—do you know your lesson?"

"I have learnt it," said Gavrila, hanging his head.

"Well, Parlay—voo—fransay?"

"Vee, moossyu, zhe—le—parl—on—peu. . . ."

I don't know whether it was Gavrila's mournful face as he uttered the French phrase, or whether they were all aware of Foma's desire that they should laugh, but anyway they all burst into a roar of laughter as soon as Gavrila opened his lips. Even Madame la Générale deigned to be amused. Anfisa Petrovna, sinking back on the sofa, shrieked, hiding her face behind her fan. What seemed most ludicrous was that Gavrila, seeing what his examination was being turned into, could not restrain himself from spitting and commenting reproachfully: "To think of having lived to such disgrace in my old age!"

Foma Fomitch was startled.

"What? What did you say? So you think fit to be rude?"

"No, Foma Fomitch," Gavrila replied with dignity. "My words were no rudeness, and it's not for me, a serf, to be rude to you, a gentleman born. But every man bears the image of God upon him, His image and semblance. I am sixty-three years old. My father remembers Pugatchev, the monster, and my grandfather helped his master, Matvey Nikititch—God grant him the kingdom of heaven—to hang Pugatchev on an aspen tree, for which my father was honoured beyond all others by our late master, Afanasy Matveyitch: he was his valet, and ended his life as butler. As for me, Foma Fomitch, sir, though I am my master's bondman, I have never known such a shame done me from my birth upward till now."

And at the last word Gavrila spread out his hands and hung his head. My uncle was watching him uneasily.

"Come, that's enough, Gavrila," he cried. "No need to say more, that's enough!"

"Never mind, never mind," said Foma, turning a little pale and giving a forced smile. "Let him speak, these are the fruits of your . . ."

"I will tell you everything," said Gavrila with extraordinary fervour, "I will conceal nothing! You may bind the hands, but there is no binding the tongue. Though I may seem beside you, Foma Fomitch, a low man, in fact a slave, yet I can feel insulted! Service and obedience I am always bound to give you, because I am born a slave and must do my duty in fear and trembling. You sit writing a book, it's my duty not to let you be interrupted—that is my real duty. Any service that is needed I am pleased to do. But in my old age to bleat in some outlandish way and be put to shame before folk! Why, I can't

88

go into the servants' room now: 'You are a Frenchy!' they say, 'a Frenchy!' No, Foma Fomitch, sir, it's not only a fool like me, but all good folks have begun to say the same: that you have become now a wicked man and that our master is nothing but a little child before you, that though you are a gentleman by birth and a general's son, and yourself may be near being a general too, yet you are as wicked as a real fury must be."

Gavrila had finished. I was beside myself with delight. Foma Fomitch sat pale with rage in the midst of the general discomfiture and seemed unable to recover from Gavrila's sudden attack upon him; he seemed at that moment to be deliberating how far his wrath should carry him. At last the outburst followed.

"What, he dares to be rude to me—me! but this is mutiny!" shrieked Foma, and he leapt up from his chair.

Madame la Générale followed his example, clasping her hands. There was a general commotion, my uncle rushed to turn the culprit out.

"Put him in fetters, put him in fetters!" cried Madame la Générale. "Take him to the town at once and send him for a soldier, Yegorushka, or you shall not have my blessing. Fix the fetters on him at once, and send him for a soldier."

"What!" cried Foma. "Slave! Lout! Hamlet! He dares to be rude to me! He, he, a rag to wipe my boots! He dares to call me a fury!"

I slipped forward with unusual determination.

"I must confess that in this affair I am completely of Gavrila's opinion," I said, looking Foma Fomitch straight in the face and trembling with excitement.

He was so taken aback by this onslaught that for the first minute he seemed unable to believe his ears.

"What's this now?" he cried out at last, pouncing upon me in a frenzy, and fixing his little bloodshot eyes upon me. "Why, who are you?"

"Foma Fomitch . . ." my uncle, utterly distracted, began, "this is Seryozha, my nephew. . . ."

"The learned gentleman!" yelled Foma. "So he's the learned gentleman! Liberté—égalité—fraternité. Journal des Débats! No, my friend, you won't take me in! I am not such a fool. This isn't Petersburg, you won't impose upon us. And I spit on your des Débats. You have your des Débats, but to us that's all fiddlesticks, young man! Learned! You know as much as I have forgotten seven times over. So much for your learning!''

If they had not held him back I believe he would have fallen upon me with his fists.

"Why, he is drunk," I said, looking about me in bewilderment.

"Who, I?" cried Foma, in a voice unlike his own.

"Yes, you!"

"Drunk?"

"Yes, drunk."

This was more than Foma could endure. He uttered a screech as though he were being murdered and rushed out of the room. Madame la Générale seemed desirous of falling into a swoon, but reflected that it would be better to run after Foma Fomitch. She was followed by all the others, and last of all by my uncle. When I recovered myself and looked round I saw in the room no one but Yezhevikin. He was smiling and rubbing his hands.

"You promised just now to tell me about the Jesuits," he said in an insinuating voice.

"What?" I asked, not understanding what he was talking about.

"About the Jesuits, you promised just now to tell me . . . some little anecdote. . . ."

I ran out into the veranda and from there into the garden. My head was going round. . . .

CHAPTER VIII

A DECLARATION OF LOVE

I WANDERED about the garden for about a quarter of an hour, feeling irritated and extremely dissatisfied with myself, and deliberating what I should do now. The sun was setting. Suddenly at a turning into a dark avenue I met Nastenka face to face. She had tears in her eyes, in her hand a handkerchief with which she was wiping them.

"I was looking for you," she said.

"And I for you," I answered. "Tell me, am I in a madhouse?"

"Certainly not in a madhouse," she answered resentfully, with an intent glance at me.

"Well, if that's so, what's the meaning of it all? For Christ's

sake give me some advice. Where has my uncle gone now?
Can I go to him? I am very glad that I have met you; perhaps
you will be able to suggest what I ought to do."

"No, better not go to him. I have just come away from
them."

"Why, where are they?"

"Who knows? Perhaps by now they have run into the
kitchen garden again," she said irritably.

"Into the kitchen garden!"

"Why, last week, Foma Fomitch began shouting that he
wouldn't stay in the house, and all at once he ran into the
kitchen garden, found a spade in the shed and began digging
the beds. We were all amazed, and wondered whether he
hadn't gone out of his mind. 'That I may not be reproached
for doing nothing for my keep,' said he, 'here I will dig and
pay for the bread I have eaten, and then I will go away. That's
what you have driven me to.' And then they all began crying
and almost falling on their knees before him; they took the
spade away from him; but he would go on digging; he dug up
all the turnips, that was all he did. They humoured him once,
he may do it again. That would be just like him."

"And you . . . you tell that with such coolness!" I cried out,
with intense indignation.

She looked at me with flashing eyes.

"Forgive me, I really don't know what I am saying! Listen!
do you know what I've come here for?"

"N-no," she answered, flushing crimson, and some painful
feeling was reflected in her charming face.

"You must excuse me," I went on. "I am upset, I feel that
this is not how I ought to have begun speaking of this . . .
especially with you. . . . But never mind! To my thinking,
openness in such matters is best. I confess . . . that is, I
meant to say . . . you know my uncle's design? He has told
me to ask for your hand. . . ."

"Oh, what nonsense! don't speak of it, please," she said,
hurriedly interrupting me and flushing crimson.

I was disconcerted.

"How nonsense? But he wrote to me, you see."

"So he wrote to you?" she asked eagerly. "Oh, what a
man! How he promised that he would not write! What nonsense! Good heavens, what nonsense!"

"Forgive me," I muttered, not knowing what to say. "Perhaps I have acted incautiously, crudely . . . but, you see, it's

such a moment! Only think, goodness knows what's going on around us. . . ."

"Oh, for God's sake don't apologise! Believe me that it is painful for me to hear this apart from that, and yet, do you know, I wanted to speak to you myself, to find out something. . . . Oh, how vexatious! So he really wrote to you? That's what I was most afraid of! My God, what a man he is! And you believed him and galloped here full speed? Well, that's the last straw!"

She did not conceal her annoyance. My position was not an attractive one.

"I must confess I did not expect . . ." I blurted out in the utmost confusion, "such a turn . . . I expected, on the contrary . . ."

"Ah, so that's what you expected? . . ." she brought out with light irony, biting her lip. "And do you know, you must show me the letter he wrote."

"Very good."

"And please don't be angry with me, don't be offended; I have trouble enough without that!" she said in an imploring voice, though a mocking smile faintly gleamed on her pretty lips.

"Oh, please don't take me for a fool," I cried hotly. "But perhaps you are prejudiced against me, perhaps someone has spoken against me? Perhaps you say this because I put my foot in it just now? But that is nothing, I assure you. I know what a fool I must look to you now. Don't laugh at me, please! I don't know what I am saying, and it is all because I am twenty-two, damn it."

"Oh, mercy on us, why?"

"You ask why? Anyone who is twenty-two, you know, has it written in his face; as I had, for instance, when I bounced out just now in the middle of the room, or as when I stand before you now. . . . It's a damnable age!"

"Oh, no, no!" answered Nastenka, hardly able to restrain her laughter. "I am sure that you are kind and nice and clever, and I say that sincerely, I do really! But . . . you are only very vain. You may get over that in time."

"I fancy I am only as vain as I ought to be."

"Oh, no. Think how embarrassed you were just now, and what for? Because you stumbled as you came in! . . . What right had you to turn into ridicule your good generous uncle who has done you so much kindness? Why did you try to turn the laugh against him when you were laughable yourself? That was horrid, shameful! It does not do you credit, and I must own I disliked you very much at that minute, so there!"

"That's true! I was a blockhead! more than that—I did a mean thing! You noticed it, and that is my punishment. Abuse me, laugh at me, but listen; perhaps you will change your opinion of me in the end," I added, carried away by a strange feeling. "You know so little of me as yet; afterwards when you know more of me, then . . . perhaps . . ."

"For God's sake let us stop this conversation!" cried Nastenka, with visible impatience.

"Very well, very well, let us stop! But . . . where can I see you?"

"Where can you see me?"

"Why, you know, this cannot be the last word we have to say to each other, Nastasya Yevgrafovna! For God's sake, let me meet you again to-day, for instance. But it's already getting dark. So if it is anyhow possible let it be to-morrow early, I will ask to be called earlier on purpose. You know there's an arbour over there by the pond. You see, I remember it, I know the way. I used to stay here when I was little."

"Meet you! What for? Why, we are talking now."

"But I know nothing yet, Nastasya Yevgrafovna, I will first find out everything from my uncle. Why, he is bound to tell me everything now. And then, perhaps, I shall have something very important to tell you. . . ."

"No, no! You mustn't, you mustn't!" cried Nastenka. "Let us end it all at once now, so that we may never think of it again. And don't go to that arbour for nothing; I assure you I shall not go. And please put all this nonsense out of your head—I beg you in earnest. . . ."

"So then uncle has behaved like a madman to me!" I cried in an excess of insufferable vexation. "Why did he send for me? But listen, what is that noise?"

We were close to the house; from the open windows came the sounds of shrieking and extraordinary outcries.

"My God!" she said, turning pale, "again! I foresaw it would be so!"

"You foresaw it? Nastasya Yevgrafovna, one more question. Of course I have not the least right to do so, but I venture to put this last question to you for the good of us all. Tell me—

and I will keep it secret to the grave—tell me frankly: is my uncle in love with you or not?"

"Oh! Please, please put that nonsense out of your head once for all," she cried, flushing crimson with anger. "And you, too! If he were in love with me, he wouldn't have wanted to have married me to you," she added with a bitter smile. "And what put that idea into your head? Don't you know what the trouble's about? Do you hear those shouts?"

"But. . . . It's Foma Fomitch. . . ."

"Yes, of course it is Foma Fomitch; but now the trouble is over me because they are saying the same thing as you, the same senseless thing; they, too, suspect that he is in love with me. And as I am poor and of no consequence, and as it costs nothing to throw dirt on me and they want to marry him to someone else, they are insisting that he should send me home to my father to make things sure. And when they talk to him of that he flies into a rage at once; he's ready to tear Foma Fomitch to pieces even. They are quarrelling about that now; I feel that it is about that."

"So that's the truth! So he really is going to marry that Tatyana, then."

"That Tatyana?"

"Yes, that silly fool!"

"Not a silly fool at all! She is good; you have no right to talk like that! She has a noble heart, nobler than many other people. It's not her fault that she is unfortunate."

"Forgive me. Supposing you are quite right about that, yet aren't you mistaken about the chief point? Tell me, how is it, then, that they make your father welcome, as I noticed? Why, if they were so set against you as you say and were turning you out, they would be angry with him too, and would give him a cold welcome."

"Why, don't you see what my father is doing for my sake? He is playing the fool before them! He is received just because he has succeeded in ingratiating himself with Foma Fomitch; and as Foma Fomitch was a buffoon himself, you see it flatters him to have buffoons about him now. For whose sake do you suppose my father does it? He does it for me, only for me. He wants nothing; he wouldn't bow down to anyone for himself. He may be very absurd in some people's eyes, but he is a noble man, the noblest of men! He thinks—goodness knows why, and certainly not because I get a good salary here, I assure you —he thinks that it is best for me to stay here in this house;

but now I have quite brought him round. I wrote to him firmly. He has come on purpose to take me; and if it comes to extremes, to-morrow. For things have got beyond everything; they are ready to tear me to pieces, and I am certain that they are quarrelling about me now. They are at *him,* on my account, they will be the death of *him!* And he is like a father to me— do you hear? more even than my own father. I won't stay to see it. I know more than other people. To-morrow, to-morrow I am going! Who knows: perhaps that will make them put off, if only for a time, his marriage to Tatyana Ivanovna. . . . Here I have told you all about it now. Tell him this, because I can't speak to him now; we are watched, especially by that Perepelitsyn woman. Tell him not to worry about me, tell him I would rather eat black bread and live in my father's hut than be the cause of his sufferings here. I am a poor girl, and I ought to live like a poor girl. But, my God, what an uproar! What shouting! What is happening? Yes, come what may I shall go in! I will tell them all this straight to their faces myself, whatever happens! I ought to do it! Good-bye."

She ran away. I remained standing on the same spot, fully conscious of the absurdity of the part it had just been my lot to play, and completely puzzled to think how it would all be settled. I was sorry for the poor girl, and I was afraid for my uncle. All at once I found Gavrila at my side; he was still holding the exercise book in his hand.

"Please come to your uncle," he said in a dejected voice.

I pulled myself together.

"To my uncle? Where is he? What's happening to him now?"

"In the tea-room. Where your honour had tea this afternoon."

"Who is with him?"

"His honour's alone. He is waiting."

"For whom? For me?"

"He has sent for Foma Fomitch. Happy days have come for us," he added, with a deep sigh.

"Foma Fomitch? H'm! Where are the others? Where's your mistress?"

"In her own apartments. Her honour's fallen into a swoon, and now she is lying unconscious and crying."

Conversing in this way, we reached the veranda. It was almost completely dark outside. My uncle really was alone in the very room in which my encounter with Foma Fomitch had

95

taken place, and he was striding up and down it. There were lighted candles on the tables. He was pale and breathing hard; his hands were trembling, and from time to time a nervous shudder ran over his whole frame.

CHAPTER IX

YOUR EXCELLENCY

"MY dear boy, it's all over, it's all settled," he pronounced in a tragic half-whisper.

"Uncle," I said, "I heard shouts and uproar."

"Yes, my boy, shouts there were; shouts of all sorts! Mamma is in a swoon, and everything is upside down now. But I have made up my mind, and shall insist on my own way. I am afraid of no one now, Seryozha. I want to show them that I, too, have a will of my own, and I will show them! And so I have sent for you on purpose that you may help me show them. . . . My heart is broken, Seryozha . . . but I ought, I am bound to act with severity. Justice is inexorable."

"But whatever has happened, uncle?"

"I am parting with Foma," my uncle pronounced in a resolute voice.

"Uncle," I cried, delighted, "you could have thought of nothing better! And if I can assist in any way to carry out your decision . . . make use of me now and always."

"Thank you, my boy, thank you! But now it is all settled. I am waiting for Foma, I have already sent for him. Either he or I! We must part. Either Foma leaves this house to-morrow or I swear I'll throw up everything and go into the Hussars again. They will take me and give me a division. Away with all this bobbery! A fresh start in every way now. What have you got that French exercise book for?" he cried furiously, addressing Gavrila. "Away with it! Burn it, stamp on it, tear it to pieces! *I* am your master, and *I* order you not to learn French. You can't disobey me, you dare not, for *I* am your master, and not Foma Fomitch!"

"I thank Thee, O Lord!" Gavrila muttered to himself.

Evidently things had got beyond a joke.

"My dear," my uncle went on, with deep feeling, "they are asking me the impossible. You shall decide; you stand between me and them now as an impartial judge. You don't know what they have insisted on my doing, you don't know, and at last they have formally demanded it, they have spoken out. But it's repugnant to humanity, to decent feeling, to honour. . . . I will tell you all about it, but first . . ."

"I know about it already, uncle!" I cried, interrupting him. "I can guess . . . I have just been talking to Nastasya Yevgrafovna."

"My dear, not a word, not a word of that now!" he interrupted me hurriedly, as though he were frightened. "I will explain about it later on, but meanwhile. . . . Well?" he cried to Vidoplyasov, who walked in. "Where is Foma Fomitch?"

Vidoplyasov entered with the information "that Foma Fomitch did not wish to come, and considered that the insistence on his doing so was rude to the point of impertinence, so that his honour, Foma Fomitch, was greatly offended by it."

"Bring him! Drag him! Fetch him here! Drag him here by force!" cried my uncle, stamping.

Vidoplyasov, who had never seen his master in such a rage, retreated in alarm. I was surprised.

"Something very important must have happened," I thought, "if a man of his character is capable of being moved to such wrath and such determination."

For some moments my uncle walked up and down the room as though struggling with himself.

"Don't tear up your exercise book though," he said to Gavrila as last. "Wait a little and stay here. You may perhaps be wanted. My dear," he went on, turning to me, "I think I was too noisy just now. Everything must be done with dignity and manliness, but without shouting and insulting people. Do you know what, Seryozha; wouldn't it be better if you were to go out? It will be just the same to you. I will tell you all about it later on—eh? What do you think? Do that for my sake, please."

"Are you frightened, uncle? Are you repenting?" I said, looking at him intently.

"No, no, my dear boy, I am not repenting," cried my uncle, with redoubled earnestness. "I am afraid of nothing now. I have taken decisive steps, the most decisive! You don't know, you can't imagine what they have demanded of me! Ought I to consent? No, I will show them. I have made a stand against them and I will show them. I was bound to show them sooner or later! But you know, my dear boy, I am sorry I sent for you; it will be very hard, perhaps, for Foma if you are here, so to say, the witness of his humiliation. You see, I want to turn him out of the house in a gentlemanly way, without humiliating him at all. Though, indeed, it is only a form of words to say, without humiliation. The position is such, my boy, that however honied one's speech is it will still be insulting. I am coarse, uneducated perhaps, I may do something in my foolishness that I may regret later. Anyway he has done a great deal for me. . . . Go away, my dear. . . . Here, they are bringing him! Seryozha, I entreat you, go away; I will tell you all about it afterwards. For Christ's sake go away!"

And uncle led me out on to the veranda at the very moment when Foma walked into the room. But I must confess I did not go away; I made up my mind to stay on the veranda, where it was very dark, and so it was difficult to see me from within. I made up my mind to play the eavesdropper! I do not justify my action, but I can boldly say that I consider I performed an heroic feat in standing that whole half-hour on the veranda without losing patience.

From my position I could not only hear well, but could even see well; the doors were of glass. I now beg the reader to imagine Foma Fomitch after he had been *commanded* to come, and threatened with force if he refused.

"Can my ears have heard that threat aright, Colonel?" cried Foma, entering the room. "Was that your message?"

"Yes, Foma, yes; calm yourself," my uncle answered valiantly. "Sit down; we must have a little serious friendly talk like brothers. Sit down, Foma."

Foma Fomitch majestically sat down on a low chair. My uncle walked about the room with rapid and uneven steps, evidently puzzled how to begin.

"Like brothers, precisely," he repeated. "You understand me, Foma; you are not a boy, I am not a boy either—in fact, we are both getting on. . . . H'm! You see, Foma, we don't get on together on certain points . . . yes, on certain points, precisely, and so, Foma, would it not be better to part? I am convinced that you are a generous man, that you wish me well, and so . . . But why prolong the discussion? Foma, I am your friend now and always, and I swear that by all the saints! Here are fifteen thousand roubles in silver; it's all I have to bless myself with. I have scraped together every farthing, I have robbed my own children. Take it boldly! I ought—it is my duty—to secure your future. It's almost all in bank-notes and very little in cash. Take it boldly; you owe me nothing, for I shall never be able to repay you for all you have done for me. Yes, yes, precisely, I feel that, though now we are in disagreement over the most important point. To-morrow or the day after, or when you like, let us part. Drive to our little town, Foma, it is not eight miles away; there behind the church in the first side-street there is a little house with green shutters, a charming little house belonging to the widow of a priest, that looks as though it had been built for you. She is selling it, and I will buy it for you in addition to this money. Settle there near us. Work at literature, study science, you will win fame. . . . The officials there are gentlemanly, agreeable, disinterested men; the head priest is learned. You shall come and stay with us for the holidays—and we shall all live as in paradise. Will you?"

"So these are the terms on which Foma is to be kicked out!" I thought. "Uncle did not say a word to me about money."

For a long time a profound silence reigned. Foma sat in his easy-chair as though struck dumb, gazing fixedly at my uncle, who was evidently becoming uncomfortable from that silence and that stare.

"The money!" Foma articulated at last in an affectedly faint voice. "Where is it? Where is that money? Give it me, give it here at once!"

"Here it is, Foma, everything I have to the last farthing, just fifteen thousand. Here are notes and securities; you can see for yourself . . . here!"

"Gavrila, take that money," Foma said mildly, "it may be of use to you, old man. But no!" he cried all at once, raising his voice to an extraordinary squeal and leaping up from his chair; "no, give me that money first, Gavrila! Give it me. Give it me. Give me those millions that I may trample them underfoot; give them to me that I may tear them to pieces, spit on them, fling them away, spurn them, scorn them! . . . They offer money to me—to me! They try to buy me to leave this house! Have I heard that? Have I lived to see this last ignominy? Here they are, here are your millions! Look! there, there, there, there. That is how Foma Opiskin behaves if you did not know it before, Colonel!"

And Foma threw the whole roll of notes about the room. It was noticeable that he did not tear or spit on one of the notes as he had boasted of doing; he only crumpled them a little, and even that rather carefully. Gavrila flew to pick up the notes from the floor, and later on, after Foma's departure, he carefully restored them to his master.

Foma's action produced an overwhelming impression upon my uncle. In his turn, he now stood facing him, immovably, senselessly, open-mouthed. Foma meanwhile had replaced himself in his arm-chair and was panting as though from unutterable agitation.

"You are a man of lofty feelings, Foma!" my uncle cried out at last, recovering himself. "You are the noblest of men!"

"I know it," Foma answered in a faint voice, but with ineffable dignity.

"Foma, forgive me! I have been a mean wretch to you, Foma!"

"Yes, to me," Foma assented.

"Foma, it is not your disinterestedness that I marvel at," my uncle went on enthusiastically, "but that I could have been so coarse, blind and mean as to offer you money in such circumstances. But, Foma, you are mistaken about one thing; I was not bribing you, I was not paying you for leaving this house, but just simply I wanted you to have money that you might not be in straits when you leave me. I swear that! On my knees, on my knees I am ready to beg your forgiveness, Foma; and if you like, I am ready to go down on my knees before you this moment . . . if you wish me to. . . ."

"I don't want your kneeling, Colonel."

"But, my God! Foma, consider: you know I was carried away, overwhelmed, I was not myself. . . . But do tell me, do say in what way I can, in what way I may be able to efface this insult! Instruct me, admonish me. . . ."

"In no way, in no way, Colonel! And rest assured that to-morrow morning I shall shake the dust from off my boots on the threshold of this house."

And Foma began to get up from his chair. My uncle rushed in horror to make him sit down again.

"No, Foma, you will not go away, I assure you!" cried my uncle. "It is no use talking about dust and boots, Foma! You are not going away, or I will follow you to the utmost ends of the earth, and I will follow you till such time as you forgive me . . . I swear it, Foma, and I will do it!"

"Forgive you? You are to blame?" said Foma. "But do you yet understand the wrong you have done me? Do you understand that even the fact that you have given me a piece of bread here has become a wrong to me now? Do you understand that now in one minute you have poisoned every morsel I have tasted in your house? You reproached me just now with those morsels, with every mouthful of the bread I have eaten; you have shown me now that I have been living like a slave in your house, like a flunkey, like a rag to wipe your polished boots! And yet I, in the purity of my heart, imagined up to now that I was residing in your house as a friend and a brother! Did you not, did you not yourself in your snake-like speeches assure me a thousand times of that brotherly relation? Why did you mysteriously weave for me the snare in which I have been caught like a fool? Why have you dug in the darkness this wolf-pit into which you have yourself thrust me now? Why did you not strike me down with one blow before? Why did you not wring my neck at the very beginning like a cock, because he . . . well, for instance, simply because he doesn't lay eggs? Yes, that's just it! I stick to that comparison, Colonel, though it is taken from rustic life and recalls the trivial tone of modern literature; I stick to it, because one sees in it all the senselessness of your accusation; for I am as much in fault as this supposititious cock who displeases his frivolous owner by not laying eggs! Upon my word, Colonel! Does one pay a friend, a brother, with money—and what for? That's the point, what for? 'Here, my beloved brother, I am indebted to you; you have even saved my life; here are a few of Judas's silver pieces for you, only get away out of my sight!' How naïve! How crudely you have behaved to me! You thought that I was thirsting for your gold, while I was cherishing only the heavenly feeling of securing your welfare. Oh, how you have broken my heart! You have played with my finest feelings like some wretched boy with a ninepin! Long, long ago, Colonel, I foresaw all this—that is why I have long choked over your bread, I have been suffocated by your bread! That is why your feather beds have stifled me, they have stifled me instead of lulling me to slumber! That is why your sugar, your sweetmeats have been cayenne pepper to me and not sweetmeats! No, Colonel! live alone, prosper alone, and let Foma go his sorrowful way with a wallet on his back. So it shall be, Colonel!"

"No, Foma, no! It shall not be so, it cannot be so!" moaned my uncle, utterly crushed.

"Yes, Colonel, yes! So it shall be, for so it must be. To-morrow I shall depart from you. Scatter your millions, strew all my way, all the high road to Moscow with your bank-notes—and I will walk proudly and scornfully over your notes; this very foot, Colonel, will trample your notes into the mud and crush them; for Foma Opiskin the nobility of his own soul will be enough! I have said it and I have shown it! Farewell, Colonel, fa-re-we-ell!"

And Foma began again getting up from his chair.

"Forgive me, forgive me, Foma; forget it! . . ." repeated my uncle, in an imploring voice.

"Forgive you! Why, what use will my forgiveness be to you? Why, supposing I do forgive you: I am a Christian; I cannot refuse to forgive; I have almost forgiven you already. But consider yourself: is it in the least consistent with common sense and gentlemanly feeling for me to stay one minute longer in your house? Why, you have turned me out of it!"

"It is consistent, it is consistent, Foma! I assure you that it is consistent!"

"It is? But are we equals now? Don't you understand that I have, so to speak, crushed you by my generosity, and you have crushed yourself by your degrading action? You are crushed and I am uplifted. Where is the equality? Is friendship possible without equality? I say this, uttering a cry of lamentation from my heart, and not triumphing, not exalting myself over you, as you perhaps imagine."

"But I am uttering a cry of lamentation from my heart too, Foma, I assure you."

"And this is the man," Foma went on, changing his severe tone for a sanctimonious one, "this is the man for whom I so often kept vigil at night! How many times on my sleepless nights have I arisen from my bed, have lighted a candle and said to myself, 'Now he is sleeping peacefully, trusting in you. Do not you, Foma, sleep, be valiant for him; maybe you will think of something more for the welfare of that man.' That is what Foma thought on his sleepless nights, Colonel! And this is how that colonel has repaid him! But enough, enough . . ."

"But I will deserve your friendship again, Foma; I will deserve it, I swear to you."

"You will deserve it? Where is the guarantee? As a Christian I will forgive you, and even love you; but as a man and a gentleman I shall not be able to help despising you. I must, I am bound to, in the name of morality, because—I repeat it—you have disgraced yourself, while my action has been most high-minded. Why, who out of *your set* would perform such an action? Would any one of them refuse an immense sum of money which poor destitute Foma, despised by all, has refused from devotion to true greatness? No, Colonel; to be on a level with me you must perform now a regular series of heroic deeds. And what are you capable of when you cannot even address me as your equal, but call me Foma like a servant. . . ."

"Foma! but I call you so from affection!" wailed my uncle. "I did not know you disliked it. My God! if I had only known! . . ."

"You," Foma pursued, "you who could not, or rather, would not, grant the most insignificant, the most trivial request when I asked you to address me like a general as 'your Excellency' . . ."

"But, Foma, you know that is really, so to say, high treason, Foma!"

"High treason! You have learnt some phrase out of a book and repeat it like a parrot! But, do you know, you put me to shame, covered me with ignominy by your refusal to call me 'your Excellency'; you covered me with ignominy because without understanding my reasons you made me look a capricious fool worthy of a madhouse. Why, do you suppose I don't understand that I should have been ridiculous if I had wanted to be styled 'Excellency'—I who despise all these ranks and earthly grandeurs, insignificant in themselves if they are not lighted up by virtue? For a million I would not accept the rank of general, without virtue. And meanwhile you looked upon me as a madman! It was for your benefit I sacrificed my pride and allowed you, *you* to be able to look upon me as a madman, you and your learned gentlemen! It was solely in order to enlighten your mind, to develop your morals, and to shed upon you the light of new ideas that I made up my mind to demand from you a general's title. I wanted you for the future not to regard generals as the highest luminaries on this earthly sphere; I wanted to show you that rank is nothing without greatness of soul, and that there is no need to rejoice at the arrival of your general when there are, perhaps, standing at your side, people made illustrious by virtue! But you have so constantly prided yourself before me on your rank of colonel that it was hard for you to say to me: 'your Excellency.' That was the root of it! That was where one must look for the reason, and not in any breach of the decrees of Providence! The whole reason is, that you are a colonel and I am simply Foma. . . ."

"No, Foma; no, I assure you that it is not so. You are a learned man . . . you are not simply Foma. . . . I respect you. . . ."

"You respect me! Good! Then tell me, since you respect me, what is your opinion, am I worthy of the rank of a general or am I not? Answer at once and straightforwardly, am I or not? I want to see your intelligence, your development."

"For honesty, for disinterestedness, for intelligence, for lofty nobility of soul you are worthy of it," my uncle brought out with pride.

"Well, if I am worthy of it, why will you not say 'your Excellency' to me?"

"Foma, I will, perhaps."

"But, I insist! And I insist now, Colonel, I require it and insist. I see how hard it is for you, that is why I insist. That sacrifice on your side will be the first step in your moral victory, for—don't forget it—you will have to gain a series of moral victories to be on a level with me; you must conquer yourself, and only then I shall feel certain of your sincerity. . . ."

"To-morrow, then, I will call you 'your Excellency', Foma."

"No, not to-morrow, Colonel, to-morrow can take care of itself. I insist that you now at once address me as 'your Excellency'."

"Certainly, Foma, I am ready; only what do you mean by 'at once', Foma?"

"Why not at once, or are you ashamed? That's an insult to me if you are ashamed."

"Oh, well, if you like, Foma. I am ready . . . I am proud to do so, indeed; only it's queer, Foma, apropos of nothing, 'Good-day, your Excellency.' You see, one can't."

"No, not 'Good-day, your Excellency.' That's an offensive tone, it is like a joke, a farce. I do not permit such jokes with me. You forget yourself, Colonel, you forget yourself. Change your tone!"

"And you are not joking, Foma?"

"In the first place, I am not Foma, Yegor Ilyitch, and don't you forget it. I am Foma Fomitch."

"Oh, Foma Fomitch, I am delighted, really, I am altogether delighted, only what am I to say?"

"You are puzzled what to add to the phrase, 'your Excellency'. That I understand. You should have explained yourself long ago. It is excusable indeed, especially if a man is not a *literary character*, to put it politely. Well, I will help you, since you are not a literary character. Repeat after me, 'Your Excellency!' . . ."

"Well, your Excellency . . ."

"No, not 'Well, your Excellency,' but simply 'your Excellency!' I tell you, Colonel, you must change your tone. I hope, too, that you will not be offended if I suggest that you should make a slight bow. And at the same time bend forward, expressing in that way respectfulness and readiness, so to say, to fly on his errands. I have been in the society of generals myself, and I know all that, so then 'your Excellency.' "

"Your Excellency . . ."

"How inexpressibly delighted I am that I have at last an opportunity of asking your forgiveness for not having recognised from the first moment your Excellency's soul. I make bold to assure you that I will not for the future spare my poor efforts for the public welfare. . . . Well, that's enough!"

Poor uncle! He had to repeat all this rigmarole phrase by phrase, word by word. I stood and blushed as though I were guilty. I was choking with rage.

"Well, don't you feel now," the torturer went on, "that your heart is suddenly lighter, as though an angel had flown into your soul? . . . Do you feel the presence of that angel? Answer."

"Yes, Foma, I certainly feel more at ease," answered my uncle.

"As though after you have conquered yourself your heart were, so to say, steeped in holy oil?"

"Yes, Foma; certainly it all seems as it were in butter."

"As it were in butter? H'm. I wasn't talking of butter, though. . . . Well, never mind! You see, Colonel, the value of a duty performed! Conquer yourself. You are vain, immensely vain!"

"I see I am, Foma," my uncle answered, with a sigh.

"You are an egoist, and indeed a gloomy egoist. . . ."

"An egoist I am, it is true, Foma, and I see it; ever since I have come to know you, I have learned to know that too."

"I am speaking to you now like a father, like a tender mother. . . . You repel people and forget that a friendly calf sucks two mothers."

"That is true too, Foma!"

"You are coarse. You jar so coarsely upon the human heart,

you so egoistically insist upon attention, that a decent man is ready to run from you to the utmost ends of the earth.''

My uncle heaved another deep sigh.

''Be softer, more attentive, more loving to others; forget yourself for the sake of others, then they will think of you. Live and let others live—that is my rule! Suffer, labour, pray and hope—those are the truths which I would like to instil into all mankind at once! Model yourself on them and then I shall be the first to open my heart to you, I shall weep on your bosom . . . if need be. . . . As it is, it is always 'I' and 'I' and 'my gracious self' with you. But, you know, one may get sick at last of your gracious self, if you will allow me to say so.''

''A sweet-tongued gentleman,'' Gavrila brought out, awe-struck.

''That's true, Foma, I feel all that,'' my uncle assented, deeply touched. ''But I am not altogether to blame, Foma. I've been brought up like this, I have lived with soldiers; but I swear, Foma, I have not been without feeling. When I said good-bye to the regiment, all the hussars, all my division, simply shed tears and said they would never get another like me. I thought at the time that I too was not altogether a lost soul.''

''Again a piece of egoism! Again I catch you in vanity. You are boasting and at the same time reproaching me with the hussars' tears. Why don't I boast of anyone's tears? And yet there may have been grounds, there may have been grounds for doing so.''

''I meant nothing, Foma, it was a slip of the tongue. I couldn't help remembering those old happy times.''

''Happy times do not fall from heaven, we make them ourselves; it lies in our hearts, Yegor Ilyitch. That is why I am always happy and, in spite of my sufferings, contented, tranquil in spirit, and am not a burden to anyone unless it is to fools, upstarts and *learned gentlemen*, on whom I have no mercy and don't care to have. I don't like fools! And what are these learned gentlemen? 'A man of learning'; and his learning turns out to be nothing but a hoaxing trick, and not learning. Why, what did *he* say just now? Let him come here! Let all these men of learning come here! I can refute them all; I can refute all their propositions! I say nothing of greatness of soul . . .''

''Of course, Foma. Who doubts it?''

"This afternoon, for instance, I showed intelligence, talent, colossal erudition, knowledge of the human heart, knowledge of contemporary literature; I showed and displayed in a brilliant fashion how some wretched Komarinsky may furnish a lofty topic of conversation for a man of talent. And did any one of them appreciate me as I deserved? No, they turned away! Why, I am certain he has told you already that I know nothing, and yet perhaps Macchiavelli himself or some Mercadante was sitting before him and only to blame for being poor and in obscurity. . . . That does not penetrate to them! . . . I hear of Korovkin too. What sort of queer fish is he?"

"He is a clever man, Foma, a man of learning. . . . I am expecting him. He will certainly be a nice man, Foma."

"H'm, I doubt it. Most likely some modern ass laden with books; there is no soul in them, Colonel, no heart in them! And what is learning without virtue?"

"No, Foma, no. How he talked of family happiness! The heart feels it of itself, Foma."

"H'm! We will have a look at him; we will examine Korovkin too. But enough," Foma concluded, getting up from his easy-chair. "I cannot altogether forgive you yet, Colonel; the insult was too deadly; but I will pray, and perhaps God will shed peace on the wounded heart. We will speak further of this to-morrow, but now permit me to withdraw. I am tired and exhausted. . . ."

"Oh, Foma!" cried my uncle in a fluster, "why, of course you are tired! I say, won't you have something to support you, a snack of something? I will order something at once."

"A snack! Ha-ha-ha!" answered Foma, with a contemptuous laugh. "First they offer you a drink of poison, and then they ask you if you won't have a snack of something. They want to heal the wounds of the heart with stewed mushrooms or pickled apples! What a pitiful materialist you are, Colonel!"

"Oh, Foma, I spoke in all simplicity . . ."

"Oh, very well. Enough of that. I will withdraw, and you go at once to your mother; fall on your knees, sob, weep, but beg for her forgiveness, that is your duty, that is a moral obligation."

"Oh, Foma, I have been thinking of nothing but that all the time; even now while I have been talking to you I have been thinking of it. I am ready to implore her on my knees till dawn. But only think, Foma, what they are expecting of me.

Why, you know it's unjust, Foma, it's cruel. Be entirely magnanimous, make me completely happy, think a little, decide, and then . . . then . . . I swear! . . ."

"No, Yegor Ilyitch, no, it's no business of mine," answered Foma. "You know that I do not meddle in the slightest degree in all that; you may be persuaded that I am at the bottom of it all, but I assure you that from the very beginning I have held entirely aloof from this affair. It is solely the desire of your mother, and she, of course, wishes for nothing but your good. . . . Go to her, make haste, fly and rectify the position by your obedience . . . and let not the sun go down upon your wrath; while I . . . I shall be all night long praying for you. I have known no sleep for many a night, Yegor Ilyitch. Good night! I forgive you too, old man," he said, turning to Gavrila. "I know you did not do it of yourself. You forgive me too if I have offended you. . . . Good night, good night, all, and may the Lord bless you."

Foma went out. I rushed at once into the room.

"You've been listening!" cried my uncle.

"Yes, uncle, I have been listening! And you, you could call him 'your Excellency'?"

"What could I do, brother? Indeed, I am proud of it. . . . That was no great act of sacrifice. But what a noble, what a disinterested, what a great man! Sergey, why, you heard yourself . . . and how I could, how I could thrust that money on him, I simply don't understand! My dear, I was carried away, I was in a rage. I did not understand him; I suspected him, I accused him. . . . But no, he could not be antagonistic to me—I see that now . . . and do you remember what a noble expression there was on his face when he was refusing the money?"

"Very well, uncle, you can be as proud as you like, but I am going; my patience is at an end. For the last time I say it, tell me what you want of me? Why did you send for me, and what do you expect? And if it is all over and I am of no use to you, then I am going. I can't endure such exhibitions! I am going this very day."

"My dear!" My uncle was in a fluster as usual. "Only wait two minutes; I am going now, dear boy, to mamma, to settle there . . . a grave, important, immense question! . . . And you meanwhile go to your room. Here, Gavrila will take you to the summer lodge. You know the summer lodge, it is in the garden. I have given orders, and your trunk has been taken there; and I am going in to beg forgiveness and settle one question—I know now what to do—and then I will be with you in a flash, and then I'll tell you everything, I'll open my whole soul to you and . . . and . . . happy days will come for us too, some time! Two minutes, only two minutes, Sergey!''

He pressed my hand and hurriedly went out. There was nothing to be done, I had to go off with Gavrila again.

CHAPTER X

MIZINTCHIKOV

THE lodge to which Gavrila conducted me was called "the new lodge" only from old habit, because it was built long ago in the time of the former owners. It was a pretty little wooden house, standing in the garden a few paces from the old house. It was surrounded on three sides by tall old lime trees which touched the roof with their branches. All the four rooms of this little house were kept ready for visitors, and were not badly furnished. Going into the room assigned me, to which my portmanteau had been already taken, I saw on a little table before the bedstead a sheet of notepaper, covered with magnificent handwriting in various styles framed in garlands and flourishes. The capital letters and the garlands were illuminated in various colours. The whole made a very pretty specimen of calligraphy. From the first words I read I saw that it was a begging letter addressed to me, and that in it I was styled "Enlightened benefactor". It was headed "The Plaints of Vidoplyasov". Though I tried with strained attention to make out something of what was written, my efforts were all in vain, it was the most inflated nonsense, written in a high-flown flunkey lingo. I could only surmise that Vidoplyasov was in trouble of some sort, was begging for my assistance, was building great hopes upon me, "by reason of my enlightenment", and in conclusion begged me to interest myself on his behalf with my uncle and to work upon him with "my machinery", as he expressed it at the end of this epistle. I was still reading it when the door opened and Mizintchikov walked in.

"I hope you will allow me to make your acquaintance," he

said in a free and easy way, though with extreme courtesy, offering me his hand. "I could not say two words to you this afternoon, and yet from the first glance I felt a desire to know you better."

I answered at once that I was delighted and so on, though I was, in fact, in an extremely bad temper. We sat down.

"What have you got here?" he said, glancing at the sheet of paper which I was still holding in my hand. "Not 'the plaints of Vidoplyasov'? That's what it is. I was certain that Vidoplyasov was attacking you too. He presented me with just such a document with the same complaints; and he has been expecting you a long time and most likely got ready beforehand. You need not be surprised: there's a great deal that's queer here, and really there is plenty to laugh at."

"Only to laugh at?"

"Oh, well, surely not to cry over. If you like I will give you Vidoplyasov's history, and I am certain that you will laugh."

"I confess I am not interested in Vidoplyasov just now," I answered with vexation.

It was evident to me that Mr. Mizintchikov's friendliness and his polite conversation were all assumed by him with some object, and that he was simply trying to get something out of me. He had sat scowling and serious in the afternoon; now he was good-humoured, smiling, and ready to tell me long stories. It was evident from the first glance that the man was perfectly self-possessed, and he seemed to understand human nature.

"That cursed Foma!" I said, banging my fist on the table with fury. "I am positive that he is at the bottom of every sort of mischief here and mixed up in it all! Cursed brute!"

"I think your anger is excessive," Mizintchikov observed.

"My anger excessive!" I cried, instantly firing up. "I let myself go too far this afternoon, of course, and so gave everyone a right to blame me. I know very well that I plunged in and put my foot in it on every point, and I think there is no need to tell me that! . . . I know, too, that that's not the way to behave in decent society; but how could I help letting myself go? tell me that. Why, this is a madhouse, if you care to know! And . . . and . . . in fact . . . I am simply going away, so there."

"Do you smoke?" Mizintchikov asked calmly.

"Yes."

"Then you will probably allow me to smoke? They won't let me in there, and I am wretched without it. I agree," he went on, as he lighted a cigarette, "that all this is like a madhouse; but believe me, I do not venture to criticise you, just because in your place I should perhaps be three times as excited and violent as you."

"And why were you not violent if you really were angry too? I remember you very cool, on the contrary, and, I confess, I even thought it strange that you did not stand up for my poor uncle, who is ready to befriend . . . all and everyone!"

"You are right: he has befriended many people; but I consider it perfectly useless to stand up for him: in the first place it would be useless and even derogatory for him in a way; and in the second I should be kicked out to-morrow. And I tell you frankly my circumstances are such that to be a guest here is a great advantage for me."

"But I do not make the slightest claim on your frankness in regard to your circumstances . . . I should, however, have liked to ask, since you have been here a month . . ."

"Please, do, ask anything: I am at your service," Mizintchikov answered, hurriedly moving up a chair.

"Well, explain this, for instance: Foma Fomitch has just refused fifteen thousand roubles which were in his hands—I saw it with my own eyes."

"What? Impossible!" cried Mizintchikov. "Tell me, please."

I told him, saying nothing about "your Excellency". Mizintchikov listened with greedy curiosity. He positively changed countenance when the fifteen thousand were mentioned.

"That's smart!" he said, when he heard my story. "I really did not expect it of Foma."

"He did refuse the money, though! How do you explain that? Surely not by the nobility of his soul?"

"He refused fifteen thousand to take thirty later. Though, do you know," he added after a moment's thought, "I doubt whether Foma had any mercenary design in it. He is not a practical man; he is a sort of poet, too, in his own way. Fifteen thousand . . . h'm. He would have taken the money, do you see, but he couldn't resist the temptation to strike an attitude and give himself airs. I tell you he's a sentimental mush, and the sloppiest old sniveller and all that, with the most unbounded vanity!"

Mizintchikov was positively roused to anger. It was evident that he was very much annoyed and even envious. I looked at him with curiosity.

"H'm! We may expect great changes," he added, musing. "Now Yegor Ilyitch is ready to worship Foma. I shouldn't wonder if he does get married now that his heart is softened," he muttered through his teeth.

"So you think that this abominable, unnatural marriage with that crazy fool really will come off?"

Mizintchikov looked at me searchingly.

"The scoundrels!" I cried emphatically.

"There is a fairly sound idea at the back of it, though. They maintain that he ought to do something for his family."

"As though he hadn't done enough for them," I cried indignantly. "And you, you talk of there being a sound idea in marrying a vulgar fool!"

"Of course I agree with you that she is a fool. . . . H'm! It's a good thing that you are so fond of your uncle; I sympathise with him myself . . . though he could round off his estate finely with her fortune! They have other reasons, though; they are afraid that Yegor Ilyitch may marry that governess . . . do you remember, an attractive girl?"

"But is that likely to be true? . . ." I asked in agitation. "It seems to me that it's spiteful gossip. Tell me, for goodness' sake, it interests me extremely. . . ."

"Oh, he is head over ears in love with her! Only, of course, he conceals it."

"He conceals it? You think that he is concealing it? And she? Does she love him?"

"It is very likely she does. It is all to her advantage to marry him, though; she is very poor."

"But what grounds have you for your supposition that they love each other?"

"Oh, you know, you can't help seeing it; besides, I believe they meet in secret. They do say that she has illicit relations with him, in fact. Only, please, don't repeat that. I tell you as a secret."

"Is it possible to believe that?" I cried. "And you, you acknowledge that you believe it?"

"Of course I do not fully believe it, I wasn't there. But it's very possible, though."

"Very possible? Think of my uncle's sense of honour, his noble character."

"I agree; but one may be carried away, with a conviction that one is going to make it right with matrimony afterwards. People often are. But, I repeat, I don't insist on the absolute certainty of the facts, especially as they have blackened her character in all sorts of ways here; they even say that she had an intrigue with Vidoplyasov."

"There, you see," I cried, "with Vidoplyasov. Why, as though it were possible! Isn't it revolting even to listen to such a thing? Surely you can't believe it?"

"I tell you that I do not quite believe it," answered Mizintchikov calmly, "but it might happen. Anything may happen in this world. I was not there, and besides, I consider it not my business. But as I see you take great interest in all this, I feel I ought to add that I really don't put much faith in the story about Vidoplyasov. It's all the invention of Anna Nilovna, that Miss Perepelitsyn; it's she who has set those rumours going here out of envy because she dreamed in the past of marrying Yegor Ilyitch herself—yes, by Jove, on the ground that she is a major's daughter. Now she is disappointed and awfully furious. But I believe I have told you all about that business now, and I confess I greatly dislike gossip, especially as we are losing precious time. I have come to ask you a trifling favour, you see."

"A favour? Certainly; any way in which I can be of use to you."

"I understand, and indeed I hope to interest you, for I see you love your uncle and take great interest in his fate in the matrimonial line; but before I ask you that favour I will ask you another, a preliminary one."

"What is that?"

"I'll tell you; perhaps you will consent to grant my chief request, and perhaps not; but in any case, before telling it you I will humbly ask you to grant one great favour, to give me your word of honour as a nobleman and a gentleman that all you hear from me shall remain a dead secret, and that you will not betray the secret in any case or for the sake of any person, and will not take advantage for your own benefit of the idea which I now find it necessary to communicate to you. Do you agree or not?"

It was a solemn introduction. I gave my assent.

"Well?" . . . I said.

"It is really a very simple matter," Mizintchikov began. "I want to elope with Tatyana Ivanovna and to marry her;

in short, there is to be something in the Gretna Green style, do you understand?"

I stared Mizintchikov straight in the face, and for some time I could not utter a word.

"I confess I don't understand at all," I brought out at last; "and what's more," I went on, "expecting that I had to do with a sensible man, I did not in the least expect . . ."

"Expecting you did not expect," interrupted Mizintchikov; "which may be translated, that I and my project are stupid—that's so, isn't it?"

"Oh, not at all . . . but . . ."

"Oh, please, don't mind speaking plainly! Don't be uneasy; you will do me a great pleasure by plain speaking, in fact, for so we shall get nearer our object. I agree with you, though, that all this must seem somewhat strange at the first glance. But I venture to assure you that so far from being foolish, my project is extremely sensible; and if you will be so good as to listen to all the circumstances . . ."

"Oh, certainly! I am listening eagerly."

"There is scarcely anything to tell, though. You see, I am in debt and haven't a farthing. I have, besides, a sister, a girl of nineteen, fatherless and motherless, living in a family and entirely without means, you know. For that I am partly to blame. We inherited a property of forty serfs. Just at that time I was promoted to be a cornet. Well, at first, of course, I mortgaged, and then I squandered our money in other ways too. I lived like a fool, set the fashion, gave myself airs, gambled, drank—it was idiotic, in fact, and I am ashamed to remember it. Now I have come to my senses and want to change my manner of life completely. But to do so it is absolutely essential to have a hundred thousand roubles. As I shall never get anything in the service, since I am not qualified for anything and have scarcely any education, there are, of course, only two resources left to me: to steal or to marry a rich wife. I came here almost without boots to my feet, I walked, I could not drive. My sister gave me her last three roubles when I set off from Moscow. Here I saw Tatyana Ivanovna, and at once the idea dawned upon me. I immediately resolved to sacrifice myself and marry her. You will agree that all that is nothing but good sense. Besides, I am doing it more for my sister's sake . . . though, of course, for my own too."

"But allow me to ask, do you mean to make a formal proposal to Tatyana Ivanovna? . . ."

"God forbid, they would kick me out at once; but if I suggest an elopement, a runaway match, she will marry me at once. That's the whole point, that there should be something romantic and sensational about it. Of course it would all immediately end in legal matrimony. If only I can allure her away from here!"

"But why are you so sure that she will elope with you?"

"Oh, don't trouble about that! I am perfectly sure of that. The whole plan rests on the idea that Tatyana Ivanovna is ready to carry on an intrigue with anyone she meets, with anyone, in fact, to whom it occurs to respond to her. That is why I first asked you to give me your word of honour that you would not take advantage of the idea. You will understand, of course, that it would be positively wicked of me not to take advantage of such an opportunity, especially in my circumstances."

"So then she is quite mad. . . . Oh, I beg your pardon," I added, catching myself up. "Since you now have intentions. . . ."

"Please don't mind speaking out, as I have asked you already. You ask, is she quite mad? What shall I tell you? Of course she is not mad, since she is not yet in a madhouse; besides, I really don't see anything particularly mad in this mania for love affairs. She is a respectable girl in spite of everything. You see, till a year ago she was horribly poor, and from her birth up has lived in bondage to the ladies who befriended her. Her heart is exceptionally susceptible; no one has asked her in marriage. . . . Well, you understand: dreams, desires, hopes, the fervour of feelings which she has always had to conceal, perpetual agonies at the hands of the ladies who befriended her—all that of course might well drive a sensitive character to derangement. And all at once she comes in for a fortune; you'll allow that is enough to upset anyone. Well, now of course people make up to her and hang about her, and all her hopes have risen up. She told us this afternoon about a dandy in a white waistcoat; that's a fact which happened literally as she described. From that fact you can judge of the rest. With sighs, notes, verses you can inveigle her at once; and if with all that you hint at a silken rope ladder, a Spanish serenade and all that nonsense, you can do what you like with her. I have put it to the test, and at once obtained a secret interview. But meanwhile I have put it off till the right moment. But I must carry her off within four days. The evening before I shall begin to make tender speeches, to sigh: I can sing and play the guitar pretty well. At night there will be a meeting in the arbour, and at dawn the coach will be in readiness; I shall entice her away, we shall get into the coach and drive off. You understand that there is no risk about it whatever; she is of age, and what's more, completely her own mistress. And if once she ran away with me she would, of course, be bound to me. I should take her to a poor but respectable family, thirty miles away, who would look after her, and not let anyone come near her till the wedding; and meanwhile I shan't lose time, we'll get married within three days—it can be done. Of course, first of all, money is needed; but I have reckoned that I shall not need more than five hundred roubles for the whole business, and for that I rely on Yegor Ilyitch. He will give it, of course, without knowing what is up. Do you understand now?"

"I do," I answered, taking it all in fully. "But tell me, in what way can I be of use to you?"

"Oh, in a great deal, I assure you, or I would not have asked you. I told you that I had in view a poor but very respectable family. You can help me both here and there, and as a witness. I must own that without your help I should be at a loss."

"Another question, why have you done me the honour to select me to receive your confidence, though you know nothing of me, since I have only been here a few hours?"

"Your question," Mizintchikov answered with the most polite smile, "your question, I frankly confess, gives me great satisfaction, because it affords me an opportunity of expressing my special regard for you."

"Oh, you do me too much honour!"

"No; you see, I have been studying you a little this afternoon. Admitting you are both hasty and . . . and . . . well, young, I tell you what I am thoroughly certain of: when you have given me your word that you will tell no one you will certainly keep it. You are not Obnoskin—that's the first point. Secondly, you are honest and will not take advantage of my idea—for yourself, of course, I mean—unless you would like to enter into a friendly compact with me. In that case I will perhaps agree to yield to you my idea—that is, Tatyana Ivanovna—and be ready to help you zealously in the elopement, only on condition of receiving from you a month after your marriage fifty thousand roubles, for which you would of course give me security beforehand in the shape of an I O U."

"What!" I cried out. "So now you are offering her to me?"

"Naturally, I can give it up to you if on reflection you wish it. I should of course be a loser, but . . . the idea belongs to me, and you know one is paid for one's ideas. Thirdly and lastly I asked you because I had no choice. And taking into consideration the position here, it was impossible to delay long; besides which it will soon be the fast of the Assumption, and they won't celebrate weddings. I hope you fully understand me now?"

"Perfectly. And once more, I feel bound to keep your secret quite sacred; but I cannot be your accomplice in the business, and I think it my duty to tell you so at once."

"Why so?"

"You ask, why so?" I cried, giving the rein to my pent-up feelings at last. "Why, surely you must understand that such an act is positively dishonourable. Supposing you were quite correct in your calculations, reckoning on the lady's weakness of mind and unhappy mania, why it's that very thing which ought to restrain you as an honourable man! You say your-self that she is worthy of respect in spite of being ridiculous, and you are taking advantage of her misfortune to rob her of a hundred thousand. You will not, of course, be a real husband to her, carrying out your obligations: you will certainly leave her . . . it's so dishonourable that, excuse me, I can't even understand how you could bring yourself to ask me to assist you."

"Ough! my goodness! how romantic!" cried Mizintchikov, looking at me with unfeigned surprise. "Though, indeed, it's not that it's romantic, but simply I believe that you don't understand the position. You say that it's dishonourable, and yet all the advantages are not on my side, but hers . . . only consider . . ."

"Of course, if one looks at it from your point of view I dare say it will appear that you will be doing something most mag-nanimous in marrying Tatyana Ivanovna," I answered, with a sarcastic smile.

"Well, what else? Just so, it is something most mag-nanimous," cried Mizintchikov, growing hot in his turn. "Only consider: in the first place, I am sacrificing myself in consent-ing to be her husband. Is not that some sacrifice? In the second place, although she has certainly a hundred thousand in silver roubles I shall only take a hundred thousand in paper, and I have sworn that I won't take another farthing from her all my life, though I could; that's some sacrifice again. Lastly, look into it more deeply. Could she anyway lead a peaceful life? For her to live in peace one would have to take her money from her and put her in a madhouse, for one may expect any minute that some worthless fellow, some scheming rogue, some adventurer, will turn up with a moustache and an imperial, with a guitar and serenades, someone in the style of Obnoskin, who will inveigle her, marry her and strip her completely, and then turn her out into the gutter. This, for instance, is a most respectable household, and yet they are only keeping her here because they are speculating on her fortune. From such risks she must be saved, rescued. Well, you see, as soon as she marries me such risks are over, it will be my duty to see that no trouble comes near her. In the first place, I shall settle her at once in Moscow, in a poor but honourable family—not the one I have spoken of to you, but another; my sister will be constantly with her; they will look after her and pay her every attention. She will have two hundred and fifty thousand, possibly three hundred, in paper left, one can do well on that, you know! Every pleasure will be provided for her, all sorts of entertainment, balls, masquerades and concerts. She may even dream of love affairs, only of course I shall look after that. She may dream as much as she likes, but not so in reality! Now, for instance, anyone can ill-treat her, but no one will be able to then; she will be my wife, she will be a Mizintchikov, and I won't allow my name to be insulted! That alone is worth something, isn't it? Naturally I am not going to live with her. She will live in Moscow, and I shall live somewhere in Petersburg. I admit that, because I am doing things straightforwardly with you. But what if we do live apart? Look at her character and just consider, is she fit to be a wife and live with a husband? Is it possible to go on living with her continually? Why, she is the most light-headed creature in the world. She must have incessant change; she is capable next day of forgetting that she was married yesterday and made a lawful wife. Why, I should make her wretched in the end if I were to live with her and insist on her strictly performing her wifely duties. Naturally I shall go and see her once a year or oftener, and not to get money, I assure you. I have told you that I am not going to take more than a hundred thousand in paper from her, and I shan't either! On the money side I shall treat her in the most honourable way. If I come to see her for two or three days, my visit will actually be a pleasure to her and not a bore; I shall laugh with her, tell her stories, take her to a ball, make love to her, give her little souvenirs, sing songs to her, make her a present of a lapdog, have a romantic parting from her, and keep up an exchange of love letters. Why, she will be in ecstasies over such a romantic, devoted, and amusing husband. To my thinking, that is the rational way to proceed; that's how all husbands ought to behave. Husbands are only precious to their wives when they are absent, and following my system, I shall engage Tatyana Ivanovna's heart in the most honied way for the whole of her life. What more can she want? tell me that. Why, it is paradise, not life!"

I listened in silence and with wonder; I realised that it was impossible to turn Mr. Mizintchikov from his plan. He was fanatically persuaded of the rectitude and even the greatness of his project, and spoke of it with the enthusiasm of an inventor. But there was still one rather delicate question which it was essential to clear up.

"Have you reflected," I said, "that she is almost betrothed to my uncle? It will be a great insult to him if you elope with her; you will be carrying her off almost on the eve of her wedding, and what's more, will borrow from him to carry out your exploit."

"That is just where I have you!" Mizintchikov cried out with heat. "You needn't trouble, I foresaw your objection. But first and foremost, your uncle has not yet made her an offer, consequently there is no need for me to know that they are intending her for a match for him; moreover, I beg you to note that I thought of this enterprise three weeks ago, when I knew nothing of their intentions, so I am perfectly justified from the moral point of view as regards them. And in fact, strictly speaking, it is rather he who is carrying off my betrothed than I his, whom, take note, I have already met in secret at night in the arbour. And lastly, allow me to ask, were not you yourself in a perfect frenzy at your uncle's being forced to marry Tatyana Ivanovna? And now you are all at once standing up for the marriage, and talking of honour, of some insult to the family! Why, on the contrary, I am doing your uncle the greatest service, I am saving him—you ought to understand that. He looks on the match with aversion, and what's more, is in love with another young lady! Why, what sort of wife would Tatyana Ivanovna be to him? And she would be wretched with him too, because, say what you like, she would then have to be restrained from throwing roses at young men. And you know if I elope with her in the night, then no Madame la Générale, no Foma Fomitch, will be able to do anything. To bring back a bride who has run away from the wedding would be too discreditable. Isn't that a service, isn't it a benefit to Yegor Ilyitch?''

I must own this last argument had a great effect on me.

"But what if he makes her an offer to-morrow?" I said. "You see, it would be rather too late then; she will be formally betrothed to him.''

"To be sure it will be, but that is just why we must work to prevent it. What am I asking you to help me for? It's hard for me alone, but the two of us together can arrange things and prevent Yegor Ilyitch from making a proposal. We must do everything we can to prevent it, even if it comes to thrashing Foma Fomitch and so distracting the general attention from all thoughts of the match. Of course that is only in the last extremity, I only give that for the sake of example. This is what I am relying on you for.''

"One more last question: have you told no one but me of your scheme?''

Mizintchikov scratched the back of his head and made a very wry face.

"I must confess that question is worse than the bitterest pill for me. That's just the trouble, that I have given away the idea . . . in fact, I have been the most awful fool! And to whom, do you suppose? To Obnoskin! I can scarcely believe it myself. I don't know how it happened! He is always about the place, I did not know him so well, and when this inspiration dawned upon me I was, of course, greatly excited; and as I realised even then that I should need someone to help me, I appealed to Obnoskin . . . it was unpardonable, unpardonable!''

"Well, and what did Obnoskin say?''

"He agreed with enthusiasm, but next day early in the morning he disappeared. Three days later he turned up again with his mamma. He doesn't say a word to me, and in fact avoids me as though he were afraid of me. I saw at once what was up. And his mother is a regular shark, she's been in tight places before now. I used to know her in the past. Of course he has told her all about it. I am waiting and keeping quiet; they are spying on me, and things are in rather a strained position . . . that's why I am in a hurry.''

"What is it exactly you fear from them?"

"They can't do a great deal, of course, but that they will do something nasty—that is certain. They will insist on having money for keeping quiet and helping, that I expect. . . . Only I can't give them a great deal, and I am not going to. I have made up my mind about that. I can't give more than three thousand paper roubles. Judge for yourself: three thousand to them, five hundred in silver for the wedding, for I must pay your uncle back in full; then my old debts; then at least something for my sister, something at least. There won't be much left out of a hundred thousand, will there? Why, it will be ruin! . . . The Obnoskins have gone away, though."

"Gone away?" I asked with curiosity.

"Just after tea, damn them! but they will turn up again to-morrow, you will see. Well, how is it to be, then? Do you agree?"

"I must own," I answered, shrugging, "I really don't know what to say. It's a delicate matter. . . . Of course I will keep it all secret, I am not Obnoskin; but . . . I think it's no use your building hopes on me."

"I see," said Mizintchikov, getting up from his chair, "that you are not yet sick of Foma Fomitch and your grandmother; and though you do care for your kind and generous uncle, you have not yet sufficiently realised how he is being tormented. You are new to the place. . . . But patience! You will be here to-morrow, look about you, and by evening you'll consent. Your uncle is lost if you don't, do you understand? They will certainly force him to marry her. Don't forget that to-morrow he may perhaps make her an offer. It will be too late, we must settle things to-day."

"Really, I wish you every success, but as for helping you . . . I don't know in what way."

"We know! But let us wait till to-morrow," said Mizintchikov, smiling ironically. *"La nuit porte conseil.* Good-bye for the present. I will come to you early in the morning, and you think things over. . . ."

He turned and went out whistling.

I almost followed him out, to get a breath of fresh air. The moon had not yet risen; it was a dark night, warm and stifling. The leaves on the trees did not stir. In spite of being terribly tired I wanted to walk to distract my mind, collect my thoughts; but I had not gone above ten paces when I suddenly heard my uncle's voice. He was mounting the steps of the lodge in company with someone, and speaking with great animation. I turned back and called to him. My uncle was with Vidoplyasov.

CHAPTER XI

THE EXTREME OF PERPLEXITY

"UNCLE," I said, "at last I have got you."

"My dear boy, I was rushing to you myself. Here, I will just finish with Vidoplyasov, and then we can talk to our hearts' content. I have a great deal to tell you."

"What, Vidoplyasov now! Oh, get rid of him, uncle."

"Only another five or ten minutes, Sergey, and I shall be entirely at your disposal. You see, it's important."

"Oh, no doubt, it is his foolishness," I said, with vexation.

"What can I say to you, my dear? The man has certainly found a time to worry me with his nonsense! Yes, my good Grigory, couldn't you find some other time for your complaints? Why, what can I do for you? You might have compassion even on me, my good boy. Why, I am, so to say, worn out by you all, devoured alive, body and soul! They are too much for me, Sergey!" And my uncle made a gesture of the profoundest misery with both hands.

"But what business can be so important that you can't leave it? And, uncle, I do so want . . ."

"Oh, my dear boy, as it is they keep crying out that I take no trouble over my servants' morals! Very likely he will complain of me to-morrow that I wouldn't listen to him, and then . . ." and my uncle waved his hand in despair again.

"Well, then, make haste and finish with him! Perhaps I can help you; let us go up the steps. What is it? What does he want?" I said as we went into the room.

"Well, you see, my dear, he doesn't like his own surname, and asks leave to change it. What do you think of that?"

"His surname! What do you mean? . . . Well, uncle, before I hear what he has to say himself, allow me to remark that it is only in your household such queer things can happen," I said, flinging up my hands in amazement.

"Oh, my dear boy, I might fling up my hands like you, but that's no good," my uncle said with vexation. "Come, talk to him yourself, you have a try. He has been worrying me for two months past. . . ."

"It's not a respectable surname," Vidoplyasov observed.

"But why is it not respectable?" I asked him in surprise.

"Oh, because it suggests all sorts of abomination."

"But why abomination? And how can you change it? Does anyone change his surname?"

"Well, really, sir, do other people have such surnames?"

"I agree that your surname is a somewhat strange one," I went on, in complete bewilderment; "but there is no help for it now, you know. Your father had the same surname, I suppose, didn't he?"

"That is precisely so that through my parent I have in that way had to suffer all my life, inasmuch as I am destined by my name to accept many jeers and to endure many sorrows," answered Vidoplyasov.

"I bet, uncle, that Foma Fomitch has a hand in this!" I cried with vexation.

"Oh, no, my boy; oh, no, you are mistaken. Foma certainly has befriended him. He has taken him to be his secretary, that's the whole of his duty. Well, of course he has developed him, has filled him with noble sentiments, so that he is even in some ways cultivated. . . . You see, I will tell you all about it. . . ."

"That is true," Vidoplyasov interrupted, "that Foma Fomitch is my true benefactor, and being a true benefactor to me, he has brought me to understand my insignificance, what a worm I am upon the earth, so that through his honour I have for the first time learned to comprehend my destiny."

"There you see, Seryozha, there you see what it all means," my uncle went on, growing flustered as he always did. "He lived at first in Moscow, almost from childhood, in the service of a teacher of calligraphy. You should see how he has learned to write from him, and he illuminates in colours and gold with cupids round, you know—in fact he is an artist, you know Ilyusha has lessons from him; I pay him a rouble and a half a lesson. Foma himself fixed on a rouble and a half. He goes to three gentlemen's houses in the neighbourhood; they pay him too. You see how he is dressed! What's more, he writes poetry."

"Poetry! That's the last straw!"

"Poetry, my dear boy, poetry. And don't imagine I am joking; real poetry, so to say, versifications, and so well composed, you know, on all sorts of subjects. He'll describe any subject you like in a poem. It's a real talent! On mamma's nameday he concocted such a harangue that we listened with our mouths open; there was something from mythology in it, and the Muses flying about, so that indeed, you know, one could see the . . . what do you call it? . . . polish of form—in fact it was perfectly in rhyme. Foma corrected it. Well, I have nothing against that, and indeed I am quite pleased. Let him compose, as long as he doesn't get into mischief. You see, Grigory, my boy, I speak to you like a father. Foma heard of it, looked at his poetry, encouraged him, and chose him as his reader and copyist—in fact he has educated him. It is true, as he says, that Foma has been a benefactor to him. Well, and so, you know, he has begun to have gentlemanly and romantic sentiments, and a feeling of independence—Foma explained it all to me, but I have really forgotten; only I must own that I wanted, apart from Foma, to give him his freedom. I feel somehow ashamed, you know! . . . but Foma opposes that and says that he finds him useful, that he likes him; and what's more he says: 'It's a great honour to me, as his master, to have poets among my own servants; that that's how some barons somewhere used to live, and that it is living *en grand.*' Well, *en grand* so be it, then! I have begun to respect him, my boy —you understand. . . . Only goodness knows how he is behaving! The worst of it is that since he has taken to poetry he has become so stuck-up with the rest of the servants that he won't speak to them. Don't you take offence, Grigory, I am speaking to you like a father. Last winter, he promised to marry a serf girl here, Matryona, and a very nice girl she is, honest, hard-working and merry. But now it is 'No, I won't'. That's all about it, he has given her up. Whether it is that he has grown conceited, or has planned first to make a name and then to seek a match in some other place.''

"More through the advice of Foma Fomitch," observed Vidoplyasov, "seeing that his honour is my true well-wisher.''

"Oh, of course Foma Fomitch has a hand in everything," I could not help exclaiming.

"Ough, my dear boy, that's not it!" my uncle interrupted me hurriedly. "Only, you see, now he has no peace. She's a bold, quarrelsome girl, she has set them all against him, they mimic him, bait him, even the serf boys look upon him as a buffoon. . . .''

"It's chiefly owing to Matryona," observed Vidoplyasov; "for Matryona's a real fool, and being a real fool, she's a woman of unbridled character. Through her I have come in this manner to endure such prolonged sufferings."

"Ough, Grigory, my boy, I have talked to you already," my uncle went on, looking reproachfully at Vidoplyasov. "You see, Sergey, they have made up some horrid rhyme on his surname. He comes to me and complains, asks whether he cannot somehow change his surname, says that he has long been upset at its ugly sound. . . ."

"It's an undignified name," Vidoplyasov put in.

"Come, you be quiet, Grigory! Foma approved of it too . . . that is, he did not approve exactly, but, you see, this was his idea: that in case he were to publish his poems—and Foma has a project of his doing so—such a surname perhaps might be a drawback, mightn't it?"

"So he wants to publish his verses, uncle?"

"Yes, my boy. It's settled already—at my expense, and on the title-page will be put, 'the serf of so-and-so', and in the preface, the author's thanks to Foma for his education. It's dedicated to Foma. Foma is writing the preface himself. Well, so just fancy if on the title-page there stands, 'The Poems of Vidoplyasov'."

"The Plaints of Vidoplyasov," Vidoplyasov corrected.

"There, you see, plaints too! Well, Vidoplyasov is no use for a surname, it positively revolts the delicacy of one's feelings, so Foma says. And all these critics, they say, are such fellows for picking holes and jeering; Brambeus, for instance. . . . They don't stick at anything, you know! They will make a laughing-stock of him for his surname alone; they'll tickle your sides for you till you can do nothing but scratch them, won't they? What I say is, put any surname you like on your poems—a pseudonym it's called, isn't it? I don't remember; some word ending in *nym*. 'But no,' he says; 'give the order to the whole servants' hall to call me by a new name hereafter, for ever, so that I may have a genteel surname to suit my talent.'"

"I bet that you consented, uncle. . . ."

"I did, Seryozha, my boy, to avoid quarrelling with them; let them do as they like. You see, at that time there was a misunderstanding between Foma and me. So since then it has come to a new surname every week, and he keeps choosing such dainty ones as Oleandrov, Tulipov. . . . Only think, Grigory, at first you asked to be called 'Vyerny' (*i.e.* true, faithful)—'Grigory Vyerny'; afterwards you didn't like the name yourself because some simpleton found a rhyme to it, 'skverny' (*i.e.* nasty, horrid). You complained, and the fellow was punished. You were a fortnight thinking of a new name— what a selection you had!—at last you made up your mind and came to be asked to be called 'Ulanov'. Come, tell me, my boy, could anything be sillier than 'Ulanov'? I agreed to that too, and gave instructions a second time about changing your surname to Ulanov. It was simply to get rid of him," added my uncle, turning to me. "You spoilt all the walls, all the window-sills in the arbour scribbling 'Ulanov' in pencil, they have had to paint it since. You wasted a whole quire of good paper on signing your name 'Ulanov'. At last that was a failure too, they found a rhyme for you: 'Bolvanov' (*i.e.* fool, blockhead). He didn't want to be a blockhead, so the name must be changed again! What did you choose next? I have forgotten."

"Tantsev," answered Vidoplyasov. "If I am destined through my surname to be connected with dancing, it would be more dignified in the foreign form: 'Tantsev'."

"Oh, yes, 'Tantsev'. I agreed to that too, Sergey. Only they found a rhyme to that which I don't like to repeat. To-day he comes forward again, he has thought of something new. I bet he has got some new surname. Have you, Grigory? Confess!"

"I have truly been meaning for a long time to lay at your feet a new name, a genteel one."

"What is it?"

"Essbouquetov."

"Aren't you ashamed, really ashamed, Grigory? A surname off a pomatum pot! And you call yourself a clever man. How many days he must have been thinking about it! Why, that's what is written on scent-bottles."

"Upon my word, uncle," I said in a half-whisper, "why, he is simply a fool, a perfect fool."

"It can't be helped," my uncle answered, also in a whisper. "They declare all round that he is clever, and that all this is due to the working of noble qualities. . . ."

"But for goodness' sake, get rid of him!"

"Listen, Grigory! I have really no time, my boy," my uncle began in something of an imploring tone, as though he were afraid even of Vidoplyasov. "Come, judge for yourself, how can I attend to your complaints now? You say that they have insulted you in some way again. Come, I give you my word that to-morrow I will go into it all; and now go, and God be with you. . . . Stay! What is Foma Fomitch doing?"

"He has lain down to rest. He told me that if I was asked about him, I was to say that he is at prayer, that he intends to be praying a long time to-night."

"H'm! Well, you can go, you can go, my boy! You see, Seryozha, he is always with Foma, so that I am actually afraid of him. And that's why the servants don't like him, because he is always telling tales to Foma. Now he has gone away, and very likely to-morrow he will have spun some fine yarn about something! I've made it all right, my boy, and feel at peace now. . . . I was in haste to get to you. Now at last I am with you again," he brought out with feeling, pressing my hand. "And you know I thought, my dear, that you were desperately angry with me, and would be sure to slip off. I sent them to keep an eye on you. But now, thank God! And this afternoon, Gavrila, what a to-do.! and Falaley, and you, and one thing after another! Well, thank God! thank God! At last we can talk to our hearts' content. I will open my heart to you. You mustn't go away, Seryozha; you are all I have, you and Korovkin. . . ."

"But excuse me, uncle, how have you put things right, and what have I to expect here after what has happened? I must own my head's going round."

"And do you suppose that mine isn't? It has been waltzing round for the last six months, my head has, my boy! But, thank God, everything is settled now. In the first place, they have forgiven me, completely forgiven me, on certain conditions of course; but now I am scarcely afraid of anything. Sashenka has been forgiven too. Ah, Sasha, Sasha, this afternoon . . . a passionate little heart! She went a little too far, but she has a heart of gold! I am proud of that girl, Seryozha. May the blessing of God be with her for ever. You too have been forgiven, and even—do you know—you can do just what you like; you can go all over the house and into the garden, and even among the guests. In fact, you can do just as you like; but only on one condition, that you will say nothing to-morrow in the presence of mamma or Foma—that's an absolute condition, that is literally not half a word, I have promised for you already—but will only listen to what your elders . . . that is, I mean, what others may say. They say that you are young. Don't you be offended, Seryozha; you know you really are young. . . . That's what Anna Nilovna says. . . ."

127

Of course I was very young, and showed it at once by boiling over with indignation at such insulting conditions.

"Listen, uncle," I cried, almost breathless. "Tell me one thing and set my mind at rest: am I really in a madhouse or not?"

"There you are, my boy, criticising at once! You can't be patient," my uncle answered, in distress. "It's not a madhouse at all, it's nothing but over-hastiness on both sides. But you must consider, my boy, how you have behaved yourself. You remember what a sousing you gave him—a man, so to say, of venerable years?"

"Such men have no venerable years, uncle."

"Oh, there, my boy, you go too far! That's really free-thinking. I have nothing against rational free-thinking myself, my boy, but really that is beyond the mark; you really surprise me, Sergey."

"Don't be angry, uncle. I beg pardon, but I only beg your pardon. As for your Foma Fomitch . . ."

"There, now, it is *your!* Oh, Sergey, my boy, don't judge him too harshly; he is a misanthropical man and nothing more, morbid! You musn't judge him too severely. But he is a high-minded man; in fact, he is simply the most high-minded of men! Why, you saw it yourself just now; he was simply glorious. And as for the tricks he plays sometimes, it is no use noticing it. Why, it happens to everyone."

"On the contrary, uncle, it happens to nobody."

"Ough, he keeps on at the same thing! There is not much good nature in you, Seryozha; you don't know how to forgive. . . ."

"Oh, all right, uncle, all right! Let us leave that. Tell me, have you seen Nastasya Yevgrafovna?"

"Oh, my dear, the whole bother has been about her. I tell you what, Seryozha, and first, what is most important: we've all decided to congratulate him to-morrow on his birthday— Foma, I mean—for to-morrow really is his birthday. Sashenka is a good girl, but she is mistaken; so we will go, the whole tribe of us, rather early, before mass. Ilyusha will recite some verses to him which will be like oil on his heart—in fact, it will flatter him. Oh, if only you, Seryozha, would congratulate him with us! He would perhaps forgive you altogether. How splendid it would be if you were reconciled! Forget your wrongs, Seryozha; you insulted him too, you know . . . he is a most worthy man. . . ."

"Uncle! uncle!" I cried, losing all patience, "I want to talk of what is important, and you. . . . Do you know, I say again, what is happening to Nastasya Yevgrafovna?"

"Why, what is the matter, my boy? Why are you shouting? All the trouble has arisen over her, though indeed it arose some time ago. I did not want to tell you about it before, so as not to frighten you, for they wanted simply to turn her out, and they insisted on my sending her away too. You can imagine my position. . . . Oh, well, thank God, all that is set right now. They thought, you see—I will confess it all to you—that I was in love with her myself, and wanted to marry her; that I was, in short, rushing to ruin, and that really would be rushing to my ruin, they have explained it so to me. And so, to save me, they meant to turn her out. It was mamma's doing, and most of all Anna Nilovna's. Foma says nothing so far. But now I have convinced them all that they are wrong; and I must confess I have told them already that you are making Nastenka a formal proposal and that is what you have come for. Well, that has pacified them to some extent, and now she will remain, though not altogether; that is, so far only on probation. Still, she will remain. And indeed you have risen in general esteem since I told her you were courting her. Anyway, mamma seems pacified. Only Anna Nilovna goes on grumbling! I really don't know what to think of to satisfy her. And what is it she really wants, Anna Nilovna?"

"Uncle, you are greatly in error! Why, do you know that Nastasya Yevgrafovna is going away to-morrow if she has not gone away already? Do you know that her father came to-day on purpose to take her away? That it's all a settled thing, that she told me of it to-day herself, and in conclusion asked me to give you her greetings? Do you know that or not?"

My uncle stood blankly facing me with his mouth open. I fancied that he shuddered, and a moan broke from his lips.

Without loss of time I hastened to describe to him all my conversation with Nastenka; my attempt to pay her my addresses, her resolute refusal, her anger with my uncle for having summoned me. I explained that she was hoping by her departure to save him from marrying Tatyana Ivanovna. In fact I concealed nothing from him; indeed I purposely exaggerated everything that was unpleasant in my story. I wanted to impress my uncle so as to wring some resolute step out of him, and I really did impress him. He cried out and clutched at his head.

"Where is she, don't you know? Where is she now?" he brought out at last, turning pale with alarm. "And I, like a fool came here quite easy in my mind, I thought everything had been set right," he added in despair.

"I don't know where she is now; only when the uproar was beginning she went to you: she meant to proclaim all this aloud, before them all. Most likely they would not let her go in."

"No, indeed! What might she not have done! Ah, the hot-headed proud little thing! And what is she going to? What is she going to? And you, you are a pretty fellow. Why, what did she refuse you for? It's nonsense! You ought to have made her like you. Why doesn't she like you? For God's sake, answer, why are you standing there?"

"Have mercy on me, uncle! How can you ask such questions?"

"But you know this is impossible! You must marry her, you must. What did I bring you from Petersburg for? You must make her happy! Now they will drive her away, but when she is your wife, my own niece, they won't drive her away. If not, what has she to go to? What will become of her? To be a governess. Why, that is simply senseless nonsense, being a governess. While she is looking for a place, what is she going to live upon at home? Her old father has got nine to keep; they go hungry themselves. She won't take a farthing from me, you know, if she goes away through this disgusting gossip; she won't, nor will her father. And to go away like this—it is awful! It will cause a scandal—I know. And her salary has been paid for a long time in advance for necessities at home; you know she is their breadwinner. Why, supposing I do recommend her as a governess, and find an honest and honourable family. . . . But where the devil is one to find them, honourable, really honourable people? Well, granting that there are many—indeed it's a blasphemy to doubt it, but, my dear boy, you see it's risky—can one rely on people? Besides, anyone poor is suspicious, and apt to fancy he is being forced to pay for food and kindness with humiliation! They will insult her; she is proud, and then . . . and what then? And what if some scoundrelly seducer turns up? She would spurn him, I know she would, but yet he would insult her, the scoundrel! And some discredit, some slur, some suspicion may be cast upon her all the same, and then. . . . My head is going round! Ah, my God!"

"Uncle,. forgive me for one question," I said solemnly. "Don't be angry with me; understand that your answer to this question may decide much. Indeed, I have a right in a way to demand an answer from you, uncle!"

"What, what it is? What question?"

"Tell me as in God's presence, openly and directly; don't you feel that you are a little in love with Nastasya Yevgrafovna yourself and would like to marry her? Just think; that is why she is being turned away from here."

My uncle made a vigorous gesture of the most violent impatience.

"I? In love? With her? Why, they have all gone off their heads, or are in a conspiracy against me. And why did I. write to you to come if not to prove to them that they were all off their heads? Why am I making a match for her with you? I? In love? With her? They are all crazy, that's all about it!"

"But if it is so, uncle, do allow me to speak freely. I declare to you solemnly that I see absolutely nothing against the suggestion. On the contrary, you would make her happy, if only you love her and—and—God grant it may be so. And God give you love and good counsel!"

"But upon my word, what are you talking about?" cried my uncle, almost with horror. "I wonder how you can say such a thing coolly . . . and . . . you are altogether, my boy, in too great a hurry, I notice that characteristic in you! Why, aren't you talking nonsense? How, pray, am I to marry her when I look upon her as a daughter and nothing else? It would be shameful for me, indeed, to look upon her in any other light; it would be a sin in fact! I am an old man, while she is a flower! Indeed, Foma made that clear to me in those very words. My heart glows with a father's love for her, and here you talk of marriage! Maybe out of gratitude she would not refuse me, but you know she would despise me afterwards for taking advantage of her gratitude. I should spoil her life, I should lose her affection! And I would give my soul for her, she is my beloved child! I love her just as I do Sasha, even more, I must own. Sasha is my daughter by right, by law, but this one I have made my daughter by love. I took her out of poverty, I have brought her up. Katya, my lost angel, loved her; she left her to me as a daughter. I have given her a good education: she speaks French and plays the piano, she has read books and everything. . . . Such a sweet smile she has! Have you noticed it, Seryozha? As though she were laughing at one, but yet she is not laughing, but on the contrary, loving one. . . . You see I thought that you would come and make her an offer; they would be convinced that I had no intentions in regard to her, and would give over spreading these disgusting stories. She would remain with us then in peace, in comfort, and how happy we should be! You are both my children, both almost orphans, you have both grown up under my guardian-ship . . . I should have loved you so! I would have devoted my life to you; I would not part from you; I would follow you anywhere! Oh, how happy we might have been! And why are these people always so cross, always so angry, why do they hate each other? If only I could explain it all to them! If only I could make them see the whole truth! Ah, my God!"

"Yes, uncle, yes, that is all so; but, you see, she has refused me."

"Refused you! Hm. . . . Do you know, I had a sort of presentiment that she would refuse you," he said, musing. "But no!" he cried. "I don't believe it. It's impossible. In that case, all our plans are upset! But you must have begun injudiciously somehow, even offended her perhaps. Perhaps you tried your hand at paying compliments. . . . Tell me how it was again, Sergey."

I repeated the whole story in full detail again. When I came to Nastenka's hoping by her departure to save my uncle from Tatyana Ivanovna, he gave a bitter smile.

"Save me!" he said. "Save me till to-morrow morning. . . ."

"But you don't mean to say that you are going to marry Tatyana Ivanovna!" I cried in alarm.

"How else could I have paid for Nastasya's not being sent away to-morrow? To-morrow I make the offer—the formal proposal."

"And you have made up your mind to it, uncle?"

"What could I do, my boy, what could I do? It rends my heart, but I have made up my mind to it. The proposal will be to-morrow; they suggest that the wedding should be a quiet one, at home; it would certainly be better at home. You will perhaps be best man. I have already dropped a hint about you, so they won't drive you away before then. There is no help for it, my boy. They say, 'It's a fortune for your children!' Of course one would do anything for one's children. One would turn head over heels, especially as really, perhaps, what they say is right. You know, I really ought to do something for my family. One can't sit an idle drone for ever!"

"But, uncle, she is mad, you know!" I cried, forgetting myself, and there was a sickly pang at my heart.

"Oh, mad, is she now? She is not mad at all; it's only, you know, that she has had trouble. . . . There is no help for it, my boy. Of course I should have been glad of one with sense. . . . Though, after all, some who have sense are no better! If only you knew what a kind-hearted creature she is, noble-hearted!"

"But, my God! he is resigning himself to the thought of it already," I said in despair.

"And what else is there to do? You know they are doing their utmost for my benefit, and, indeed, I felt beforehand that sooner or later they would force me to marry, that there is no getting out of it. So better now than make more quarrelling about it. I am telling you everything quite openly, Seryozha. In a way I am actually glad. I have made up my mind, somehow. Why, I came here with my mind almost at ease. It seems, it's my fate. And the great thing to make up for it was that Nastenka would stay on. You know I agreed on that condition. And now she wants to run away of herself! But that shall not be!" my uncle cried, stamping. "Listen, Sergey," he added with a determined air; "wait for me here, don't go away. I will come back to you in an instant."

"Where are you off to, uncle?"

"Perhaps I shall see her, Sergey; it will all be cleared up, believe me that it will all be cleared up, and . . . and . . . you shall marry her, I give you my word of honour!"

My uncle went quickly out of the room, and turned not towards the house, but into the garden. I watched him from the window.

CHAPTER XII

THE CATASTROPHE

I WAS left alone. My position was insufferable; I had been rejected, and my uncle meant to marry me almost by force. I was perplexed and lost in a tangle of ideas. Mizintchikov and his proposition was not absent from my mind for an instant. At all costs uncle must be saved! I even thought of going to look for Mizintchikov and telling him all about it. But where had my uncle gone, though? He had said himself that he was going to look for Nastenka, but had turned in the direction of the garden. The thought of secret meetings flashed through my mind, and a very unpleasant feeling clutched at my heart. I remembered what Mizintchikov had said of a secret liaison. After a moment's thought I rejected my suspicions with indignation. My uncle was incapable of deceit: that was obvious. My uneasiness grew greater every moment. Unconsciously I went out on to the steps, and walked into the garden down the very avenue into which my uncle had disappeared. The moon was beginning to rise. I knew that garden through and through, and was not afraid of losing myself. As I drew near the old arbour which stood in solitude on the bank of the neglected scum-covered pond, I suddenly stood rooted to the spot; I heard voices in the arbour. I cannot describe the strange feeling of annoyance that took possession of me. I felt convinced that my uncle and Nastenka were there, and went on going nearer, appeasing my conscience by thinking that I was walking at the same pace as before and not trying to approach stealthily. Suddenly there was the distinct sound of a kiss, then stifled exclamations, and immediately afterwards a shrill feminine shriek. At that instant a woman in a white dress ran out of the arbour and flashed by me like a swallow. It even seemed to me that she hid her face in her hands that she might not be recognised: probably I had been noticed from the arbour. But what was my amazement when in the swain who emerged after the flying lady I recognised—Obnoskin, Obnoskin, who, according to Mizintchikov's words, had gone away some hours before. Obnoskin on his side was greatly confused when he saw me; all his impudence vanished instantly.

"Excuse me, but . . . I did not in the least expect to meet you," he brought out, smiling and hesitating.

"Nor I you," I answered ironically, "especially as I heard you had already gone away."

"No. . . . It was just . . . I went a little on the way with my mother. But may I appeal to you as an absolutely honourable man?"

"What about?"

"There are cases—and you will agree yourself that it is so—when a truly honourable man is forced to appeal to the highest sense of honour of another truly honourable man. . . . I hope you understand me. . . ."

"Do not hope, I understand absolutely nothing. . . ."

"You saw the lady who was here with me in the arbour?"

"I saw her, but I did not recognise her."

"Ah, you did not recognise her. . . . That lady I shall shortly call my wife."

"I congratulate you. But in what way can I be of use to you?"

"Only in one way, by keeping it a dead secret that you have seen me with that lady."

"Who can she be?" I wondered. "Surely not . . ."

"I really don't know," I answered Obnoskin. "I hope that you will excuse me for not being able to promise."

"Yes, please, for God's sake," Obnoskin besought me. "Understand my position, it's a secret. You may be betrothed too: then I . . ."

"Sh! someone is coming!"

"Where?"

We did indeed catch a glimpse thirty paces away of the shadow of someone passing.

"It . . . it must be Foma Fomitch!" Obnoskin whispered, trembling all over. "I know him from his walk. My God! And steps again from the other direction! Do you hear? . . . Good-bye! I thank you . . . and I entreat you . . ."

Obnoskin vanished. A minute later, as though he had sprung out of the earth, my uncle was before me.

"Is it you?" he greeted me. "It is all over, Seryozha, it is all over!"

I noticed, too, that he was trembling from head to foot.

"What is all over, uncle?"

"Come along!" he said, gasping for breath, and clutching my hand tightly he drew me after him. He did not utter a word all the way to the lodge, nor did he let me speak. I was expecting something monstrous, and my expectations were almost realised.

When we went indoors he was overcome with giddiness, he was deathly pale. I promptly sprinkled him with water. "Something very awful must have happened," I thought, "for a man like this to faint."

"Uncle, what is the matter with you?" I asked him at last.

"All is over, Seryozha! Foma found me in the garden with Nastenka, at the very moment when I was kissing her."

"Kissing her! In the garden!" I cried, looking at my uncle in amazement.

"In the garden, my boy. The Lord confounded me! I went

there to be sure of seeing her. I wanted to speak openly to her, to make her see reason—about you, I mean. And she had been waiting for me a whole hour, on the broken seat, beyond the pond. . . . She often goes there when she wants to speak to me."

"Often, uncle?"

"Yes, often, my boy! Of late we have been meeting almost every night. Only they must have watched us—in fact, I know that they watched us and that it was Anna Nilovna's doing. We gave it up for a time. The last four days we have not met; but to-day it was necessary again. You saw yourself how necessary it was; how else could I have said anything to her? I went in the hope of finding her, and she had been sitting there a whole hour, waiting for me: she, too, wanted to tell me something. . . ."

"Good heavens, how incautious! Why, you knew that you were being watched!"

"But, you see, it was a critical matter, Seryozha; there was a great deal we had to discuss together. I don't dare to look at her in the daytime. She looks in one corner and I look in another, as though she did not exist. But towards night we meet and have a talk. . . ."

"Well, what happened, uncle?"

"Before I could utter a couple of words, you know, my heart began throbbing and the tears gushed from my eyes. I began trying to persuade her to marry you, and she answered me: 'You certainly don't love me—you must be blind.' And all of a sudden she flings herself on my neck, throws her arms round me, and begins crying and sobbing! 'I love no one but you,' she said, 'and won't marry anyone. I have loved you for ever so long, but I will never marry you. And to-morrow I am going away and going into a nunnery.'"

"My goodness! Did she really say that? Well, what then, uncle, what then?"

"I looked up and there was Foma facing us! And where had he sprung from? Could he have been sitting behind a bush, and waiting for some such lapse?"

"The scoundrel!"

"I was petrified, Nastenka ran away, while Foma Fomitch passed by without a word and held up his finger at me. Sergey, do you understand what a hubbub there will be to-morrow?"

"I should think I do!"

"Do you understand?" he cried in despair, leaping up from

his seat. "Do you understand that they will try to ruin her, to disgrace her, to dishonour her; they are looking for a pretext to accuse her of something disgraceful, and now the pretext is found. You know they will say that she is carrying on an abominable intrigue with me! You know, the scoundrels made out that she had an intrigue with Vidoplyasov! It's all Anna Nilovna's tales. What will happen now? What will happen to-morrow? Will Foma really tell them?"

"He'll certainly tell them, uncle."

"If he does, if he really does tell . . ." he brought out, biting his lips and clenching his fists. "But no, I don't believe it! He won't tell, he will understand . . . he is a man of the loftiest character! He will spare her. . . ."

"Whether he spares her or whether he doesn't," I answered resolutely, "it is your duty in any case to make Nastasya Yevgrafovna an offer to-morrow."

My uncle looked fixedly at me.

"Do you understand, uncle, that you have ruined the girl's reputation if this story gets about? Do you understand that you ought to prevent that calamity as quickly as possible; that you ought to look them all in the face boldly and proudly, ought to offer her your hand publicly, to spurn their arguments and pound Foma to a jelly if he hints a word against her?"

"My dear boy," cried my uncle, "I thought of that as I came along here!"

"And did you make up your mind?"

"Yes, and finally! I had made up my mind before I began speaking to you."

"Bravo, uncle!"

And I rushed to embrace him.

We talked for a long time. I put before him all the arguments, all the absolute necessity for marrying Nastenka, which, indeed, he understood far better than I did. But my eloquence was aroused. I was delighted on my uncle's account. He was impelled by a sense of duty or he would never have taken a stand. He had the deepest reverence for duty, for obligation. But in spite of that I was quite unable to imagine how things would be settled. I knew and blindly believed that nothing would induce my uncle to fall short of what he had once recognised as his duty; but yet I could not believe that he would have the strength to stand out against his household. And so I did my utmost to incite him and urge him on, and set to work with all the fervour of youth.

"The more so," I said, "as now everything is settled and your last doubts have vanished! What you did not expect, though in reality everyone else saw it, and everyone noticed it before you did, has happened; Nastasya Yevgrafovna loves you! Surely," I cried, "you will not let that pure love be turned into shame and disgrace for her?"

"Never! But, my dear boy, can I really be going to be so happy?" cried my uncle, throwing himself on my neck. "And how is it she loves me, and what for? What for? It seems to me there is nothing in me likely to . . . I am an old man compared to her; I certainly did not expect it! My angel, my angel! . . . Listen, Seryozha! you asked me this evening whether I were not in love with her: had you any idea?"

"All I saw, uncle, was that you love her as much as anyone can love: you love her and at the same time you don't know it yourself. Upon my word! You invite me, you want to marry me to her solely in order that she may become your niece, and so you may have her always with you. . . ."

"But you . . . you do forgive me, Sergey?"

"Oh, uncle. . . ."

And he embraced me again.

"Mind, uncle, they will all be against you: you must stand up for yourself and resist them, and no later than to-morrow!"

"Yes . . . yes, to-morrow . . ." he repeated somewhat pensively. "And you know we must attack the business with manliness, with true nobility of soul, with strength of will . . . Yes, with strength of will!"

"Don't be frightened, uncle."

"I am not frightened, Seryozha! There's one thing I don't know how to begin, how to proceed."

"Don't think about it, uncle. To-morrow will settle everything. Set your mind at rest for to-day. The more you think the worse it will be. And if Foma begins—kick him out of the house at once and pound him to a jelly."

"And can't we avoid kicking him out? What I have decided, my boy, is this. To-morrow I shall go to him early, at dawn, I shall tell him all about it, just as I have told you here. Surely he cannot but understand me, he is a high-minded man, the most high-minded of men. But I tell you what does worry me: what if mamma speaks to Tatyana Ivanovna to-day of the offer to be made to her to-morrow? That would be unlucky, wouldn't it?"

"Don't worry yourself about Tatyana Ivanovna, uncle."

138

And I told him about the scene in the arbour with Obnoskin. My uncle was extremely surprised. I did not say a word about Mizintchikov.

"A fantastical person. A really fantastical person!" he cried. "Poor thing! They ingratiate themselves with her and try to take advantage of her simplicity. Was it really Obnoskin? But, you know, he has gone away. . . . Strange, awfully strange! I am astonished, Seryozha. . . . We must look into it to-morrow and take steps. . . . But are you perfectly certain that it was Tatyana Ivanovna?"

I answered that I had not seen her face, but for certain reasons I was positive that it was Tatyana Ivanovna.

"H'm. Wasn't it a little intrigue with one of the servant girls and you fancied it was Tatyana Ivanovna? Wasn't it Dasha, the gardener's daughter? A sly hussy! She has been remarked upon, that's why I say so. Anna Nilovna caught her! . . . But it wasn't she, though! He said he meant to marry her. Strange, strange!"

At last we parted. I embraced my uncle and gave him my blessing.

"To-morrow, to-morrow," he repeated, "it will all be settled; before you are up it will be settled. I shall go to Foma and take a chivalrous line, I will speak frankly as I would to my own brother, I will lay bare the inmost recesses of my heart. Good-bye, Seryozha. You go to bed, you are tired; but I am sure I shan't shut my eyes all night."

He went away. I went to bed at once, tired out and utterly exhausted. It had been a hard day. My nerves were over-wrought, and before I fell really asleep I kept starting and waking up again. But strange as my impressions were on going off to sleep, the strangeness of them was as nothing beside the queerness of my awakening next morning.

PART II

CHAPTER I

THE PURSUIT

I SLEPT soundly without dreaming. Suddenly I felt as though a load of some hundredweights was lying on my feet. I cried out and woke up. It was daylight; the sun was peeping brightly into the room. On my bed, or rather on my feet, was sitting Mr. Bahtcheyev.

It was impossible to doubt that it was he. Managing somehow to release my legs, I sat up in bed and looked at him with the blank amazement of a man just awake.

"And now he is looking about him," cried the fat man. "Why are you staring at me? Get up, sir, get up. I have been waking you for the last half-hour; rub away at your eyes!"

"Why, what has happened? What's the time?"

"It's still early by the clock, but our Fevronya did not wait for dawn, but has given us the slip. Get up, we are going in pursuit!"

"What Fevronya?"

"Why, our young lady, the crazy one! She has given us the slip! She was off before dawn. I came to you, sir, only for a minute, to wake you, and here I have been busy with you a couple of hours. Get up, your uncle's waiting for you. They waited for the festive day!" he added, with a malignant quiver in his voice.

"But whom and what are you talking about?" I asked impatiently, though I was beginning to guess. "Surely not Tatyana Ivanovna?"

"To be sure. She it is. I said so, I foretold it; they wouldn't listen to me. A nice treat she has given us for the festive day now! She is mad on *amour*, and has *amour* on the brain. Tfoo! And that fellow, what do you say to that fellow? With his little beard, eh?"

"Can you mean Mizintchikov?"

"Tfoo, plague take it! Why, my dear sir, you had better rub your eyes and pull yourself together—if only for the great holy festive day. You must have had a great deal too much at supper last night if you are still hazy this morning! With Mizintchikov! It's with Obnoskin, not Mizintchikov. Ivan Ivanovitch Mizintchikov is a moral young man and he is coming with us in pursuit."

"What are you saying?" I cried, jumping up in bed. "Is it really with Obnoskin?"

"Tfoo, you annoying person!" answered the fat man, leaping up from his seat. "I come to him as to a man of culture to inform him of what has happened, and he still doubts it. Well, sir, if you want to come with us, get up, shoot into your breeches. It's no good my spending more words on you; I've wasted golden time on you as it is."

And he went out in extreme indignation.

Amazed by the news, I jumped out of bed, hurriedly dressed, and ran downstairs. Thinking to find my uncle in the house, where everyone still seemed asleep and knowing nothing of what had happened, I cautiously mounted the front steps, and in the hall I met Nastenka. She seemed to have dressed hurriedly in some sort of *peignoir* or *schlafrock*. Her hair was in disorder; it was evident that she had only just jumped out of bed, and she seemed to be waiting for someone in the hall.

"Tell me, is it true that Tatyana Ivanovna has run away with Obnoskin?" she asked hurriedly in a breaking voice, looking pale and frightened.

"I am told it is true. I am looking for my uncle, we want to go after them."

"Oh, bring her back, make haste and bring her back. She will be ruined if you don't fetch her back."

"But where is uncle?"

"Most likely in the stable; they are getting the carriage out. I have been waiting for him here. Listen: tell him from me that I must go home to-day; I have quite made up my mind. My father will take me; I shall go at once if I can. Everything is hopeless now. All is lost!"

Saying this, she looked at me as though she were utterly lost, and suddenly dissolved into tears. I think she began to be hysterical.

"Calm yourself," I besought her. "Why, it's all for the best —you will see. What is the matter with you, Nastasya Yevgrafovna?"

"I . . . I don't know . . . what is the matter with me," she said, sighing and unconsciously squeezing my hands. "Tell him . . ."

At that instant there was a sound from the other side of the door on the right.

She let go of my hand and, panic-stricken, ran away upstairs without finishing her sentence.

I found the whole party—that is, my uncle, Bahtcheyev, and Mizintchikov—in the back yard by the stable. Fresh horses had been harnessed in Bahtcheyev's carriage. Everything was ready for setting off; they were only waiting for me.

"Here he is!" cried my uncle on my appearance. "Have you heard, my boy?" he asked, with a peculiar expression on his face.

Alarm, perplexity, and, at the same time, hope were expressed in his looks, in his voice and in his movements. He was conscious that a momentous crisis had come in his life.

I was immediately initiated into all the details of the case. Mr. Bahtcheyev, who had spent a very bad night, left his house at dawn to reach the monastery five miles away in time for early mass. Just at the turning from the high road to the monastery he suddenly saw a chaise dashing along at full trot, and in the chaise Tatyana Ivanovna and Obnoskin. Tatyana Ivanovna, with a tear-stained and as it seemed frightened face, uttered a shriek and stretched out her hands to Mr. Bahtcheyev as though imploring his protection—so at least it appeared from his story; "while he, the scoundrel, with the little beard," he went on, "sits more dead than alive and tries to hide himself. But you are wrong there, my fine fellow, you can't hide yourself." Without stopping, Stepan Alexyevitch turned back to the road and galloped to Stepantchikovo and woke my uncle, Mizintchikov, and finally me. They decided to set off at once in pursuit.

"Obnoskin, Obnoskin," said my uncle, looking intently at me, looking at me as though he would like to say something else as well. "Who would have thought it?"

"Any dirty trick might have been expected of that low fellow!" cried Mizintchikov with the most vigorous indignation, and at once turned away to avoid my eye.

"What are we going to do, go or not? Or are we going to stand here till night babbling!" interposed Mr. Bahtcheyev as he clambered into the carriage.

"We are going, we are going," cried my uncle.

"It's all for the best, uncle," I whispered to him. "You see how splendidly it has all turned out?"

"Hush, my boy, don't be sinful. . . . Ah, my dear! They

142

will simply drive *her* away now, to punish her for their failure, you understand. It's fearful, the prospect I see before me!''

"Well, Yegor Ilyitch, are you going on whispering or starting?" Mr. Bahtcheyev cried out a second time. "Or shall we unharness the horses and have a snack of something? What do you say; shall we have a drink of vodka?"

These words were uttered with such furious sarcasm that it was impossible not to satisfy Bahtcheyev at once. We all promptly got into the carriage, and the horses set off at a gallop.

For some time we were all silent. My uncle kept looking at me significantly, but did not care to speak to me before the others. He often sank into thought; then as though waking up, started and looked about him in agitation. Mizintchikov was apparently calm, he smoked a cigar, and his looks expressed the indignation of an unjustly treated man. But Bahtcheyev had excitement enough for all of us. He grumbled to himself, looked at everyone and everything with absolute indignation, flushed crimson, fumed, continually spat aside, and could not recover himself.

"Are you sure, Stepan Alexyevitch, that they have gone to Mishino?" my uncle asked suddenly. "It's fifteen miles from here, my boy," he added, addressing me. "It's a little village of thirty souls, lately purchased from the former owners by a provincial official. The most pettifogging fellow in the world. So at least they say about him, perhaps mistakenly. Stepan Alexyevitch declares that that is where Obnoskin has gone, and that that official will be helping him now."

"To be sure," cried Bahtcheyev, starting. "I tell you, it is Mishino. Only by now maybe there is no trace of him left at Mishino. I should think not, we have wasted three hours chattering in the yard!"

"Don't be uneasy," observed Mizintchikov. "We shall find them."

"Find them, indeed! I dare say he will wait for you. The treasure is in his hands. You may be sure we have seen the last of him!"

"Calm yourself, Stepàn Alexyevitch, calm yourself, we shall overtake them," said my uncle. "They have not had time to take any steps yet, you will see that is so."

"Not had time!" Mr. Bahtcheyev brought out angrily. "She's had time for any mischief, for all she's such a quiet one! 'She's a quiet one,' they say, 'a quiet one,' he added in a mincing voice, as though he were mimicking someone. 'She has had troubles.' Well, now, she has shown us her heels, for all her troubles. Now you have to chase after her along the high roads with your tongue out before you can see where you are going! They won't let a man go to church for the holy saint's day. Tfoo!''

"But she is not under age," I observed; "she is not under guardianship. We can't bring her back if she doesn't want to come. What are we going to do?''

"Of course," answered my uncle; "but she will want to—I assure you. What she is doing now means nothing. As soon as she sees us she will want to come back—I'll answer for it. We can't leave her like this, my boy, at the mercy of fate, to be sacrificed; it's a duty, so to say. . . .''

"She's not under guardianship!" cried Bahtcheyev, pouncing on me at once. "She is a fool, my dear sir, a perfect fool—it's not a case of her being under guardianship. I didn't care to talk to you about her yesterday, but the other day I went by mistake into her room and what did I see, there she was before the looking-glass with her arms akimbo dancing a schottische! And dressed up to the nines: a fashion-plate, a regular fashion-plate! I simply spat in disgust and walked away. Then I foresaw all this, as clear as though it were written in a book!''

"Why abuse her so?" I observed with some timidity. "We know that Tatyana Ivanovna . . . is not in perfect health . . . or rather she has a mania. . . . It seems to me that Obnoskin is the one to blame, not she.''

"Not in perfect health! Come, you get along," put in the fat man, turning crimson with wrath. "Why, he has taken an oath to drive a man to fury! Since yesterday he has taken an oath to! She is a fool, my dear sir, I tell you, an absolute fool. It's not that she's not in perfect health; from early youth she has been mad on Cupid. And now Cupid has brought her to this pass. As for that fellow with the beard, it's no use talking about him. I dare say by now he is racing off double quick with the money in his pocket and a grin on his face.''

"Do you really think, then, that he'll cast her off at once?''

"What else should he do? Is he going to drag such a treasure about with him? And what good is she to him? He'll fleece her of everything and then sit her down somewhere under a bush on the high road—and make off. While she can sit there under the bush and sniff the flowers.''

"Well, you are too hasty there, Stepan, it won't be like that!" cried my uncle. "But why are you so cross? I wonder at you, Stepan. What's the matter with you?"

"Why, am I a man or not? It does make one cross, though it's no business of mine. Why, I am saying it perhaps in kindness to her. . . . Ech, damnation take it all! Why, what have I come here for? Why, what did I turn back for? What is it to do with me? What is it to do with me?"

So grumbled Mr. Bahtcheyev, but I left off listening to him and mused on the woman whom we were now in pursuit of— Tatyana Ivanovna. Here is a brief biography of her which I gathered later on from the most trustworthy sources, and which is essential to the explanation of her adventures.

A poor orphan child who grew up in a strange unfriendly house, then a poor girl, then a poor young woman, and at last a poor old maid, Tatyana Ivanovna in the course of her poor life had drained the over-full cup of sorrow, friendlessness, humiliation and reproach, and had tasted to the full the bitterness of the bread of others. Naturally of a gay, highly susceptible and frivolous temperament, she had at first endured her bitter lot in one way or another and had even been capable at times of the gayest careless laughter; but with years destiny at last got the upper hand of her. Little by little Tatyana Ivanovna grew thin and sallow, became irritable and morbidly susceptible, and sank into the most unrestrained, unbounded dreaminess, often interrupted by hysterical tears and convulsive sobbing. The fewer earthly blessings real life left to her lot, the more she comforted and deluded herself in imagination. The more certainly, the more irretrievably her last hopes in real life were passing and at last were lost, the more seductive grew her dreams, never to be realised. Fabulous wealth, unheard-of beauty, rich, elegant, distinguished suitors, always princes and sons of generals, who for her sake had kept their hearts in virginal purity and were dying at her feet from infinite love; and finally, *he—he*, the ideal of beauty combining in himself every possible perfection, passionate and loving, an artist, a poet, the son of a general—all at once or all by turns—began to appear to her not only in her dreams but almost in reality. Her reason was already beginning to fail, unable to stand the strain of this opiate of secret incessant dreaming. . . . And all at once destiny played a last fatal jest at her expense. Living in the last extreme of humiliation, in melancholy surroundings that crushed the heart, a companion to a toothless old lady, the most peevish in the world, scolded for everything, reproached for every crust she ate, for every threadbare rag she wore, insulted with impunity by anyone, protected by no one, worn out by her miserable existence and secretly plunged in the luxury of the maddest and most fervid dreams—she suddenly heard the news of the death of a distant relation, all of whose family had died long before (though she in her frivolous way had never taken the trouble to ascertain the fact); he was a strange man, a phrenologist and a money-lender, who led a solitary, morose, unnoticed life, in seclusion somewhere very remote in the wilds. And now all at once immense wealth fell as though by miracle from heaven and scattered gold at Tatyana Ivanovna's feet; she turned out to be the sole legitimate heiress of the dead money-lender. A hundred thousand silver roubles came to her at once. This jest of destiny was the last straw. Indeed, how could a mind already tottering doubt the truth of dreams when they were actually beginning to come true? And so the poor thing took leave of her last remaining grain of common sense. Swooning with bliss, she soared away beyond recall into her enchanted world of impossible imaginations and seductive fancies. Away with all reflection, all doubt, all the checks of real life, all its laws clear and inevitable as twice two make four. Thirty-five years and dreams of dazzling beauty, the sad chill of autumn and the luxuriance of the infinite bliss of love—all blended in her without discord. Her dreams had once already been realised in life; why should not all the rest come true? Why should not *he* appear? Tatyana Ivanovna did not reason, but she had faith. But while waiting for *him*, the ideal—suitors and knights of various orders and simple gentlemen, officers and civilians, infantry men and cavalry men, grand noblemen and simply poets who had been in Paris or had been only in Moscow, with beards and without beards, with imperials and without imperials, Spaniards and not Spaniards (but Spaniards, by preference), began appearing before her day and night in horrifying numbers that awakened grave apprehensions in onlookers; she was but a step from the madhouse. All these lovely phantoms thronged about her in a dazzling, infatuated procession. In reality, in actual life, everything went the same fantastic way: anyone she looked at was in love with her; anyone who passed by was a Spaniard; if anyone died it must be for love of her. As ill-luck would have it, all this was confirmed in her eyes by the fact that men such as Obnoskin,

Mizintchikov, and dozens of others with the same motives began running after her. Everyone began suddenly trying to please her, spoiling her, flattering her. Poor Tatyana Ivanovna refused to suspect that all this was for the sake of her money. She was fully convinced that, as though at some signal, people had·suddenly reformed, and all, every one of them, grown gay and kind, friendly and good. *He* had not appeared himself in person; but though there could be no doubt that *he* would appear, her daily life as it was was so agreeable, so alluring, so full of all sorts of distractions and diversions, that she could wait. Tatyana Ivanovna ate sweetmeats, culled the flowers of pleasure, and read novels. The novels heated her imagination and were usually flung aside at the second page; she could not read longer, but was carried to dreamland by the very first lines, by the most trivial hint at love, sometimes simply by the description of scenery, of a room, of a toilette. New finery, lace, hats, hair ornaments, ribbons, samples, paper patterns, designs, sweetmeats, flowers, lapdogs were being continually sent her. Three girls spent whole days sewing for her in the maid's room, while their lady was trying on bodices and flounces, and twisting and turning before the looking-glass from morning to night, and even in the night. She actually seemed younger and prettier on coming into her fortune. To this day I don't know what was her relationship to the late General Krahotkin. I have always been persuaded that it was the invention of Madame la Générale, who wanted to get possession of Tatyana Ivanovna and at all costs to marry her to my uncle for her money. Mr. Bahtcheyev was right when he spoke of its being Cupid that had brought Tatyana Ivanovna to the last point; and my uncle's idea on hearing of her elopement with Obnoskin—to run after her and bring her back even by force—was the most rational one. The poor creature was not fit to live without a guardian, and would have come to grief at once if she had fallen into evil hands.

It was past nine when we reached Mishino. It was a poor little village, lying in a hole two miles from the high road. Six or seven peasants' huts, begrimed with smoke, slanting on one side and barely covered with blackened thatch, looked dejectedly and inhospitably at the traveller. There was not a garden, not a bush, to be seen for a quarter of a mile round. Only an old willow hung drowsily over the greenish pool that passed for a pond. Such a new abode could hardly make a cheering impression on Tatyana Ivanovna. The manor house consisted of a new long, narrow, wooden building with six windows in a row, and had been roughly thatched. The owner, the official, had only lately taken possession. The yard was not even fenced, and only on one side a new hurdle had been begun from which the dry leaves of the nut branches had not yet dropped. Obnoskin's chaise was standing by the hurdle. We had fallen on the fugitives like snow on the head. From an open window came the sound of cries and weeping.

The barefoot boy who met us dashed away at breakneck speed. In the first room Tatyana Ivanovna with a tear-stained face was seated on a long chintz-covered sofa without a back. On seeing us she uttered a shriek and hid her face in her hands. Beside her stood Obnoskin, frightened and pitifully confused. He was so distraught that he flew to shake hands with us, as though overjoyed at our arrival. From the door that opened into the other room we had a peep of some lady's dress; some-one was listening and looking through a crack imperceptible to us. The people of the house did not put in an appearance; it seemed as though they were not in the house; they were all in hiding somewhere.

"Here she is, the traveller! Hiding her face in her hands too!" cried Mr. Bahtcheyev, lumbering after us into the room.

"Restrain your transports, Stepan Alexyevitch! They are quite unseemly. No one has a right to speak now but Yegor Ilyitch; we have nothing to do here!" Mizintchikov observed sharply.

My uncle, casting a stern glance at Mr. Bahtcheyev, and seeming not to observe the existence of Obnoskin who had rushed to shake hands with him, went up to Tatyana Ivanovna, whose face was still hidden in her hands, and in the softest voice, with the most unaffected sympathy, said to her—

"Tatyana Ivanovna, we all so love and respect you that we have come ourselves to learn your intentions. Would you care to drive back with us to Stepantchikovo? It is Ilyusha's name-day, mamma is expecting you impatiently, while Sasha and Nastenka have no doubt been crying over you all the morning. . . ."

Tatyana Ivanovna raised her head timidly, looked at him through her fingers, and suddenly bursting into tears, flung herself on his neck.

"Oh, take me away, make haste and take me away from here!" she said, sobbing. "Make haste, as much haste as you can!"

"She's gone off on the spree and made an ass of herself!"
hissed Mr. Bahtcheyev, nudging my arm.

"Everything is at an end, then," said my uncle, turning
dryly to Obnoskin and scarcely looking at him. "Tatyana
Ivanovna, please give me your arm. Let us go!"

There was a rustle the other side of the door; the door creaked
and opened wider.

"If you look at it from another point of view though,"
Obnoskin observed uneasily, looking at the open door, "you
will see yourself, Yegor Ilyitch . . . your action in my house
. . . and in fact I was bowing to you, and you would not even
bow to me, Yegor Ilyitch. . . ."

"Your action in *my* house, sir, was a low action," said my
uncle, looking sternly at Obnoskin, "and this house is not
yours. You have heard: Tatyana Ivanovna does not wish to
remain here a minute. What more do you want? Not a word—
do you hear? not another word, I beg! I am extremely
desirous of avoiding further explanations, and indeed it would
be more to your interest to do so."

But at this point Obnoskin was so utterly crestfallen that he
began uttering the most unexpected drivel.

"Don't despise me, Yegor Ilyitch," he began in a half-
whisper, almost crying with shame and continually glancing
towards the door, probably from fear of being overheard. "It's
not my doing, but my mother's. I didn't do it from mercenary
motives, Yegor Ilyitch; I didn't mean anything; I did, of
course, do it from interested motives, Yegor Ilyitch . . . but I
did it with a noble object, Yegor Ilyitch. I should have
used the money usefully . . . I should have helped the
poor. I wanted to support the movement for enlightenment,
too, and even dreamed of endowing a university scholarship.
. . . That was what I wanted to turn my wealth to, Yegor
Ilyitch; and not to use it just for anything, Yegor Ilyitch."

We all felt horribly ashamed. Even Mizintchikov reddened
and turned away, and my uncle was so confused that he did
not know what to say.

"Come, come, that's enough," he said at last. "Calm yourself, Pavel Semyonitch. It can't be helped! It might happen
to anyone. . . . If you like, come to dinner . . . and I shall
be delighted."

But Mr. Bahtcheyev behaved quite differently.

"Endow a scholarship!" he bawled furiously. "You are not
the sort to endow a scholarship! I bet you'd be ready to fleece

anyone you come across. . . . Not a pair of breeches of his own, and here he is bragging of scholarships! Oh, you rag-and-bone man! So you've made a conquest of a soft heart, have you? And where is she, the parent? Hiding, is she? I bet she is sitting somewhere behind a screen, or has crept under the bed in a fright. . . ."

"Stepan, Stepan!" cried my uncle.

Obnoskin flushed and was on the point of protesting; but before he had time to open his mouth the door was flung open and Anfisa Petrovna herself, violently irritated, with flashing eyes, crimson with wrath, flew into the room.

"What's this?" she shouted. "What's this going on here? You break into a respectable house with your rabble, Yegor Ilyitch, frighten ladies, give orders! . . . What's the meaning of it? I have not taken leave of my senses yet, Yegor Ilyitch! And you, you booby," she went on yelling, pouncing on her son, "you are snivelling before them already. Your mother is insulted in her own house, and you stand gaping. Do you call yourself a gentlemanly young man after that? You are a rag, and not a young man, after that."

Not a trace of the mincing airs and fashionable graces of the day before, not a trace of the lorgnette even was to be seen about Anfisa Petrovna now. She was a regular fury, a fury without a mask.

As soon as my uncle saw her he made haste to take Tatyana Ivanovna on his arm, and would have rushed out of the room, but Anfisa Petrovna at once barred the way.

"You are not going away like that, Yegor Ilyitch," she clamoured again. "By what right are you taking Tatyana Ivanovna away by force? You are annoyed that she has escaped the abominable snares you had caught her in, you and your mamma and your imbecile Foma Fomitch; you would have liked to marry her yourself for the sake of filthy lucre. I beg your pardon, but our ideas here are not so low! Tatyana Ivanovna, seeing that you were plotting against her, that you were bringing her to ruin, confided in Pavlusha of herself. She herself begged him to save her from your snares, so to say; she was forced to run away from you by night—that's a pretty thing! That's what you have driven her to, isn't it, Tatyana Ivanovna? And since that's so, how dare you burst, a whole gang of you, into a respectable gentleman's house and carry off a young lady by force in spite of her tears and protests? I will not permit it! I will not permit it! I have not taken leave of my senses! Tatyana Ivanovna will remain because she wishes it! Come, Tatyana Ivanovna, it is useless to listen to them, they are your enemies, not your friends! Come along, don't be frightened! I'll see them all out directly! . . ."

"No, no!" cried Tatyana Ivanovna, terrified, "I don't want to, I don't want to! He is no husband for me. I don't want to marry your son! He's no husband for me!"

"You don't want to!" shouted Anfisa Petrovna, breathless with rage. "You don't want to! You have come and you don't want to! Then how dared you deceive us like this? Then how dared you give him your promise? You ran away with him by night, you forced yourself upon him, and have led us into embarrassment and expense. My son has perhaps lost an excellent match through you! He may have lost a dowry of ten thousand through you! . . . No! you must pay for it, you ought to pay for it; we have proofs; you ran away at night. . . ."

But we did not hear this tirade to the end. All at once, grouping ourselves round my uncle, we moved forward straight upon Anfisa Petrovna and went out on to the steps. The carriage was at hand at once.

"None but dishonourable people, none but scoundrels behave like that," cried Anfisa Petrovna from the steps, in an absolute frenzy. "I will lodge a petition, you shall pay for it . . . you are going to a disreputable house, Tatyana Ivanovna. You cannot marry Yegor Ilyitch; under your very nose he is keeping his governess as his mistress."

My uncle shuddered, turned pale, bit his lip and rushed to assist Tatyana Ivanovna into the carriage. I went round to the other side of the carriage, and was waiting for my turn to get in, when I suddenly found Obnoskin by my side, clutching at my hand.

"Allow me at least to seek your friendship!" he said warmly, squeezing my hand, with an expression of despair on his face.

"What's that, friendship?" I said, lifting my foot to the carriage step.

"Yes! I recognised in you yesterday a man of culture; do not condemn me. . . . My mother led me on, I had nothing to do with it. My inclinations are rather for literature—I assure you; this was all my mother. . . ."

"I believe you, I believe you," I said. "Good-bye!"

We got in and the horses set off at a gallop. The shouts and curses of Anfisa Petrovna resounded for a long way after us, and unknown faces suddenly poked out of all the windows of the house and stared after us with wild curiosity.

There were five of us now in the carriage, but Mizintchikov got on to the box, giving up his former seat to Mr. Bahtcheyev, who had now to sit directly facing Tatyana Ivanovna. The latter was greatly relieved that we had taken her away, but she was still crying. - My uncle consoled her as best he could. He was himself sad and brooding; it was evident that Anfisa Petrovna's frantic words about Nastenka were echoing painfully and bitterly in his heart. Our return journey would, however, have ended without any disturbance if only Mr. Bahtcheyev had not been with us.

Sitting opposite Tatyana Ivanovna, he seemed not himself, he could not look indifferent, he shifted in his seat, turned as red as a crab, and rolled his eyes fearfully, particularly when my uncle began trying to console Tatyana Ivanovna. The fat man was absolutely beside himself, and growled like a bull-dog when it is teased. My uncle looked at him apprehensively. At last Tatyana Ivanovna, noticing the extraordinary state of mind of her *vis-à-vis*, began watching him intently; then she looked at us, smiled, and all at once picking up her parasol gracefully gave Mr. Bahtcheyev a light tap on the shoulder.

"Crazy fellow!" she said with a most enchanting playfulness, and at once hid her face in her fan.

This sally was the last straw.

"Wha-a-at?" roared the fat man. "What's that, madam? So you are after me now!"

"Crazy fellow! crazy fellow!" repeated Tatyana Ivanovna, and she suddenly burst out laughing and clapped her hands.

"Stop!" cried Bahtcheyev to the coachman, "stop!"

We stopped. Bahtcheyev opened the door, and hurriedly began clambering out of the carriage.

"Why, what is the matter, Stepan Alexyevitch? Where are you off to?" cried my uncle in astonishment.

"No, I have had enough of it," answered the fat man, trembling with indignation. "Deuce take it all! I am too old, madam, to be besieged with amours. I would rather die on the high road! Good-bye, madam. *Comment vous portez-vous?*"

And he actually began walking on foot. The carriage followed him at a walking pace.

"Stepan Alexyevitch!" cried my uncle, losing all patience at last. "Don't play the fool, come, get in! Why, it's time we were home."

"Bother you!" Stepan Alexyevitch brought out, breathless with walking, for owing to his corpulence he had quite lost the habit of exercise.

"Drive on full speed," Mizintchikov shouted to the coachman.

"What are you doing? Stop!" my uncle cried out as the carriage dashed on.

Mizintchikov was not out in his reckoning, the desired result followed at once.

"Stop! Stop!" we heard a despairing wail behind us. "Stop, you ruffian! Stop, you cut-throat . . ."

The fat man came into sight at last, half dead with exhaustion, with drops of sweat on his brow, untying his cravat and taking off his cap. Silently and gloomily he got into the carriage, and this time I gave him my seat; he was not anyway sitting directly opposite Tatyana Ivanovna, who all through this scene had been gushing with laughter and clapping her hands. She could not look gravely at Stepan Alexyevitch all the rest of the journey. He for his part sat without uttering a single word all the way home, staring intently at the hind wheel of the carriage.

It was midday when we got back to Stepantchikovo. I went straight to my lodge, where Gavrila immediately made his appearance with tea. I flew to question the old man, but my uncle walked in almost on his heels and promptly sent him away.

CHAPTER II

NEW DEVELOPMENTS

"I HAVE come to you for a minute, dear boy," he began, "I was in haste to tell you. . . . I have heard all about everything. None of them have even been to mass to-day, except Ilyusha, Sasha and Nastenka. They tell me mamma has been in convulsions. They have been rubbing her, it was all they could do to bring her to by rubbing. Now it has been settled for us all to go together to Foma, and I have been summoned. Only I don't know whether to congratulate Foma on the name-day or not—it's an important point! And in fact how are they going to take this whole episode? It's awful, Seryozha, I fore-see it. . . ."

"On the contrary, uncle," I hastened in my turn to reply, "everything is settling itself splendidly. You see you can't marry Tatyana Ivanovna now—that's a great deal in itself. I wanted to make that clear to you on our way."

"Oh, yes, my dear boy. But that's not the point; there is the hand of Providence in it no doubt, as you say, but I wasn't thinking of that. . . . Poor Tatyana Ivanovna! What adventures happen to her, though! . . . Obnoskin's a scoundrel, a scoundrel! Though why do I call him 'a scoundrel'? Shouldn't I have been doing the same if I married her? . . . But that, again, is not what I have come about. . . . Did you hear what that wretch Anfisa Petrovna shouted about Nastenka this morning?"

"Yes, uncle. Haven't you realised now that you must make haste?"

"Certainly, at all costs!" answered my uncle. "It is a solemn moment. Only there is one thing, dear boy, which we did not think of, but I was thinking of it afterwards all night. Will she marry me, that's the point?"

"Mercy on us, uncle! After she told you herself that she loves you . . ."

"But, my dear boy, you know she also said at once that nothing would induce her to marry me."

"Oh, uncle, that's only words; besides, circumstances are different to-day."

"Do you think so? No, Sergey, my boy, it's a delicate business, dreadfully delicate! H'm. . . . But do you know, though I was worrying, yet my heart was somehow aching with happiness all night. Well, good-bye, I must fly. They are wait-ing for me; I am late as it is. I only ran in to have a word with you. Oh, my God!" he cried, coming back, "I have forgotten what is most important! Do you know what? I have written to him, to Foma!"

"When?"

"In the night, and in the morning, at daybreak, I sent the letter by Vidoplyasov. I put it all before him on two sheets of paper, I told him everything truthfully and frankly, in short that I ought, that is, absolutely must—do you understand—make Nastenka an offer. I besought him not to say a word about our meeting in the garden, and I have appealed to all the generosity of his heart to help me with mamma. I wrote a poor letter, of course, my boy, but I wrote it from my heart and, so to say, watered it with my tears. . . ."

"Well? No answer?"

"So far no; only this morning when we were getting ready to set off, I met him in the hall in night attire, in slippers and nightcap—he sleeps in a nightcap—he had come out of his room. He didn't say a word, he didn't even glance at me. I peeped up into his face, not a sign."

"Uncle, don't rely on him; he'll play you some dirty trick."

"No, no, my boy, don't say so!" cried my uncle, gesticulating. "I am sure of him. Besides, you know, it's my last hope. He will understand, he'll appreciate it. He's peevish, he's capricious, I don't deny it; but when it comes to a question of nobility, then he shines out like a pearl. . . . Yes, like a pearl. You think all that, Sergey, because you have never seen him yet when he is most noble . . . but, my God! if he really does spread abroad my secret of yesterday, then . . . I don't know what will happen then, Sergey! What will be left me in the world that I can believe in? But no, he cannot be such a scoundrel. I am not worth the sole of his shoe. Don't shake your head, my boy; it's true—I am not."

"Yegor Ilyitch! Your mamma is anxious about you." We hear from below the unpleasant voice of Miss Perepelitsyn, who had probably succeeded in hearing the whole of our conversation from the open window. "They are looking for you all over the house, and cannot find you."

"Oh, dear, I am late! How dreadful!" cried my uncle in a fluster. "My dear boy, for goodness' sake dress and come too. Why, it was just for that I ran in, so that we might go together. . . . I fly, I fly! Anna Nilovna, I fly!"

When I was left alone, I recalled my meeting with Nastenka that morning and was very glad I had not told my uncle of it; I should have upset him even more. I foresaw a great storm, and could not imagine how my uncle would arrange his plans and make an offer to Nastenka. I repeat: in spite of my faith in his honour, I could not help feeling doubtful of his success.

However, I had to make haste. I considered myself bound to assist him, and at once began dressing; but as I wanted to be as well-dressed as possible, I was not very quick in spite of my haste. Mizintchikov walked in.

"I have come for you," he said. "Yegor Ilyitch begs you to come at once."

"Let us go!"

155

I was quite ready, we set off.

"What news there?" I asked on the way.

"They are all in Foma's room, the whole party," answered Mizintchikov. "Foma is not in bad humour, but he is somewhat pensive and doesn't say much, just mutters through his teeth. He even kissed Ilyusha, which of course delighted Yegor Ilyitch. He announced beforehand through Miss Perepelitsyn that they were not to congratulate him on the nameday, and that he had only wanted to test them. . . . Though the old lady keeps sniffing her smelling-salts, she is calm because Foma is calm. Of our adventure no one drops a hint, it is as though it had never happened; they hold their tongues because Foma holds his. He hasn't let anyone in all the morning, though. While we were away the old lady implored him by all the saints to come that she might consult him, and indeed she hobbled down to the door herself; but he locked himself in and answered that he was praying for the human race, or something of the sort. He has got something up his sleeve, one can see that from his face. But as Yegor Ilyitch is incapable of seeing anything from anyone's face, he is highly delighted now with Foma's mildness; he is a regular baby! Ilyusha has prepared some verses, and they have sent me to fetch you."

"And Tatyana Ivanovna?"

"What about Tatyana Ivanovna?"

"Is she there? With them?"

"No; she is in her own room," Mizintchikov answered dryly. "She is resting and crying. Perhaps she is ashamed too. I believe that . . . governess is with her now. I say! surely it is not a storm coming on? Look at the sky!"

"I believe it is a storm," I answered, glancing at a stormcloud that looked black on the horizon.

At that moment we went up on to the terrace.

"Tell me, what do you think of Obnoskin, eh?" I went on, not able to refrain from probing Mizintchikov on that point.

"Don't speak to me of him! Don't remind me of that blackguard," he cried, suddenly stopping, flushing red and stamping. "The fool! the fool! to ruin such a splendid plan, such a brilliant idea! Listen: I am an ass, of course, for not having detected what a rogue he is!—I admit that solemnly, and perhaps that admission is just what you want. But I swear if he had known how to carry it through properly, I should perhaps have forgiven him. The fool! the fool! And how can such people be allowed in society, how can they be endured! How is it they are not sent to Siberia, into exile, into prison! But that's all nonsense, they won't get over me! Now I have experience anyway, and we shall see who gets the best of it. I am thinking over a new idea now. . . . You must admit one can't lose one's object simply because some outside fool has stolen one's idea and not known how to set about it. Why, it's unjust! And, in fact, this Tatyana will inevitably be married, that's her pre-destined fate. And if no one has put her into a madhouse up to now, it was just because it is still possible to marry her. I will tell you my new idea. . . ."

"But afterwards, I suppose," I interrupted him, "for here we are."

"Very well, very well, afterwards," Mizintchikov answered, twisting his lips into a spasmodic smile. "And now. . . . But where are you going? I tell you, straight to Foma Fomitch's room! Follow me; you have not been there yet. You will see another farce. . . . For it has really come to a farce."

CHAPTER III

ILYUSHA'S NAMEDAY

FOMA occupied two large and excellent rooms; they were even better decorated than any other of the rooms in the house. The great man was surrounded by perfect comfort. The fresh and handsome wall-paper, the parti-coloured silk curtains on the windows, the rugs, the pier-glass, the fireplace, the softly upholstered elegant furniture—all testified to the tender solicitude of the family for Foma's comfort. Pots of flowers stood in the windows and on little marble tables in front of the windows. In the middle of the study stood a large table covered with a red cloth and littered with books and manuscripts. A handsome bronze inkstand and a bunch of pens which Vidoplyasov had to look after—all this was to testify to the severe intellectual labours of Foma Fomitch. I will mention here by the way that though Foma had sat at that table for nearly eight years, he had composed absolutely nothing that was any good. Later on, when he had departed to a better world, we went through his manuscripts; they all turned out to be extraordinary trash. We found, for instance, the beginning of an historical novel, the scene of which was laid in Novgorod, in the seventh century;

then a monstrous poem, "An Anchorite in the Churchyard", written in blank verse; then a meaningless meditation on the significance and characteristics of the Russian peasant, and how he should be treated; and finally "The Countess Vlonsky", a novel of aristocratic life, also unfinished. There was nothing else. And yet Foma Fomitch had made my uncle spend large sums every year on books and journals. But many of them were actually found uncut. Later on, I caught Foma Fomitch more than once reading Paul de Kock, but he always slipped the book out of sight when people came in. In the further wall of the study there was a glass door which led to the courtyard of the house.

They were waiting for us. Foma Fomitch was sitting in a comfortable arm-chair, wearing some sort of long coat that reached to his heels, but yet he wore no cravat. He certainly was silent and thoughtful. When we went in he raised his eyebrows slightly and bent a searching glance on me. I bowed; he responded with a slight bow, a fairly polite one, however. Grandmother, seeing that Foma Fomitch was behaving graciously to me, gave me a nod and a smile. The poor woman had not expected in the morning that her paragon would take the news of Tatyana Ivanovna's "escapade" so calmly, and so she was now in the best of spirits, though she really had been in convulsions and fainting fits earlier in the day. Behind her chair, as usual, stood Miss Perepelitsyn, compressing her lips till they looked like a thread, smiling sourly and spitefully and rubbing her bony hands one against the other. Two always mute lady companions were installed beside Madame la Générale. There was also a nun of sorts who had strayed in that morning, and an elderly lady, a neighbour who had come in after mass to congratulate Madame la Générale on the nameday and who also sat mute. Aunt Praskovya Ilyinitchna was keeping in the background somewhere in a corner, and was looking with anxiety at Foma Fomitch and her mother. My uncle was sitting in an easy-chair, and his face was beaming with a look of exceptional joy. Facing him stood Ilyusha in his red holiday shirt, with his hair in curls, looking like a little angel. Sasha and Nastenka had in secret from everyone taught him some verses to rejoice his father on this auspicious day by his progress in learning. My uncle was almost weeping with delight. Foma's unexpected mildness, Madame la Générale's good humour, Ilyusha's nameday, the verses, all moved him to real enthusiasm, and with a solemnity worthy of the occasion he had asked them to send for me that I might hasten to share the general happiness and listen to the verses. Sasha and Nastenka, who had come in just after us, were standing near Ilyusha. Sasha was continually laughing, and at that moment was as happy as a little child. Nastenka, looking at her, also began smiling, though she had come into the room a moment before pale and depressed. She alone had welcomed Tatyana Ivanovna on her return from her excursion, and until then had been sitting upstairs with her. The rogue Ilyusha seemed, too, as though he could not keep from laughing as he looked at his instructresses. It seemed as though the three of them had prepared a very amusing joke which they meant to play now. . . . I had forgotten Bahtcheyev. He was sitting on a chair at a little distance, still cross and red in the face; holding his tongue, sulking, blowing his nose and altogether playing a very gloomy part at the family festivity. Near him Yezhevikin was fidgeting about; he was fidgeting about everywhere, however, kissing the hands of Madame la Générale and of the visitors, whispering something to Miss Perepelitsyn, showing attention to Foma Fomitch, in fact he was all over the place. He, too, was awaiting Ilyusha's verses with great interest, and at my entrance flew to greet me with bows as a mark of the deepest respect and devotion. Altogether there was nothing to show that he had come to protect his daughter, and to take her from Stepantchikovo for ever.

"Here he is!" cried my uncle gleefully on seeing me. "Ilyusha has got a poem for us, that's something unexpected, a real surprise! I am overpowered, my boy, and sent for you on purpose, and have put off the verses till you came. . . . Sit down beside me! Let us listen. Foma Fomitch, confess now, it must have been you who put them all up to it to please an old fellow like me. I'll wager that is how it is!"

Since my uncle was talking in such a tone and voice in Foma's room one would have thought that all must be well. But unluckily my uncle was, as Mizintchikov expressed it, incapable of reading any man's face. Glancing at Foma's face, I could not help admitting that Mizintchikov was right and that something was certainly going to happen. . . .

"Don't trouble about me, Colonel," Foma answered in a faint voice, the voice of a man forgiving his enemies. "I approve of the surprise, of course; it shows the sensibility and good principles of your children. . . . Poetry is of use, too, even for the pronunciation. . . . But I have not been busy over verses this morning, Yegor Ilyitch; I have been praying . . .

you know that. . . . I am ready to listen to the verses, however."

Meanwhile I had congratualted Ilyusha and kissed him.

"Quite so, Foma, I beg your pardon! Kiss him once more, though I am sure of your affection, Foma! Kiss him once more, Seryozha! Look what a fine big boy! Come, begin, Ilyusha! What is it about? I suppose it is something solemn from Lomonosov?"

And my uncle drew himself up with a dignified air. He could scarcely sit still in his seat for impatience and delight.

"No, papa, not from Lomonosov," said Sashenka, hardly able to suppress her laughter; "but as you have been a soldier and fought the enemy, Ilyusha has learnt a poem about warfare. . . The siege of Pamba, papa!"

"The siege of Pamba! I don't remember it. . . . What is this Pamba, do you know, Ilyusha? Something heroic, I suppose."

And my uncle drew himself up again.

"Begin, Ilyusha!" Sasha gave the word of command.

Ilyusha began in a little, clear, even voice, without stops or commas, as small children generally recite verses they have learned by heart—

> "Nine long years Don Pedro Gomez
> Has besieged the fort of Pamba,
> On a diet of milk supported.
> And Don Pedro's gallant warriors,
> Brave Castilians, full nine thousand,
> All to keep the vow they've taken
> Taste no bread nor other victuals,
> Milk they drink and milk alone."

"What? What's that about milk?" cried my uncle, looking at me in perplexity.

"Go on reciting, Ilyusha!" cried Sashenka.

> "Every day Don Pedro Gomez,
> In his Spanish cloak enveloped,
> Bitterly his lot bewails.
> Lo, the tenth year is approaching;
> Still the fierce Moors are triumphant;
> And of all Don Pedro's army
> Only nineteen men are left. . . ."

"Why, it's a regular string of nonsense!" cried my uncle uneasily. "Come, that's impossible. Only nineteen men left out of a whole army, when there was a very considerable corps before? What is the meaning of it, my boy?"

But at that point Sasha could not contain herself, and went off into the most open and childish laughter; and though there was nothing very funny, it was impossible not to laugh too as one looked at her.

"They are funny verses, papa," she cried, highly delighted with her childish prank. "The author made them like that on purpose to amuse everybody."

"Oh! Funny!" cried my uncle, with a beaming face. "Comic, you mean! That's just what I thought. . . . Just so, just so, funny! And very amusing, extremely amusing: he starved all his army on milk owing to some vow. What possessed them to take such a vow? Very witty, isn't it, Foma? You see, mamma, these are jesting verses, such as authors sometimes do write, don't they, Sergey? Extremely amusing. Well, well, Ilyusha, what next?"

> "Only nineteen men are left!
> Them Don Pedro doth assemble
> And says to them: 'Noble Nineteen!
> Let us raise aloft our standards!
> Let us blow on our loud trumpets!
> And with clashing of our cymbals
> Let us from Pamba retreat!
> Though the fort we have not taken,
> Yet with honour still untarnished
> We can swear on faith and conscience
> That our vow we have not broken;
> Nine long years we have not eaten,
> Not a morsel have we eaten,
> Milk we've drunk and milk alone!' "

"What a noodle! What comfort was it for him that he had drunk milk for nine years?" my uncle broke in again. "What is there virtuous in it? He would have done better to have eaten a whole sheep, and not have been the death of people! Excellent! capital! I see, I see now: it's a satire on . . . what do they call it? an allegory, isn't it? And perhaps aimed at some foreign general," my uncle added, addressing me, knitting his brows significantly and screwing up his eyes, "eh? What do you think? But of course a harmless, good, refined satire that injures nobody! Excellent! excellent, and what matters most, it is refined. Well, Ilyusha, go on. Ah, you rogues, you rogues!" he added with feeling, looking at Sasha and stealthily also at Nastenka, who blushed and smiled.

> "And emboldened by that saying,
> Those nineteen Castilian warriors,
> Each one swaying in his saddle,
> Feebly shouted all together:
> 'Sant' Iago Compostello!
> Fame and glory to Don Pedro!
> Glory to the Lion of Castile!'
> And his chaplain, one Diego,
> Through his teeth was heard to mutter:
> 'But if I had been commander,
> I'd have vowed to eat meat only,
> Drinking good red wine alone.' "

"There! Didn't I tell you so?" cried my uncle, extremely delighted. "Only one sensible man was found in the whole army, and he was some sort of a chaplain. And what is that, Sergey: a captain among them, or what?"

"A monk, an ecclesiastical person, uncle."

"Oh, yes, yes. Chaplain! I know, I remember. I have read of it in Radcliffe's novels. They have all sorts of orders, don't they. . . . Benedictines, I believe? . . . There are Benedictines, aren't there?"

"Yes, uncle."

"H'm! . . . I thought so. Well, Ilyusha, what next? Excellent! capital!"

> "And Don Pedro overhearing,
> With loud laughter gave the order:
> 'Fetch a sheep and give it to him!
> He has jested gallantly!' "

'What a time to laugh! What a fool! Even he saw it was funny at last! A sheep! So they had sheep; why did he not eat some himself! Well, Ilyusha, go on. Excellent! capital! Extraordinarily cutting!"

"But that's the end, papa!"

"Oh, the end. Indeed there wasn't much left to be done—was there, Sergey? Capital, Ilyusha! Wonderfully nice. Kiss

me, darling. Ah, my precious! Who was it thought of it:
you, Sasha?"

"No, it was Nastenka. We read it the other day. She read
it and said: 'What ridiculous verses! It will soon be Ilyusha's
nameday, let us make him learn them and recite them. It will
make them laugh!"

"Oh, it was Nastenka? Well, thank you, thank you," my
uncle muttered, suddenly flushing like a child. "Kiss me again,
Ilyusha. You kiss me too, you rogue," he said, embracing
Sashenka and looking into her face with feeling. "You wait a
bit, Sashenka, it will be your nameday soon," he added, as
though he did not know what to say to express his pleasure.

I turned to Nastenka and asked whose verses they were.

"Yes, yes, whose are the verses?" my uncle hurriedly chimed
in. "It must have been a clever poet who wrote them, mustn't
it, Foma?"

"H'm . . ." Foma grunted to himself.

A biting sarcastic smile had not left his face during the whole
time of the recitation of the verses.

"I have really forgotten," said Nastenka, looking timidly at
Foma Fomitch.

"It's Mr. Kuzma Prutkov wrote it, papa; it was published
in the *Contemporary*," Sashenka broke in.

"Kuzma Prutkov! I don't know his name," said my uncle.
"Pushkin I know! . . . But one can see he is a gifted poet—
isn't he, Sergey? And what's more, a man of refined qualities,
that's as clear as twice two! Perhaps, indeed, he is an officer.
. . . I approve of him. And the *Contemporary* is a first-rate
magazine. We certainly must take it in if poets like that are
among the contributors. . . . I like poets! They are fine fellows!
They picture everything in verse. Do you know, Sergey, I met
a literary man at your rooms in Petersburg. He had rather a
peculiar nose, too . . . really! . . . What did you say, Foma?"

Foma Fomitch, who was getting more and more worked up,
gave a loud snigger.

"No, I said nothing . . ." he said, as though hardly able to
suppress his laughter. "Go on, Yegor Ilyitch, go on! I will
say my word later. . . . Stepan Alexyevitch is delighted to
hear how you made the acquaintance of literary men in
Petersburg."

Stepan Alexyevitch, who had been sitting apart all the time
lost in thought, suddenly raised his head, reddened, and turned
in his chair with exasperation.

"Don't you provoke me, Foma, but leave me in peace," he said, looking wrathfully at Foma, with his little bloodshot eyes. "What is your literature to me? May God only give me good health," he muttered to himself, "and plague take them all . . . and their authors too. . . . Voltairians, that's what they are!"

"Authors are Voltairians?" said Yezhevikin immediately at his side. "Perfectly true what you have been pleased to remark, Stepan Alexyevitch. Valentin Ignatyitch was pleased to express the same sentiments the other day. He actually called me a Voltairian, upon my soul he did! And yet, as you all know, I have written very little so far. . . . If a bowl of milk goes sour—it's all Voltaire's fault! That's how it is with everything here."

"Well, no," observed my uncle with dignity, "that's an error, you know! Voltaire was nothing but a witty writer; he laughed at superstitions; and he never was a Voltairian! It was his enemies spread that rumour about him. Why were they all against him, really, poor fellow? . . ."

Again the malignant snigger of Foma Fomitch was audible. My uncle looked at him uneasily and was perceptibly embarrassed.

"Yes, Foma, I am thinking about the magazine, you see," he said in confusion, trying to put himself right somehow. "You were perfectly right, my dear Foma, when you said the other day that we ought to subscribe to one. I think we ought to, myself. H'm . . . after all, they do assist in the diffusion of enlightenment; one would be a very poor patriot if one did not support them. Wouldn't one, Sergey. H'm . . . Yes . . . The *Contemporary*, for instance. But, do you know, Seryozha, the most instruction, to my thinking, is to be found in that thick magazine—what's its name?—in a yellow cover . . ."

"*Notes of the Fatherland*, papa."

"Oh, yes, *Notes of the Fatherland*, and a capital title, Sergey, isn't it? It is, so to say, the whole Fatherland sitting writing notes. . . . A very fine object. A most edifying magazine. And what a thick one! What a job to publish such an omnibus! And the information in it almost makes one's eyes start out of one's head. I came in the other day, the volume was lying here, I took it up and from curiosity opened it and reeled off three pages at a go. It made me simply gape, my dear! And, you know, there is information about everything; what is meant, for instance, by a broom, a spade, a ladle, an ovenrake. To my thinking, a broom is a broom and an ovenrake an ovenrake!

No, my boy, wait a bit. According to the learned, an ovenrake turns out not an ovenrake, but an emblem or something mythological; I don't remember exactly, but something of the sort. . . . So that's how it is! They have gone into everything!"

I don't know what precisely Foma was preparing to do after this fresh outburst from my uncle, but at that moment Gavrila appeared and stood with bowed head in the doorway.

Foma Fomitch glanced at him significantly.

"Ready, Gavrila?" he asked in a faint but resolute voice.

"Yes, sir," Gavrila answered mournfully, and heaved a sigh.

"And have you put my bundle on the cart?"

"Yes, sir."

"Well, then, I am ready too!" said Foma, and he deliberately go up from his easy-chair. My uncle looked at him in amazement. Madame la Générale jumped up from her seat and looked about her uneasily.

"Allow me, Colonel," Foma began with dignity, "to ask you to leave for a moment the interesting subject of literary ovenrakes; you can continue it after I am gone. As I am *taking leave of you for ever*, I should like to say a few last words to you. . . ."

Every listener was spellbound with alarm and amazement.

"Foma! Foma! but what is the matter with you? Where are you going?" my uncle cried at last.

"I am about to leave your house, Colonel," Foma brought out in a perfectly composed voice. "I have made up my mind to go where fortune takes me, and so I have hired at my own expense a humble peasant's cart. My bundle is lying in it already, it is of no great dimensions: a few favourite books, two changes of linen—that is all! I am a poor man, Yegor Ilyitch, but nothing in the world would induce me now to take your gold, which I refused even yesterday!"

"But for God's sake, Foma, what is the meaning of it?" cried my uncle, turning as white as a sheet.

Madame la Générale uttered a shriek and looked in despair at Foma Fomitch, stretching out her hands to him. Miss Perepelitsyn flew to support her. The lady companions sat petrified in their chairs. Mr. Bahtcheyev got up heavily from his seat.

"Well, here's a pretty to-do!" Mizintchikov whispered beside me.

At that moment a distant rumble of thunder was heard; a storm was coming on.

CHAPTER IV

THE EXPULSION

"YOU ask me, I believe, Colonel, what is the meaning of this?" Foma brought out with a solemn dignity, as though enjoying the general consternation. "I am surprised at the question! Will you on your side explain how it is *you* can bring yourself to look me in the face now? Explain to me this last psychological problem in human shamelessness, and then I shall depart, the richer for new knowledge of the depravity of the human race."

But my uncle was not equal to answering him. With open mouth and staring eyes he gazed at Foma, alarmed and annihilated.

"Merciful heavens! What passions!" hissed Miss Perepelitsyn.

"Do you understand, Colonel," Foma went on, "that you had better let me go now, simply without asking questions? In your house even I, a man of years and understanding, begin to feel the purity of my morals gravely endangered. Believe me, that your questions can lead to nothing but putting you to shame."

"Foma! Foma!" cried my uncle, and a cold perspiration came out on his forehead.

"And so allow me without further explanation to say a few farewell words at parting, my last words in your house, Yegor Ilyitch. The thing is done and there is no undoing it! I hope that you understand to what I am referring. But I implore you on my knees: if one spark of moral feeling is left in your heart, curb your unbridled passions! And if the noxious poison has not yet caught the whole edifice, then, as far as possible, extinguish the fire!"

"Foma, I assure you that you are in error!" cried my uncle, recovering himself little by little and foreseeing with horror the climax.

"Moderate your passions," Foma continued in the same solemn voice, as though he had not heard my uncle's exclamation, "conquer yourself. 'If thou would'st conquer all the world —conquer thyself.' That is my invariable rule. You are a land-owner; you ought to shine like a diamond in your estate, and what a vile example of unbridled passion you set your inferiors! I have been praying for you the whole night, and trembled as

166

I sought for your happiness. I did not find it, for happiness lies in virtue. . . ."

"But this is impossible, Foma!" my uncle interrupted him again. "You have misunderstood and what you say is quite wrong."

"And so remember you are a landowner," Foma went on, still regardless of my uncle's exclamations. "Do not imagine that repose and sensuality are the destined vocation of the landowning class. Fatal thought! Not repose, but zealous work, zealous towards God, towards your sovereign, and towards your country! Hard work, hard work is the duty of the landowner, he should work as hard as the poorest of his peasants!"

"What, am I to plough for the peasant, or what?" growled Bahtcheyev. "Why, I am a landowner, too. . . ."

"I turn to you now, servants of the house," Foma went on, addressing Gavrila and Falaley, who had appeared in the doorway. "Love your master and and his family, and obey them humbly and meekly, and they will reward you with their love. And you, Colonel, be just and compassionate to them. A fellow-man—the image of God—like a child of tender years, so to say, is entrusted to you by your sovereign and your country. Great is the duty, but great also is the merit."

"Foma Fomitch, my dear man, what notion is this?" cried Madame la Générale in despair, almost swooning with horror.

"Well, that is enough, I think," Foma concluded, paying no attention even to Madame la Générale. "Now to lesser things; they may be small, but they are essential, Yegor Ilyitch. Your hay on the Harinsky waste has not been cut yet. Do not be too late with it: mow it and mow it quickly. That is my advice. . . ."

"But, Foma . . ."

"You meant to cut down the Zyryanovsky copse, I know; don't cut it—that's a second piece of advice. Preserve forest land, for trees retain humidity on the surface of the earth. It is a pity that you have sown the spring corn so late; it's amazing how late you have been in sowing the spring corn! . . ."

"But, Foma . . ."

"But enough! One cannot convey everything, and indeed there is not time. I will send you written instructions in a special book. Well, good-bye, good-bye all, God be with you, and the Lord bless you. I bless you too, my child," he went on, turning to Ilyusha; "and may God keep you from the noxious poison of your passions. I bless you too, Falaley; forget the Komarinsky! . . . And all of you. . . . Remember Foma. . . . Well, let us go, Gavrila! Come and help me in, old man."

And Foma turned towards the door. Madame la Générale gave a piercing shriek and flew after him.

"No, Foma, I will not let you go like this," cried my uncle, and overtaking him, he seized him by the hand.

"So ̤ou mean to have resort to force?" Foma asked haughtily.

"Yes, Foma. . . even to force," answered my uncle, quivering with emotion. "You have said too much, and must explain your words! You have misunderstood my letter, Foma! . . ."

"Your letter!" squealed Foma, instantly flaring up as though he had been awaiting that minute for an explosion; "your letter! Here it is, your letter! Here it is. I tear this letter, I spit upon it! I trample your letter under my foot, and in doing so fulfil the most sacred duty of humanity. That is what I will do if you compel me by force to an explanation! Look! Look! Look! . . . ."

And scraps of paper flew about the room.

"I repeat, Foma, you have misunderstood it," cried my uncle, turning paler and paler. "I am making an offer of marriage, Foma, I am seeking my happiness."

"Marriage! You have seduced this young girl, and are trying to deceive me by offering her marriage, for I saw you with her last night in the garden, under the bushes."

Madame la Générale uttered a scream and fell fainting into an arm-chair. A fearful hubbub arose. Poor Nastenka sat deathly pale. Sasha, frightened, clutched Ilyusha and trembled as though she were in a fever.

"Foma!" cried my uncle in a frenzy, "if you divulge that secret you are guilty of the meanest action on earth!"

"I do divulge that secret," squealed Foma, "and I am performing the most honourable action! I am sent by God Himself to unmask your villainies to all the world. I am ready to clamber on some peasant's thatched roof and from there to proclaim your vile conduct to all the gentlemen of the neighbourhood and all the passers-by. . . . Yes, let me tell you all, all of you, that yesterday in the night I found him in the garden, under the bushes with this young girl whose appearance is so innocent. . . ."

168

"Oh, what a disgrace!" piped Miss Perepelitsyn.

"Foma! Don't be your own destruction!" cried my uncle, with clenched fists and flashing eyes.

"He," squealed Foma, "he, alarmed at my having seen him, had the audacity to try with a lying letter to persuade me into conniving at his crime—yes, crime! . . . for you have turned a hitherto innocent young girl into a . . ."

"Another insulting word to her and I will kill you, Foma, I swear! . . ."

"I say that word, since you have succeeded in turning the most innocent young girl into a most depraved girl."

Foma had hardly uttered this last word when my uncle seized him by the shoulder, turned him round like a straw, and flung him violently at the glass door, which led from the study into the courtyard. The shock was so violent that the closed door burst open, and Foma, flying head over heels down the stone steps, fell full length in the yard. Bits of broken glass were scattered tinkling about the steps.

"Gavrila, pick him up!" cried my uncle, as pale as a corpse. "Put him in the cart, and within two minutes let there be no trace of him in Stepantchikovo!"

Whatever Foma's design may have been, he certainly had not expected such a climax.

I will not undertake to describe what happened for the first minutes after this episode. The heart-rending wail of Madame la Générale as she rolled from side to side in an arm-chair; the stupefaction of Miss Perepelitsyn at this unexpected behaviour of my hitherto submissive uncle; the sighs and groans of the lady companions; Nastenka almost fainting with fright while her father hovered over her; Sashenka terror-stricken; my uncle in indescribable excitement pacing up and down the room waiting for his mother to come to herself; and lastly, the loud weeping of Falaley in lamentation over the troubles of his betters—all this made up an indescribable picture. I must add, too, that at this moment a violent storm broke over us; peals of thunder were more and more frequent, and big drops of rain began pattering on the window.

"Here's a nice holiday!" muttered Mr. Bahtcheyev, bowing his head and flinging wide his arms.

"It's a bad business," I whispered to him, beside myself with excitement too. "But anyway they have turned Foma out, and he won't come back again."

"Mamma! Are you conscious? Are you better? Can you

169

listen to me at last?" asked my uncle, stopping before the old lady's arm-chair.

She raised her head, clasped her hands, and looked with imploring eyes at her son, whom she had never in her life before seen moved to such wrath.

"Mamma," he went on, "it was the last straw, you have seen for yourself. It was not like this that I meant to approach this subject, but the hour has come, and it is useless to put it off. You have heard the calumny, hear my defence. Mamma, I love this noble and high-minded girl, I have loved her a long while, and I shall never cease to love her. She will make the happiness of my children, and will be a dutiful daughter to you. And so now, before you, and in the presence of my friends and my family, I solemnly plead at her feet, and beseech her to do me infinite honour by consenting to be my wife."

Nastenka started, then flushed crimson all over and got up from her seat. Madame la Générale stared some time at her son as though she did not understand what he was saying to her, and all at once with a piercing wail flung herself on her knees.

"Yegorushka, my darling, bring Foma Fomitch back," she cried. "Bring him back at once, or without him I shall die before night."

My uncle was petrified at the sight of his self-willed and capricious old mother kneeling before him. His painful distress was reflected in his face. At last, recovering himself, he flew to raise her up and put her back in her chair.

"Bring Foma Fomitch back, Yegorushka," the old lady went on wailing. "Bring him back darling! I cannot live without him!"

"Mamma," my uncle cried sorrowfully, "have you heard nothing of what I have just said to you? I cannot bring Foma back—understand that. I cannot and I have not the right to after his low and scoundrelly slander on this angel of honour and virtue. Do you understand, mamma, that it is my duty, that my honour compels me now to defend virtue? You have heard: I am asking this young lady to be my wife, and I beg you to bless our union."

Madame la Générale got up from her seat again and fell on her knees before Nastenka.

"My dear girl!" she wailed, "do not marry him. Do not marry him, but entreat him, my dear, to fetch back Foma Fomitch. Nastasya Yevgrafovna, darling! I will give up everything, I will sacrifice everything if only you will not marry him. Old as I am, I have not spent everything, I had a little left me when my poor husband died. It's all yours, my dear, I will give you everything, and Yegorushka will give you something too, but do not lay me living in my grave, beg him to bring back Foma Fomitch."

And the old woman would have gone on wailing and drivelling if Miss Perepelitsyn and all the lady companions had not, with shrieks and moans, rushed to lift her up, indignant that she should be on her knees before a hired governess. Nastenka was so frightened that she could hardly stand, while Miss Perepelitsyn positively shed tears of fury.

"You will be the death of your mamma," she screamed at my uncle. "You will be the death of her. And you, Nastasya Yevgrafovna, ought not to make dissension between mother and son; the Lord has forbidden it. . . ."

"Anna Nilovna, hold your tongue!" cried my uncle. "I have put up with enough!"

"Yes, and I have had enough to put up with from you too. Why do you reproach me with my friendless position? It is easy to insult the friendless. I am not your slave yet. I am the daughter of a major myself. You won't see me long in your house, this very day . . . I shall be gone. . . ."

But my uncle did not hear her; he went up to Nastenka and with reverence took her by the hand.

"Nastasya Yevgrafovna! You have heard my offer?" he said, looking at her with anguish, almost with despair.

"No, Yegor Ilyitch, no! We had better give it up," said Nastenka, utterly dejected too. "It is all nonsense," she said, pressing his hand and bursting into tears. "You only say this because of yesterday . . . but it cannot be. You see that yourself. We have made a mistake, Yegor Ilyitch. . . . But I shall always think of you as my benefactor and . . . I shall pray for you always, always! . . ."

At this point tears choked her. "My poor uncle had evidently foreseen this answer; he did not even think of protesting, of insisting. He listened, bending down to her, still holding her hand, crushed and speechless. There were tears in his eyes.

"I told you yesterday," Nastya went on, "that I could not be your wife. You see that I am not wanted here . . . and I foresaw all this long ago; your mamma will not give you her blessing . . . *others* too. Though you would not regret it afterwards, because you are the most generous of men, yet you would be made miserable through me . . . with your soft-heartedness. . . ."

"Just because of your *soft-heartedness!* Just because you are so *soft-hearted!* That's it, Nastenka, that's it!" chimed in her old father, who was standing on the other side of her chair. "That's just it, that's just the right word."

"I don't want to bring dissension into your house on my account," Nastenka went on. "And don't be uneasy about me, Yegor Ilyitch; no one will interfere with me, no one will insult me . . . I am going to my father's . . . this very day. . . . We had better say good-bye, Yegor Ilyitch. . . ."

And poor Nastenka dissolved into tears again.

"Nastasya Yevgrafovna! Surely this not not your final answer!" said my uncle, looking at her in unutterable despair. "Say only one word and I will sacrifice everything for you! . . ."

"It is final, it is final, Yegor Ilyitch . . ." Yezhevikin put in again, "and she has explained it all very well to you, as I must own I did not expect her to. You are a very soft-hearted man, Yegor Ilyitch, yes, very soft-hearted, and you have graciously done us a great honour! A great honour, a great honour! . . . But all the same we are not a match for you, Yegor Ilyitch. You ought to have a bride, Yegor Ilyitch, who would be wealthy and of high rank, and a great beauty and with a voice too, who would walk about your rooms all in diamonds and ostrich feathers. . . . Then perhaps Foma Fomitch would make a little concession and give his blessing! And you will bring Foma Fomitch back! It was no use, no use your insulting him. It was from virtue, you know, from excess of fervour that he said too much, you know. You will say yourself that it was through his virtue—you will see! A most worthy man. And here he is getting wet through now. It would be better to fetch him back now. . . . For you will have to fetch him back, you know. . . ."

"Fetch him back, fetch him back!" shrieked Madame la Générale. "What he says is right, my dear! . . ."

"Yes," Yezhevikin went on. "Here your illustrious parent has upset herself about nothing. . . . Fetch him back! And Nastaya and I meanwhile will be on the march. . . ."

"Wait a minute, Yevgraf Larionitch!" cried my uncle, "I entreat you. There is one thing more must be said, Yevgraf, one thing only. . . ."

Saying this, he walked away, sat down in an arm-chair in

the corner, bowed his head, and put his hands over his eyes as though he were thinking over something.

At that moment a violent clap of thunder sounded almost directly over the house. The whole building shook. Madame la Générale gave a scream, Miss Perepelitsyn did the same, the lady companions, and with them Mr. Bahtcheyev, all stupefied with terror, crossed themselves.

"Holy Saint, Elijah the prophet!" five or six voices murmured at once.

The thunder was followed by such a downpour that it seemed as though the whole lake were suddenly being emptied upon Stepantchikovo.

"And Foma Fomitch, what will become of him now out in the fields?" piped Miss Perepelitsyn.

"Yegorushka, fetch him back!" Madame la Générale cried in a voice of despair, and she rushed to the door as though crazy. Her attendant ladies held her back; they surrounded her, comforted her, whimpered, squealed. It was a perfect Bedlam!

"He went off with nothing over his coat. If he had only taken an overcoat with him!" Miss Perepelitsyn went on. "He did not take an umbrella either. He will be struck by lightning! . . ."

"He will certainly be struck!" Bahtcheyev chimed in. "And he will be soaked with rain afterwards, too."

"You might hold you tongue!" I whispered to him.

"Why, he is a man, I suppose, or isn't he?" Bahtcheyev answered wrathfully. "He is not a dog. I bet you wouldn't go out of doors yourself. Come, go and have a bath for your *plaisir.*"

Foreseeing how it might end and dreading the possibility, I went up to my uncle, who sat as though chained to his chair.

"Uncle," I said, bending down to his ear, "surely you won't consent to bring Foma Fomitch back? Do understand that that would be the height of unseemliness, at any rate as long as Nastasya Yevgrafovna is here."

"My dear," answered my uncle, raising his head and looking at me resolutely," I have been judging myself at this moment and I know what I ought to do. Don't be uneasy, there shall be no offence to Nastenka, I will see to that. . . ."

He got up from his seat and went to his mother.

"Mamma," he said, "don't worry yourself, I will bring Foma Fomitch back, I will overtake him; he cannot have gone far yet.

But I swear he shall come back only on one condition, that here publicly in the presence of all who were witnesses of the insult he should acknowledge how wrong he has been, and solemnly beg the forgiveness of this noble young lady. I will secure that, I will make him do it! He shall not cross the threshold of this house without it! I swear, too, mamma, solemnly, that if he consents to this of his own free will, I shall be ready to fall at his feet, and will give him anything, anything I can, without injustice to my children. I myself will renounce everything from this very day. The star of my happiness has set. I shall leave Stepantchikovo. You must all live here calmly and happily. I am going back to my regiment, and in the turmoil of war, on the field of battle, I will end my despairing days. . . . Enough! I am going!"

At that moment the door opened, and Gavrila, soaked through and incredibly muddy, stood facing the agitated company.

"What's the matter? Where have you come from? Where is Foma?" cried my uncle, rushing up to Gavrila.

Everyone followed him, and with eager curiosity crowded round the old man, from whom dirty water was literally trickling in streams. Shrieks, sighs, exclamations accompanied every word Gavrila uttered.

"I left him at the birch copse, a mile away," he began in a tearful voice. "The horse took fright at the lightning and bolted into a ditch."

"Well? . . . " cried my uncle.

"The cart was upset. . . ."

"Well? . . . and Foma?"

"He fell into the ditch."

"And then? Tell us, you tantalising old man!"

"He bruised his side and began crying. I unharnessed the horse, got on him and rode here to tell you."

"And Foma remained there?"

"He got up and went on with his stick," Gavrila concluded; then he heaved a sigh and bowed his head.

The tears and sobs of the tender sex were indescribable.

"Polkan!" cried my uncle, and he flew out of the room. Polkan was brought, my uncle leapt on him barebacked, and a minute later the thud of the horse's hoofs told us that the pursuit of Foma Fomitch had begun. My uncle had actually galloped off without his cap.

The ladies ran to the windows. Among the sighs and groans

were heard words of advice. There was talk of a hot bath, of Foma Fomitch being rubbed with spirits, of some soothing drink, of the fact that Foma Fomitch "had not had a crumb of bread between his lips all day and that he is wet through on an empty stomach." Miss Perepelitsyn found his forgotten spectacles in their case, and the find produced an extraordinary effect: Madame la Générale pounced on them with tears and lamentations, and still keeping them in her hand, pressed up to the window again to watch the road. The suspense reached the utmost pitch of intensity at last. In another corner Sashenka was trying to comfort Nastya; they were weeping in each other's arms. Nastenka was holding Ilyusha's hand and kissing him from time to time. Ilyusha was in floods of tears, though he did not yet know why. Yezhevikin and Mizintchikov were talking of something aside. I fancied that Bahtcheyev was looking at the girls as though he were ready to blubber himself. I went up to him.

"No, my good sir," he said to me, "Foma Fomitch may leave here one day perhaps, but the time for that has not yet come; they haven't got gold-horned bulls for his chariot yet. Don't worry yourself, sir, he'll drive the owners out of the house and stay there himself!"

The storm was over, and Mr. Bahtcheyev had evidently changed his views.

All at once there was an outcry: "They are bringing him, they are bringing him," and the ladies ran shrieking to the door. Hardly ten minutes had passed since my uncle set off; one would have thought it would have been impossible to bring Foma Fomitch back so quickly; but the enigma was very simply explained later on. When Foma Fomitch had let Gavrila go he really had "set off walking with his stick", but finding himself in complete solitude in the midst of the storm, the thunder, and the pouring rain, he was ignominiously panic-stricken, turned back towards Stepantchikovo and ran after Gavrila. He was already in the village when my uncle came upon him. A passing cart was stopped at once; some peasants ran up and put the unresisting Foma Fomitch into it. So they conveyed him straight to the open arms of Madame la Générale, who was almost beside herself with horror when she saw the condition he was in. He was even muddier and wetter than Gavrila. There was a terrific flurry and bustle; they wanted at once to drag him upstairs to change his linen; there was an outcry for elder-flower tea and other invigorating beverages, they scurried in all directions without doing anything sensible; they all talked at once. . . . But Foma seemed to notice nobody and nothing. He was led in, supported under the arms. On reaching his easy-chair, he sank heavily into it and closed his eyes. Someone cried out that he was dying; a terrible howl was raised, and Falaley was the loudest of all, trying to squeeze through the crowd of ladies up to Foma Fomitch to kiss his hand at once. . . .

CHAPTER V

FOMA FOMITCH MAKES EVERYONE HAPPY

"WHERE have they brought me?" Foma articulated at last, in the voice of a man dying in a righteous cause.

"Damnable humbug!" Mizintchikov whispered beside me. "As though he didn't see where he had been brought! Now he will give us a fine exhibition!"

"You are among us, Foma, you are in your own circle!" cried my uncle. "Don't give way, calm yourself! And really, Foma, you had better change your things, or you will be ill. . . . And won't you take something to restore you, eh? Just something . . . a little glass of something to warm you. . . ."

"I could drink a little Malaga," Foma moaned, closing his eyes again.

"Malaga? I am not sure there is any," my uncle said, anxiously looking towards Praskovya Ilyinitchna.

"To be sure there is!" the latter answered. "There are four whole bottles left." And jingling her keys she ran to fetch the Malaga, followed by exclamations of the ladies, who were clinging to Foma like flies round jam. On the other hand, Mr Bahtcheyev was indignant in the extreme.

"He wants Malaga!" he grumbled almost aloud. "And asks for a wine that no one drinks. Who drinks Malaga nowadays but rascals like him? Tfoo, you confounded fellow! What am I standing here for? What am I waiting for?"

"Foma," my uncle began, stumbling over every word, "you see now . . . when you are rested and are with us again . . . that is, I meant to say, Foma, that I understand how accusing, so to say, the most innocent of beings . . ."

"Where is it, my innocence, where?" Foma interrupted, as though he were feverish and in delirium. "Where are my golden days? Where art thou, my golden childhood, when innocent and lovely I ran about the fields chasing the spring butterflies? Where are those days? Give me back my innocence, give it me back! . . ."

And Foma, flinging wide his arms, turned to each one of us in succession as though his innocence were in somebody's pocket. Bahtcheyev was ready to explode with wrath.

"Ech, so that's what he wants!" he muttered in a fury. "Give him his innocence! Does he want to kiss it, or what? Most likely he was as great a villain when he was a boy as he is now! I'll take my oath he was."

"Foma!" . . . my uncle was beginning again.

"Where, where are they, those days when I still had faith in love and loved mankind?" cried Foma; "when I embraced man and wept upon his bosom? But now where am I? Where am I?"

"You are with us, Foma, calm yourself," cried my uncle. "This is what I wanted to say to you, Foma. . . ."

"You might at least keep silent now," hissed Miss Perepelitsyn, with a spiteful gleam in her viperish eyes.

"Where am I?" Foma went on. "Who are about me? They are bulls and buffaloes turning their horns against me. Life, what art thou? If one lives one is dishonoured, disgraced, humbled, crushed; and when the earth is scattered on one's coffin, only then men will remember one and pile a monument on one's poor bones!"

"Holy saints, he is talking about monuments!" whispered Yezhevikin, clasping his hands.

"Oh, do not put up a monument to me," cried Foma, "do not! I don't need monuments. Raise up a monument to me in your hearts, I want nothing more, nothing more!"

"Foma," my uncle interposed, "enough, calm yourself! There is no need to talk about monuments. Only listen. You see, Foma, I understand that you were perhaps, so to say, inspired with righteous fervour when you reproached me, but you were carried away, Foma, beyond the limit of righteousness—I assure you you were mistaken, Foma. . . ."

"Oh, will you give over?" hissed Miss Perepelitsyn again. "Do you want to murder the poor man because he is in your hands? . . ."

After Miss Perepelitsyn, Madame la Générale made a stir, and all her suite followed her example; they all waved their hands at my uncle to stop him.

"Anna Nilovna, be silent yourself, I know what I am saying!" my uncle answered firmly. "This is a sacred matter! A question of honour and justice. Foma! you are a sensible man, you must at once ask the forgiveness of the virtuous young lady whom you have insulted."

"What young lady? What young lady have I insulted?" Foma articulated in amazement, staring round at everyone as though he had entirely forgotten everything that had happened, and did not know what was the matter.

"Yes, Foma; and if now of your own accord you frankly acknowledge you have done wrong, I swear, Foma, I will fall at your feet and then . . ."

"Whom have I insulted?" wailed Foma. "What young lady? Where is she? Where is the young lady? Recall to me something about the young lady! . . ."

At that instant, Nastenka, confused and frightened, went up to Yegor Ilyitch and pulled him by the sleeve.

"No, Yegor Ilyitch, leave him alone, there is no need of an apology. What is the object of it all?" she said in an imploring voice. "Give it up!"

"Ah, now I begin to remember," cried Foma. "My God, I understand. Oh, help me, help me to remember!" he implored, apparently in great excitement. "Tell me, is it true that I was turned out of this house, like the mangiest of curs? Is it true that I was struck by lightning? Is it true that I was kicked down the steps? Is it true? Is that true?"

The weeping and wailing of the fair sex were the most eloquent reply to Foma Fomitch.

"Yes, yes," he repeated, "I remember . . . I remember now that after the lightning and my fall I was running here, pursued by the thunder, to do my duty and then vanish for ever! Raise me up! Weak as I may be now, I must do my duty."

He was at once helped up from his chair. Foma stood in the attitude of an orator and stretched out his hands.

"Colonel," he cried, "now I have quite recovered. The thunder has not extinguished my intellectual capacities; it has left, it is true, a deafness in my right ear, due perhaps not so much to the thunder as to my fall down the steps, but what of that? And what does anyone care about Foma's right ear!"

Foma threw such a wealth of mournful irony into these last words, and accompanied them with such a pathetic smile, that the groans of the deeply-moved ladies resounded again. They all looked with reproach, and some also with fury, at my uncle, who was beginning to be crushed by so unanimous an expression of public opinion. Mizintchikov, with a curse, walked away to the window. Bahtcheyev kept prodding me more and more violently with his elbow; he could hardly stand still.

"Now listen to my whole confession!" yelled Foma, turning upon all a proud and determined gaze, "and at the same time decide the fate of poor Opiskin! Yegor Ilyitch, for a long time past I have been watching over you, watching over you with a tremor at my heart, and I have seen everything, everything, while you were not suspecting that I was watching over you. Colonel! Perhaps I was mistaken, but I knew your egotism, your boundless vanity, your phenomenal sensuality, and who would blame me for trembling for the honour of an innocent young person?"

"Foma, Foma! . . . you need not enlarge on it, Foma," cried my uncle, looking uneasily at Nastenka's suffering face.

"What troubled me was not so much the innocence and trustfulness of the person in question as her inexperience," Foma went on, as though he had not heard my uncle's warning. "I saw that a tender feeling was blossoming in her heart, like a rose in spring, and I could not help recalling Petrarch's saying, 'Innocence is often but a hair's breadth from ruin.' I sighed, I groaned, and though I was ready to shed the last drop of my blood to safeguard that pure pearl of maidenhood, who could answer to me for you, Yegor Ilyitch? I know the unbridled violence of your passions, and knowing that you are ready to sacrifice everything for their momentary gratification, I was plunged in the depths of alarm and apprehension for the fate of the noblest of girls. . . ."

"Foma! Could you really imagine such a thing?" cried my uncle.

"With a shudder at my heart I watched over you. And if you want to know what I have been suffering, go to Shakespeare: in his *Hamlet* he describes the state of my soul. I became suspicious and terrible. In my anxiety, in indignation, I saw everything in the blackest colour and that not the 'black colour' sung of in the well-known song—I can assure you. That was the cause of the desire you saw in me to remove *her* far away from this house: I wanted to save her; that was why you have seen me of late irritable and bitter against the whole human race. Oh! who will reconcile me with humanity? I feel that I was perhaps over-exacting and unjust to your guests, to your nephew, to Mr. Bahtcheyev, when I expected from him a knowledge of astronomy; but who will blame me for my state of mind at the time? Going to Shakespeare again, I may say that the future looked to my imagination like a gloomy gulf of unfathomed depth with a crocodile lying at the bottom. I felt that it was my duty to prevent disaster, that I was destined, appointed for that purpose—and what happened? You did not understand the generous impulse of my heart, and have been repaying me all this time with anger, with ingratitude, with jeers, with slights . . ."

"Foma! If that is so . . . of course I feel . . ." cried my uncle, in extreme agitation.

"If you really do feel it, Colonel, be so kind as to listen and not interrupt me. I will continue. My whole fault lay in the fact, therefore, that I was too much troubled over the fate and the happiness of this child; for compared with you she is a child. It was the truest love for humanity that turned me all this time into a fiend of wrath and suspicion. I was ready to fall on people and tear them to pieces. And you know, Yegor Ilyitch, all your actions, as though of design, made me more suspicious every hour, and confirmed my fears. You know, Yegor Ilyitch, when you showered your gold upon me yesterday to drive me from you, I thought: 'He is driving away in my person his conscience, so as more easily to perpetrate this wickedness. . . .'"

"Foma, Foma, can you have thought that yesterday?" my uncle cried out with horror. "Merciful heavens! and I hadn't the faintest suspicion . . ."

"Heaven itself inspired those suspicions," Foma went on. "And judge for yourself: what could I suppose when chance led me that very evening to that fatal seat in the garden? What were my feelings at that moment—oh, my God!—when I saw with my own eyes that all my suspicions were justified in the most flagrant manner? But I had still one hope left, a faint one indeed, but still it was a hope, and—this morning you shattered it into dust and ashes! You sent me your letter, you alleged your intention to marry; you besought me not to make it public. . . . 'But why?' I wondered. 'Why did he write now after I have found him out and not before? Why did he not run to me before, happy and comely—for love adorns the countenance—why did he not fly to my embrace, why did he not weep upon my bosom tears of infinite bliss and tell me all about it, all about it?' Or am I a crocodile who would have devoured you instead of giving you good advice? Or am I some loathsome beetle who would only have bitten you and not assisted your happiness? 'Am I his friend or the most repulsive of insects?' that was the question I asked myself this morning. 'With what object,' I asked myself, 'with what object did he invite his nephew from Petersburg and try to betroth him to this girl, if not to deceive us and his *frivolous* nephew, and meanwhile in secret to persist in his criminal designs?' Yes, Colonel, if anyone confirmed in me the thought that your mutual love was criminal, it was you yourself and you only! What is more, you have behaved like a criminal to this young girl; for through your tactlessness and selfish mistrustfulness you have exposed her, a modest and high-principled girl, to slander and odious suspicions.''

My uncle stood silent with bowed head, Foma's eloquence was evidently getting the better of his convictions, and he was beginning to regard himself as a complete criminal. Madame la Générale and her followers were listening to Foma in awe-struck silence, while Miss Perepelitsyn looked with spiteful triumph at poor Nastenka.

"Overwhelmed, nervously exhausted and shattered," Foma went on, "I locked myself in this morning and prayed, and the Lord showed me the right path. At last I decided: for the last time and publicly to put you to the test. I may have gone about it with too much fervour, I may have given way too much to my indignation; but for my well-meaning effort, you flung me out of the window! As I fell out of the window I thought to myself: 'This is how virtue is rewarded all the world over.' Then I struck the earth, and I scarcely remember what happened to me afterwards.''

Shrieks and groans interrupted Foma Fomitch at this tragic recollection. Madame la Générale made a dash at him with a bottle of Malaga in her hand, which she had just snatched from Praskovya Ilyinitchna, but Foma majestically waved aside the hand and the Malaga and Madame la Générale herself.

"Let me alone,'' he shouted; "I must finish. What happened after my fall—I don't know. I know one thing only, that now, wet through and on the verge of fever, I am standing here to secure your mutual happiness. Colonel! From many signs which I do not wish now to particularise, I am convinced at last that your love was pure and even exalted, though at the same time criminally distrustful. Beaten, humiliated, suspected of insulting a young lady in defence of whose honour I am ready like a medieval knight to shed the last drop of my blood, I have made up my mind to show you how Foma Opiskin revenges an injury. Give me your hand, Colonel!"

"With pleasure, Foma!" cried my uncle. "And since you have now fully cleared the honour of this young lady from every aspersion, why . . . of course . . . here is my hand, Foma, together with my regrets. . . ."

And my uncle gave him his hand warmly, not yet suspecting what was to come of it.

"Give me your hand too," went on Foma in a faint voice, parting the crowd of ladies who were pressing round him and appealing to Nastenka.

Nastenka was taken aback and confused, she looked timidly at Foma.

"Approach, approach, my sweet child! It is essential for your happiness," Foma added caressingly, still holding my uncle's hand in his.

"What's he up to now?" said Mizintchikov.

Nastenka, frightened and trembling, went slowly up to Foma and timidly held out her hand.

Foma took her hand and put it in my uncle's.

"I join your hands and bless you," he pronounced in the most solemn voice. "And if the blessing of a poor sorrow-stricken sufferer may avail you, be happy. This is how Foma Opiskin takes his revenge! Hurrah!"

The amazement of everyone was immense. The conclusion was so unexpected that everyone was struck dumb. Madame la Générale stood rooted to the spot, with her mouth open and the bottle of Malaga in her hand. Miss Perepelitsyn turned pale and trembled with fury. The lady companions clasped their hands and sat petrified in their seats. My uncle trembled and tried to say something, but could not. Nastya turned deathly pale and timidly murmured that "it could not be" . . . but it was too late. Bahtcheyev was the first—we must do him that credit—to second Foma's hurrah. I followed suit, and after me Sashenka shouted at the top of her ringing voice as she flew to embrace her father; then Ilyusha joined in, then Yezhevikin, and last of all Mizintchikov.

"Hurrah!" Foma cried once more; "hurrah! And on your knees, children of my heart, on your knees before the tenderest of mothers! Ask her blessing, and if need be I will kneel before her by your side. . . ."

My uncle and Nastya, not looking at each other, and seeming not to understand what was being done to them, fell on their knees before Madame la Générale, the whole company flocked round them; but the old lady seemed to be stupefied, not knowing what to do. Foma came to the rescue at this juncture too; he plumped down himself before his patroness. This at once dispelled all her hesitation. Dissolving into tears, she said at last that she consented. My uncle jumped up and clasped Foma in his arms.

"Foma, Foma! . . ." he began, but his voice broke and he could not go on.

"Champagne!" bawled Mr. Bahtcheyev. "Hurrah!"

"No, sir, not champagne," Miss Perepelitsyn caught him up. She had by now recovered herself, and realised the position and at the same time its consequences. "Put up a candle to God, pray to the holy image and bless with the holy image, as is done by all godly people. . . ."

At once all flew to carry out the sage suggestion; a fearful bustle followed. They had to light the candle. Mr. Bahtcheyev drew up a chair and got up on it to put the candle before the holy image, but immediately broke the chair and came down heavily on the floor—still on his feet, however. Not in the least irritated by this, he at once respectfully made way for Miss Perepelitsyn. The slender Miss Perepelitsyn had done the job in a flash: the candle was lighted. The nun and the lady companions began crossing themselves and bowing down to the ground. They took down the image of the Saviour and carried it to Madame la Générale. My uncle and Nastya went down on their knees again and the ceremony was carried out under the pious instructions of Miss Perepelitsyn, who was saying every minute: "Bow down to her feet, kiss the image, kiss your mamma's hand." Mr. Bahtcheyev thought himself bound to kiss the image after the betrothed couple, and at the same time he kissed the hand of Madame la Générale.

"Hurrah!" he shouted again. "Come, now we will have some champagne."

Everyone, however, was delighted. Madame la Générale was weeping, but it was now with tears of joy. Foma's blessing had at once made the union sanctified and suitable, and what mattered most to her was that Foma Fomitch had distinguished himself and that now he would remain with her for ever. All the lady companions, in appearance at least, shared the general satisfaction. My uncle at one moment was on his

knees kissing his mother's hands, at the next was flying to
embrace me, Bahtcheyev, Mizintchikov and Yezhevikin.
Ilyusha he almost smothered in his embraces. Sasha ran to hug
and kiss Nastenka. Praskovya Ilyinitchna dissolved into tears.
Bahtcheyev, noticing this, went up to kiss her hand. Poor old
Yezhevikin was completely overcome, he was weeping in a
corner and was wiping his eyes with the same check handkerchief. In another corner Gavrila was whimpering and gazing
reverently at Foma Fomitch, and Falaley was sobbing loudly
and going up to each of the company in turn, kissing his hand.
All were overwhelmed with feeling; no one yet had begun to
talk, or explain things; it seemed as though everything had
been said; nothing was heard but joyful exclamations. No one
understood yet how all this had been so quickly arranged. They
knew one thing only, that it had all been arranged by Foma
Fomitch, and that this was a solid fact which could not be
changed.

But not five minutes had passed after the general rejoicing,
when suddenly Tatyana Ivanovna made her appearance
among us. In what way, by what intuition could she, sitting
in her own room upstairs, have so quickly divined love and
marriage below? She fluttered in with a radiant face, with
tears of joy in her eyes, in a fascinating and elegant get-up (she
had had time to change her dress before coming down), and
flew straight to embrace Nastenka with loud exclamations.

"Nastenka, Nastenka! You loved him and I did not know!"
she cried. "Goodness! They loved each other, they suffered
in silence! They have been persecuted. What a romance!
Nastya, darling, tell me the whole truth: do you really love
this crazy fellow?"

By way of reply Nastya hugged and kissed her.

"My goodness, what a fascinating romance!" And Tatyana
Ivanovna clapped her hands in delight. "Nastya, listen, my
angel: all these men, all, every one, are ungrateful wretches,
monsters, and not worthy of our love. But perhaps he is the
best of them. Come to me, you crazy fellow!" she cried,
addressing my uncle and clutching him by the arm. "Are you
really in love? Are you really capable of loving? Look at me,
I want to look into your eyes, I want to see whether those
eyes are lying or not? No, no, they are not lying; there is the
light of love in them. Oh, how happy I am! Nastenka, my
dear, you are not rich—I shall make you a present of thirty
thousand roubles. Take it, for God's sake. I don't want it, I

don't want it; I shall have plenty left. No, no, no," she cried, waving her hand as she saw Nastenka was meaning to refuse. "Don't you speak, Yegor Ilyitch, it is not your affair. No, Nastya, I had made up my mind already to give you the money; I have been wanting to make you a present for a long time, and was only waiting for you to be in love. . . . I shall see your happiness. You will wound me if you don't take it; I shall cry, Nastya. No, no, no and no!"

Tatyana Ivanovna was so overjoyed that for the moment at least it was impossible, it would have been a pity indeed, to cross her. They could not bring themselves to do it, but put it off. She flew to kiss Madame la Générale, Miss Perepelitsyn and all of us. Mr. Bahtcheyev squeezed his way up to her very respectfully and asked to kiss her hand.

"My dear, good girl! Forgive an old fool like me for what happened this morning. I didn't know what a heart of gold you had."

"Crazy fellow! I know you," Tatyana Ivanovna lisped with gleeful playfulness. She gave Mr. Bahtcheyev a flick on the nose with her glove, and swishing against him with her gorgeous skirts, fluttered away like a zephyr.

The fat man stepped aside respectfully.

"A very worthy young lady!" he said with feeling. "They have stuck a nose on to the German! You know!" he whispered to me confidentially, looking at me joyfully.

"What nose? What German?" I asked in surprise.

"Why, the one I ordered, the German kissing his lady's hand while she is wiping away a tear with her handkerchief. Only yesterday my Yevdokem mended it; and when we came back from our expedition this morning I sent a man on horseback to fetch it. . . . They will soon be bringing it. A superb thing."

"Foma!" cried my uncle in a frenzy of delight. "It is you who have made our happiness. How can I reward you?"

"Nohow, Colonel," replied Foma, with a sanctimonious air. *"Continue to pay no attention to me* and be happy without Foma."

He was evidently piqued; in the general rejoicing he seemed, as it were, forgotten.

"It is all due to our joy, Foma," cried my uncle. "I don't know whether I am on my head or my feet. Listen, Foma, I have insulted you. My whole blood is not enough to atone for my wrong to you, and that is why I say nothing and do not even beg your pardon. But if ever you have need of my head, my life, if you ever want someone to throw himself over a precipice for your sake, call upon me, and you shall see. . . . I will say nothing more, Foma."

And my uncle waved his hand, fully recognising the impossibility of adding anything that could more strongly express his feeling. He only gazed at Foma with grateful eyes full of tears.

"See what an angel he is!" Miss Perepelitsyn piped in her turn in adulation of Foma.

"Yes, yes," Sashenka put in. "I did not know you were such a good man, Foma Fomitch, and I was disrespectful to you. But forgive me, Foma Fomitch, and you may be sure I will love you with all my heart. If you knew how much I respect you now!"

"Yes, Foma," Bahtcheyev chimed in. "Forgive an old fool like me too. I didn't know you, I didn't know you. You are not merely a learned man, Foma, but also—simply a hero. My whole house is at your service. But there, the best of all would be, if you would come to me the day after to-morrow, old man, with Madame la Générale too, and the betrothed couple—the whole company, in fact. And we will have a dinner, I tell you. I won't praise it beforehand, but one thing I can say, you will find everything you want unless it is bird's milk. I give you my word of honour."

In the midst of these demonstrations, Nastenka, too, went up to Foma Fomitch and without further words warmly embraced him and kissed him.

"Foma Fomitch," she said, "you have been a true friend to us, you have done so much for us, that I don't know how to repay you for it all; but I only know that I will be for you a most tender and respectful sister . . ."

She could say no more, she was choked by tears. Foma kissed her on the head and grew tearful.

"My children, the children of my heart," he said. "Live and prosper, and in moments of happiness think sometimes of the poor exile. For myself, I will only say that misfortune is perhaps the mother of virtue. That, I believe, is said by Gogol, a frivolous writer, but from whom one may sometimes glean fruitful thoughts. Exile is a misfortune. I shall wander like a pilgrim with my staff over the face of the earth, and who knows?—perchance my troubles will make me more righteous yet! That thought is the one consolation left me!"

"But . . . where are you going, Foma?" my uncle asked in alarm.

All were startled, and pressed round Foma.

"Why, do you suppose I can remain in your house after your behaviour this morning?" Foma inquired with extraordinary dignity.

But he was not allowed to finish, outcries from all the company smothered his voice. They made him sit down in an easychair, they besought him, they shed tears over him, and I don't know what they didn't do. Of course he hadn't the faintest intention of leaving "this house", just as he had not earlier that morning, nor the day before, nor on the occasion when he had taken to digging in the garden. He knew now that they would reverently detain him, would clutch at him, especially since he had made them all happy, since they all had faith in him again and were ready to carry him on their shoulders and to consider it an honour and a happiness to do so. But most likely his cowardly return, when he was frightened by the storm, was rankling in his mind and egging him on to play the hero in some way. And above all, there was such a temptation to give himself airs; the opportunity of talking, of using fine phrases and laying it on thick, of blowing his own trumpet, was too good for any possibility of resisting the temptation. He did not resist it; he tore himself out of the grasp of those who held him. He asked for his staff, besought them to let him have his freedom, to let him wander out into the wide wide world, declared that in *that house* he had been dishonoured, beaten, that he had only come back to make everyone happy, and, he asked, could he remain in this "house of ingratitude and eat soup, sustaining, perhaps, but seasoned with blows?" At last he left off struggling. He was reseated in his chair, but his eloquence was not arrested.

"Have I not been insulted here?" he cried. "Have I not been taunted? Haven't you, you yourself, Colonel, have you not every hour pointed the finger of scorn and made the long nose of derision at me, like the ignorant children of the working class in the streets of the town? Yes, Colonel, I insist on that comparison, because if you have not done so physically it has yet been a moral long nose, and in some cases a moral long nose is more insulting than a physical one. I say nothing of blows . . ."

"Foma, Foma," cried my uncle, "do not crush me with

these recollections. I have told you already that all my blood is not enough to wash out the insults. Be magnanimous! Forgive, forget, and remain to contemplate our happiness! Your work, Foma . . ."

"I want to love my fellow-man, to love him," cried Foma, "and they won't give me him, they forbid me to love him, they take him from me. Give me, give me my fellow-man that I may love him! Where is that fellow-man? Where is he hidden? Like Diogenes with his candle, I have been looking for him all my life and cannot find him; and I can love no one, to this day I cannot find the man. Woe to him who has made me a hater of mankind! I cry: give me my fellow-man that I may love him, and they thrust Falaley upon me! Am I to love Falaley? Do I want to love Falaley? Could I love Falaley, even if I wanted to? No. Why not? Because he is Falaley. Why do I not love humanity? Because all on earth are Falaleys or like Falaley. I don't want Falaley, I hate Falaley, I spit on Falaley, I trample Falaley under my feet. And if I had to choose I would rather love Asmodeus than Falaley. Come here, come here, my everlasting torment, come here," he cried, suddenly addressing Falaley, who was in the most innocent way standing on tiptoe, looking over the crowd that was surrounding Foma Fomitch. "Come here. I will show you, Colonel," cried Foma, drawing towards him Falaley, who was almost unconscious with terror, "I will show you the truth of my words about the everlasting long nose and finger of scorn! Tell me, Falaley, and tell the truth: what did you dream about last night? Come, Colonel, you will see your handiwork! Come, Falaley, tell us!"

The poor boy, shaking with terror, turned despairing eyes about him, looking for someone to rescue him; but everyone was in a tremor waiting for his answer.

"Come, Falaley, I am waiting."

Instead of answering, Falaley screwed up his face, opened his mouth wide, and began bellowing like a calf.

"Colonel! Do you see this stubbornness? Do you mean to tell me it's natural? For the last time I ask you, Falaley, tell me: what did you dream of last night?"

"O-of . . ."

"Say you dreamed of me," said Bahtcheyev.

"Of your virtue, sir," Yezhevikin prompted in his other ear.

Falaley merely looked about him.

"O-of . . . of your vir . . . of a white bu-ull," he roared at last, and burst into scalding tears.

Everyone groaned. But Foma Fomitch was in a paroxysm of extraordinary magnanimity.

"Anyway, I see your sincerity, Falaley," he said. "A sincerity I do not observe in others. God bless you! If you are purposely mocking at me with that dream at the instigation of others, God will repay you and those others. If not, I respect your truthfulness; for even in the lowest of creatures like you it is my habit to discern the image and semblance of God. . . . I forgive you, Falaley. Embrace me, my children. I will remain with you."

"He will remain!" they all cried in delight.

"I will remain and I will forgive. Colonel, reward Falaley with some sugar, do not let him cry on such a day of happiness for all."

I need hardly say that such magnanimity was thought astounding. To take *so much* thought at *such* a moment, and for whom? For Falaley. My uncle flew to carry out his instruction in regard to the sugar. Immediately a silver sugar-basin— I don't know where it came from—appeared in the hands of Praskovya Ilyinitchna. My uncle was about to take out two pieces with a trembling hand, then three, then he dropped them, at last, seeing he was incapable of doing anything from excitement.

"Ah!" he cried, "for a day like this! Hold out your coat, Falaley," and he poured into his coat all the contents of the sugar-basin. "That's for your truthfulness," he said, by way of edification.

"Mr. Korovkin!" Vidoplyasov announced, suddenly appearing in the doorway.

A slight flutter of consternation followed—Korovkin's visit was obviously ill-timed. They all looked inquiringly at my uncle.

"Korovkin!" cried my uncle, in some embarrassment. "Of course I am delighted . . ." he added, glancing timidly towards Foma; "but really I don't know whether to ask him in at such a moment. What do you think, Foma?"

"Oh, yes, why not," said Foma amicably. "Invite Korovkin too; let him, too, share in the general rejoicing."

In short, Foma Fomitch was in an angelic frame of mind.

"I most respectfully make bold to inform you," observed Vidoplyasov, "that the gentleman is not quite himself."

189

"Not quite himself? How? What nonsense are you talking?" cried my uncle.

"It is so, indeed; he is not quite in a sober condition."

But before my uncle had time to open his mouth, flush red, and show his alarm and extreme embarrassment, the mystery was explained. Korovkin appeared in the doorway, pushed Vidoplyasov aside and confronted the astonished company. He was a short, thick-set gentleman of forty, with dark hair touched with grey and closely cropped, with a round purple face and little bloodshot eyes, wearing a high horsehair cravat, fastened at the back with a buckle, an extraordinarily threadbare swallow-tail coat covered with fluff and hay and disclosing a bad rent under the arm, and unspeakable trousers, and carrying an incredibly greasy cap which he was holding out at arm's length. This gentleman was completely drunk. Advancing into the middle of the room, he stood still, staggering, nodding his head as though he were pecking at something with his nose in drunken hesitation; then he slowly grinned from ear to ear.

"Excuse me, ladies and gentlemen," he began, "I . . . er . . ." (here he gave a tug at his collar) "got 'em!"

Madame la Générale immediately assumed an air of offended dignity. Foma, sitting in his easy-chair, ironically looked the eccentric visitor up and down. Bahtcheyev stared at him in perplexity, through which some sympathy was, however, apparent. My uncle's embarrassment was incredible; he was deeply distressed on Korovkin's account.

"Korovkin," he began. "Listen."

"*Attendez!*" Korovkin interrupted him. "Let me introduce myself: a child of nature. . . . But what do I see? There are ladies here. . . . Why didn't you tell me, you rascal, that you had ladies here?" he added with a roguish smile. "Never mind! Don't be shy. Let us be presented to the fair sex. Charming ladies," he began, articulating with difficulty and stumbling over every word, "you see a luckless mortal . . . who . . . and so on. . . . The rest must remain unsaid. . . . Musicians! A polka!"

"Wouldn't you like a nap?" asked Mizintchikov, quietly going up to Korovkin.

"A nap? You say that to insult me?"

"Not at all. You know a little sleep is a good thing after a journey . . ."

"Never!" Korovkin answered with indignation. "Do you

think I am drunk?—not a bit. But where do they sleep here?"

"Come along, I'll take you at once."

"Where? In the coach-house? No, my lad, you won't take me in! I have spent a night there already. . . . Lead the way, though. Why not go along with a good fellow. . . . I don't want a pillow. A military man does not want a pillow. . . . But you produce a sofa for me, old man . . . a sofa. And, I say," he added, stopping, "I see you are a jolly fellow; produce something else for me . . . you know? A bit of the rummy, enough to drown a fly in, only enough for that, only one little glass, I mean."

"Very well, very well!" answered Mizintchikov.

"Very well. But you wait a bit, I must say good-bye. *Adieu, mesdames* and *mesdemoiselles*. You have, so to speak, smitten. . . . But there, never mind! We will talk about that afterwards . . . only do wake me when it begins . . . or even five minutes before it begins . . . don't begin without me! Do you hear? Don't begin! . . ."

And the merry gentleman vanished behind Mizintchikov.

Everyone was silent. The company had not got over their astonishment. At last Foma without a word began noiselessly chuckling, his laughter grew into a guffaw. Seeing that, Madame la Générale, too, was amused, though the expression of insulted dignity still remained on her face. Irrepressible laughter arose on all sides. My uncle stood as though paralysed, flushing almost to tears, and was for some time incapable of uttering a word.

"Merciful heavens!" he brought out at last. "Who could have known this? But you know . . . you know it might happen to anyone. Foma, I assure you that he is a most straightforward, honourable man, and an extremely well-read man too, Foma . . . you will see! . . ."

"I do see, I do see," cried Foma, shaking with laughter; "extraordinarily well-read. Well-read is just the word."

"How he can talk about railways!" Yezhevikin observed in an undertone.

"Foma," my uncle was beginning, but the laughter of all the company drowned his words. Foma Fomitch was simply in fits, and looking at him, my uncle began laughing too.

"Well, what does it matter?" he said enthusiastically. "You are magnanimous, Foma, you have a great heart; you have made me happy . . . you forgive Korovkin too."

Nastenka was the only one who did not laugh. She looked

with eyes full of love at her future husband, and looked as though she would say—

"How splendid, how kind you are, the most generous of men, and how I love you!"

CHAPTER VI

CONCLUSION

FOMA'S triumph was complete and beyond attack. Certainly without him nothing would have been settled, and the accomplished fact stifled all doubts and objections. The gratitude of those he had made happy was beyond all bounds. My uncle and Nastya waved me off when I attempted to drop a faint hint at the process by which Foma's consent to their marriage had been obained. Sashenka cried: "Good, kind Foma Fomitch; I will embroider him a cushion in woolwork!" and even reproached me for my hard-heartedness. I believe that Bahtecheyev in the fervour of his conversion would have strangled me if I had ventured to say anything disrespectful about Foma Fomitch. He followed Foma about like a little dog, gazed at him with devout reverence, and at every word the latter uttered he would exclaim: "You are a noble man, Foma. You are a learned man, Foma." As for Yezhevikin, he was highly delighted. The old man had for a long time past seen that Nastenka had turned Yegor Ilyitch's head, and from that time forward his one dream, waking and sleeping, was to bring about this marriage. He had clung to the idea to the last, and had only given it up when it had been impossible not to do so. Foma had changed the aspect of the affair. I need hardly say that in spite of his delight the old man saw through Foma; in short, it was clear that Foma Fomitch would be supreme in that household for ever, and that there would be no limit to his despotism. We all know that even the most unpleasant and ill-humoured people are softened, if only for a time, when their desires are gratified. Foma Fomitch, on the contrary, seemed to grow stupider when he was successful, and held his nose higher in the air than ever. Just before dinner, having changed all his clothes, he settled down in an arm-chair, summoned my uncle, and in the presence of the whole family began giving him another lecture.

"Colonel," he began, "you are about to enter upon holy matrimony. Do you realise the obligation . . ."

And so on and so on. Imagine ten pages of the size of the *Journal des Débats*, of the smallest print, filled with the wildest nonsense, in which there was absolutely nothing dealing with the duties of marriage, but only the most shameful eulogies of the intellect, mildness, magnanimity, manliness and disinterestedness of himself, Foma Fomitch. Everyone was hungry, they all wanted their dinners; but in spite of that no one dared to protest, and everyone heard the twaddle reverently to the end. Even Bahtcheyev, in spite of his ravenous appetite, sat without stirring, absolutely respectful. Gratified by his own eloquence, Foma Fomitch grew livelier, and even drank rather heavily at dinner, proposing the most extraordinary toasts. He proceeded to display his wit by being jocose, at the expense of the happy pair, of course. Everybody laughed and applauded. But some of the jokes were so gross and suggestive that even Bahtcheyev was embarrassed by them. At last Nastenka jumped up from the table and ran away, to the indescribable delight of Foma Fomitch, but he immediately pulled himself up. Briefly but in strong terms he dwelt upon Nastenka's virtues, and proposed a toast to the health of the absent one. My uncle, who a minute before had been embarrassed and unhappy, was ready to hug Foma Fomitch again. Altogether the betrothed pair seemed somewhat ashamed of each other and their happiness—and I noticed that they had not said a word to each other from the time of the blessing, they even seemed to avoid looking at one another. When they got up from dinner, my uncle vanished, I don't know where. I strolled out on to the terrace to look for him. There I found Foma sitting in an easy-chair, drinking coffee and holding forth, extremely exhilarated. Only Yezhevikin, Bahtcheyev and Mizintchikov were by him. I stopped to listen.

"Why," asked Foma, "am I ready at this moment to go through fire for my convictions? And why it it that none of you are capable of going through fire? Why is it? Why is it?"

"Well, but it's unnecessary, Foma Fomitch, to go through fire," Yezhevikin said banteringly. "Why, what's the sense of it? In the first place it would hurt, and in the second it would burn—what would be left?"

"What would be left? Noble ashes would be left. But how should you understand, how should you appreciate me? To you, no great men exist but perhaps some Cæsar or Alexander of Macedon. And what did your Cæsars do? Whom did they make happy? What did your vaunted Alexander of Macedon do? He conquered the whole earth? But give me such a phalanx and I could be a conqueror too, and so could you, and so could he. . . . On the other hand, he killed the virtuous Clitus, but I have not killed the virtuous Clitus. . . . A puppy, a scoundrel! He ought to have had a thrashing, and not to have been glorified in universal history . . . and Cæsar with him!"

"You might spare Cæsar, anyway, Foma Fomitch!"

"I won't spare the fool!" cried Foma.

"No, don't spare him!" Bahtcheyev, who had also been drinking, backed him up. "There is no need to spare them, they are all flighty fellows, they care for nothing but pirouetting on one leg! Sausage-eaters! Here, one of them was wanting to found a scholarship just now—and what is a scholarship? The devil only knows what it means! I bet it's some new villainy! And here is another who in honourable society is staggering about and asking for rum. I have no objection to drinking. But one should drink and drink and then take a rest, and afterwards, maybe, drink again. It's no good sparing them! They are all scoundrels. You are the only enlightened one among them, Foma!"

If Bahtcheyev surrendered to anyone he surrendered unconditionally and absolutely without criticism.

I looked for my uncle in the garden, by the pond in the most secluded spot. He was with Nastenka. Seeing me, Nastenka shot into the bushes as though she were in fault. My uncle came to meet me with a beaming face; there were tears of happiness in his eyes. He took both my hands and warmly pressed them.

"My dear," he said, "I still cannot believe in my happiness. . . . Nastya feels the same. We only marvel and glorify the Almighty. She was crying just now. Would you believe it, I hardly know what I am doing yet, I am still utterly beside myself, and don't know whether to believe it or not! And why has this come to me? Why? What have I done? How have I deserved it?"

"If anyone deserves anything, it is you, uncle," I said with conviction. "I have never seen such an honest, such a fine, such a kind-hearted man as you."

"No, Seryozha, no, it is too much," he answered, as it were

with regret. "What is bad is that we are kind (I am talking only about myself really) when we are happy; but when we are unhappy it is best not to come near us! Nastenka and I were only just talking of that. Though I was dazzled by Foma, up to this very day perhaps, would you believe it, I did not quite believe in him, though I did assure you of his perfection; even yesterday I did not believe in him when he refused such a present! To my shame I say it. My heart shudders at the memory of this morning, but I could not control myself. . . . When he spoke of Nastya something seemed to stab me to the very heart. I did not understand and behaved like a tiger. . . ."

"Well, uncle, perhaps that was only natural."

My uncle waved away the idea.

"No, no, my boy, don't say so. The fact of it is, all this comes from the depravity of my nature, from my being a gloomy and sensual egoist and abandoning myself to my passions without restraint. That's what Foma says." (What could one answer to that?) "You don't know, Seryozha," he went on with deep feeling, "how often I have been irritable, unfeeling, unjust, haughty, and not only to Foma. Now it has all come back to my mind, and I feel ashamed that I have done nothing hitherto to deserve such happiness. Nastya has just said the same thing, though I really don't know what sins she has, as she is an angel, not a human being! She has just been saying that we owe a terrible debt of gratitude to God; that we must try now to be better and always to be doing good deeds. . . . And if only you had heard how fervently, how beautifully she said all that! My God, what a wonderful girl!"

He stopped in agitation. A minute later he went on.

"We resolved, my dear boy, to cherish Foma in particular, mamma and Tatyana Ivanovna. Tatyana Ivanovna! What a generous-hearted creature! Oh, how much I have been to blame towards all of them! I have behaved badly to you too. . . . But if anyone should dare to insult Tatyana Ivanovna now, oh! then. . . . Oh, well, never mind! . . . We must do something for Mizintchikov too."

"Yes, uncle, I have changed my opinion of Tatyana Ivanovna now. One cannot help respecting her and feeling for her."

"Just so, just so," my uncle assented warmly. "One can't help respecting her! Now Korovkin, for instance, no doubt you laugh at him," he added, glancing at me timidly, "and we all laughed at him this afternoon. And yet, you know, that was perhaps unpardonable. . . . You know, he may be an excellent, good-hearted man, but fate . . . he has had misfortunes. . . . You don't believe it, but perhaps it really is so."

"No, uncle, why shouldn't I believe it?"

And I began fervently declaring that even in the creature who has fallen lowest there may still survive the finest human feelings; that the depths of the human soul are unfathomable; that we must not despise the fallen, but on the contrary ought to seek them out and raise them up; that the commonly accepted standards of goodness and morality were not infallible, and so on, and so on; in fact I warmed up to the subject, and even began talking about the realist school. In conclusion I even repeated the verses: 'When from dark error's subjugation' . . ."

My uncle was extraordinarily delighted.

"My dear, my dear," he said, much touched, "you understand me fully, and have said much better than I could what I wanted to express. Yes, yes! Good heavens! Why is it man is wicked? Why is it that I am so often wicked when it is so splendid, so fine to be good? Nastya was saying the same thing just now. . . . But look, though, what a glorious place this is," he added, looking round him. "What scenery! What a picture! What a tree! Look: you could hardly get your arms round it. What sap! What foliage! What sunshine! How gay everything is, washed clean after the storm! . . . One would think that even the trees understand something, have feeling and enjoyment of life. . . . Is that out of the question —eh? What do you think?"

"It's very likely they do, uncle, in their own way, of course. . . ."

"Oh, yes, in their own way, of course. . . . Marvellous, marvellous is the Creator! You must remember all this garden very well, Seryozha; how you used to race about and play in it when you were little! I remember, you know, when you were little," he added, looking at me with an indescribable expression of love and happiness. "You were not allowed to go to the pond alone. But do you remember one evening dear Katya called you to her and began fondling you. . . . You had been running in the garden just before, and were flushed; your hair was so fair and curly. . . . She kept playing with it, and said: 'It is a good thing that you have taken the little orphan to live with us!' Do you remember?"

"Faintly, uncle."

"It was evening, and you were both bathed in the glow of sunset, I was sitting in a corner smoking a pipe and watching you. . . . I drive into the town every month to her grave. . . ." he added, dropping his voice, which quivered with suppressed tears. "I was just speaking to Nastya about it; she said we would go together. . . ."

My uncle paused, trying to control his emotion. At that instant Vidoplyasov came up to us.

"Vidoplyasov!" said my uncle, starting. "Have you come from Foma Fomitch?"

"No, I have come more on my own affairs."

"Oh, well, that's capital. Now we shall hear about Korovkin. I wanted to inquire. . . . I told him to look after him—Korovkin I mean. What's the matter, Vidoplyasov?"

"I make bold to remind you," said Vidoplyasov, "that yesterday you were graciously pleased to refer to my petition and to promise me your noble protection from the daily insults I receive."

"Surely you are not harping on your surname again?" cried my uncle in alarm.

"What can I do? Hourly insults . . ."

"Oh, Vidoplyasov, Vidoplyasov! What am I to do with you?" said my uncle in distress. "Why, what insults can you have to put up with? You will simply go out of your mind. You will end your days in a madhouse!"

"I believe I am in my right mind . . ." Vidoplyasov was beginning.

"Oh, of course, of course," my uncle interposed. "I did not say that to offend you, my boy, but for your good. Why, what sort of insults do you complain of? I am ready to bet that it is only some nonsense."

"They won't let me pass."

"Who interferes with you?"

"They all do, and chiefly owing to Matryona. My life is a misery through her. It is well known that all discriminating people who have seen me from my childhood up have said that I am exactly like a foreigner, especially in the features of the face. Well, sir, now they won't let me pass on account of it. As soon as I go by, they all shout all sorts of bad words after me; even the little children, who ought to be whipped, shout

after me. . . . As I came along here now they shouted. . . .
I can't stand it. Defend me, sir, with your protection!"

"Oh, Vidoplyasov! Well, what did they shout? No doubt
it was some foolishness that you ought not to notice."

"It would not be proper to repeat."

"Why, what was it?"

"It's a disgusting thing to say."

"Well, say it!"

"Grishka the dandy has eaten the candy."

"Foo, what a man! I thought it was something serious!
You should spit, and pass by."

"I did spit, they shouted all the more."

"But listen, uncle," I said. "You see he complains that he
can't get on in this house; send him to Moscow for a time, to
that calligrapher. You told me that he was trained by a
calligrapher."

"Well, my dear, that man, too, came to a tragic end."

"Why, what happened to him?"

"He had the misfortune," Vidoplyasov replied, "to appro-
priate the property of another, for which in spite of his talent
he was put in prison, where he is ruined irrevocably."

"Very well, Vidoplyasov, calm yourself now, and I will go
into it all and set it right," said my uncle, "I promise! Well,
what news of Korovkin? Is he asleep?"

"No, sir, his honour has just gone away. I came to tell
you."

"What? Gone away! What do you mean? How could
you let him go?" cried my uncle.

"Through the kindness of my heart, sir, it was pitiful to see
him, sir. When he came to himself and remembered all the
proceedings, he struck himself on the forehead and shouted at
the top of his voice . . ."

"At the top of his voice! . . ."

"It would be more respectful to express it, he gave utterance
to many varied lamentations. He cried out: how could he
present himself now to the fair sex? And then he added:
'I am unworthy to be a man!' and he kept talking so pitifully
in choice language."

"A man of refined feeling! I told you, Sergey. . . . But
how could you let him go, Vidoplyasov, when I told you particularly to look after him? Oh, dear! oh, dear!"

"It was through the pity of my heart. He begged me not
to tell you. His cabman fed the horses and harnessed them.

And for the sum lent him three days ago, he begged me to thank you most respectfully and say that he would send the money by one of the first posts."

"What money is that, uncle?"

"He mentioned twenty-five silver roubles," answered Vidoplyasov.

"I lent it him at the station, my dear; he hadn't enough with him. Of course he will send it by the first post. . . . Oh, dear, how sorry I am! Shouldn't we send someone to overtake him, Seryozha?"

"No, uncle, better not send."

"I think so too. You see, Seryozha, I am not a philosophei of course, but I believe there is much more good in every man than appears on the surface. Korovkin now: he couldn't face the shame of it. . . . But let us go to Foma! We have lingered here a long time; he may be wounded by our ingratitude, and neglect. . . . Let us go. Oh, Korovkin, Korovkin!"

My story is ended. The lovers were united, and their good genius in the form of Foma Fomitch held undisputed sway. I might at this point make very many befitting observations; but in reality all such observations are now completely superfluous. Such, anyway, is my opinion. I will instead say a few words about the subsequent fortunes of all the heroes of my tale. As is well known, no story is finished without this, and indeed it is prescribed by the rules.

The wedding of the couple who had been so graciously "made happy" took place six weeks after the events I have described. It was a quiet family affair, without much display or superfluous guests. I was Nastenka's best man, Mizintchikov was my uncle's. There were some visitors, however. But the foremost, the leading figure, was of course Foma Fomitch. He was made much of; he was carried on their shoulders. But it somehow happened that on this one occasion he was overcome by champagne. A scene followed, with all the accompaniment of reproaches, lamentations and outcries. Foma ran off to his room, locked himself in, cried that he was held in contempt, that now "new people had come into the family and that he was therefore nothing, not more than a bit of rubbish that must be thrown away." My uncle was in despair; Nastenka wept; Madame la Générale, as usual, had an attack of hysterics. . . . The wedding festival was like a funeral. And seven years of living like that with their benefactor, Foma

Fomitch, fell to the lot of my poor uncle and poor Nastenka. Up to the time of his death (Foma Fomitch died a year ago), he was sulky, gave himself airs, was ill-humoured and quarrelsome; but the reverence for him of the couple he had "made happy", far from diminishing, actually increased every day with his caprices. Yegor Ilyitch and Nastenka were so happy with each other that they were actually afraid of their happiness, and thought that God had given them too much, that they were not worthy of such blessings; and were inclined to expect that their latter days would be spent in hardship and suffering to atone for them. It will be readily understood that in this meek household, Foma Fomitch could do anything that took his fancy. And what did he not do in those seven years! One could never imagine to what unbridled absurdities his pampered, idle soul led him in inventing the most perverse, morally Sybaritic caprices. My grandmother died three years after my uncle's marriage. Foma was stricken with despair at his bereavement. His condition at the time is described with horror in my uncle's household to this day. When they were throwing earth into the grave, he leapt into it, shouting that he would be buried in it too. For a whole month they would not give him a knife or fork; and on one occasion four of them forced open his mouth and took out of it a pin which he was trying to swallow. An outsider who witnessed the conflict, observed that Foma Fomitch might have swallowed the pin a thousand times over during the struggle, but did not, however, do so. But everyone heard this criticism with positive indignation, and at once charged the critic with hard-heartedness and bad manners. Only Nastenka held her peace and gave a faint smile, while my uncle looked at her with some uneasiness. It must be observed that though Foma gave himself airs, and indulged his whims in my uncle's house as before, yet the insolent and despotic presumption with which he used to rail at my uncle was now a thing of the past. Foma complained, wept, blamed, reproached, cried shame, but did not scold as he had done—there was never another scene like the one concerned with "your Excellency", and this, I think, was due to Nastenka. Almost imperceptibly she compelled Foma to yield some points and to recognise some limits. She would not see her husband humiliated, and insisted on her wishes being respected. Foma perceived clearly that she almost understood him. I say *almost*, for Nastenka, too, humoured Foma and even seconded her husband whenever he sang the praises of his mentor. She tried to make other people, too, respect everything in her husband, and so publicly justified his devotion to Foma Fomitch. But I am sure that Nastenka's pure heart had forgiven all the insults of the past; she forgave Foma everything when he brought about her marriage. And what is more, I believe she seriously with all her heart entered into my uncle's idea that too much must not be expected from a "victim" who had once been a buffoon, but on the contrary, balm must be poured on his wounded heart. Poor Nastenka had herself been one of the *humiliated,* she had suffered and she remembered it. A month after the death of his old patroness, Foma became quieter, even mild and friendly; but on the other hand, he began to have quite sudden attacks of a different sort —he would fall into a sort of magnetic trance, which alarmed everyone extremely. Suddenly, for instance, the sufferer, while saying something, or even laughing, would in one instant become unconscious and rigid, and rigid in the very position he happened to be in a moment before the attack. If, for instance, he was laughing, he would remain with a smile on his lips; if he were holding something, a fork for instance, the fork would remain in his raised hand. Later on, of course, the hand would drop, but Foma Fomitch felt nothing and knew nothing of its dropping. He would sit, stare, even blink, but would say nothing, hear nothing, and understand nothing. This would last sometimes for a whole hour. Of course everyone in the house nearly died of fright, held their breath, walked about on tiptoe and shed tears. At last Foma would wake up feeling terribly exhausted, and would declare that he had seen and heard absolutely nothing all that time. The man must have been so perverse, so eager to show off, that he endured whole hours of voluntary agony, solely in order to say afterwards: "Look at me, I even feel more intensely than you." Finally Foma cursed my uncle for the "hourly slights and insults" he received from him, and went to stay with Mr. Bahtcheyev. The latter, who had quarrelled with Foma Fomitch many times since my uncle's marriage, but always ended by begging his pardon, on this occasion took the matter up with extraordinary warmth; he welcomed Foma with enthusiasm, stuffed him with good things, and at once resolved on a formal breach with my uncle, and even on lodging a complaint against him. There was a bit of land in dispute between them, though they never disputed about it, for my uncle had yielded all claim to it and had freely given it to Mr. Bahtcheyev. Without saying a word to anyone, Mr. Bahtcheyev ordered out his carriage, drove off to the town, there scribbled off a petition and handed it in, appealing to the court to adjudge him the land formally with compensation for loss and damage and so to punish contumacy and robbery. Meanwhile next day Foma Fomitch, getting bored at Mr. Bahtcheyev's, forgave my uncle, who came to apologise, and went back to Stepantchikovo. The wrath of Mr. Bahtcheyev, when he returned from the town and did not find Foma, was terrible; but three days later, he turned up at Stepantchikovo to apologise, begged my uncle's pardon with tears in his eyes, and quashed his petition. My uncle made the peace between him and Foma Fomitch the same day, and Bahtcheyev followed Foma Fomitch about like a little dog, and again said at every word: "You are a clever fellow, Foma! You are a learned man, Foma!"

Foma Fomitch is now lying in his grave near his old patroness; over him stands an expensive monument of white marble covered with lamentations and eulogistic inscriptions. Yegor Ilyitch and Nastenka sometimes go for a walk to the cemetery to pay reverent homage to his memory. They cannot even now speak of him without great feeling; they recall all his sayings, what he ate, what he liked. His things have been preserved as priceless treasures. Feeling so bereaved, my uncle and Nastya grew even more attached to each other. God has not granted them children; they grieve over this, but dare not repine. Sashenka has long been married to an excellent young man. Ilyusha is studying in Moscow. And so my uncle and Nastya are alone together, and are devoted to each other. Their anxiety over each other is almost morbid. Nastya prays unceasingly. If one of them dies first, I think the other will not survive a week. But God grant them long life. They receive everyone with a most cordial welcome, and are ready to share all they have with anyone who is unfortunate. Nastenka is fond of reading the lives of the saints, and says with compunction that to do ordinary good work is not enough, that one ought to give everything to the poor and be happy in poverty. But for his concern for Ilyusha and Sashenka, my uncle would have done this long ago, for he always agrees with his wife in everything. Praskovya Ilyinitchna lives with them, and enjoys looking after their comfort; she superintends the management of the place. Mr. Bahtcheyev made her an offer of marriage very soon after my uncle's wedding, but she refused him point-blank. It was concluded from that that she would go into a nunnery, but that did not come off either. There is one striking peculiarity about Praskovya Ilyinitchna's character: the craving to obliterate herself completely for the sake of those she loves, to efface herself continually for them, to watch for their every inclination, to humour all their caprices, to wait upon them and serve them. Now, on the death of her mother, she considers it her duty not to leave her brother, and to take care of Nastenka in every way. Old Yezhevikin is still living, and has taken to visiting his daughter more and more frequently of late. At first he drove my uncle to despair by absenting himself from Stepantchikovo almost entirely, and also keeping away his "small fry" (as he called his children). All my uncle's invitations were in vain; he was not so much proud as sensitive and touchy. His over-sensitive amour-propre sometimes approached morbidity. The idea that he, a poor man, should be entertained in a wealthy house from kindness, that he might be regarded as an intrusive and unwelcome guest, was too much for him; he sometimes even declined Nastenka's help, and only accepted what was absolutely essential. From my uncle he would take absolutely nothing. Nastenka was quite mistaken when she told me that time in the garden that her father played the fool for *her sake*. It was true that he was extremely eager at that time to marry Nastenka to Yegor Ilyitch; but he acted as he did simply through an inner craving to give vent to his accumulated malice. The impulse to jeer and mock was in his blood. He posed as the most abject, grovelling flatterer, but at the same time made it perfectly clear that he was only doing this for show; and the more cringing his flattery, the more malignantly and openly apparent was the mockery behind it. It was his way. All his children were successfully placed in the best scholastic establishments in Moscow and Petersburg. But this was only after Nastenka had made it perfectly clear to him that it was being paid for out of her own pocket, that is, out of the thirty thousand given her by Tatyana Ivanovna. That thirty thousand she had actually never taken from Tatyana Ivanovna; but not to grieve and mortify her, they appeased her by promising to appeal to her at any sudden emergency. What they did was this: to satisfy her, considerable sums were borrowed from her on two occasions. But Tatyana Ivanovna died three years ago, and Nastya received her thirty thousand all the same. The death of poor Tatyana Ivanovna was sudden. The whole family were getting ready for a ball given by a neighbour, and she had hardly decked herself out in her ball-dress and put on a fascinating wreath of white roses, when she suddenly felt giddy, sat down in an easy-chair and died. They buried her in the wreath. Nastya was in despair. Tatyana Ivanovna had been cherished and looked after like a little child in the house. She astonished everyone by the good sense of her will. Apart from Nastenka's thirty thousand, her whole fortune of three hundred thousand was devoted to the education of poor orphan girls and the provision of a sum of money for each on leaving the institution. In the year that she died Miss Perepelitsyn was married; on the death of Madame la Générale she had remained in the family in the hope of ingratiating herself with Tatyana Ivanovna. Meanwhile the petty official who had bought Mishino, the little village in which our scene with Obnoskin and his mother over Tatyana Ivanovna took place, was left a widower. This individual was terribly fond of going to law, and had six children. Supposing that Miss Perepelitsyn had money, he began making proposals to her through a third person and she promptly accepted them. But Miss Perepelitsyn was as poor as a hen, her whole fortune was three hundred silver roubles, and that was given her by Nastenka on her wedding day. Now the husband and wife are quarrelling from morning till night. She pulls his children's hair, and boxes their ears; as for him, she scratches his face (so people say), and is constantly throwing her superior station as a major's daughter in his face. Mizintchikov has also established himself. He very sensibly gave up all his hopes of Tatyana Ivanovna, and began little by little to learn farming. My uncle recommended him to a wealthy count, who had an estate of three thousand serfs, sixty miles from Stepantchikovo, and who occasionally visited his property. Observing Mizintchikov's abilities, and influenced by my uncle's recommendation of him, the count offered him the post of steward on his estate, dismissed his former German steward, who in spite of the vaunted German honesty stripped his master like a lime tree. Five years later the estate was unrecognisable: the peasants were prosperous; the farming was developed in ways previously impossible; the returns were almost doubled; in fact the new steward distinguished himself, and was talked of for his abilities as a farmer all over the province. Great was the amazement and chagrin of the count when at the end of the five years Mizintchikov insisted on giving up his situation in spite of all protests and offers of increased salary! The count imagined that he had been lured away by a rival landowner in his own neighbourhood or in another province. And everyone was astonished when, two months after giving up his post, Mizintchikov acquired an excellent estate of a hundred serfs, about thirty miles from the count's, purchased from a hussar, a friend of his who had squandered all his fortune! The hundred serfs he promptly mortgaged, and a year later he had acquired another property of sixty serfs in the neighbourhood. Now he is a landowner, and the management of his estate is unequalled. Everyone wonders how he came by the money all at once. Some people shake their heads. But Mizintchikov is perfectly self-possessed, and feels that he is absolutely right. He has sent for his sister from Moscow, the sister who gave him her last three roubles to buy boots when he was setting off for Stepantchikovo—a very sweet girl, no longer in her first youth, gentle and loving, well-educated, but extremely timid. She had been all the time dragging out a miserable existence in Moscow as a companion to some charitable lady. Now she worships her brother, and keeps house for him; she regards his will as law and thinks herself happy. Her brother does not spoil her, he makes her work rather hard, but she does not notice it. She has become a great favourite at Stepantchikovo, and I am told that Mr. Bahtcheyev is not indifferent to her. He would make her an offer, but is afraid of being refused. We hope, however, to give a fuller account of Mr. Bahtcheyev's doings in another story.

Well, I think I have dealt with all the characters of Stepantchikovo. . . . Oh! I had forgotten: Gavrila has greatly aged and completely forgotten his French; Falaley has made a very decent coachman; while poor Vidoplyasov was for many years in a madhouse and, I believe, died there. In a few days I am going to Stepantchikovo, and will certainly inquire about him from my uncle.

NYETOCHKA NYEZVANOV

—

CHAPTER I

I DON'T remember my father. He died when I was two years old. My mother married a second time. This second marriage brought her a great deal of sorrow, though it was a marriage of love. My stepfather was a musician. His history was a remarkable one: he was the strangest, the most extraordinary man I have ever known'. His image is very vivid among the earliest impressions of my childhood, so vivid that those impressions have had an influence on the whole of my life. First of all, to make my story intelligible, I will give a sketch of his biography. Everything which I am now going to tell you I learned later on from the celebrated violinist B., who was a comrade and an intimate friend of my stepfather's in his youth.

My stepfather's surname was Yefimov. He was born on the estate of a very rich landowner and was the son of a poor musician, who after years of wandering had settled on the estate of this landowner and played in the latter's orchestra. The landowner lived in luxurious style, and loved music passionately, above everything. The story was told of him that, though he never left home even to go to Moscow, yet on one occasion he took it into his head to go to some watering-place abroad, and that he went there for no longer than a few weeks with the sole object of hearing a famous violinist who, as the newspapers announced, was going to give three concerts at the watering-place. He had himself a fairly good orchestra of musicians, on which he spent almost the whole of his income. This orchestra my stepfather entered as clarinet player. He was twenty-two years old when he made the acquaintance of a strange man. In the same district there was living a wealthy count, who ruined himself over keeping up a private theatre in his house. This count had dismissed the conductor of his orchestra, an Italian, for bad conduct. This Italian certainly was a bad man. After he had been turned off he sank into complete degradation. He took to going from one village tavern to another, got drunk, sometimes begged, and there was no one in the whole province who would employ him. It was with this fellow that my stepfather made friends. This connection was strange and inexplicable, for no one noticed that he changed for the worse in his behaviour through imitation of his friend; and even his patron himself, who had at first forbidden him to associate with the Italian, afterwards winked at their friendship. At last the Italian met with a sudden death. One morning he was found by some peasants in a ditch by the dam. An inquest was held, and it appeared that he had died of an apoplectic fit. His belongings were in the keeping of my stepfather, who promptly produced evidence that he was entitled to take possession of them: the Italian had left a note in his own handwriting bequeathing everything he had to my stepfather in case of his death. The property consisted of a black frock-coat which had been carefully preserved by its late owner, as he never gave up hope of getting a situation, and of a rather ordinary-looking violin. Nobody disputed the inheritance. But a short time afterwards, the first violin of the count's orchestra came to the landowner with a letter from the count, in which the latter begged him to persuade Yefimov in sell the violin left him by the Italian, as he greatly desired to obtain it for his orchestra. He offered three thousand roubles, and added that he had several times already sent for Yegor Yefimov in order that he might arrange the sale with him personally, but had always met with an obstinate refusal from the latter. The count concluded by saying that the price he offered was what the violin was worth, that he was not trying to get it for less than its value, and that in Yefimov's refusal he saw an insulting suspicion that he, the count, was trying to take advantage of the musician's simplicity and ignorance, and he therefore begged Yefimov's patron to bring him to reason.

The landowner promptly sent for my stepfather.

"Why won't you sell the violin?" he asked him. "It's no use to you. You'll be given three thousand roubles, that's what it is worth, and you are making a mistake if you think you will get more. The count isn't going to cheat you."

Yefimov answered that he would not go to the count of his own accord, but that if he were sent, he must do his master's bidding; he would not sell the fiddle to the count, but if they should take it from him by force, then again he must submit to his master's will.

It was clear that by this answer he had touched a very sensitive spot in his patron's character. The fact was that the latter had always said with pride that he knew how to treat his musicians, for they were all genuine artists, every one of them, and that thanks to them his orchestra was not only better than the count's, but equal to any in Petersburg or Moscow.

"Very well," answered the landowner. "I will inform the count that you won't sell the violin because you won't, for you have a perfect right to sell it or not to sell it, you understand? But I ask you myself, what use is the violin to you? The clarinet is your instrument, though you are a poor player. Let me have it. I'll give you three thousand" (who could have told it was such a valuable instrument?).

Yefimov gave a laugh.

"No, sir, I won't sell it you," he answered. "Of course you are the master . . ."

"Why, I am not forcing you, am I? I am not compelling you, am I?" cried the landowner, losing his temper, the more readily as the conversation took place before the count's musician, who might from this scene draw very disadvantageous conclusions as to the position of the musicians in the landowner's orchestra. "Be off, you ungrateful fellow! Don't let me see you again. But for me what would have become of you with your clarinet, which you can't play? With me you are fed and clothed and get a salary; you live like a gentleman, but you don't care to understand that, and you don't feel it. Be off, and do not exasperate me with your presence here!"

The landowner used to drive everyone with whom he got angry out of his presence, because he was afraid of himself and his own hastiness. And on no account would he have behaved too severely with "artists", as he called his musicians.

The bargain did not come off, and it seemed as though that was the end of the matter, when a month later the count's violinist got up a horrible plot. On his own initiative, he made a statement to the police, in which he charged my stepfather with being responsible for the Italian's death, and with having murdered him with the mercenary object of acquiring a rich inheritance. He asserted that the will had been extorted by force, and swore that he could produce witnesses in support of his accusation. Neither the warnings nor the entreaties of the count and the landowner on behalf of my stepfather could move the informer from his purpose. They pointed out to him that the inquest on the Italian had been properly conducted, that he was flying in the face of facts, possibly through personal spite and disappointment at not getting the valuable instrument which was to have been bought for him. The musician stuck to his point, swore that he was right, asserted that the apoplectic fit had been due not to drunkenness but to poison, and demanded a second inquest. At the first glance there seemed to be something in his story. The case was followed up, of course. Yefimov was taken and sent to prison in town. The trial, in which the whole province took an interest, began. It was soon over, and ended in the musician being convicted of false witness. He was sentenced to a fitting punishment, but he stuck to the story to the end, and maintained that he was right. Finally he acknowledged that he had no proofs, that the evidence he had brought forward had been invented by himself, but that he had been led by suppositions, by surmises, to invent it all; for up to the time of the second inquest, when Yefimov's innocence was formally proved, he had been fully convinced that Yefimov had caused the death of the luckless Italian, though he had perhaps not poisoned him, but murdered him in some other way. But the informer's sentence was not carried out, he was suddenly taken ill with inflammation of the brain, went out of his mind, and died in the prison hospital.

During the whole of this affair, the landowner behaved in the most generous way. He defended my stepfather as though he had been his own son. Several times he went to the prison, to comfort him, to give him money, and learning that Yefimov was fond of smoking, took him the best cigars, and when he was acquitted gave a fête to the orchestra. The landowner looked upon the Yefimov affair as a matter concerning the whole orchestra, because he prized good behaviour in his musicians, if not more than, at least as much as their talents. A whole year passed, and suddenly a rumour went round the province, that a famous violinist, a Frenchman, had arrived in the chief town of the province and was going to give a few concerts there. The landowner began at once trying to get him to pay him a visit. Everything seemed favourable; the Frenchman promised to come. All the preparations were made, almost the whole district had been invited to meet him, but all at once things took quite a different turn.

One morning it was announced that Yefimov had disappeared, no one knew where. A search was made, but there was no trace of him. The orchestra was in a desperate plight, there was no one to play the clarinet; when, three days after Yefimov's disappearance, the landowner received a letter from the French violinist in which the latter haughtily refused the invitation, adding, in a roundabout way of course, that he would for the future be extremely careful in his relations with gentlemen who keep their own orchestras of musicians, that it was an offence against good taste to see real talent under the control of a man who did not know its value, and that the example of Yefimov, a true artist and the best violinist he had met in Russia, was a proof of the justice of his words.

The landowner was thrown into the utmost amazement by reading this letter. He was mortified to the depths of his soul. What! Yefimov, the Yefimov for whom he had done so much, on whom he had heaped such kindness, had so mercilessly and shamelessly slandered him to a European artist, the sort of man whose opinion he most valued! And the letter was inexplicable in another way: he was informed that Yefimov was an artist of real talent, that he was a violinist, but that his talent had not been recognised and he had been forced to play another instrument. All this so much astounded the landowner that he immediately prepared to go to the town for a personal interview with the Frenchman, when he received a letter from the count in which the latter invited him to come to his house at once, and told him that he knew all about the affair, that the famous Frenchman was now in his house with Yefimov, that, being astonished at the latter's impudence and slander, he, the count, had ordered him to be detained, and that the presence of the landowner was essential, since he, the count, was also implicated in Yefimov's accusation. He added that the affair was very important, and must be cleared up as soon as possible.

The landowner, promptly setting off to the count's, at once made the acquaintance of the Frenchman there and told him all my stepfather's story, adding that he had never suspected so great a talent in Yefimov, that the latter had been on the contrary a very poor clarinet player, and that he heard now for the first time that his runaway musician was a violinist. He added further that Yefimov was a free man, that he enjoyed complete liberty, and could leave him at any moment if he really were oppressed. The Frenchman was surprised. They sent for Yefimov, and he was almost unrecognisable: he behaved conceitedly, answered with derision and persisted in the truth of all he had told the Frenchman. All this intensely exasperated the count, who told my stepfather in so many words that he was a scoundrel and a slanderer, and that he deserved an ignominious punishment.

"Don't excite yourself, your Excellency. I know you well enough already, and understand you thoroughly," my stepfather answered. "Thanks to you, I was within an inch of being sentenced for murder. I know at whose instigation Alexey Nikiforitch, your late musician, trumped up a false charge against me."

The count was beside himself with rage on hearing this horrible accusation. He could hardly control himself; but a government official who had come to the count's on business and happened to be in the room, declared that he could not let this pass without investigation, that Yefimov's insulting rudeness was equivalent to malice, wilful slander and libel, and he respectfully asked to be allowed to arrest him on the spot in the count's house. The Frenchman showed great indignation, and said that he could not understand such black ingratitude. Then my stepfather replied emphatically that to be punished, to be tried, even though it were again on a charge of murder, was better than such an existence as he had hitherto endured, belonging to the landowner's orchestra, and being unable to leave it owing to his extreme poverty. And with these words he went out of the room, accompanied by the man who arrested him. They shut him up in a room apart, and threatened to take him to the town next day.

About midnight the prisoner's door was opened. The landowner walked in. He was in his dressing-gown and slippers and was carrying a lighted lantern. It appeared that he could not sleep, and that he was so terribly worried that he had been driven to leave his bed at such an hour. Yefimov was not asleep and he looked with amazement at his visitor, who put down the lantern and in great agitation sat down in a chair facing him.

"Yegor," he said to him, "why have you done me this wrong?"

Yefimov did not answer. The landowner repeated his question, and there was a note of deep feeling, of strange misery in his words.

"God knows why I have, sir!" my stepfather answered at last, with a despairing gesture. "I suppose that the devil confounded me! I don't know myself who drove me to do it! But I can't go on living with you, I can't bear it . . . The devil himself has got hold of me!"

"Yegor," the landowner began again, "come back to me. I will forget everything, I will forgive everything. Listen: you shall be my leading musician, I offer you a salary above all the others. . . ."

"No, sir, no, and don't speak of it; your house is not for me to live in! I tell you that the devil has got hold of me. I shall set fire to the house if I stay with you. Such misery comes over me at times that it would have been better if I had never been born. I cannot answer for myself now; you had better leave me alone, sir. It has been like this with me ever since that devil made a friend of me. . . ."

"Who?" asked the landowner.

"Why, who died like a forsaken dog, the Italian."

"It was he who taught you to play, Yegorushka."

"Yes! Many things he taught me to my ruin. It would have been better for me not to have seen him."

"Was he a first-rate violinist too, Yegorushka?"

"No, he couldn't do much himself, but he taught well. I learned by myself, he only showed me, and better for me if my hand had been withered than what I have learned. I don't myself know now what I want. Here, sir, if you were to ask me: 'What do you want, Yegorka? I can give you anything,' I shouldn't say a word in answer, because I don't know myself what I want. No, sir, I tell you again you had better leave me alone. I shall do myself some mischief, so as to be sent far away, and that will be the end of it!"

"Yegor," said the landowner after a minute's silence, "I cannot leave you like this. Since you don't want to be in my service, go your own way, you are a free man, I cannot keep you; but I cannot part from you like this. Play me something, Yegor, play on your violin. For God's sake play something. I am not ordering you, understand me, I am not compelling you, I beg you with tears: play me, Yegorushka, for God's sake, what you played to the Frenchman. Give me the pleasure. You are obstinate and I am obstinate. I have my ways too, Yegorushka. I feel for you, you too might have feeling. I can't bear it if of your own free will and pleasure you do not play me what you played the Frenchman."

"Well, so be it," said Yefimov. "I had vowed to myself never to play before you, sir, before you above all, but now my heart has melted. I will play to you only for the first and last time, and you will never hear me again anywhere, sir, not if you pay me a thousand roubles."

Then he took his violin and began playing variations on Russian songs. B. said that these variations were his first and best piece for the violin, and that he never played anything so well and with such inspiration. The landowner, who could not listen to any music with indifference, shed tears. When the performance was over, he got up from his chair, took out three hundred roubles, gave them to my stepfather and said:

"Now go your way, Yegor. I will let you out from here and will make everything right with the count; but listen: never meet me again. A wide road lies open to you, but if we run against each other on it, it will be mortifying for you and also for me. Well, good-bye. . . . Wait a moment, one more piece of advice for you on your way, one only. Don't drink, but study, study every hour. Don't grow conceited. I speak to you as your own father would speak to you. Mind, I tell you once again, study and don't take to drink; but if you once take to it from grief (and you will have much trouble) you may reckon all is lost, everything will go to the devil, and maybe you yourself will die in the ditch like your Italian. Come, now, good-bye! . . . Stay, kiss me."

They kissed each other, and then my stepfather went away in freedom.

Scarcely had he found himself at liberty when he began by squandering his three hundred roubles on debauchery in the nearest town, associating with a very low, dirty crew of rollicking companions. Being left penniless with no one to help him, he ended by being compelled to go into a wretched band attached to a strolling provincial company, as the first and perhaps the only violinist. All this was utterly inconsistent with his original intentions, which were to go as soon as possible to study in Petersburg, to obtain a good situation, and to develop into a first-rate artist. But he did not get on in the little orchestra. He soon quarrelled with the manager of the company, and left. Then he completely lost heart, and even brought himself to a desperate step very galling to his pride. He wrote a letter to the landowner, his former patron, describing his position and asking for money. The letter was written in a rather independent style, but no answer came to him. Then he wrote a second letter in which in the most cringing phrases, calling the landowner his benefactor and a true connoisseur of the arts, he begged him again for assistance. At last an answer came. The landowner sent him a hundred roubles and a few lines in the handwriting of his valet, in which he told him not to trouble him with begging letters in the future. When he got this money, my stepfather meant to set off for Petersburg at once, but after paying his debts he had so little money left that the journey was out of the question.

He was obliged to remain in the provinces, again went into some provincial orchestra, then again could not get on in it, and passing from one place to another, spent six whole years in the provinces, all the while cherishing the dream of getting in a short time to Petersburg. At last he was attacked by something like terror. With despair he noticed how his talent was suffering, continually hampered by his disorderly and beggarly existence; and one morning he abandoned his manager, took his violin and, almost begging his way, at last reached Petersburg. He installed himself somewhere in a garret, and it was here that he made the acquaintance of B., who had just arrived from Germany and was also striving to make a career. They soon made friends, and B. recalls their acquaintance with deep feeling even now. Both were young; they had the same hopes and the same object. But B. was still in his first youth; he had had little experience of poverty and sorrow; moreover he was pre-eminently a German and worked for his object obstinately and systematically, with a complete consciousness of his powers, and almost able to calculate beforehand the degree of success he could attain; while his companion, Yefimov, who was thirty, was already tired and weary, had lost all capacity for persistent effort, and had exhausted his early health and vigour in the seven years during which he had been forced for a crust of bread to lead a vagabond existence shifting about from one provincial company or private orchestra to another. He had been supported by the one perpetual unchanging hope of struggling out of his wretched position, saving money and getting to Petersburg. But this hope had been dim and vague, it was a sort of irresistible inner impulse which had with years lost its first definiteness even in Yefimov's own eyes; and by the time he came to Petersburg he was acting almost unconsciously through a sort of everlasting habit of everlasting yearning and brooding over the journey, and scarcely knew himself what he was going to do in the capital. His enthusiasm was somehow spasmodic, jaundiced, and came by fits and starts, as though he were trying to deceive himself by this enthusiasm, and to persuade himself that his vigour, his first fervour, his first inspiration, had not yet disappeared. His incessant ecstasies impressed the cool and methodical B.; he was dazzled, and hailed my stepfather as the coming musical genius. At first B. could imagine no other future for him. But before long his eyes were opened, and he saw through my step father completely. He saw clearly that all this jerkiness, feverish haste, and impatience were nothing but unconscious despair at the thought of his wasted talents; and that possibly the talent itself had not been even at the very first so great, that there had been in it a great deal of blindness, of mistaken self-confidence, of premature self-satisfaction and of incessant dreaming, incessant brooding over his own genius. "But," B. used to tell me, "I could not help wondering at the strange character of my companion. A desperate feverish contest between violently over-strained will and inner impotence was taking place in actual life before my eyes. The unhappy man had for seven whole years been content with mere dreams of his future glory, so much so that he did not even notice how he had lost what is most fundamental in our art, how he had let slip even the most fundamental mechanism of his work. And yet the most colossal plans for the future were continually taking shape in his disordered imagination. It was not enough for him to want to be a genius of the first rank, one of the first violinists in the world; it was not enough for him that he already considered himself such a genius—on the top of all that, he dreamed of becoming also a composer, though he knew nothing about counterpoint. But what astounded me most of all," B. added, "was that this man, with his complete impotence, with his really insignificant knowledge of the technique of his art, had yet so deep, so clear, and so instinctive an understanding of music. He felt and understood it so deeply that it was no wonder if he went astray in his own estimate of himself, and took himself not merely for a profound instinctive critic of music, but for a high priest of that art, for a genius. Sometimes in his coarse, plain language, untouched by any education, he would utter such profound truths that I was struck dumb, and could not understand how he had divined it all, never having read anything and never having been taught anything. And I was indebted to him," B. would add, "to him and his counsels, for much of my own progress. As for me," B. continued, "I was not troubled on my own account. I, too, loved my art passionately, though from the very beginning of my career I knew that I should be in a real sense a humble labourer in the field of art and that I wanted nothing more; but on the other hand, I was proud of the fact that I had not, like the ungrateful servant, buried what had been given me by nature, but had increased it a hundred-fold. And if the finish of my execution were praised, if the perfection of my mechanism were admired, all that I owed to unceasing, unflagging toil, to the clear recognition of my own powers, to voluntary self-subordination and to a persistent struggle against conceit, against premature self-satisfaction, and the indolence that is the natural consequence of that self-satisfaction.''

B. in his turn tried to give good advice to the friend by whom he was at first so dominated, but only succeeded in irritating him to no purpose. A coolness between them followed. B. soon observed that his friend was beginning to be more and more a prey to apathy, misery and boredom, that his bouts of enthusiasm were becoming less and less frequent, and that all this was followed by a gloomy, savage despondency. Finally Yefimov took to abandoning his violin and sometimes would not touch it for a whole week. Complete moral collapse was not far off, and before long the wretched man had sunk into every vice. What his former patron had foretold came true. He gave way to excessive drinking. B. looked on at him with horror; his advice had no effect, and indeed he was afraid to say a word. Little by little Yefimov became utterly shameless; he did not scruple to live at B.'s expense, and even behaved as though he had a complete right to do so. Meanwhile B.'s resources were being exhausted, he lived from hand to mouth by giving lessons, or by playing at evening parties for merchants, for Germans, and for petty officials who, though they paid little, paid him something. Yefimov seemed unwilling to notice his friend's straits: he behaved sullenly with him, and for weeks together did not deign to say a word to him. One day B. observed to him in the mildest way that it would not be amiss for him to take up his violin occasionally, that he might not lose his skill with the instrument altogether; then Yefimov flew into a rage and declared that he would never touch his violin again, as though he imagined that someone would implore him on his knees to do so. On another occasion B. needed someone to play with him at an evening party, and he asked Yefimov. This invitation moved Yefimov to fury. He declared that he was not a street musician, and would not demean himself like B. to degrade his noble art by playing to low tradesmen who would not understand his talent and his playing. B. did not say one word in answer; but Yefimov, brooding over this suggestion in the absence of his friend, who had gone to play, imagined that all this was only a hint at the fact that he was living at B.'s expense, and a desire to make him feel that he, too, ought to try to earn some money. When B.

came back, Yefimov began to reproach him for the meanness of his conduct, and declared that he would not remain with him another minute. He actually did disappear for two days, but on the third turned up again as though nothing had happened, and went on living as before.

Only their former intimacy and affection, and the compassion which B. felt for the ruined man, restrained him from making up his mind to put an end to this disorderly existence and to part with Yefimov for ever. At last they did part. Fortune smiled on B., he obtained powerful patronage and succeeded in giving a brilliant concert. By that time he was a first-rate performer, and his rapidly growing reputation soon afterwards gained him a place in the orchestra of an opera-house where he quickly won well-deserved success. At parting he gave Yefimov money, and begged him with tears in his eyes to return to the right path. B. cannot to this day remember him without marked feeling. His friendship with Yefimov was one of the strongest impressions of his youth. They had begun their career together, had become warmly attached to one another, and even Yefimov's strangeness, his coarse and glaring defects, drew B. more warmly to him. B. understood him; he saw through him, and knew beforehand how it would end. They embraced, and both shed tears at parting. Then Yefimov said through tears and sobs that he was a ruined and most unhappy man, that he had known it a long time, and that only now he saw his ruin clearly.

"I have no talent!" he said, turning as pale as death.

B. was deeply moved.

"Listen, Yegor Petrovitch," he said to him. "What are you doing to yourself? You will only ruin yourself with your despair; you have no patience, no courage. Now you are saying in a fit of despondency that you have no talent. It's not true. You have talent, I assure you you have. You have it. I can tell that merely from the way you feel and understand music. I will prove you that by the whole of your life. You have told me about the way you lived in the past; then, too, you were haunted by the same despair. Then your first teacher, that strange man of whom you have told me so much, first roused in you a love for music and divined your talent. You felt it then as intensely and painfully as you feel it now, but you did not understand what was happening to you. You could not bear living in your patron's house, and you did not know yourself what you wanted. Your teacher died too

217

early. He left you with nothing but vague yearnings and, worst of all, did not explain you to yourself. You felt that you needed some other wider path, that you were destined for other aims, but you did not understand how this could come about, and in your misery you came to hate everything that surrounded you. Your six years of poverty and hardship have not been lost; you have studied, you have thought, you have become conscious of yourself and your powers, you understand music and your vocation now. My friend, you must have patience and courage. A lot far more to be envied than mine awaits you; you are a hundred times more of an artist than I; but God gave you but the tenth part of my patience. Study and do not drink, as your kind old patron told you; and above all, begin from the beginning again, from the A B C. What worries you? Is it poverty, privation? But poverty and privation form the artist. They are inevitable at first. No one wants you now, no one cares to know you; that is the way of the world. Wait a bit, it will be different presently when they find out that you have a gift. Envy, petty meanness, and, worst of all, stupidity will weigh upon you more heavily than privation. Talent wants sympathy, it wants to be understood, and you will see what people will press round you when you attain ever so little of your aim. They will set at nought and despise what you have gained by bitter toil, privations, hunger, sleepless nights. They will not encourage you, they will not comfort you, your future comrades, they will not point out to you what is good and true in you; but with spiteful glee will catch up every mistake you make, will urge you to what is bad in you, to what you are mistaken about, and under an outward show of coolness and contempt will rejoice as though it were a festivity over every mistake you make. (As though anyone were free from mistakes!) You are conceited, you are often proud when there is no need to be, and may offend the amour-propre of some nonentity, and then there will be trouble —you will be one and they will be many. They will torment you with pin-pricks. Even I am beginning to have experience of that. Cheer up! You are not so poor, you can live. Don't look down on humble work, slave away as I have done at poor artisans' entertainments. But you are impatient, you are sick with your impatience, you are not simple enough, you are too subtle, you think too much, you give your brain too much work. You are audacious in words, and faint-hearted when you take up your bow. You are vain, and yet not bold enough.

Courage! wait a bit, study; and if you do not rely on your own powers, then trust to luck: you have fervour, you have feeling. You may reach your goal, and if not, anyway try your luck, you will not lose in any case, for the stake is too great. Trusting to *luck*, brother, is a great thing."

Yefimov listened to his comrade with deep feeling. But as the latter talked, the pallor left his cheeks; they flushed red; his eyes flashed with unaccustomed fire, courage and hope. This courage soon passed into self-confidence, and then into his habitual arrogance; and at last, when B. was finishing his exhortation, Yefimov listened to him absent-mindedly and impatiently. He warmly pressed his hand, however, thanked him, and always rapid in his transitions from the lowest self-abasement and despondency to extreme arrogance and insolence, declared conceitedly that his friend need not trouble himself about his future, that he knew how to manage his own affairs, that he hoped very shortly to get powerful support, that he would give a concert and so at once obtain fame and money. B. shrugged his shoulders but did not contradict him; and they parted, though of course not for long. Yefimov at once spent the money that had been given to him and came to borrow more; then a second time, and a fourth, and a tenth, till at last B. lost patience and said he was not at home. From that time he lost sight of him completely.

Several years passed. One day, as B. was coming home from a rehearsal, at the entrance of a dirty tavern in a back street he jostled against a badly dressed drunken man who called him by his name. It was Yefimov. He was greatly changed, his face looked yellow and bloated. It could be seen that his reckless life was putting a stamp upon him that could never be effaced. B. was overjoyed, and before he had time to say a couple of words to him, had followed him into the tavern into which Yefimov dragged him. There in a little grimy room apart B. scrutinised his companion more closely. The latter was almost in rags, in broken boots; his frayed shirt-front was covered with wine-stains. His hair was thin and beginning to turn grey.

"How are you getting on? Where are you now?" B. asked him.

Yefimov was overcome with embarrassment, even scared at first; he answered jerkily and incoherently, so much so that B. began to think that he was out of his mind. At last Yefimov confessed that he could not talk until he had had a drink of vodka, and that they had long since refused him credit in the tavern. Saying this, he flushed crimson, though he tried to carry it off with a jaunty gesture; but it gave an effect of insolence, artificiality and importunity, so that it was all very pitiful and excited the compassion of kind-hearted B., who saw that his worst apprehensions were fulfilled. He ordered vodka, however. Yefimov's face was transformed with gratitude, and he was so overcome that he was ready with tears in his eyes to kiss his benefactor's hand. Over dinner B. learned to his great surprise that the wretched man was married. But he was still more amazed when he heard that his wife was the cause of all his misery and misfortunes, and that his marriage had destroyed all his talent.

"How is that?" asked B.

"It's two years since I have taken up my violin, brother," Yefimov answered. "She's a common woman, a cook, a coarse, uneducated woman. Damn her. . . . We do nothing but quarrel."

"Then why did you marry her if that is how it is?"

"I had nothing to eat. I got to know her; she had about a thousand roubles. I rushed headlong into matrimony. It was she fell in love with me. She flung herself on my neck. No one drove her to it. The money has gone on food and on drink, and—it's all up with my talent! All is lost."

B. saw that Yefimov seemed in a hurry to justify himself.

"I have thrown it all up, thrown it all up," he added. Then he informed him that of late years he had attained almost perfection on the violin, that though B. was one of the first violinists in the town, yet he would not have been able to hold a candle to him, Yefimov, perhaps, if the latter had cared to outshine him.

"Then what's the difficulty?" said B., surprised. "You should get a post!"

"It's not worth while," said Yefimov, with a wave of his hand. "There isn't one of you there who knows anything about it. What do you know? Bosh! nothing, that's all you know. To scrape out some jig in a ballet—that's your job. You have never seen and never heard good violinists. What's the good of bothering you: you can stay as you like!"

At this point Yefimov waved his arm again and gave a lurch in his chair, for he was quite drunk. Then he began inviting B. to come and see him. But the latter refused, taking his address and promising to go to him next day. Yefimov, who by now had eaten his fill, looked sarcastically at his old friend, and did everything he could to stick pins into him. When they were going away he took B.'s expensive fur coat and handed it to him like a menial to his superior. As they passed through the outer room he stopped and introduced him to the people of the tavern and the company generally as the greatest violinist in Petersburg. In fact he was very disgusting at that moment.

B. did, however, seek him out next morning, and found him in a garret where we were all living at that time in great poverty. I was four years old then, and my mother had been married to Yefimov two years. She was an unhappy woman. In the past she had been a governess, very well educated, and good-looking, and had through poverty married an old government clerk, my father. She only lived with him a year. When my father died suddenly and his meagre fortune was divided among his heirs, my mother was left to face the world alone with me, with a trifling sum of money, all that came to her share. To get a situation as a governess again, with a very young child, was difficult. It was then that in some casual way she met Yefimov, and really did fall in love with him. She was an enthusiast and a dreamer; she saw in Yefimov a genius and believed in him on the strength of his conceited talk of a brilliant future. Her imagination was flattered by the glorious task of being the prop, the guide of a man of genius, and she married him.

All her dreams and hopes vanished in the first month, and there was left before her the pitiful reality. Yefimov, who really had, perhaps, married my mother because she had about a thousand roubles, folded his hands as soon as the money was spent; and as though delighted at the excuse, declared to each and all that marriage was the death of his talent, that he could not work in a stuffy room face to face with his starving family, that songs and music would not come into his mind in such surroundings, and that evidently he was fated to be unlucky. I believe he persuaded himself of the justice of his complaints, and it seemed as though he were glad of an excuse. It seemed as though this unhappy ruined genius were seeking for an external cause upon which the blame for all his failures, all his calamities, could be cast. He could not face the awful thought that he had been ruined for art long ago and for ever. He struggled convulsively with that fearful conviction as with a delirious nightmare, and when at last the reality overcame him, when at moments his eyes were opened, he felt ready to go mad with horror. He could not so easily lose his belief in what had so long been the centre of his life, and to his last hour imagined that the moment had not passed. In times of doubt he gave himself up to drink, which drove away his depression with its vile, stupefying fumes. In fact he did not know how necessary his wife was to him at that time. She was a living pretext, and in reality my stepfather became almost insane over the idea that when he buried his wife *who had ruined* him all would go well again. My poor mother did not understand him. Like a regular dreamer, she broke down at the first step into hostile reality; she became hot-tempered, bitter, shrewish. She was continually quarrelling with her husband, who took a sort of pleasure in tormenting her, and was continually egging him on to work. But my stepfather's blind obsession, his fixed idea, his craze, made him almost inhuman and unfeeling. He only laughed, and swore he would not touch his violin till the death of his wife, and he told her this with brutal frankness. My mother, who in spite of everything loved him passionately to the day of her death, could not endure such a life. She became permanently ill and suffering, lived continually on the rack, and in addition to all this misery, the whole anxiety of maintaining the family fell upon her alone. She took to preparing meals for persons who would come and fetch them. But her husband carried off all her money on the sly, and she was often compelled to send back empty dishes instead of dinner to those for whom she cooked. When B. visited us she was busy washing linen and remaking old clothes. We lived like this from hand to mouth in our garret.

B. was struck by the poverty of the family.

"I say, it's all nonsense what you tell me," he said to my stepfather. "It's not a case of ruining your talent. She is keeping you, and what are you doing?"

"Oh, nothing," answered my stepfather.

But B. did not know all my mother's troubles yet. Her husband often brought home a regular rabble of ragamuffins and rowdies, and what scenes there were then!

B. spent a long time persuading his old comrade to reform. At last he told him if he wouldn't mend his ways he, B., would not help him; he declared without beating about the bush that he would not give him money, because it would be spent on drink; and he asked him finally to play him something on the violin, that he might see what could be done for him. While my stepfather went for his violin, B. began secretly giving money to my mother, but she would not take it. It was the first time she had had to take charity. Then B. gave the money to me, and the poor woman melted into tears. My stepfather brought his violin, but asked for vodka, saying he could not play without it. They sent for vodka. He drank it, and began getting excited. "I will play you something of my own composition, because you are a friend," he said to B., and he drew out from under a chest of drawers a thick dusty manuscript book.

"I wrote all that myself," he said, pointing to the book. "There you shall see! It's very different from your ballets, my boy."

B. looked at a few pages without a word; then he opened the music he had with him, and asked Yefimov to lay aside his own composition for the time and to play something of what he had brought.

My stepfather was a little offended; however, afraid of losing a powerful friend, he did as B. told him. B. perceived that his old friend had really worked and made much progress since they had parted, though he did boast that he hadn't touched the violin since his marriage. The joy of my poor mother was worth seeing. She looked at her husband and was proud of him again. The kind-hearted B., genuinely delighted, determined to set my stepfather on his feet again. Even then he had powerful connections, and promptly began recommending his poor friend and asking for help for him, making him promise beforehand that he would behave himself. And meanwhile at his own expense he rigged him out in better clothes, and took him to see several prominent persons upon whom the appointment he wanted to get for him depended. The fact was that Yefimov's bravado was only in words, and he seems to have gladly accepted his old friend's proposition. B. told me that the flattery and cringing obsequiousness with which my stepfather tried to conciliate him, from fear of losing his favour, made him feel ashamed. Yefimov realised that he was being put on the right path, and even left off drinking.

At last a place was found for him in the orchestra of a theatre. He stood the test well, for in one month of diligence and hard work he regained all that he had lost in a year and a half of idleness, and he promised to work for the future and be punctual in the discharge of his new duties. But the position of my mother and me was not in the least improved. My stepfather did not give my mother a farthing of his salary; he spent it all on himself, eating and drinking with his new companions, of whom he soon had a regular circle. He associated chiefly with the theatre attendants, chorus singers, supers—in short, with people amongst whom he could be first; and he avoided men of real talent. He succeeded in inspiring in them a peculiar respect for himself; he at once impressed upon them that he was an unrecognised genius, that he had been ruined by his wife, and finally that their conductor knew nothing at all about music. He laughed at all the players in the orchestra, at the selection of plays that were produced, and even at the composers of the operas they played. Finally, he propounded a new theory of music; in short, he made all the orchestra sick of him. He quarrelled with his superiors and with the conductor, was rude to the manager, gained the reputation of being the most troublesome, the most nonsensical, and at the same time the most worthless person, and made himself insufferable to everybody.

And indeed it was extremely strange to see such an insignificant man, such a poor and useless performer and careless musician, with such immense pretensions, with such boastfulness and swagger, with such an overbearing manner.

It ended in my stepfather's quarrelling with B., inventing the most horrible slander, the most disgusting calumny against him, and circulating it as authentic fact. After six months of desultory work he was discharged from the orchestra, for drunkenness and negligence in the discharge of his duties. But he still hung round the place. He was soon seen in his old rags, for his decent clothes were all sold or pawned. He took to visiting his former associates, regardless of whether they were pleased to see him or not; he spread spiteful gossip, babbled nonsense, wept over his hard lot, and invited them all to come and see his wicked wife. Of course there were people found to listen, people who took pleasure in giving drink to the discharged musician, and making him talk all sorts of nonsense. Besides, he always talked wittily and cleverly, and interspersed his talk with biting sarcasm and cynical sallies which pleased listeners of a certain class. He was taken for something like a crazy buffoon, whom it was sometimes pleasant to set talking to pass an idle hour. They liked teasing him by talking before him of some new violinist who had come to Petersburg. When he heard this, Yefimov's face fell, he grew depressed and would begin inquiring who had come, and who was this new celebrity, and at once began to feel jealous of his fame. I believe that

224

this was the beginning of his real permanent madness—the fixed idea that he was the finest violinist, at least in Petersburg, but that he was persecuted by fate and ill-used, that owing to various intrigues he was not understood and left in obscurity. The last idea positively flattered him, for there are natures who are very fond of thinking themselves injured and oppressed, complaining aloud of it, or consoling themselves by gloating in secret over their unrecognised greatness. He could count over all the violinists in Petersburg on his fingers, and according to his notions could not find a rival in any one of them. Connoisseurs and musical amateurs who knew the poor crazy fellow liked to talk before him of some celebrated violinist so as to set him talking. They liked his malice, his biting remarks, they liked the apt and clever things he said as he criticised the playing of his supposed rivals. Often they did not understand him, but they were convinced that no one else could hit off the musical celebrities of the day so neatly and with such smart caricature. Even the musicians at whom he laughed were a little afraid of him, for they knew his biting wit. They recognised the aptness of his attacks and the justice of his criticism when there was something to find fault with. People grew used to seeing him in the corridors of the theatre and behind the scenes. The attendants let him pass unquestioned as though he were someone indispensable, and he became something like a Russian Thersites. This manner of life lasted for two or three years, but at last he bored everyone in this latter pose as well. His complete ostracism followed, and for the last two years of his life my stepfather seemed to have vanished entirely and was seen nowhere. B., however, met him on two occasions, but in such a pitiful plight that compassion once more got the upper hand of his repugnance. He called out his name, but my stepfather was offended and affected not to have heard him, pulled his old battered hat over his eyes and passed by. At last, on the morning of one of the chief holidays, B. was informed that his old friend Yefimov had come with his greetings. B. went out to him. Yefimov was drunk, and began making extremely low bows almost down to the ground, murmured something inarticulate, and obstinately refused to go into the room. What his behaviour was meant to convey was: "How should poor wretches like us associate with great people like you? the flunkey's place is good enough for the likes of us; just to greet you on a holiday, we make our bow and take ourselves off." In fact, it was all horrid, stupid, and revoltingly nasty. From that time B. did not see him again, till the catastrophe by which this miserable, morbid, and delirious life was ended. It ended strangely. This catastrophe is closely interwoven not only with the earliest impressions of my childhood, but with my whole life. This is how it came to pass. But I ought first to explain what my childhood was like, and what this man, whose image is so painfully reflected in my earliest impressions, and who was the cause of my mother's death, meant to me.

CHAPTER II

I BEGIN to remember myself very late, not till I was nearly nine years old. I don't know how it was, but everything that happened to me before that age has left no impression I can recall now. But from the time I was eight and a half I remember everything very distinctly, day by day, without a break, as though everything that happened then had occurred not longer ago than yesterday. It is true I can, as though in a dream, remember something earlier—a little lamp always burning in a dark corner before an old-fashioned ikon; then my being once kicked in the street by a horse, from which, as I was told afterwards, I lay ill in bed for three months; then, too, during that illness my waking up at night beside my mother with whom I was sleeping, and being suddenly terrified by my sick dreams, the stillness of the night, and the mice scratching in the corner, and trembling with terror all night, huddling under the bedclothes but not daring to wake my mother, from which I conclude that my fear of her was greater than any other terror. But from the minute when I began to be conscious of myself I developed rapidly, surprisingly, and was terribly capable of receiving many quite unchildlike impressions. Everything became clear before my eyes, everything became intelligible to me extremely quickly. The time from which I begin to remember my feelings well made a vivid and sorrowful impression on me; this impression was repeated every day afterwards and grew stronger every day; it threw a strange and gloomy colour over the whole time I lived with my parents, and over the whole of my childhood too.

It seems to me now that I became suddenly conscious, as

though awaking from deep sleep (though at the time, of course, the change cannot have been so startling). I found myself in a big room with a low-pitched ceiling, stuffy and unclean. The walls were coloured a dirty grey tint; in the corner stood a huge Russian stove; the windows looked out into the street, or more accurately, on to the roof of the house opposite, and were low and broad, like chinks. The window-sills were so high from the floor that I remember I had to push the table up, set a stool on it, and so clamber up to the window, in which I was very fond of sitting when there was no one at home. From our room one could see half the town; we lived just under the roof of a very huge six-storey house. Our furniture consisted of a relic of a sofa with the stuffing coming out, covered with American leather and coated with dust, a plain white table, two chairs, my mother's bed, in the corner a little cupboard with things in it, a chest of drawers which always stood tilted to one side, and a torn paper screen.

I remember that it was dusk; everything was in disorder and had been flung about—brushes, rags, our wooden bowls and spoons, a broken bottle, and I don't know what else besides. I remember that my mother was intensely excited and was crying about something. My stepfather was sitting in a corner in the tattered frock-coat he always wore. He said something sarcastic, which made her angrier than ever, and then brushes and bowls began flying about again. I burst out crying, I began screaming and rushed at them both. I was in a terrible panic, and put my arms round my stepfather to shield him. God knows why, but it seemed to me that my mother had no reason to be angry with him, that he was not to blame; I wanted to beg forgiveness for him, to bear any punishment for his sake. I was dreadfully frightened of my mother, and imagined that everyone else was equally afraid of her. At first my mother was astonished, then she took me by the hand and dragged me away behind the screen. I knocked my arm against the bedstead rather painfully, but my terror was greater than the pain and I did not even wince. I remember, too, that my mother began hotly and bitterly saying something to my father and pointing at me. (I will henceforward call him my father, as it was only much later that I learned that he was not related to me.) The whole scene lasted about two hours and, quivering with suspense, I did my very utmost to guess how it would end. At last the quarrel subsided, and my mother went out. Then my father called me, kissed me, stroked my head, took me on his knee, and I nestled closely, sweetly to his bosom. It was perhaps the first caress I had ever received from either parent, and perhaps that is why I began to remember everything so distinctly from that time. I observed, too, that I had gained my father's favour by defending him; and the idea occurred to me, I believe for the first time, that he had a great deal to put up with, and suffered at my mother's hands. From that time this idea was always with me, and made me more indignant every day.

From that moment I began to feel a boundless love for my father; but a strange sort of love, not a childlike feeling. I should say that it was rather a compassionate, *motherly* feeling, if such a definition of my love were not rather absurd as applied to a child. My father always seemed to me so much to be pitied, so persecuted, so crushed, such a victim, that it seemed to me a terrible and unnatural thing not to love him passionately, not to comfort him and be kind to him, not to do one's utmost for him. But I don't understand to this day how the idea entered my head that my father was such a victim, the most unhappy man in the world! Who had instilled that idea into me? In what way could a child such as I was have any understanding of his failures? But I did understand them, though I interpreted them and changed them in my imagination; but to this day I cannot conceive how this impression was formed. Perhaps my mother was too severe with me, and I attached myself to my father as a creature suffering together with me from the same cause.

I have already described my first awakening from the sleep of childhood, the first stirrings of life in me. My heart was wounded from the first moment, and my development began with inconceivable and exhausting rapidity. I could no longer be satisfied with external impressions alone. I began to think, to reason, to notice, but this noticing began so unnaturally early, that my imagination could not but interpret in its own way what was noticed, and I found myself all at once in a world apart. Everything around me began to be like the fairy tale which my father used often to tell me, and which I could not but take for the holy truth. A strange idea arose in me. I became fully aware—though I don't know how it came about —that I was living in a strange home, and that my parents were utterly unlike the other people I had chanced to meet at that time. Why is it, I wondered, why is it I see other people unlike my parents even in appearance? How is it that

I have noticed laughter on other faces, and how is it that I was at once struck by the fact that in our corner they never laughed, they never rejoiced? What force, what cause drove me, a child of nine, to look about me so diligently and listen to every word uttered by the people I chanced to meet on the stairs, or in the street when, covering my rags with my mother's old jacket, I went out in the evening with a few coppers to buy a few ha'p'orths of sugar, tea, or bread? I understood—and I don't remember how I came to—that there was everlasting, unbearable sorrow in our garret. I racked my brains trying to guess why it was so, and I don't know who helped me to solve the riddle in my own way; I blamed my mother and accepted her as my father's evil genius; and I repeat, I don't know how so monstrous an idea could have taken shape in my brain. And the more attached I became to my father, the more I grew to hate my mother. The memory of all this is a deep and bitter anguish to me to this day. Here is another incident, which did even more than the first to strengthen my strange devotion to my father. About nine o'clock one evening my mother sent me out to the shop for some yeast. My father was not at home. On my way back I fell down in the street and spilt the whole cupful. My first thought was, how angry my mother would be. At the same time I felt a horrible pain in my left arm, and could not get up. Passers-by stopped round me; an old woman began picking me up, and a boy running by hit me on the head with a key. At last I was set upon my feet. I picked up the pieces of the broken cup and walked on staggering, hardly able to put one leg before the other. Suddenly I caught sight of my father. He was standing in a crowd before a grand house that was opposite our lodging. This house belonged to people of consequence and was brilliantly lighted up; a great number of carriages had driven up to the entrance, and strains of music floated down from the windows into the street. I clutched my father by the skirt of his frock-coat, pointed to the pieces of the broken cup, and with tears began saying that I was afraid to go in to mother. I felt somehow sure that he would stand up for me. But why was I convinced of it? Who had suggested to me, who had instilled into me that he loved me more than my mother did? Why was it I approached him without fear? He took me by the hand, began comforting me, then said that he wanted to show me something, and lifted me up in his arms. I could not see anything, for he took me by my bruised arm and it hurt me frightfully; but I did not cry out for fear of wounding him. He kept asking me whether I saw something. I did my utmost to answer so as to please him, and said that I could see red curtains. When he wanted to carry me to the other side of the street nearer to the house, I suddenly, I don't know why, began crying, hugging him, and entreating him to make haste and take me up to mother. I remember that my father's caresses were bitter to me at the time, and I could not bear the thought that one of the two people I so longed to love loved me and was kind to me, while I dared not go to the other and was afraid. But my mother was scarcely angry at all, and sent me to bed at once. I remember that the pain in my arm, growing more and more acute, made me feverish. Yet I was particularly happy that it had all gone off so well, and dreamed all night of the house with the red curtains.

And when I woke next morning my first thought, my first care, was the house with the red curtains. As soon as my mother had gone out I clambered up to the little window and began looking at it. The house had long ago excited my childish curiosity. I liked looking at it particularly in the evening, when the street was lighted up, and when the crimson red curtains behind the plate-glass windows of the brightly lighted house began to gleam with a peculiar blood-red glow. Sumptuous carriages with lovely proud horses were continually driving up to the front door, and everything attracted my curiosity: the clamour and bustle at the entrance, and the different coloured lamps of the carriages, and the grandly dressed women who arrived in them. All this took, in my childish imagination, an air of royal magnificence and fairy-tale enchantment. Now since my meeting with my father before the grand house it became doubly marvellous and interesting. Now strange conceptions and theories began to stir in my excited imagination. And I am not surprised that, between two such strange people as my father and mother, I became such a strange, fantastic child. I was peculiarly affected by the contrast of their characters. I was struck, for instance, by the fact that my mother was continually working and worrying to gain our poor livelihood, was continually reproaching my father that she was the only one to toil for us all; and I could not help asking myself the question: why was it my father did not help her at all, why was it that he lived like a stranger in our home? One or two words dropped by my mother gave me a notion about this, and with some astonishment I learned that my father was an artist (that word I retained in my memory), that my father was a man of genius; the notion that an artist was a special sort of man, unlike others, shaped itself immediately in my imagination. Possibly my father's behaviour led me to that reflection; perhaps I had heard something which now has escaped my memory; but the meaning of my father's words uttered before me on one occasion with peculiar feeling was strangely intelligible to me. The words were: "The time would come when he would not be in poverty, when he would be a gentleman and wealthy; and, in fact, he would rise again when my mother died." I remember that at first I was fearfully frightened at those words. I could not stay in the room, I ran out into our cold passage and there burst into sobs, with my elbows on the window-sill and my face in my hands. But afterwards, when I had pondered continually over it, when I had grown used to my father's horrible desire, my wild imagination came to my assistance. Yes, I could not long remain in the agony of uncertainty, and absolutely had to fix upon some supposition. And so, I don't know how it all began at first—but in the end I fastened upon the idea that when my mother died, my father would leave this dreary garret and would go away somewhere with me. But where? Up to the last I could not clearly picture. I remember only that everything with which I could beautify the place to which we were going (and I made up my mind for certain that we were going together), everything brilliant, luxurious and magnificent I could create in my wild imagination—all this was brought into play in these day-dreams. I fancied that we should at once become rich; I should not have to go on errands to the shops (which was very hard for me, because the children living in the next house tormented me whenever I went out, and I was dreadfully afraid particularly when I was carrying milk or oil and knew that if I spilt it I should be severely punished); then in my dreams I decided that my father would at once get new clothes, that we should go to live in a splendid house. And here the grand house with the red curtains, and my meeting near it with my father who wanted to show me something in it, came to the assistance of my imagination, and it followed immediately in my conjectures that we should move into that house and should live in it in perpetual bliss, keeping a sort of perpetual holiday. From that time forth I used to look out of window in the evenings with intense curiosity at that house which seemed to me enchanted, recalling the crowd of visitors more grandly dressed than I had ever seen before; I imagined those strains of sweet music floating out of the windows, and watched the shadows flitting on the window curtains, and kept trying to guess what was going on there, and it always seemed to me that over there it was paradise and a perpetual holiday. I grew to hate our poor abode, the rags in which I went about; and one day when my mother scolded me and told me to get down from the window, to which I had climbed up as usual, the idea came into my head at once that she did not want me to look at that house, that she did not want me to think of it, that she disliked the thought of our happiness, that she wanted to prevent it. . . . I looked at my mother intently and suspiciously all that evening.

And how could such unfeeling callousness in regard to a creature so continually suffering as my mother have arisen in me? It is only now that I understand what a misery her life was, and I cannot think of her martyrdom without pain. Even then in the dark period of my strange childhood, in the period of this unnatural development, my heart often ached from pain and pity—and uneasiness, bewilderment and doubt lay heavily on my soul. Even then conscience was rising up within me, and often with distress and misery I felt my injustice towards my mother. But we had somehow become estranged from one another, and I cannot remember ever being affectionate to her. Now even the most trifling recollection lacerates and tears at my heart.

I remember once (of course what I am describing now is trivial, paltry, coarse, but it is just such reminiscences which torture me especially, and are imprinted upon my memory more poignantly than anything), one evening when my father was not at home, my mother sent me to the shop to buy her tea and sugar, but she kept hesitating, unable to decide, and counting over her coppers—the pitiful sum she could spend. She was calculating, I think, for half an hour, and seemed still unable to reckon it to her satisfaction. Moreover, there were moments when probably she sank into a sort of stupor. As I remember now, she kept talking on, reckoning in low measured tones, as though dropping her words accidentally; her lips and her cheeks were pale, her hands always trembled, and she always kept shaking her head when she was thinking in solitude.

"No, no need," she said, looking at me. "I had better go to bed. Eh? Are you asleep, Nyetochka?"

I did not answer; then she lifted up my head and looked at me, so gently, so caressingly, her face lighted up and glowed with such a motherly smile, that my heart ached and began beating fast. Besides, she had called me Nyetochka, which meant that she was feeling particularly fond of me. She had invented that name herself, lovingly transforming my name Anna into the diminutive Nyetochka, and when she called me that, it meant that she felt affectionate. I was touched, I longed to hug her, to nestle up to her and weep with her. And for a long time she stroked my head, poor woman, perhaps mechanically in the end, forgetting that she was fondling me, while she kept repeating: "My child, Anneta, Nyetochka." The tears were gushing from my eyes, but I made an effort and controlled myself. I was somehow stubborn in not displaying my feelings before her, though I was inwardly distressed. But that could not have been natural hard-heartedness in me. She could not have so turned me against her simply by her severity to me. No! I was corrupted by my fantastic exclusive love for my father.

I sometimes woke at night in my short little bed under the chilly quilt, and I was always frightened. Half asleep I remembered how, not long ago, when I was smaller, I slept with my mother and was not so frightened when I woke up at night; I had only to nestle up to her, shut my eyes and hug her tight, and I would go to sleep again at once. I still felt as though I could not help loving her in secret. I have noticed since that many children are abnormally unfeeling, and if they love anyone they love that one exclusively. That is how it was with me.

Sometimes there would be a deathlike silence in our garret for a whole week. My father and mother were weary of quarrelling, and I lived between them as before, always silent, always brooding, always fretting and always struggling to arrive at something in my dreams. Watching them I fully grasped their attitude to one another. I understood the obscure never-ending antagonism between them, understood all the sorrow and all the stupefying influences of the disordered existence which had made our garret its home. Of course, I understood it without grasping cause or effect, I understood it, of course, only as far as I was capable of understanding. Sometimes on the long winter evenings, huddled in some corner, I would watch them

eagerly for hours together and gaze into my father's face, trying all the while to guess what he was thinking about, what was
interesting him. Then I was impressed and frightened by my
mother. She kept walking up and down the room without
stopping, for hours at a time, often even at night, in the attacks
of sleeplessness from which she suffered; she would walk up
and down whispering to herself as though she were alone in the
room, flinging wide her arms or folding them across her bosom,
or wringing her hands in terrible, never-ending misery. Sometimes tears streamed down her cheeks, tears which perhaps
she herself did not understand. She was suffering from a very
complicated disease which she neglected entirely.

I remember that I became more and more oppressed by my
solitude and the silence I did not dare to break. I had been
for a whole year living a conscious life, always thinking,
dreaming and tormented in secret by unintelligible, obscure
impulses which had suddenly sprung up in me. I was as wild
as though I were in a forest. At last my father was the first
to notice me; he called me to him and asked me why I stared
at him so. I don't remember what answer I made. I remember
he seemed to reflect, and said at last that next day he would
bring me an alphabet and teach me to read. I looked forward
to this alphabet with impatience and dreamed about it all
night, with no clear idea what an alphabet was. At last next
day my father really did begin to teach me. Grasping in a
couple of words what was required of me, I learned rapidly,
for I knew I should please him by doing so. This was the
happiest time of my life then. When he praised me for my
quickness, patted me on the head and kissed me, I began
crying with delight at once. Little by little my father began
to be fond of me; I grew bold enough to talk to him, and often
we talked together for an hour without weariness, though sometimes I did not understand a word of what he said to me. But
I was somehow afraid of him, afraid he might think I was dull
with him, and so I did my very best to pretend to understand
everything. To sit with me in the evenings became at last a
habit with him. As soon as it began to get dark and he came
home, I went to him at once with my reading-book. He would
make me sit down on a little stool facing him, and after the
lesson he would begin to read me a book. I did not understand a word of it, but I laughed continually, thinking to
please him very much by doing so. I certainly did interest
him, and it amused him to see my laughter. About this time,

he began one evening telling me a story. It was the first story it had been my lot to hear. I sat as though spellbound, and burning with impatience as I followed the story, I was carried away to some other realm as I listened to him, and by the end of the tale I was in a perfect rapture. It was not that the story affected me so greatly, no; but I took it all for truth, at once gave full rein to my fertile fancy, and mixed up reality with fiction. The house with the red curtains, too, at once rose before my imagination; then, I don't know in what way, my father who told me the story appeared as a character acting in it, as well as my mother who seemed to be preventing us going, I don't know where, and last, or rather first, I myself, with my marvellous day-dreams, with my fantastic brain full of wild impossible phantoms, took a part in it, too. All this was so muddled together in my head that it soon turned into a formless chaos, and for a time I lost all touch, all feeling of the present, of the actual, and lived in an unreal world. At that time I was dying with impatience to speak to my father of what was awaiting us in the future, what he was himself expecting, and where he would take me with him when at last we should leave our garret. For my part I was convinced that all this would soon come to pass, but how and in what form all this would be I could not tell, and worried myself racking my brains over it. At times—and it would happen particularly in the evenings—it seemed to me that in another minute father would beckon me on the sly, and call me out into the passage; unseen by my mother I would snatch up my reading-book as I went, and also our picture, a wretched lithograph which had been hanging unframed on the wall from time immemorial, and which I was quite determined to take with us, and we should run away in secret and never come back home to mother again. One day when mother was not at home I chose a moment when father was in a particularly good humour— that happened to him when he had just drunk wine—went up to him and began speaking about something with the intention of immediately turning the conversation to my treasured secret; and hugging him tight with a throbbing heart, frightened as though I were going to speak of something mysterious and terrible, I began, speaking disconnectedly and faltering over every word, to ask him : where we were going, whether it would be soon, what we should take with us, how we should live, and finally whether we were going to live in the house with the red curtains?

"House? Red curtains? What do you mean? What nonsense are you talking, silly?"

Then, more frightened than ever, I began explaining to him that when mother died we should not go on living in the garret, that he would take me away somewhere, that we should both be rich and happy, and assured him at last that he had promised me all this. And as I did so I was fully persuaded that my father really had spoken of it before, anyway I fancied it was so.

"Your mother? Dead? When your mother is dead?" he repeated, looking at me in amazement, changing his countenance somewhat, and knitting his thick grizzled eyebrows. "What are you saying, poor, foolish child?"

Then he began scolding me, and told me over and over again that I was a silly child, that I did not understand anything . . . and I don't remember what else, but he was very much upset.

I did not understand a word of his reproaches, I did not understand how it wounded him that I had listened to what he had said to my mother in anger and intense misery, had remembered his words and had brooded over them by myself. Whatever he was at that time, however far his own madness had gone, yet all this must naturally have been a shock to him. Yet though I did not understand why he was angry, it made me horribly sad and miserable; I began to cry; it seemed to me that all that was awaiting us was so important that a silly child like me must not dare to talk of it. Moreover, although I did not understand this at the first word, yet I felt in an obscure way that I had wronged my mother. I was overcome by dread and horror, and doubt crept into my heart. Then, seeing that I was crying and miserable, he began comforting me, wiped away my tears with his sleeve, and told me not to cry. We sat for a little time in silence, however; he frowned and seemed to be pondering something, then began speaking to me again; but however much I tried to attend, everything he said seemed to me extremely obscure. From some words of that conversation which I have remembered to this day, I conclude that he explained to me that he was a great artist, that nobody understood him, and that he was a man of great talent. I remember, too, that, asking whether I understood, and receiving, of course, a satisfactory answer, he made me repeat "of talent", at which he laughed a little, for perhaps in the end it struck him as funny that he should have

236

talked with me of a matter so important to him.

Our conversation was interrupted by the arrival of Karl Fyodoritch, and I laughed and grew cheerful again when father, pointing to him, said to me:

"Now Karl Fyodoritch, here, hasn't a ha'p'orth of talent!"

This Karl Fyodoritch was a very interesting person. I had seen so few people at that period of my life that I could not possibly forget him. I can picture him now: he was a German whose surname was Meyer, he was born in Germany and had come to Russia, set upon getting into a ballet. But he was a very poor dancer, so he could not get taken on for any part in which dancing was necessary, and was only employed as a super in the theatres. He played various dumb parts such as one of the suite of Fortinbras, or one of those knights of Verona who to the number of twenty flourish cardboard daggers and shout all at once, "We will die for our king!" But certainly no actor in the world was more passionately devoted to his parts than Karl Fyodoritch. The most dreadful misfortune and sorrow of his life was that he could not get into a ballet. He put the art of the ballet above every other, and was in his way as devoted to it as my father was to the violin. He had made friends with my father when they were both employed at the theatre, and the unsuccessful dancer had never given him up since. They saw each other very often, and together bewailed their hard lot and that their talents were not recognised.

The German was the most sentimental, soft-hearted man in the world, and he cherished for my stepfather the most ardent and disinterested affection; but father, I fancy, was not particularly attached to him, and only put up with his company for lack of any other. Moreover, father was so exclusive that he could not see that the art of the ballet was an art at all, and this wounded the poor German to tears. Knowing his weak spot, he always touched upon it, and laughed at the luckless Karl Fyodoritch when the latter grew hot and excited trying to refute him. I heard a great deal about Karl Fyodoritch later on from B., who always called him the Nüremberg skipjack. B. told me a great deal about this friendship with my father; more than once they met, and after drinking a little, shed tears over their fate, over the fact that they were not recognised. I remember such interviews, I remember also that, looking at the two eccentric creatures, I began whimpering too, though I did not know why. This always happened when mother was not at home; the German was dreadfully frightened of her, and would always stand outside in the passage waiting till someone went out to him, and if he heard that mother was at home he ran downstairs again at once. He always brought some German poetry with him, and became intensely excited reading it aloud to us; and then recited it, translated into broken Russian for our benefit. This greatly amused father, and I laughed till I cried. But once they got hold of something in Russian over which they were both very enthusiastic, so that they almost always read it over when they met. I remember that it was a drama in verse by some celebrated Russian writer. I knew the first few lines of this drama so well that when I came across it many years afterwards I recognised it without difficulty. This drama treated of the troubles of a great artist, Gennaro or Giacobi, who cried on one page: "I am not recognised!" and on another, "I am famous!" or, "I have no talent!" and a few lines farther on, "I have talent!" All ended very pathetically. The play was, of course, a very poor one; but strange to say, it affected in the most naïve and tragic way the two readers, who found in the leading character a great resemblance to themselves. I remember that sometimes Karl Fyodoritch was so ecstatic that he would leap up from his seat, run into the opposite corner of the room, and urgently, insistently, with tears in his eyes, beg father and me, whom he always called "Mademoiselle", at once upon the spot to judge between him and his fate and the public. Thereupon he would fall to dancing and executing various steps, crying out to us to tell him at once whether he was an artist or not, and whether anything could be said to the contrary—that is, that he had no talent. Father would at once grow merry, and wink at me on the sly as though to let me know that he would make fun of the German in a most amusing way. I was immensely diverted, but father would hold up his hand and I would control myself, choking with laughter. I cannot help laughing even now at the mere memory of it. I can see that poor Karl Fyodoritch now. He was a very little, extremely lean, grey-headed man, with a red hooked nose stained with snuff, and grotesque bow-legs; but in spite of that he seemed to be proud of their shape and wore tightly fitting trousers. When he stopped at the last caper in an attitude, holding out his hands to us and smiling as dancers smile on the stage when they have finished their steps, father for some moments remained silent as though he could not make up his mind to pronounce judgment, and purposely left the unrecognised dancer in his attitude so that the latter began swaying from side to side on one leg, doing his utmost to preserve his balance. At last father would glance towards me with a very serious face, as though inviting me to be an impartial witness of his judgment, and at the same time the timid imploring eyes of the dancer were fastened upon me.

"No, Karl Fyodoritch, you haven't done it!" father would say at last, pretending that it grieved him to utter the bitter truth.

Then a genuine groan broke from the chest of Karl Fyodoritch; but he recovered himself instantly, with still more rapid gesticulations begged our attention again, declared that he had been dancing on the wrong system, and besought us to criticise him once more. Then he ran off again to the other corner, and sometimes hopped so zealously that he knocked his head against the ceiling and bruised himself badly, but heroically bore the pain like a Spartan, again stopped in an attitude, again with a smile stretched out trembling hands to us, and again begged us to decide his fate. But father was relentless, and answered gloomily as before:

"No, Karl Fyodoritch, it seems it's your fate: you've not done it!"

Then I could restrain myself no longer and broke into peals of laughter in which my father joined. Karl Fyodoritch noticed at last that we were laughing at him, turned crimson with indignation, and with tears in his eyes, with intense though comic feeling which made me feel miserable afterwards on the poor fellow's account, said to father:

"You are a treacherous friend!"

Then he would snatch up his hat and run away from us, swearing by everything in the world that he would never come again. But these quarrels did not last long. A few days later he would come to see us again, and the reading of the celebrated drama would begin once more, once more tears would be shed, and once more the simple-hearted Karl Fyodoritch would ask us to judge between him and the public and his fate, only he would entreat us this time to judge seriously, as true friends should, and not to laugh at him.

One day mother sent me to the shop to make some purchase, and I came back carrying carefully the small silver change I had been given. As I went up the stairs I met my father, who was coming up from the yard. I laughed to him because I could not restrain my feeling when I saw him, and bending down to kiss me, he noticed the silver money in my hand. . . . I had forgotten to say that I had studied the expression of his face so carefully that I could detect almost all his wishes at the first glance. When he was sad, I was racked with misery. He was most often and most acutely depressed when he had no money, and so could not get a drop of the drink to which he had accustomed himself. But at the moment when I met him on the stairs it seemed to me that something particular was passing in his mind. His lustreless eyes shifted uneasily; for the first moment he did not notice me; but when he saw the shining coins in my hand, he suddenly flushed, then turned pale, stretched out his hand to take the money from me, then at once drew it back. Evidently there was a struggle going on within him. Then apparently he mastered himself, told me to go upstairs, went down a few steps, but suddenly stopped and hurriedly called me. He was very much confused.

"Listen, Nyetochka," he said; "give me that money. I'll give it to you back. You will give it to Daddy, won't you? You are a good little thing, Nyetochka."

I felt that I had known this was coming. But for the first instant, the thought of mother's anger, timidity, and, above all, an instinctive shame on my own account and my father's restrained me from giving him the money. He saw that in a flash, and said hastily:

"Oh, you needn't, you needn't! . . ."

"No, no, Daddy, take it; I will say I lost it, that the children next door took it."

"Oh, very well, very well; I knew you were a clever girl," he said, smiling with quivering lips, no longer concealing his delight when he felt the money in his hands. "You are a kind girl, you are my little angel! There, let me kiss your hand."

Then he seized my hand and would have kissed it, but I quickly pulled it away. I was overcome by a sort of pity, and began being more and more agonisingly ashamed. I ran upstairs in a sort of panic, abandoning my father without saying good-bye to him. When I went into the room my cheeks were burning and my heart was throbbing with an overwhelming sensation I had never known till then. However, I had the boldness to tell my mother that I had dropped the money in the snow and could not find it. I expected a beating at least, but it did not come off. Mother certainly was beside herself with distress at first, for we were dreadfully poor. She began scolding me, but at once seemed to change her mind and left off, only observing that I was a clumsy careless girl, and that it seemed I did not love her much since I took so little care of her property. This observation hurt me more than a beating would have done. But mother knew me. She had noticed my sensibility, which often reached the pitch of morbid irritability, and thought by bitter reproaches for not loving her to impress me more strongly and make me more careful in the future.

Towards dusk, when father was to come home, I waited for him as usual in the passage. This time I was in a terrible state of mind. My feelings were troubled by something which sickeningly tortured my conscience. At last my father came in, and I was greatly relieved at his coming. I seemed to think it would make me feel better. He had already been drinking, but on seeing me at once assumed a mysterious and embarrassed air; and drawing me aside into a corner, looking timidly towards our door, took out of his pocket a cake he had bought and began in a whisper bidding me never to take money again and hide it from mother, that that was bad and shameful and very wrong; that it had been done this time because Daddy needed the money very much, but that he would give it back; that I could say afterwards I had found it again. And to take from mother was shameful, and that for the future I must not dream of it, and that if I were obedient for the future he would buy me some cakes again. In the end he even added that I must feel for mother, that mother was so ill and so poor, that she worked for us all. I listened in terror, trembling all over, and tears rushed into my eyes. I was so overwhelmed that I could not say a word, and could not move from the spot. At last, he went into the room, told me not to cry nor say anything about it to mother. I noticed that he was fearfully upset himself. All the evening I was in a panic, and did not dare to look at him or go near him. He, too, evidently avoided my eyes. Mother was walking up and down the room and was talking to herself as usual, as though she were in a dream. That day she was feeling worse, she had had some sort of attack. At last my mental sufferings began to make me feverish. When night came on I could not go to sleep. I was tormented by delirious dreams. At last I could not bear it, and began crying bitterly. My sobs wakened my mother; she called to me and asked me what was the matter. I did not answer, but wept more bitterly. Then she lighted a candle, came up to me and began trying to soothe me, thinking

I was frightened by something I had dreamed. "Oh, you silly little thing," she said, "you still cry when you have a bad dream. Come, give over!" And then she kissed me, saying I should sleep with her. But I would not, and dared not hug her or go to her. My heart was torn in unimaginable tortures. I longed to tell her all about it. I was on the point of doing so, but the thought of father and his prohibition restrained me. "Oh, you poor little Nyetochka!" said my mother, tucking me up in my bed and covering me up with her old jacket as she noticed that I was shivering with feverish chilliness. "I am afraid you will be an invalid like me!" Then she looked at me so mournfully that I could not bear her eyes, I frowned and turned away. I don't remember how I fell asleep, but half awake I heard my poor mother trying for a long time to lull me to sleep. I had never suffered such anguish before. My heart ached painfully. Next morning I felt better. I talked to my father without referring to what had happened the day before, for I divined beforehand that this would please him. He immediately became very cheerful, for he had been frowning whenever he looked at me. Now a sort of joy, an almost childish satisfaction came over him at my light-hearted air. My mother soon went out, and then he could restrain himself no longer. He began kissing me, so that I was almost hysterically delighted and laughed and cried together. At last he said that he wanted to show me something very nice, that I should be very much pleased to see, for my being such a good and clever girl. Then he unbuttoned his waistcoat and took out a key, which he had hanging round his neck on a black cord. Then looking mysteriously at me as though he wanted to read in my face all the delight that in his opinion I must be feeling, he opened a chest and carefully took out of it a black box of peculiar shape which I had never seen before. He took up this box with a sort of timidity and was completely transformed; the laughter vanished from his face, and was succeeded by a solemn expression. At last he opened the mysterious box with a key and took out of it a thing which I had never seen before—a thing, at the first glance, of a very queer shape. He took it in his hands carefully, with a look of reverence, and said that this was his violin, his instrument. Then he began saying a great deal to me in a quiet solemn voice; but I did not understand him, and only retained in my memory the phrases I knew already—that he was an artist, that he was a genius, that he would one day play on the violin,

242

and that at last we should all be rich and should attain some great happiness. Tears came into his eyes and ran down his cheeks. I was very much touched. At last he kissed his violin and gave it to me to kiss. Seeing that I wanted to look at it more closely, he led me to my mother's bed and put the violin in my hand, but I saw that he was trembling with fear that I might break it. I took the violin in my hands and touched the strings, which gave forth a faint sound.

"It's music," I said, looking at father.

"Yes, yes, music," he repeated, rubbing his hands joyfully. "You are a clever child, a good child!"

But in spite of his praise and his delight, I saw that he was uneasy over his violin, and I was frightened too—I made haste to give it back to him. The violin was put back in the box with the same precaution, the box was locked up and put back in the chest; father stroked me on the head again, and promised to show me the violin every time I was as now, clever, good and obedient. So the violin dispelled our common sadness. Only in the evening as father was going out he whispered to me to remember what he had told me yesterday.

This was how I grew up in our garret, and little by little my love—no, I should rather say passion, for I do not know a word strong enough to express fully the overwhelming feeling for my father which was an anguish to myself—grew into something like a morbid obsession. I had only one enjoyment—thinking and dreaming of him; only one desire—to do anything that would give him the slightest satisfaction. How often have I waited on the stairs for him to come in, often shivering and blue with cold, simply to know one instant sooner of his arrival and to look at him a little sooner. I used to be almost frantic with delight when he bestowed the slightest caress on me. And meanwhile it often distressed me dreadfully that I was so obstinately cold with my poor mother; there were moments when I was torn by pity and misery as I looked at her. I could not be unmoved by their everlasting hostility, and I had to choose between them. I had to take the side of one or of the other, and I took the side of this half-crazy man, solely from his being so pitiful, so humiliated in my eyes, and from his having so incomprehensibly impressed my imagination from the beginning. But who can tell? Perhaps I attached myself to him because he was very strange even to look at, and not so grave and gloomy as my mother; because he was almost mad, and often there was something of buffoonery, of childish make-

243

believe about him; and lastly, because I was less afraid of him and indeed had less respect for him than for my mother. He was, as it were, more on my level. Little by little I felt that the ascendancy was even on my side, and that I dominated him a little, that I was necessary to him. I was inwardly proud of this, inwardly triumphant, and realising that I was necessary to him, even played with him at times. This strange devotion of mine was indeed not unlike being in love. . . . But it was not destined to last long: a short time afterwards I lost my father and mother. Their life ended in a terrible catastrophe which is deeply and painfully printed upon my memory. This is how it happened.

CHAPTER III

JUST at the time all Petersburg was excited by a great piece of news. The rumour went about that the famous S. had arrived in the town. The whole musical world of Petersburg was astir. Singers, actors, poets, artists, musical people, and even those who were not at all musical, but with modest pride declared that they did not know one note from another, rushed with eager enthusiasm to buy tickets. The hall could not seat a tenth of the enthusiasts who were able to pay twenty-five roubles for a ticket; but the European fame of S., his old age crowned with laurels, the unflagging freshness of his talent, the rumours that of late years he rarely took up the bow for the benefit of the public, the assertion that he was making the tour of Europe for the last time and would give up playing altogether afterwards, all produced an effect. In fact, the sensation was immense.

I have mentioned already that the arrival of any new violinist, of a celebrity of any note, had a most unpleasant effect on my stepfather. He was always one of the first to hasten to hear the new arrival, so as to discover quickly the full extent of his merits. He was often made really ill by the applause bestowed upon the newcomer, and was only pacified when he could discover defects in the new violinist's playing, and greedily circulated his opinion wherever he could. The poor madman recognised in the whole world but one musical genius, and that genius was, of course, himself. But the talk about the arrival of S. the musical genius had a shattering effect upon him. I must observe that for the previous ten years

Petersburg had not heard a single famous musician, even of less distinction; consequently my father could have no conception of the play of European musicians of the first rank.

I have been told that at the first rumours of S.'s visit, my father was seen again behind the scenes of the theatre. He is said to have seemed extremely agitated, and to have inquired uneasily of S. and the approaching concert. It was a long time since he had been seen behind the scenes, and his appearance there made quite a sensation. Someone wanted to tease him, and with a challenging air said: "Now, Yegor Petrovitch, old man, you are going to hear something very different from ballet music, something that will make your life not worth living, I expect." I am told that he turned pale when he heard that jeer, but answered with an hysterical smile: "We shall see; far-off bells always ring sweet. S., you know, has only been in Paris, and the French have made a fuss of him, and we know what the French are!" And so on. There was a sound of laughter round him; the poor fellow was offended, but, controlling himself, added that he would say nothing; however, that we should see, that we should know, that the day after to-morrow was not long to wait, and that all doubts would soon be solved.

B. tells that just before dusk the same evening he met Prince X., a well-known musical amateur, a man with a deep love and understanding of music. They walked along together, talking of the newly arrived star, when all at once at a street-turning B. caught sight of my father, who was standing before a shop window, looking intently at a placard in it with an announcement in big letters of S.'s concert.

"Do you see that man?" said B., pointing to my father.

"Who is he?" asked Prince X.

"You have heard of him already. That's Yefimov, of whom I have talked to you more than once, and on whose behalf you interested yourself on one occasion."

"Ah, that's interesting," said Prince X. "You talked a great deal about him. I am told he is very interesting. I should like to hear him."

"That's not worth while," answered B., "and it's painful. I don't know how it would be with you, but he always rends my heart. His life is a terrible, hideous tragedy. I feel for him deeply, and however abject he may be, my sympathy for him is not extinct. You say, prince, that he must be interesting. That is true, but he makes too painful an impression. To begin with, he is mad, and then three crimes lie at his door, for besides his own he has ruined two existences—his wife's and his daughter's. I know him. It would kill him on the spot if he realised his crime. But the whole horror of it is that for the last eight years he has *almost* realised it, and for eight years he has been struggling with his conscience on the brink of recognising it, not almost, but fully.''

"You say he is poor?" said Prince X.

"Yes; but poverty is almost good fortune for him now, because it is an excuse. He can assure everyone now that poverty is the only thing that hinders him, and that if he were rich he would have leisure and no anxiety, and it would be seen at once how far he was a musician. He married with the strange hope that the thousand roubles his wife had could help to give him a standing. He behaved like a dreamer, like a poet, but he has always behaved like that all his life. Do you know what he has been continually saying for the last eight years? He asserts that his wife is responsible for his poverty, that she hinders him. He has folded his hands and won't work. But if you were to take his wife away he would be the most miserable creature on earth. Here, he hasn't touched his violin for several years—do you know why? Because every time he takes the bow in his hand, he is inwardly forced to admit that he is no good, a nonentity, not a musician. Now while his fiddle is laid aside he has a faint remote hope that that is false. He is a dreamer. He thinks that all at once by some miracle he will become the most celebrated man in the world. His motto is: *Aut Cæsar, aut nihil,*' as though one could become Cæsar all at once, in one minute. He thirsts for fame. And if such a feeling becomes the mainspring of an artist's activity, then he ceases to be an artist; for he has lost the chief instinct of the artist, that is, the love for art simply because it is art and nothing else, not fame. With S., on the other hand, it is quite the contrary: when he takes up his bow nothing in the world exists for him but music. Next to his violin money is the chief thing for him, and fame only comes third, I think. But he hasn't worried himself much about that. . . . Do you know what is absorbing that luckless fellow now?" added B., pointing to Yefimov. "He is engrossed by the most stupid, most trivial, most pitiful and most absurd anxiety in the world—that is, whether he is superior to S. or S. is superior to him— nothing less, for he is still persuaded that he is the foremost musician in the world. Convince him that he is not a musical genius, and I assure you he would die on the spot as though struck down by a thunderbolt; for it is terrible to part with a fixed idea to which one has sacrificed one's whole life, and which anyway rests on a deep and real foundation, for he had a genuine vocation at first."

"But it will be interesting to see what happens to him when he hears S.," observed Prince X.

"Yes," said B. thoughtfully. "But, no; he would recover at once; his madness is stronger than the truth, and he would at once invent some evasion."

"You think so," said Prince X.

At that moment they came up to my father. He was trying to pass them unnoticed, but B. stopped him and began speaking to him. B. asked him whether he would be at S.'s concert. My father answered indifferently that he did not know, that he had business of more importance than any concerts and any foreign celebrities; but, however, he would wait and see, and if he had an hour free—he might perhaps go in. Then he looked rapidly at B. and Prince X. and smiled mistrustfully, then snatched at his hat, nodded, and walked by, saying he was in a hurry.

But even the day before, I was aware of my father's anxiety. I did not know exactly what it was that was worrying him, but I saw that he was terribly uneasy; even mother noticed it. She was extremely ill at the time, and could scarcely put one foot before the other. Father was continually coming in and going out. In the morning three or four visitors, old companions in the orchestra, came to see him; at which I was greatly surprised, as except Karl Fyodoritch we scarcely ever saw anyone, and all our acquaintances had dropped us since father had quite given up the theatre. At last Karl Fyodoritch ran in panting and brought a poster. I listened and watched attentively, and all this troubled me as much as though I alone were responsible for all this commotion and for the uneasiness I read on my father's face. I longed to understand what they were talking about, and for the first time I heard the name of S. Then I grasped that the sum of fifteen roubles at least was necessary in order to see this S. I remember, too, that father could not refrain from saying with a wave of his hand that he knew these foreign prodigies, these unique geniuses, he knew S. too; that they were all Jews running after Russian money, because the Russians in their simplicity would believe in any nonsense, and especially anything the French made a fuss about. I knew already what was meant by the words, *not a genius*. The visitors began laughing, and soon all of them went away, leaving father thoroughly out of humour. I realised that he was angry with S. for some reason, and to propitiate him and to distract his attention I went up to the table, took up the poster, began spelling it out and read aloud the name of S. Then laughing and looking towards father, who was sitting on a chair brooding, said: "I expect he is another one like Karl Fyodoritch: I expect he won't hit it off either." Father started as though he were frightened, tore the poster out of my hands, shouted at me, stamped, and snatching up his hat was about to go out of the room, but came back at once, called me out into the passage, kissed me, and with uneasiness with some secret dread began saying to me that I was a good, clever child, that he was sure I had not meant to wound him, that he was reckoning on me to do him a great service, but what it was exactly he did not say. Moreover, it was bitter to me to listen to him; I saw that his words and his endearments were not genuine, and all this had a shattering effect on me.

Next day at dinner—it was the day before the concert—father seemed utterly crushed. He was completely changed, and was incessantly looking at mother. At last, to my surprise, he actually began talking to mother. I was surprised, because he hardly ever said anything to her. After dinner he began being particularly attentive to me; he was continually on various pretexts calling me into the passage and, looking about him as though he were frightened of being caught, he kept patting me on the head, kissing me and telling me that I was a good child, that I was an obedient child, that he was sure I loved my Daddy and would do what he was going to ask me. All this made me unbearably miserable. At last, when for the tenth time he called me out into the passage, the mystery was explained. With a miserable, harassed face, looking away uneasily, he asked me whether I knew where mother had put the twenty-five roubles she had brought in the morning before. I was ready to die with terror when I heard this question. But at that moment someone made a noise on the stairs, and father, alarmed, abandoned me and ran out. It was evening when he came back, confused, sad, and careworn; he sat down in silence and began looking at me with something like joy in his face. A feeling of dread came over me, and I avoided his eyes. At last mother, who had been in bed all day, called me, gave me some coppers and sent me to the shop to buy tea

248

and sugar. We rarely drank tea. Mother permitted herself this luxury, as it was for our means, only when she felt ill and feverish. I took the money, and as soon as I got into the passage set off to run as though I were afraid of being overtaken. But what I had foreseen happened: father overtook me in the street and turned me back to the stairs.

"Nyetochka," he said in a shaking voice. "My darling! Listen: give me that money and to-morrow I'll . . ."

"Daddy! Daddy!" I cried, falling on my knees and imploring him. "Daddy! I can't! I mustn't! Mother needs the tea . . . I mustn't take it from mother, I mustn't! I'll get it another time."

"So you won't? you won't?" he whispered in a sort of frenzy. "So you won't love me? Oh, very well. I shall have nothing more to do with you, then. You can stay with mother, and I shall go away and shan't take you with me. Do you hear, you wicked girl? Do you hear?"

"Daddy!" I cried, filled with horror. "Take the money. What can I do now!" I cried, wringing my hands and clutching at the skirts of his coat. "Mother will cry, mother will scold me again."

Apparently he had not expected so much resistance, yet he took the money. At last, unable to endure my sobs and lamentations, he left me on the stairs and ran down. I went upstairs, but my strength failed me at the door of our garret; I did not dare to go in. Every feeling in me was revolted and shattered. I hid my face in my hands and ran to the window, as I had done when first I heard my father say he wished for my mother's death. I was in a sort of stupor, in a state of numbness, and kept starting as I listened to every sound on the stairs. As last I heard someone coming rapidly upstairs. It was he, I recognised his step.

"You are here?" he said in a whisper.

I flew to him.

"There," he said, thrusting the money into my hand; "there! Take it back. I am not your father now, do you hear? I don't care to be your father. You love mother more than me! So go to mother! But I don't want to have anything to do with you!" As he said this he pushed me away and ran downstairs again. Weeping, I flew to overtake him.

"Daddy! Dear Daddy! I will be obedient," I cried. "I love you more than mother. Take the money back, take it!"

But he did not hear me; he had vanished. All that evening I felt more dead than alive, and shivered as though in a fever. I remember mother said something to me, called me to her; I was hardly conscious, I could hear and see nothing. It ended in violent hysterics; I began crying and screaming; mother was frightened and did not know what to do. She took me into her bed, and I don't remember how I fell asleep, with my arms round her neck, trembling and starting with fright at every instant. The whole night passed like that. In the morning I woke up very late, mother was no longer in the room. At that time she went out every day to her work. There was someone with father, and they were both talking in loud voices. I had to wait till the visitor was gone; and when we were left alone I flew to my father and begged him, sobbing, to forgive me for what had happened the day before.

"But will you be a good girl as you were before?" he asked me grimly.

"Yes, Daddy, yes," I answered. "I will tell you where mother's money is put. It was lying yesterday in a box in the little chest."

"It was? Where?" he cried, starting, and got up from his chair. "Where was it?"

"It's locked up, Father!" I said. "Wait a little: in the evening when mother goes to get change, for there are not coppers left, I saw."

"I must have fifteen roubles, Nyetochka. Do you hear? Only fifteen roubles! Get it me to-day; I will bring it all back to you to-morrow. And I will go directly and buy you some sugar-candy, I will buy you some nuts . . . I will buy you a doll too . . . and to-morrow again, and I will bring you little treats every day if you will be a good girl."

"You needn't, Daddy, you needn't! I don't want treats. I won't eat them, I shall give them you back!" I cried, choking with tears all of a sudden, for my heart seemed bursting. I felt at that moment that he had no pity for me, and that he did not love me because he saw how I loved him, but thought that I was ready to serve him for the sake of treats. At that moment I, a child, understood him through and through, and felt that that understanding had wounded me for ever, that I could not love him as before, that I had lost the old daddy. He was in a kind of ecstasy over my promise, he saw that I was ready to do anything for him, that I had done everything for him, and Gods knows how much that "everything" was to me then. I knew what that money meant to my poor mother, I knew that she might be ill with distress at losing it, and remorse was crying aloud in me and rending my heart. But he saw nothing; he thought of me as though I were a child of three, while I understood it all. His delight knew no bounds; he kissed me, tried to coax me not to cry, promised that that very day he would leave mother and go off somewhere—meaning, I suppose, to flatter the daydream that never left me. He took a poster out of his pocket, began assuring me that the man he was going to see to-day was his enemy, his mortal enemy, but that his enemies would not succeed. He was exactly like a child himself as he talked to me about his enemies. Noticing that I was not smiling as usual when he talked to me, and was listening to him in silence, he took up his hat and went out of the room, for he was in a hurry to go off somewhere; but as he went out he kissed me again and nodded to me with a smile, as though he were not quite sure of me, and, as it were, trying to prevent my changing my mind.

I have said already that he was like a madman; but that had been apparent the day before. He needed the money to get a ticket for the concert which was to decide everything for him. He seemed to feel beforehand that this concert was to decide his fate; but he was so beside himself that the day before he had tried to take those few coppers from me as though he could get a ticket with them. His strange condition showed itself even more distinctly at dinner. He simply could not sit still, and did not touch a morsel; he was continually getting up from his seat and sitting down again, as though he were hesitating. At one moment he would snatch up his hat as though he were going off somewhere, then suddenly he became strangely absent-minded, kept whispering something to himself, then suddenly glanced at me, winked, made some sign to me as though impatient to get the money as soon as possible, and was angry with me for not having obtained it yet. My mother even noticed his strange behaviour, and looked at him in surprise. I felt as though I were under sentence of death. Dinner was over; I huddled in a corner and, shivering as though I were in a fever, counted the minutes to the hour when mother usually sent me to the shop. I have never spent more agonising hours in my life; they will live in my memory for ever. What feelings did I not pass through in my imagination! There are moments in which you go through more in your inner consciousness than in whole years of actual life. I felt that I was doing something wicked; he had himself helped my good instincts when, like a coward, he had thrust me into evil-doing the first time, and frightened by it had explained to me that I had done very wrong. How could he fail to see how hard it is to deceive an impressionable nature that had already felt and interpreted much good and evil? I understood, of course, what the horrible extremity was that drove him once more to thrust me into vice, to sacrifice my poor defenceless childhood, and risk upsetting my unstable conscience again. And now, huddled in my corner, I wondered to myself why he had promised me rewards for what I had made up my mind to do of my own accord. New sensations, new impulses, unknown till then, new questions rose up crowding upon my mind, and I was tortured by these questions. Then all at once I began thinking about mother; I pictured her distress at the loss of her last earnings. At last mother laid down the work which she was doing with an effort and called me. I trembled and went to her. She took some money out of the chest of drawers, and as she gave it me, she said: "Run along, Nyetochka, only God forbid that they should give you short change as they did the other day; and don't lose it, whatever happens." I looked with an imploring face at my father, but he nodded and smiled at me approvingly, and rubbed his hands with impatience. The clock struck six, and the concert was at seven. He had had much to suffer in those hours of suspense too.

I stopped on the stairs waiting for him. He was so excited and agitated that without any precaution he ran after me at once. I gave him the money; it was dark on the stairs and I could not see his face, but I felt that he was trembling all over as he took the money. I stood as though turned to stone, and did not move from the spot. I only came to myself when he sent me upstairs again to fetch his hat.

"Daddy! . . . Surely . . . aren't you coming with me?" I asked in a breaking voice, thinking of my last hope—his protection.

"No . . . you had better go alone . . . eh? Wait a minute, wait a minute," he cried, catching himself up. "Wait a minute, I will get you something nice directly, only you go in first and bring my hat here."

I felt as though an icy hand had been laid upon my heart. I shrieked, pushed him away and rushed upstairs. When I went into the room my face was full of horror, and if I had tried to say that I had been robbed of the money mother would have believed me. But I could say nothing at that moment. In a paroxysm of convulsive despair I threw myself across my mother's bed and hid my face in my hands. A minute later the door creaked timidly and father came in. He had come for his hat.

"Where is the money?" cried my mother, suddenly guessing that something extraordinary had happened. "Where is the money? Speak, speak!" Then she snatched me up from the bed and stood me in the middle of the room.

I stood mute with my eyes on the floor; I scarcely understood what was happening to me and what they were doing to me.

"Where is the money?" she cried again, leaving me and suddenly turning on father, who had caught up his hat. "Where is the money?" she repeated. "Ah! She has given it to you. Godless wretch! You have murdered me! You have destroyed me! So you will ruin her too? A child! Her? Her? No, you shall not go off like that!"

And in one instant she had flown to the door, locked it on the inside and taken the key.

"Speak! Confess!" she said to me in a voice scarcely audible from emotion. "Tell me all about it! Speak! Speak, or I don't know what I shall do to you."

She seized my hands and wrung them as she questioned me. At that instant I vowed to be silent and not say a word about father, but timidly raised my eyes to him for the last time. . . . One look, one word from him, such as I was expecting and praying for in my heart—and I should have been happy, in spite of any agony, any torture. . . . But, my God! With a callous threatening gesture he commanded me to be silent, as though I could be afraid of any other threat at that moment! There was a lump in my throat, my breath failed me, my legs gave way under me, and I fell senseless on the floor. . . . I had a second nervous attack like the one the day before.

I came to myself when there was a sudden knock at the door of our garret. Mother unlocked the door, and saw a man in livery who, coming into the room and looking round in amazement at all three of us, asked for the musician Yefimov. My stepfather introduced himself. Then the footman gave him a note and announced that he came from B., who was at that moment at Prince X.'s. In the envelope lay an invitation ticket to S.'s concert.

The arrival of a footman in gorgeous livery who mentioned the name of Prince X. as his master, who had sent on purpose to fetch Yefimov, a poor musician—all this instantly made a great impression on my mother. I have mentioned already when describing her character that the poor woman still loved my father. And now in spite of eight years of perpetual misery and suffering her heart was still unchanged, she still could love him! God knows, perhaps at this moment she imagined a complete change in his fortunes. Even the faintest shadow of hope had an influence on her. How can one tell, perhaps she, too, was a little infected by her crazy husband's unshakable self-confidence. And indeed it would have been impossible that his self-confidence should not have had some influence on a weak woman, and on Prince X.'s attention she might instantly build a thousand plans for him. In an instant she was ready to turn to him again; she was ready to forgive him for all her life, even to overlook his last crime, the sacrifice of her only child, and in a rush of renewed enthusiasm, in a rush of new hope, to reduce that crime to an ordinary act, an act of cowardice to which he had been driven by poverty, his degraded life, and his desperate position. Everything with her was impulsive, and in an instant she had forgiveness and boundless compassion for her ruined husband.

My father began bustling about; he, too, was impressed by this attention from Prince X. and B. He turned straight away to mother, whispered something to her, and she went out of the room. She came back two minutes later, having changed the money, and father immediately gave a silver rouble to the messenger, who went away with a polite bow. Meanwhile mother, after going out for a minute, brought an iron, got out her husband's best shirt-front and began ironing it. She herself tied round his neck a white cambric cravat which had been preserved from time immemorial in his wardrobe, together with his black—by now very shabby—dress-coat which had been made for him when he was in the orchestra of a theatre. When his toilet was complete, father took his hat, but as he was going out asked for a glass of water; he was pale, and sat down on a chair for a minute, feeling faint. I had recovered sufficiently to hand him the water; perhaps the feeling of hostility had stolen back again into mother's heart and cooled her first enthusiasm.

Father went away; we were left alone. I crouched in the corner, and for a long time watched my mother in silence. I had never before seen her in such excitement; her lips were quivering, her pale cheeks suddenly glowed, and from time to time she trembled all over. At last her misery began to find an outlet in complaining, in stifled sobs and lamentation.

"It is all my fault, my fault, wretched mother that I am!" she said, talking to herself. "What will become of her? What will become of her when I die?" she went on, standing still in the middle of the room, as though thunderstruck by the very thought. "Nyetochka! my child! My poor little child! Unhappy child!" she said, taking me by the hand and embracing me convulsively. "How will you be left after I am dead, when even now I can't educate you, look after you and watch over you as I ought? Ah, you don't understand me! Do you understand? Will you remember what I have just said to you, Nyetochka? Will you remember it in the future?"

"I will, mother, I will," I said, clasping my hands and beseeching her.

She held me tight in a long embrace, as though trembling at the very thought of parting from me. My heart was bursting.

"Mammy! Mammy!" I said, sobbing. "Why is it . . . Why is it you don't love Daddy?" and my sobs prevented my finishing.

A groan broke from her bosom. Then in a new rush of terrible misery she began walking up and down the room.

"My poor, poor child! And I did not notice how she was growing up; she knows, she knows all about it! My God! What an impression, what an example!" And again she wrung her hands in despair.

Then she came up to me and with frenzied love kissed me, kissed my hands, bathed them with tears, sought my forgiveness. . . . I have never seen such suffering. . . . At last she seemed exhausted, and fell into apathy. So passed a whole hour. Then she got up, weary and exhausted, and told me to go bed. I went off into my corner, wrapped myself up in the quilt, but could not get to sleep. I was worried about her and I was worried about father. I awaited his return with impatience. I was possessed by a kind of terror at the thought of him. Half an hour later mother took a candle and came up to me to see whether I was asleep. To soothe her I shut my eyes tight and pretended to be asleep. After looking at me she went very quietly to the cupboard, opened it, and poured herself out a glass of wine. She drank it and went to sleep, leaving a candle alight on the table and the door unlocked, as she always did when father might come in late.

I lay in a sort of stupor, but sleep would not come to me.

As soon as I had closed my eyes, I woke up again trembling at some horrible vision. My misery grew more acute every minute. I wanted to cry out, but the scream died away in my breast. At last, late in the night, I heard our door open. I don't remember how long it was afterwards, but when I opened my eyes I saw father. It seemed to me that he was fearfully pale. He was sitting in a chair close to the door, and seemed to be lost in thought. There was a deathly stillness in the room. The guttering candle shed a mournful light over our abode.

I watched him a long time, but still father did not move from his seat; he was sitting motionless, still in the same position, with his head bowed, and his hands pressed rigidly against his knees. Several times I attempted to call to him, but could not. My state of numb stupor persisted. At last he suddenly came to himself, raised his head and got up from his chair. He stood for some minutes in the middle of the room as though he were making some decision; then suddenly went up to my mother's bed, listened, and assuring himself that she was asleep, went to the chest where he kept his violin.

He unlocked the chest, brought out the black violin case and put it on the table; then looked about him again. His eyes had a lustreless and wandering look, such as I had never seen in them before.

He was about to take up the violin, but at once leaving it went back and shut the door; then noticing the open cupboard, went stealthily to it, saw the glass and the wine, poured some out and drank it. Then for the third time he took up the violin, but for the third time put it down and went up to mother's bed. Rigid with terror, I watched to see what would happen.

He listened for a very long time, then put the quilt over her face and began feeling her with his hand. I started. He bent down once more and almost put his head to her, but when he got up the last time there seemed a gleam of a smile on his fearfully white face. He quietly and carefully covered the sleeping figure with the quilt, covered her head, her feet . and I began trembling with a terror I did not understand; I felt frightened for mother, I felt terrified by her deep sleep, and I looked with uneasiness at the immovable angular line of her limbs under the quilt. . . . Like lightning the fearful thought flashed through me!

When he had finished all these preliminaries he went back to the cupboard again and drank off the rest of the wine. He was trembling all over as he went to the table. His face was unrecognisable, it was so white. Then he took up the violin again. I saw the violin and knew what it was, but now I expected something awful, terrible, monstrous. . . . I shuddered at the first note. Father began playing, but the notes came, as it were, jerkily, he kept stopping as though he were recalling something; at last with a harassed agonised face put down his bow and looked strangly at the bed. Something there still troubled him. He went up to the bed again. . . . I did not miss a single movement he made, and almost swooning with a feeling of horror, watched him.

All at once he began hurriedly groping for something, and again the same fearful thought flashed through me like lightning. I wondered why mother slept so soundly. How was it she did not wake when he touched her face with his hand? At last I saw him getting together all the clothes he could. He took mother's pelisse, his old frock-coat, his dressing-gown, even the clothes that I had thrown off when I went to bed, so that he covered mother completely and hid her under the pile thrown on her. She still lay motionless, not stirring a limb.

She was sleeping soundly.

He seemed to breathe more freely when he had finished his task. This time nothing hindered him, but yet he was still uneasy. He moved the candle and stood with his face towards the door, so as not even to look towards the bed. At last he took the violin, and with a despairing gesture drew his bow across it. . . . The music began.

But it was not music. . . . I remember everything distinctly; to the last moment I remembered everything that caught my attention at the time. No, this was not music such as I have heard since. They were not the notes of the violin, but some terrible voice seemed to be resounding for the first time in our room. Either my impressions were abnormal and due to delirium, or my senses had been so affected by all I had witnessed and were prepared for terrible and agonising impressions—but I am firmly convinced that I heard groans, the cry of a human voice, weeping. Utter despair flowed forth in these sounds; and at the end, when there resounded the last awful chord which seemed to combine all the horror of lamentation, the very essence of torment, of hopeless despair, I could not bear it—I began trembling, tears spurted from my eyes, and rushing at father with a fearful, despairing shriek, I clutched at his hands. He uttered a cry and dropped the violin.

He stood for a minute as though bewildered. At last his eyes began darting and straying from side to side, he seemed to be looking for something; suddenly he snatched up the violin, brandished it above me, and . . . another minute and he would perhaps have killed me on the spot.

"Daddy!" I shouted at him; "Daddy!"

He trembled like a leaf when he heard my voice, and stepped back a couple of paces.

"Oh, so you are still left! So it's not all over yet! So you are still left with me!" he shouted, lifting me in the air above his shoulders.

"Daddy!" I cried again. "For God's sake don't terrify me! I am frightened! Oh!"

My wail impressed him; he put me down on the ground gently, and for a minute looked at me without speaking, as though recognising and remembering something. At last, as though at some sudden revulsion, as though at some awful thought, tears gushed from his lustreless eyes; he bent down and began looking intently in my face.

"Daddy," I said to him, racked by terror, "don't look like that! Let us go away from here! Let us make haste and go away! Let us go, let us run away!"

"Yes, we'll run away, we'll run away. It's high time. Come along, Nyetochka. Make haste, make haste!" And he rushed about as though he had only now grasped what he must do. He looked hurriedly around, and seeing mother's handkerchief on the ground, picked it up and put it in his pocket. Then he saw her cap, and picked that up too and put it in his pocket, as though preparing for a long journey and putting together everything he would want.

I got my clothes on in an instant, and in haste I too began snatching up everything which I fancied necessary for the journey.

"Is everything ready, everything?" asked my father. "Is everything ready? Make haste! make haste!"

I hurriedly tied up my bundle, threw a kerchief on my head, and we were about to set off when the idea occurred to me that I must take the picture which was hanging on the wall. Father instantly agreed to this. Now he was quiet, spoke in a whisper, and only urged me to make haste and start. The picture hung very high up. Together we brought a chair, put a stool on it, and clambering on it, after prolonged efforts, took it down. Then everything was ready for our journey. He took me by the hand, and we had almost started when father suddenly stopped me. He rubbed his forehead for some minutes as though trying to remember something which had not been done. At last he seemed to find what he wanted; he felt for the key which lay under mother's pillow and began hurriedly looking for something in the chest of drawers. At last he came back to me and brought me some money he had found in the box.

"Here, take this, take care of it," he whispered to me. Don't lose it, remember, remember!"

At first he put the money in my hand, then took it back and thrust it in the bosom of my dress. I remembered that I shuddered when that silver touched my body, and it seemed that only then I understood what money meant. Now we were ready again, but all at once he stopped me again.

"Nyetochka!" he said to me, as though reflecting with an effort, "my child, I have forgotten. . . . What is it? . . . I can't remember. . . . Yes, yes, I have found it, I remember! . . . Come here, Nyetochka!"

He led me to the corner where the holy image stood, and told me to kneel down.

"Pray, my child, pray! You will feel better! . . . Yes, really it will be better," he whispered, pointing to the ikon, and looking at me strangely. "Say your prayers," he said in an imploring voice.

I dropped on my knees, and clasping my hands, full of horror and despair which by now had gained complete possession of me, I sank on the floor and lay there for some moments without breathing. I strained every thought, every feeling to pray, but tears overwhelmed me. I got up exhausted with misery. I no longer wanted to go with him, I was frightened of him. At last what harassed and tortured me burst out.

"Daddy," I said, melting into tears, "and Mammy? . . . What's the matter with Mammy? Where is she? Where's my Mammy?"

I could not go on, I wept bitterly.

He shed tears too, as he looked at me. At last he took me by the hand, led me up to the bed, swept away the pile of clothes and turned down the quilt. My God! she lay dead, already cold and blue. Almost senseless, I flung myself on her and threw my arms round her dead body. My father made me kneel down.

"Bow down to her, child!" he said. "Say good-bye to her. . . ."

I bowed down. My father bowed down beside me. He was fearfully pale. His lips were trembling and whispering something.

"*It wasn't I, Nyetochka, it wasn't I*," he said, pointing at the dead body with a trembling finger. "Do you hear? *It was not I, it was not my doing*. Remember, Nyetochka!"

"Daddy, let us go," I whispered in terror, "it's time!"

"Yes, it is time now, we ought to have gone long ago!" he said, gripping me tightly by the hand, in haste to get out of the room. "Now let us set off. Thank God, thank God, now it is all over!"

We went down the stairs; the drowsy porter unlocked the gate for us, looking at us suspiciously; and father, as though afraid he would question him, ran out of the gate first, so that I had difficulty in overtaking him. We went down our street and came out on the bank of the canal. Snow had fallen on the pavement overnight, and was coming down in tiny flakes now. It was cold, I was chilled to the bone, and ran along with father clutching convulsively at the skirts of his coat. His violin was under his arm, and he was continually stopping to prevent its slipping.

We walked for a quarter of an hour; at last he turned along the sloping pavement down to the edge of the canal and sat down on the farthest part. There was a hole cut in the ice two paces from us. There was not a sound around. Oh, God! How I remember to this day the terrible feeling that over-powered me! At last everything of which I had been dreaming for a whole year had come to pass. We had left our poor home. But was this what I was expecting, was it of this I was dreaming, was this the creation of my childish imagination, when I looked into the future for the happiness of him whom I loved with a passion so unlike a child's? Above all, the thought of mother tortured me at that moment. Why had we left her alone, I wondered. We had abandoned her body like some useless thing. I remember that that harassed and tortured me more than anything.

"Daddy," I began, unable to endure my agonising thoughts, "Daddy!"

"What is it?" he said sullenly.

"Why have we left Mammy there, Daddy? Why have we deserted her?" I asked, beginning to cry. "Daddy, let us go home again. Let us fetch someone to her."

"Yes, yes," he said, starting and getting up from the post as though some new idea had come into his mind, which settled all his doubts. "Yes, Nyetochka, it won't do; we must go to Mother, she is cold there. You go to her, Nyetochka. It isn't dark, there's a candle there, don't be frightened. Fetch someone to her and then come back to me; you go alone and I will wait for you here. . . . I won't go away . . ."

I went at once, but I had scarcely reached the pavement when something seemed to stab me to the heart. . . . I turned round, and saw that he was already running in the opposite direction and was running away from me, leaving me alone, abandoning me at such a moment. I screamed as loud as I could and panic-stricken flew to overtake him. I gasped for breath; he ran faster and faster. . . . I lost sight of him. On the way I came upon his hat which he had lost in his flight. I picked it up and fell to running again. My breath failed me and my legs gave way under me. I felt as though something hideous were happening to me. It kept seeming to me that it was a dream, and at times I had the sensation I had had in dreams that I was running away from someone, but that my legs were giving way under me, that I was being overtaken and was falling senseless. An agonising sensation was rending my heart; I was sorry for him, my heart ached when I realised that he was running without an overcoat, without a hat away from me, away from his beloved child. . . . I wanted to overtake him simply to kiss him warmly once more, to tell him not to be afraid of me, to soothe him, to assure him that I would not run after him if he did not wish it, but would go back alone to mother. I made out at last that he had turned down a street. Running to it and turning down it I could still discern him before me. Then my strength failed me; I began crying and screaming. I remember that as I ran I knocked up against two passers-by, who stopped in the middle of the pavement and looked after us in amazement.

"Daddy, Daddy!" I cried for the last time, but I slipped on the pavement and fell at the gateway of a house. I felt my whole face bathed in blood. A moment later I lost consciousness.

I came to myself in a soft warm bed, and saw beside me kind welcoming faces which greeted my recovery with delight.

I made out an old woman with spectacles on her nose, a tall gentleman who looked at me with deep compassion, then a lovely young lady, and last of all a grey-headed old man who held my hand and looked at his watch. I woke up to a new life. One of the people I had rushed up against in my flight was Prince X., and I had fallen down at the gate of his house. When after long investigations it was found out who I was, the prince who had sent my father the ticket for S.'s concert, impressed by the strangeness of the coincidence, resolved to take me into his house and bring me up with his own children. Search was made to discover what had become of my father, and it was ascertained that he had been apprehended outside the town, suffering from an attack of acute mania. He was taken to the hospital, where he died two days later.

He died because such a death was a necessity to him, the natural consequence of such a life. He was bound to die like that, when everything that had supported him in life crumbled away at once and faded away like a phantom, like an insubstantial empty dream. He died when his last hope vanished, when in one instant everything with which he had deceived himself and sustained himself through life fell to pieces before his eyes. The truth blinded him with its unbearable light, and what was false was recognised as false by himself. At his last hour he had heard a marvellous genius, who had revealed to him himself and condemned him for ever. With the last sound that floated from the strings of the master's violin the whole mystery of art was revealed to him, and genius, ever youthful, powerful and true, had crushed him by its truth. It seemed as though all that had weighed upon him his whole life in mysterious unfathomable agonies, all that had hitherto tortured him impalpably, elusively, only in dreams, that had taken clear shape at times though he had run from it in horror, screening himself with a lie all his life, all of which he had had a presentiment though he had feared to face it—all this had suddenly flashed upon him at once, had been laid bare to his eyes which had till then stubbornly refused to recognise light for light, darkness for darkness. But the truth was more than his eyes could endure when he gazed upon what had been, what was, and what awaited him; it blinded and burnt up his reason. It had struck him down at once inexorably like lightning. What he had been expecting all his life with a tremor and a sinking of his heart had suddenly happened. It seemed as though an axe had been hanging over his head all his life. All his life he had been every moment expecting in unutterable anguish that it would strike him and—at last the axe had struck him! The blow was fatal. He tried to flee from the sentence passed upon him, but there was nowhere for him to flee, his last hope had vanished, his last excuse had disappeared. The woman whose life had weighed upon him so many years, who would not let him live, at whose death as he blindly believed he would suddenly revive again—died. At last he was alone, there was nothing to hamper him; at last he was free! For the last time in convulsive despair he tried to judge himself, to judge himself sternly and relentlessly, like a partial, disinterested critic; but his enfeebled bow could only faintly repeat the last musical phrase of the genius. . . . At that instant madness, which had been stalking him for ten years, clutched him beyond escape.

CHAPTER IV

I RETURNED to health slowly; and even when no longer confined to my bed, my brain remained in a sort of stupor, and for a long time I could not quite understand what had happened to me. There were moments when it seemed to me that I was dreaming, and I remember I longed that all that was happening might really turn into a dream! And as I fell asleep at night I hoped that I might somehow wake up in our poor garret and see father and mother. . . . But, at last my position grew clear to me, and little by little I understood that I had become utterly alone and was living with strangers. Then for the first time I felt that I was an orphan.

At first I looked eagerly at all the new things that so suddenly surrounded me. At first everything seemed strange and wonderful, everything bewildered me—the new faces, the new habits, and the rooms of the old princely mansion, large, lofty and richly furnished as I see now, but so gloomy and forbidding that I remember I was genuinely afraid to make my way across the long, long drawing-room in which I felt that I should be utterly lost. My illness had not yet quite passed off and my impressions were gloomy, oppressive, in perfect keeping with this solemnly dignified gloomy abode. Moreover, a depression I did not myself understand grew stronger and stronger in my little heart. I would stop in amazement before a picture, a looking-glass, a fireplace of cunning workmanship, or a statue which seemed to be hiding in some secluded niche on purpose to keep better watch on me and frighten me. I would stop and suddenly forget why I had stopped, what I wanted, what I had begun thinking about, and only when I came to myself I was sometimes overwhelmed by dread and perplexity.

Of those who from time to time came to see how I was when I was lying ill in bed, besides the old doctor, the one who impressed me most was a man, rather elderly, very serious, but very kind, who looked at me with deep compassion. I liked his face better than all the others. I longed to speak to him, but was afraid. He always looked depressed, spoke in brief snatches, and there was never a trace of a smile on his lips. This was Prince X., who had found me and was caring for me in his house. When I began to get better his visits became less and less frequent. The last time he came he brought me sweets, a child's picture-book, kissed me, made the sign of the cross over me, and begged me to be more cheerful. To comfort me he told me that I should soon have a companion, his daughter Katya, a little girl like me who was now in Moscow. Then after saying something to a middle-aged Frenchwoman, his children's nurse, and to the maid who looked after me, he commended me to them, went out, and from that time I did not see him for three weeks. The prince lived in complete solitude in his house. The princess lived in the larger part of the house; she, too, sometimes saw nothing of the prince for weeks together. Later on I noticed that all the members of the household hardly spoke of him, as though he were not in the house at all. They all respected him and loved him too, one could see that, and yet looked upon him as a strange and queer man. It seemed as though he realised himself that he was very odd, somehow not like other people, and so tried to keep out of their sight as much as possible. I shall have occasion to say a great deal and in much more detail about him.

One morning they dressed me in fine white linen, put me into a black woollen frock with white *pleureuses* at which I gazed with a sort of dejected wonder, combed my hair, and took me downstairs to the princess's apartments. I stood petrified with wonder when I was taken in to her; I had never before seen such wealth and magnificence around me. But that impression was momentary, and I turned pale when I heard the princess's voice bidding them bring me nearer. Even while I was being dressed I thought that I was being prepared for some painful ordeal, though God only knows how such an idea was suggested to me. Altogether I entered upon my new life with a strange distrust of everything surrounding me. But the princess was very gracious with me and kissed me. I looked at her a little more boldly. It was the same lovely lady whom I had seen when I regained consciousness. But I was trembling all over when I kissed her hand, and could not pluck up courage enough to answer her questions. She told me to sit down on a low stool near her. I think this place had been assigned me beforehand. One could see that the princess wished for nothing better than to care for me with her whole heart, to pet me and to take the place of a mother to me completely. But I was utterly unable to understand my good fortune, and did nothing to gain her good opinion. I was given a fine picture-book and told to look at it. The princess was writing a letter; from time to time she put down her pen and talked to me again; but I was confused and perplexed and said nothing sensible. In fact, though my story was very exceptional, and fate, moving in all sorts of mysterious ways, undoubtedly played a great part in it, and in fact there was much in it that was interesting, inexplicable, and even fantastic, yet I myself turned out, as though in despite of these melodramatic surroundings, a most ordinary child, scared, as it were crushed, and even rather stupid. The last characteristic the princess disliked particularly, and I think she was thoroughly sick of me in a little while, for which I blame myself entirely, of course! Between two and three o'clock visitors began to arrive, and the princess suddenly became more attentive and affectionate to me. To the questions asked about me she answered that it was an extremely interesting story, and then began to tell it in French. As she told the story, her visitors looked at me, shook their heads and exclaimed. One young man eyed me through his lorgnette, one grey-headed and scented old gentleman would have kissed me; while I turned pale and red and sat with my eyes cast down, afraid to stir, and trembling in every limb. My heart ached. My mind went back to the past, to our garret. I thought of my father, our long silent evenings, mother; and when I thought of mother, tears welled up into my eyes, there was a lump in my throat, and I longed to run away, to disappear, to be alone. . . . Then when the visitors had gone, the princess's face became noticeably colder. She looked at me more crossly, spoke more abruptly, and

I was particularly frightened by her piercing black eyes, sometimes fixed on me for a quarter of an hour at a stretch, and
her tightly compressed lips. In the evening I was taken
upstairs. I fell asleep in a fever, woke up in the night miserable
and crying at delirious dreams. Next morning there was the
same business, and I was taken to the princess again. At last
she seemed herself tired of telling her visitors about my adventures, and the visitors tired of commiserating me. Besides, I
was such an ordinary child, "entirely without simplicity", as I
remember the princess herself expressed it in a *tête-à-tête* to a
middle-aged lady who asked her whether she was not bored
with me. And behold, one evening I was taken away not to be
brought back again. So ended my career as favourite. I was
allowed, however, to go about the house freely wherever I
liked. I could not sit still in the same place, I was so intensely,
morbidly miserable, and I was very, very glad when at last I
could get away from everyone into the big rooms downstairs.
I remember that I had a great longing to talk to the servants,
but I was so afraid of annoying them that I preferred to remain
alone. The way I liked best to pass my time was to retreat
into some corner where I was more out of sight, to stand
behind some piece of furniture and there at once begin recalling and imagining all that had happened. But strange to say,
I seemed to have forgotten the ending of my life with my
parents and all that terrible time. Pictures flitted before my
eyes, facts stood out. I did remember it all really—the night,
the violin and father, I remembered how I had got him the
money; but somehow I could not interpret, could not explain
all that had happened. . . . Only there was a weight on my
heart, and when in my memories I came to the moment when
I said my prayers beside my dead mother a cold shiver ran
all over me; I trembled, uttered a faint scream, and then my
breathing felt choked, my whole chest ached, and my heart
thumped so that I ran out of my corner in a panic. I was
wrong, however, in saying that they left me alone, I was
zealously and watchfully looked after; and the instructions of
the prince, who had directed that I should be given complete
freedom and not be restricted in any way, but not be lost sight
of for a moment, were scrupulously carried out. I used to
notice that from time to time someone of the household would
glance into the room in which I was, and go away again without saying a word to me. I was much surprised and rather
troubled by this attention; I could not understand why this

was done. It seemed to me that I was being taken care of for some purpose, and that they meant to do something with me later on. I remember that I was always trying to get farther away, that I might know in case of need where to hide.

Once I strayed out on to the front staircase. It was wide, made of marble and covered with carpet, decorated with flowers and beautiful vases. Two tall men, very gaily dressed, and wearing gloves and the whitest of cravats, sat in silence on each landing. I gazed at them in amazement, and could not explain to myself why they sat there and did not speak, but simply stared at one another and did nothing.

I liked these solitary expeditions more and more. There was, besides, another reason for my running away from upstairs. The prince's old aunt lived on the upper floor, scarcely ever going out. This old lady has left a vivid impression on my memory. She was almost the most important person in the house. Everyone observed a ceremonious etiquette with her, and even the princess, who looked so proud and imperious, had on fixed days twice a week to go upstairs and pay a personal visit to the prince's aunt. She usually went in the morning; a frigid conversation began, frequently interrupted by solemn pauses, during which the old lady either murmured a prayer or counted her reckoning beads. The visit did not end till desired by the aunt, who rose from her seat and kissed the princess on the lips, and thereby gave her to understand that the interview was at an end. In the past the princess had had to visit her husband's aunt every day; but of late at the old lady's desire the severity of this rule had been relaxed, and the princess was only obliged on the other five days of the week to send every morning to inquire after her health. In fact, the old lady lived like a hermit. She was unmarried, and when she was five-and-thirty had retired to a convent, where she spent seventeen years but did not take the veil; then she had left the convent and gone to Moscow to live with her widowed sister, Countess L., who was growing frailer in health year by year, and to be reconciled with her second sister, another un-married Princess X. with whom she had been on bad terms for over twenty years. But the old ladies are said never to have spent a single day without quarrelling; thousands of times they were on the point of parting and could not bring themselves to do so, because they realised at last that each one of them was necessary to the other two, to ward off boredom and the infirmities of old age. But in spite of the unattractiveness of their manner of life, and the ceremonial boredom that reigned in their Moscow mansion, the whole town looked upon it as a duty not to discontinue visiting the three recluses. They were looked upon as the guardians of all the sanctities and traditions of aristocracy, and as living relics of the old nobility. Countess L. was an excellent woman, and many good things were remembered of her. People called on them first on arriving from Petersburg. Anyone who was received in their house was received everywhere. But the countess died and the remaining sisters parted; the elder princess remained in Moscow, to inherit her share of the fortune of the countess, who died without children, while the younger settled with her nephew Prince X. in Petersburg. On the other hand, the prince's two children, Katya and Alexandr, were visiting their great-aunt at Moscow, to entertain and console her in her solitude. Their mother, who loved her children passionately, did not dare to utter a word of protest at being parted from them for the whole period assigned for mourning. I have forgotten to mention that the prince's whole house was still in mourning when I came to live in it; but the time for it was soon over.

The old princess was dressed always in black, always in gowns of plain woollen stuff, and wore starched pleated collars which made her look like an inmate of an almshouse. She did not give up wearing the rosary, drove out in solemn state to mass, observed all the fasts, received visits from various ecclesiastical dignitaries and pious personages, read holy books, and altogether led the life of a nun. The stillness on the upper floor was terrible, one dared not let a door creak. The old lady's senses were as keen as though she were a girl of fifteen, and she sent immediately to find out the cause of any noise, even the faintest creak. Everyone spoke in a whisper, everyone walked on tiptoe, and the poor Frenchwoman, herself an old lady, was obliged to give up her favourite footgear—shoes with high heels. Heels were banished. A fortnight after my arrival the old princess sent to inquire who I was, what I was like, how I had come into the house, and so on. Her curiosity was immediately and respectfully gratified. Then a second messenger was sent to the French lady to inquire why she, the old princess, had not yet seen me? At once there was a great to-do; they began combing my hair, washing my face and hands, which were already very clean, showing me how to walk in, how to bow, how to look more good-humoured and gracious, how to speak—in fact, I was regularly tormented.

268

Then an envoy was sent from our part of the house to inquire whether the great lady cared to see the little orphan. The answer that followed was in the negative, but another time, the following day after mass, was fixed. I did not sleep all night, and I was told afterwards that I was light-headed all night, and raving of going to the old princess and begging her forgiveness for something. At last my presentation arrived. I saw a spare little old lady sitting in a huge easy-chair. She nodded her head to me, and put on her spectacles to look at me more closely. I remember that she did not like me at all. It was observed that I was quite a savage, that I did not know how to curtsy, nor kiss hands. Questions followed and I scarcely answered them; but when allusion was made to my father and mother, I began to cry. The old lady was much displeased at my display of feeling; however, she began trying to console me, telling me to put my trust in God. Then she asked me when I had last been to church; and as I scarcely understood her question, for my education had been greatly neglected, the old princess was horrified. She sent for her niece. A consultation followed, and it was settled that I should be taken to church on the following Sunday. Till then the old princess undertook to pray for me, but told them to take me away as, in her own words, I had made a very painful impression on her. There was nothing strange in that, it was bound to be so. But it was evident that she did not like me at all; the same day word was sent that I was too noisy in my play and could be heard all over the house, though, as I sat all day long without moving, this must have been the old lady's fancy. Yet the same message came next day. It happened about that time that I dropped a cup and broke it. The French governess and all the servants were in despair, and I was immediately sent to a room at the farther end of the house, where they all followed me in a state of panic.

I don't know how the incident ended: this was why I was glad to get downstairs and wander about the great rooms, knowing that there I should disturb no one.

I remember I was sitting one day in a big drawing-room downstairs. I hid my face in my hands, bowed my head, and sat like that I don't remember how many hours. I kept thinking and thinking; my immature mind was unable to analyse my misery, and I felt more dreary and sick at heart every day. Suddenly a soft voice rang out over me.

"What's the matter with you, my poor child?"

I raised my head; it was the prince. His gaze expressed deep sympathy and compassion; but I gazed at him with such a crushed, unhappy air that tears came into his big blue eyes.

"Poor little orphan!" he said, patting me on the head.

"No, no, not an orphan, no!" I said, and a moan broke from me and everything surged up in me and rose to the surface. I got up from my seat, clutched at his hand, and kissing it and wetting it with my tears, repeated in an imploring voice:

"No, no, not an orphan, no!"

"My child, what is the matter with you, my dear? What is it, poor Nyetochka?"

"Where is my mother? where is my mother?" I cried, sobbing loudly, unable to conceal my misery any longer, and helplessly falling on my knees before him. "Please tell me where my mother is?"

"Forgive me, my child! . . . Oh, poor little thing, I have reminded her. . . . What have I done? Come, come along with me, Nyetochka, come along with me."

He took me by the hand and led me along with him quickly. He was moved to the depths of his soul. At last we reached a room which I had not seen before.

It was the ikon room. It was dusk. The lamps gleamed brightly, with their lights reflected on the golden settings and precious stones of the ikons. The faces of the saints looked out dimly from the gold mountings. Everything here was so unlike the other rooms, so mysterious and gloomy, that I was much impressed and overcome by a sort of terror. Besides, I was in such a morbid condition. The prince quickly made me kneel down before the ikon of the Mother of God, and knelt down beside me. . . .

"Pray, my child, pray; we will both pray," he said in a soft, broken voice.

But I could not pray; I was overwhelmed, even terrified; I remembered my father's words that last night beside my mother's body, and I had a nervous seizure. I lay in bed ill, and in this second period of my illness I almost died. This was how it happened.

One day a familiar name sounded in my ears. I heard the name of S. Someone of the household pronounced the name by my bedside. I started; memories came rushing upon me, and overwhelmed by recollections, dreams, and distress, I lay for

I don't know how many hours in real delirium. I woke up very late, it was dark all round me; the night-light had gone out, and the girl who used to sit in my room was not there. All at once I heard the sound of far-away music. At times the music died away entirely, at times grew more and more distinct as though it were coming nearer. I don't remember what feeling came over me, what project sprang up in my sick brain. I got out of bed, and I don't know how I found strength to do it, but I dressed in my mourning and went groping through the rooms. I found no one in the next room nor in the room beyond. At last I made my way into the corridor. The sounds were becoming more and more distinct. In the middle of the corridor there was a staircase leading down; that was the way by which I always went down to the big rooms. The staircase was brightly lighted up; people were walking about below. I hid in a corner to avoid being seen, and only when it was possible went downstairs to the second corridor. The music was coming from the drawing-room near; in it there was noise and talk as though thousands of people were assembled. One of the drawing-room doors leading out of the corridor was draped with two curtains of crimson velvet. I raised the outer one and stood between the two. My heart beat so violently that I could hardly stand. But a few minutes later, mastering my agitation, I ventured to move a little aside the border of the second curtain. . . . My goodness! the immense gloomy room which I was so afraid to enter was gleaming now with a thousand lights. It was like a sea of light flowing upon me, and my eyes, accustomed to the darkness, were at first painfully dazzled. The perfumed air fanned my face like a hot wind. Masses of people were walking to and fro; it seemed as though all had gay and joyful faces. The women were in such rich, such light dresses. On all sides I saw eyes sparkling with delight. I stood as though spellbound. It seemed to me as though I had seen all this somewhere, in a dream. . . . There came back into my mind the dusk, our garret, the high window, the street far down below with the glittering lamp-posts, the windows of the house opposite with the red curtains, the carriages densely packed at the doors; the stamping and snorting of the proud horses, the shouts, the noise, the shadows at the windows, and the faint, distant music. . . . So here, here was that paradise! flashed through my mind. This was where I wanted to go with my poor father. . . . So it was not a dream. . . . Yes, I had seen it all before in my dreams, in

271

my fancies! My imagination, inflamed by illness, took fire, and tears of inexplicable rapture streamed from my eyes. I looked about for my father: "he must be here, he is here," I thought, and my heart beat with anticipation. . . . I could hardly breathe. . . . But the music ceased, a hum of voices began, and a murmur arose from all parts of the room. I gazed eagerly into the faces that flashed by me, and tried to recognise someone. All at once an extraordinary excitement was apparent in the room, I saw a tall lean old man on a raised platform. His pale face was smiling, he bent his angular figure, bowing in all directions. A profound silence followed as though all these people were holding their breath. All eyes were fixed on the old man, all were expectant. He raised his violin and touched the strings with his bow. The music began, and I felt all at once as though something were clutching my heart. In intense anguish, holding my breath, I listened to those sounds; something familiar was sounding in my ears, as though I had somewhere heard this before, some foreboding of something awful, horrible was reflected in my heart. At last the violin vibrated more loudly; the notes resounded faster and more shrilly. It was like a despairing wail, a pitiful lamentation, as though some prayer were being uttered in vain in all that crowd, and dying away, ceasing in despair. Something more and more familiar was taking shape in my heart, but my heart refused to believe it. I clenched my teeth to keep back a moan of pain, I clutched at the curtain that I might not fall. From time to time I closed my eyes and suddenly opened them, expecting that it was a dream, that I should wake up at some terrible moment I knew already, and that I was dreaming of that last night and hearing those same sounds. Opening my eyes, I tried to reassure myself, I looked eagerly into the crowd —no, these were different people, different faces. It seemed as though they were all, like me, expecting something—all, like me, suffering agony; that they all wanted to scream at those fearful moans and wails to stop, not to tear their hearts. But the wails and moans flowed on, more agonising, more plaintive, more prolonged. Then the last fearful prolonged cry rang out, and everything in me was shaken. . . . I had no doubt. It was the same, the same cry! I recognised it, I had heard it before, it stabbed me to the heart as it had on that night. "Father! father!" flashed like lightning through my brain; "he is here, it's he, he is calling me, it is his violin!" A groan seemed to rise from all that crowd, and terrific applause shook the room. I could restrain myself no longer, threw back the curtain and dashed into the room.

"Daddy, Daddy! it is you! Where are you?" I cried, almost beside myself.

I don't know how I reached the tall old man; people let me pass, they stood aside to make way for me. I rushed to him with an agonising shriek; I thought that I was embracing my father. . . . All at once I saw that long bony hands had seized me and were lifting me up in the air. Black eyes were fixed upon me, and seemed as though they would scorch me with their fire. I looked at the old man. No, this was not my father, it was his murderer, was the thought that flashed through my brain. I was overwhelmed by frenzy, and all at once it seemed to me as though there were a shout of laughter at me, that that laughter was re-echoed in the room in a unanimous roar. I lost consciousness.

CHAPTER V

THIS was the second and last period of my illness. When I opened my eyes again I saw bending over me the face of a child, a girl of my own age, and my first movement was to hold out my hands to her. From my first glance at her, a feeling of happiness like a sweet foreboding filled my soul. Picture to yourself an ideally charming face, startling, dazzling beauty —beauty before which one stops short as though stabbed in delighted amazement, shuddering with rapture, and to which one is grateful for its existence, for one's eyes having fallen upon it, for its passing by one. It was the prince's daughter Katya, who had only just returned from Moscow. She smiled at my gesture, and my weak nerves ached with a sweet ecstasy.

The little princess called her father, who was only two paces away talking to the doctor.

"Well, thank God, thank God," said the prince, taking my hand, and his face beamed with genuine feeling. "I am glad, very glad," he said, speaking rapidly, as he always did. "And this is Katya, my little girl; you must make friends, here is a companion for you. Make haste and get well, Nyetochka. Naughty girl, what a fright she gave me!"

My recovery followed very quickly. A few days later I was up and about. Every morning Katya came to my bedside, always with a smile, always with laughter on her lips. I awaited her coming as a joyful event; I longed to kiss her. But the naughty child never stayed for more than a few minutes, she could not sit still. She always wanted to be on the move, to be running and jumping, making a noise and an uproar all over the house. And so she informed me from the first that she found it horribly dull to sit with me, and she would not come very often, and only came because she was so sorry for me that she could not help coming, and that we should get on better when I was well again. And every morning her first word was:

"Well, are you all right now?" And as I was still pale and thin, and as the smile seemed to peep out timorously on my mournful face, the little princess frowned at once, shook her head, and stamped her foot in vexation.

"But I told you yesterday to get better, you know! I suppose they don't give you anything to eat?"

"A little," I answered timidly, for I was already overawed by her. I wanted to do my utmost to please her, and so I was timid over every word I uttered, over every movement I made. Her arrival moved me to more and more delight. I could not take my eyes off her, and when she went away I used to go on gazing at the spot where she had stood as though I were spellbound. I began to dream of her. And when I was awake I made up long conversations with her in her absence—I was her friend, played all sorts of pranks with her, wept with her when we were scolded. In short, I dreamed of her like a lover. I was desperately anxious to get well and grow fat, as she advised me.

Sometimes when Katya ran in to me in the morning and her first words were, "Aren't you well yet? As thin as ever," I was as downcast as though I were to blame. But nothing could be more genuine than Katya's astonishment that I could not get well in twenty-four hours, so that at last she began to be really angry with me.

"Well, I will bring you a cake to-day if you like," she said to me one day. "You must eat, and that will soon make you fatter."

"Do bring it," I said, delighted that I should see her a second time.

When she came to inquire after my health, Katya usually sat on a chair opposite me and began scrutinising me with her black eyes. And when first she made my acquaintance, she was continually looking me up and down from head to foot with the most naïve astonishment. But conversation between us made little progress. I was intimidated by Katya and her abrupt sallies, though I was dying with desire to talk to her.

"Why don't you talk?" Katya began after a brief silence.

"What is your father doing?" I asked, delighted that there was a sentence with which I could always begin a conversation.

"Nothing. Father's all right. I had two cups of tea this morning instead of one. How many did you have?"

"One."

Silence again.

"Falstaff tried to bite me to-day."

"Is that the dog?"

"Yes, the dog. Haven't you seen him?"

"Yes, I have seen him."

And as again I did not know what to say, Katya stared at me in amazement.

"Well? Does it cheer you up when I talk to you?"

"Yes, very much; come oftener."

"They told me that it would cheer you up for me to come and see you. But do make haste and get up. I will bring you a cake to-day. . . . Why are you always silent?"

"I don't know."

"I suppose you are always thinking?"

"Yes, I think a lot."

"They tell me I talk a lot and don't think much. There is no harm in talking, is there?"

"No. I am glad when you talk."

"H'm, I will ask Madame Leotard, she knows everything. And what do you think about?"

"I think about you," I answered after a brief pause.

"Does that cheer you up?"

"Yes."

"So you like me, then?"

"Yes."

"Well, I don't like you yet. You are so thin. But I will bring you some cakes. Well, good-bye."

And Katya, kissing me almost in the act of darting away, vanished from the room.

But after dinner the cake really did make its appearance. She ran in as though she were crazy, laughing with glee at having brought me something to eat which was forbidden.

"Eat more, eat well. That's my cake, I did not eat it myself. Well, good-bye!" And she was gone in a flash.

Another time she suddenly flew in to see me after dinner, not at her usual hour. Her black curls were flying in all directions, her cheeks glowed crimson, her eyes were sparkling; she must have been racing and skipping about for the last hour.

"Can you play battledore and shuttlecock?" she cried, panting for breath, and speaking quickly in haste to be off again.

"No," I answered, deeply regretting that I could not say yes.

"What a girl! Get well and I'll teach you. That's all I came for. I am just having a game with Madame Leotard. Good-bye, they are waiting for me."

At last I got up for good, though I was still weak and frail. My first idea was never to be parted from Katya again. Some irresistible force seemed to draw me to her. I could not take my eyes off her, and that surprised Katya. The attraction to her was so powerful, I became so increasingly ardent in my new feeling, that she could not avoid noticing it, and at first it struck her as incredibly strange. I remember that once, in the middle of some game, I could not refrain from throwing myself on her neck and kissing her. She extricated herself from my arms, caught hold of my hands, and frowning at me as though I had offended her in some way, asked me:

"What is the matter with you? Why are you kissing me?"

I was confused as though I were in fault, started at her sudden question and made no answer. Katya shrugged her shoulders in token of perplexity (a gesture that was habitual with her), compressed her pouting lips, gave up the game and sat down on the sofa in the corner, whence she scrutinised me for a long time, pondering over something as though considering a new question which had suddenly arisen in her mind. That was her habit, too, when any difficulty arose. On my side, too, I could not for a long while get used to these harsh and abrupt traits of her character.

At first I blamed myself, and thought that there really must be much that was strange in me. But though that was true, yet I was worried by not understanding why I could not be friends with Katya from the first, and make her like me once and for all. My failure to do so mortified me bitterly, and I was ready to shed tears at every hasty word from Katya, at every mistrustful glance she bent upon me. But my trouble grew not from day to day, but from hour to hour, for with Katya everything moved quickly. A few days later I began to notice that she had not taken to me at all, and was even beginning to feel an aversion for me. Everything in that child took place quickly, abruptly—some might have said roughly, if there had not been a genuine and noble grace in the rapid manifestations of her direct, naïvely open nature. It began by her feeling at first mistrust and then contempt for me. I think it arose from my complete inability to play any kind of game. Katya was fond of frolicking and racing about, she was strong, lively, agile; I was just the opposite. I was still weak from illness, quiet and dreamy; I did not enjoy playing. In short, I was entirely without the qualities that Katya liked. Moreover, I could not bear people to be displeased with me for anything, I became sad and dispirited at once, so that I had not the energy to smoothe over my offence and alter for the better the unfavourable impression I had made; in fact, I was in a hopeless plight. That Katya could not understand. At first she frightened me; in fact, she would stare at me in amazement, as her habit was after she had sometimes been struggling for a whole hour with me, showing me how to play battledore and shuttlecock without making any progress. And as I immediately became dejected, as tears were ready to gush from my eyes, she would, after considering me two or three times without arriving at any explanation either from me or her reflections, abandon me altogether and begin playing alone, and would give up asking me to join her, and not even say a word to me for days together. This made such an impression on me that I could hardly endure her scorn. My new sort of loneliness seemed almost more unbearable than the old, I began to be sad and brooding, and dark thoughts clouded my soul again.

Madame Leotard, who looked after us, noticed this change in our relations. And as first of all she noticed me and was struck by my enforced loneliness, she went straight to the little princess and scolded her for not treating me properly. Katya scowled, shrugged her little shoulders, and declared that there was nothing she could do with me—that I didn't know how to play, that I was always thinking about something, and that she had better wait till her brother Sasha came back from Moscow, and then it would be much livelier for both of them.

But Madame Leotard was not satisfied with such an answer, and said that Katya was leaving me alone, though I was still ill; that I could not be as merry and playful as Katya; that that was all the better, however, since Katya was too full of mischief; that she was always up to some prank; that the day before yesterday the bulldog had almost bitten her—in fact, Madame Leotard gave her a merciless scolding. She ended by sending her to me, bidding her make it up with me at once.

Katya listened to Madame Leotard with great attention, as though she really understood something new and just from her observations. Abandoning a hoop which she had been trundling about, she came up to me and, looking at me gravely, asked wonderingly—

"Do you want to play?"

"No," I answered. I had been frightened for myself and for Katya while Madame Leotard was scolding her.

"What do you want to do?"

"I will sit still a little; it's tiring for me to run. Only don't be cross with me, Katya, for I like you very much."

"Well, then, I will play alone," said Katya slowly and deliberately, seeming surprised that, after all, it appeared, she was not to blame. "Well, good-bye. I won't be cross with you."

"Good-bye," I said, getting up and giving her my hand.

"Perhaps you would like to kiss me?" she asked after a moment's thought, probably remembering what had happened recently, and desiring to do what would please me best in order to finish with me agreeably and as quickly as possible.

"As you like," I answered with timid hope.

She came up to me and very gravely, without a smile, kissed me. So, having accomplished all that was expected of her, having even done more than was necessary to give complete satisfaction to the poor child to whom she had been sent, she ran away from me gay and content, and her shouts and laughter were soon resounding through all the rooms again, till exhausted and out of breath she threw herself on the sofa to rest and recover. She kept looking at me suspiciously all the evening; most likely I seemed to her very queer and strange. It was evident that she wanted to talk to me, to find out the explanation of something that puzzled her about me; but on this occasion she restrained herself, I don't know why. As a rule, Katya's lessons began in the morning. Madame Leotard taught her French. The lessons consisted of repetition of grammar rules and the reading of La Fontaine. She was not taught much, for they could hardly get her to agree to sit still at her books for two hours in the day. She had at last been brought to agree to do so much, by her father's request and her mother's commands, and kept to her compact scrupulously because she

278

had given her word. She had rare abilities; she was very quick of understanding. But she had some little peculiarities on that side too; if she did not understand anything she would at once begin thinking about it by herself, and could not endure asking for explanations—she seemed ashamed to do it. I have been told that she would for days at a time be struggling over some problem which she could not solve, and be angry that she could not master it by herself unaided; and only in the last extremity, when quite tired out, she would go to Madame Leotard and ask for her help to solve the problem which had baffled her. It was the same with everything she did. She thought a great deal, though that was not at all apparent at first sight. At the same time she was naïve for her age; sometimes she would ask quite a foolish question, while at other times her answers would betray the most far-sighted subtlety and ingenuity.

When at last I was fit to have lessons too, Madame Leotard examined me as to my attainments, and finding that I read very well but wrote very badly, considered it a matter of the first necessity to teach me French.

I made no objections, so one morning I sat down to lessons at the same table with Katya. It happened, as luck would have it, she was particularly dense and inattentive that morning, so much so that Madame Leotard was surprised at her. At one sitting I almost mastered the whole French alphabet, wishing to do my utmost to please Madame Leotard by my diligence. Towards the end of the lesson Madame Leotard was really angry with Katya.

"Look at her!" she said, indicating me. "The child is ill and is having her first lesson, and yet she has done ten times as much as you. Aren't you ashamed?"

"Does she know more than I do?" Katya asked in astonishment.

"How long did it take you to learn the alphabet?"

"Three lessons."

"And she has learnt it in one. So she learns three times as quickly as you do, and will soon catch you up."

Katya pondered a little and turned suddenly fiery red, as she recognised that Madame Leotard's observation was just. To flush crimson and grow hot with shame was the first thing she did if she failed in anything, if she were vexed or her pride were wounded, or she were caught in some piece of mischief— on almost every occasion, in fact. This time tears almost came into her eyes; but she said nothing, merely looked at me as

279

though she would burn me with her eyes. I guessed at once what was wrong. The poor child's pride and amour-propre were excessive. When we left Madame Leotard I began to speak, hoping to soften her vexation and to show that I was not to blame for the governess's words, but Katya remained mute as though she had not heard me.

An hour later she came into the room where I was sitting over a book, thinking all the while of Katya, and feeling upset and frightened at her refusing to talk to me again. She looked at me from under her brows, sat down as usual on the sofa, and for half an hour did not take her eyes off me. At last I could bear it no longer, and glanced at her inquiringly.

"Can you dance?" asked Katya.

"No, I can't."

"I can."

Silence.

"And can you play the piano?"

"No, I can't do that, either."

"I can. That's very difficult to learn."

I said nothing.

"Madame Leotard says you are cleverer than I am."

"Madame Leotard is angry with you," I said.

"And will father be angry too?"

"I don't know," I answered.

Silence again; Katya tapped the floor with her little foot in her impatience.

"So you are going to laugh at me because you are quicker at learning than I am?" she asked at last, unable to restrain her annoyance.

"Oh, no, no," I cried, and I jumped up from my place to rush and hug her.

"And aren't you ashamed to imagine such a thing and ask about it, princess?" we suddenly heard the voice of Madame Leotard, who had been watching us for the last five minutes and listening to our conversation. "For shame! You are envious of the poor child, and boast to her that you can dance and play the piano. For shame! I shall tell the prince all about it."

Katya's cheeks glowed like a fire.

"It's a bad feeling. You have insulted her by your questions. Her parents were poor people and could not engage teachers for her; she has taught herself because she has a kind good heart. You ought to love her, and you want to quarrel with

her. For shame, for shame! Why, she is an orphan. She
has no one. You will be boasting next that you are a princess
and she is not. I shall leave you alone. Think over what I
have said to you, and improve.''

Katya did think for exactly two days. For two days her
laughter and shouts were not heard. Waking in the night, I
heard her even in her sleep still arguing with Madame Leotard.
She actually grew a little thinner during those two days, and
there was not such a vivid flush of red on her bright little face.
At last on the third day we met downstairs in the big rooms.
Katya was on her way from her mother's room, but seeing me,
she stopped and sat not far off, facing me. I waited in terror
for what was coming, trembling in every limb.

"Nyetochka, why did they scold me because of you?" she
asked at last.

"It was not because of me, Katenka," I said in haste to
defend myself.

"But Madame Leotard said that I had insulted you."

"No, Katenka, no; you did not insult me."

Katya shrugged her shoulders to express her perplexity.

"Why is it you are always crying?" she asked after a brief
silence.

"I won't cry if you want me not to," I answered through
my tears.

She shrugged her shoulders again.

"You were always crying before."

I made no answer.

"Why is it you are living with us?" Katya asked suddenly.

I gazed at her in bewilderment, and something seemed to
stab me to the heart.

"Because I am an orphan," I answered at last, pulling myself together.

"Used you to have a father and mother?"

"Yes."

"Well, didn't they love you?"

"No . . . they did love me," I answered with an effort.

"Were they poor?"

"Yes."

"They didn't each you anything?"

"They taught me to read."

"Did you have any toys?"

"No."

"Did you have any cakes?"

281

"No."

"How many rooms had you?"

"One."

"And had you any servants?"

"No, we had no servants."

"Who did the work?"

"I used to go out and buy things myself."

Katya's questions lacerated my heart more and more. And memories and my loneliness and the astonishment of the little princess—all this stabbed and wounded my heart, and all the blood seemed to rush to it. I was trembling with emotion, and was choking with tears.

"I suppose you are glad you are living with us?"

I did not speak.

"Did you have nice clothes?"

"No."

"Nasty ones?"

"Yes."

"I have seen your dress, they showed me it."

"Why do you ask me questions?" I said, trembling all over with a new and unknown feeling, and I got up from my seat. "Why do you ask me questions?" I went on, flushing with indignation. "Why are you laughing at me?"

Katya flared up, and she, too, rose from her seat, but she instantly controlled her feeling.

"No . . . I am not laughing," she answered. "I only wanted to know whether it was true that your father and mother were poor."

"Why do you ask me about father and mother?" I said, beginning to cry from mental distress. "Why do you ask such questions about them? What have they done to you, Katya?"

Katya stood in confusion and did not know what to answer. At that moment the prince walked in.

"What is the matter with you, Nyetochka?" he asked, looking at me and seeing my tears. "What is the matter with you?" he asked, glancing at Katya, who was as red as fire. "What were you talking about? What have you been quarrelling about? Nyetochka, what have you been quarrelling about?"

But I could not answer. I seized the prince's hand and kissed it with tears.

"Katya, tell the truth. What has happened?"

Katya could not lie.

"I told her that I had seen what horrid clothes she had when she lived with her father and mother."

"Who showed you them? Who dared to show them?"

"I saw them myself," Katya answered resolutely.

"Well, very well! You won't tell tales, I know that. What else?"

"And she cried and asked why I was laughing at her father and mother.

"Then you were laughing at them?"

Though Katya had not laughed, yet she must have had some such feeling when for the first time I had taken her words so. She did not answer a word, which meant that she acknowledged that it was the fact.

"Go to her at once and beg her forgiveness," said the prince, indicating me.

The little princess stood as white as a handkerchief and did not budge.

"Well?" said the prince.

"I won't," Katya brought out at last in a low voice, with a most determined air.

"Katya!"

"No, I won't, I won't!" she cried suddenly, with flashing eyes, and she stamped. "I won't beg forgiveness, papa. I don't like her. I won't live with her. . . . It's not my fault she cries all day. I don't want to. I don't want to!"

"Come with me," said the prince, taking her by the hand. "Nyetochka, go upstairs." And he led her away into the study.

I longed to rush to the prince to intercede for Katya, but the prince sternly repeated his command and I went upstairs, turning cold and numb with terror. When I got to our room I sank on the sofa and hid my head in my hands. I counted the minutes, waited with impatience for Katya, I longed to fling myself at her feet. At last she came back, and without saying a word passed by me and sat down in a corner. Her eyes looked red and her cheeks were swollen from crying. All my resolution vanished. I looked at her in terror, and my terror would not let me stir.

I did my utmost to blame myself, tried my best to prove to myself that I was to blame for everything. A thousand times I was on the point of going up to Katya, and a thousand times I checked myself, not knowing how she would receive me. So passed one day and then a second. On the evening of the second day Katya was more cheerful, and began bowling her hoop through the rooms, but she soon abandoned this pastime and sat down alone in her corner. Before going to bed she suddenly turned to me, even took two steps in my direction, and her lips parted to say something to me; but she stopped, turned away and got into bed. After that another day passed, and Madame Leotard, surprised, began at last asking Katya what had happened to her, and whether it was because she was ill she had become so quiet. Katya made some answer and took up the shuttlecock, but as soon as Madame Leotard turned away, she reddened and began to cry. She ran out of the room that I might not see her. And at last it was all explained: exactly three days after our quarrel she came suddenly, after dinner, into my room and shyly drew near me.

"Papa has ordered me to beg your forgiveness," she said. "Do you forgive me?"

I clutched Katya by both hands quickly, and breathless with excitement, I said—

"Yes, yes."

"Papa ordered me to kiss you. Will you kiss me?"

In reply I began kissing her hands, wetting them with my tears. Glancing at Katya, I saw in her an extraordinary change. Her lips were faintly moving, her chin was twitching, her eyes were moist; but she instantly mastered her emotion and a smile came for a second on her lips.

"I will go and tell father that I have kissed you and begged your forgiveness," she said softly, as though reflecting to herself. "I haven't seen him for three days; he forbade me to go in to him till I had," she added after a brief pause.

And saying this, she went timidly and thoughtfully downstairs, as though she were uncertain how her father would receive her.

But an hour later there was a sound of noise, shouting, and laughter upstairs, Falstaff barked, something was upset and broken, several books flew on to the floor, the hoop went leaping and resounding through all the rooms—in short, I learned that Katya was reconciled with her father, and my heart was all aquiver with joy.

But she did not come near me, and evidently avoided talking with me. On the other hand, I had the honour of exciting her curiosity to the utmost. More and more frequently she sat down opposite in order to scrutinise me the more conveniently. Her observation of me became even more naïve; the fact was that the spoilt and self-willed child, whom everyone in the house petted and cherished as a treasure, could not understand how it was that I had several times crossed her path when she had no wish at all to find me on it. But she had a noble, good little heart, which could always find the right path, if only by instinct. Her father, whom she adored, had more influence over her than anyone. Her mother doted on her, but was extremely severe with her; and it was from her mother that Katya got her obstinacy, her pride and her strength of will. But she had to bear the brunt of all her mother's whims, which sometimes reached the point of moral tyranny. The princess had a strange conception of education, and Katya's education was a strange mixture of senseless spoiling and ruthless severity. What was yesterday permitted was suddenly for no sort of reason forbidden to-day, and the child's sense of justice was wounded. . . . But I am anticipating. I will only observe here that the child already realised the difference between her relations with her mother and with her father. With the latter she was absolutely herself, always open, and nothing was kept back. With her mother it was quite the opposite—she was reserved, mistrustful, and unquestioningly obedient. Her obedience was not, however, due to sincere feeling and conviction, but was the result of a rigid system. I will explain this more fully later on. However, to the peculiar honour of my Katya, she did in fact understand her mother, and when she gave in to her it was with a full recognition of her boundless love, which at times passed into morbid hysteria—and the little princess magnanimously took that into her reckoning. Alas! that reckoning was of little avail to the headstrong girl later on!

But I scarcely understood what was happening to me. Everything within me was in a turmoil from a new and inexplicable sensation, and I am not exaggerating if I say that I suffered, that I was torn by this new feeling. In short—and may I be forgiven for saying so—I was in love with my Katya. Yes, it was love, real love, love with tears and bliss, passionate love. What was it drew me to her? What gave rise to such a love? It began from my first sight of her, when all my feelings were joyfully thrilled by the angelic beauty of the child. Everything about her was lovely; not one of her defects was innate—they were all derived from her surroundings, and all were in a state of conflict. In everything one could see a fine quality taking for the time the wrong form; but everything in her, from that conflict upwards, was radiant with joyous hope, everything foretold a reassuring future. Everyone admired her, everyone loved her—not only I. When at three o'clock we were taken out for a walk, passers-by would stop as though in amazement as soon as they saw her, and often an exclamation of admiration followed the fortunate child. She was born to be happy, she must be born to be happy—that was one's first impression on meeting her. Perhaps my æsthetic sense, my sense of the artistic, was for the first time excited; it took shape for the first time, awakened by beauty, and that was the source from which my love arose.

The little princess's chief defect, or rather the leading element in her character, which was incessantly seeking expression in its true form, and naturally was continually misdirected and in a state of conflict—was pride. This pride was carried to such a pitch that it showed itself in the simplest trifles and passed into vanity. For instance, contradiction of any sort did not annoy her or anger her, but merely surprised her. She could not conceive that anything could be different from what she wanted. But the feeling of justice always gained the upper hand in her heart. If she were convinced that she had been unjust she at once accepted her punishment without repining or hesitation. And if till then she had not in her relation to me been true to herself, I set it down to an unconquerable aversion for me which for a time disturbed the grace and harmony of her whole being. It was bound to be so. She was carried away too passionately by her impulses, and it was always only by experience that she was brought into the right path. The results of all her undertakings were fine and true, but were gained only at the cost of incessant errors and mistakes.

Katya very soon satisfied her curiosity about me, and finally decided to let me alone. She behaved as though I were not in the house; she bestowed not an unnecessary word, scarcely a necessary one, upon me. I was banished from her games, and banished not by force, but so cleverly that it seemed as though I agreed to it. The lessons took their course, and if I was held up to her as an example of quickness of understanding and gentleness of disposition, I no longer had the honour of mortifying her vanity, though it was so sensitive that it could be wounded even by the bulldog, Sir John Falstaff. Falstaff was lethargic and phlegmatic, but fierce as a tiger when he was teased, so fierce that even his master could not make him obey. Another characteristic of the beast was that he had no affection for anyone whatever. But his greatest enemy was undoubtedly the old princess. . . . I am anticipating again, however. Katya's vanity made her do her utmost to overcome Falstaff's unfriendliness. She could not bear to think that there was even an animal in the house which did not recognise her authority, her power, did not give way to her, did not like her. And so Katya made up her mind to try and conquer Falstaff. She wanted to rule and dominate everyone; how could Falstaff be an exception? But the stubborn bulldog would not give in.

One day, when we were both sitting downstairs in one of the big drawing-rooms after dinner, the bulldog was lying stretched out in the middle of the room, enjoying his after-dinner siesta. It was at this moment that Katya took it into her head to conquer him. And so she abandoned her game and began cautiously on tiptoe to approach him, coaxing him, calling him the most endearing names, and beckoning to him ingratiatingly. But even before she got near him, Falstaff showed his terrible teeth; the little princess stood still. All she meant to do was to go up to Falstaff and stroke him—which he allowed no one to do but her mother, whose pet he was—and to make him follow her. It was a difficult feat, and involved serious risks, as Falstaff would not have hesitated to bite off her hand or to tear her to pieces if he had thought fit. He was as strong as a bear, and I watched Katya's manœuvres from a distance with anxiety and alarm. But it was not easy to make her change her mind all at once, and even Falstaff's teeth, which he displayed most uncivilly, were not a sufficient argument. Seeing that she could not approach him all at once, Katya walked round her enemy in perplexity. Falstaff did not budge. Katya made another circle, considerably diminishing its diameter, then a third, but when she reached a spot which Falstaff seemed to regard as the forbidden limit, he showed his teeth again. The little princess stamped her foot, walked away in annoyance and hesitation, and sat down on the sofa.

Ten minutes later she devised a new method of seduction, she went out and returned with a supply of biscuits and cakes—in fact, she changed her tactics. But Falstaff was indifferent, probably because he already had had enough to eat. He did not even look at the piece of biscuit which was thrown; when Katya again reached the forbidden line which Falstaff seemed to regard as his boundary there followed even more show of hostility than at first. Falstaff raised his head, bared his teeth, gave a faint growl and made a slight movement, as though he were preparing to leap up. Katya turned crimson with anger, threw down the cakes, and sat down on the sofa again.

She was unmistakably excited as she sat there. Her little foot tapped on the carpet, her cheeks were flaming, and there were actually tears of vexation in her eyes. She chanced to glance at me—and the blood rushed to her head. She jumped up from her seat resolutely, and with a firm step went straight up to the fierce dog.

Perhaps astonishment had a powerful effect on Falstaff this time. He let his enemy cross the boundary, and only when Katya was two paces away greeted her with the most malignant growl. Katya stopped for a minute, but only for a minute, and resolutely advanced. I was almost fainting with terror. Katya was roused as I had never seen her before, her eyes were flashing, with victory, with triumph. She would have made a wonderful picture. She fearlessly faced the menacing eyes of the furious bulldog, and did not flinch at the sight of his terrible jaws. He sat up, a fearful growl broke from his hairy chest; in another minute he would have torn her to pieces. But the little princess proudly laid her little hand upon him and three times stroked his back in triumph. For one instant the bulldog hesitated. That moment was the most awful; but all at once he moved, got up heavily, stretched, and probably reflecting that it was not worth while having anything to do with children, walked calmly out of the room. Katya stood in triumph on the field of battle and glanced at me with an indescribable look in her eyes, a look full of the joy and intoxication of victory. I was as white as a sheet; she noticed it with a smile. But a deathly pallor overspread her cheeks too. She could scarcely reach the sofa, and sank on it almost fainting.

But my infatuation over her was beyond all bounds. From the day when I had suffered such terror on her account, I could not control my feelings. I was pining away in misery. A thousand times over I was on the point of throwing myself on her neck, but fear riveted me motionless to my seat. I remember I tried to avoid her that she might not see my emotion, but she chanced to come into the room where I was in hiding. I was so upset, and my heart began beating so violently that I felt giddy. I fancy that the mischievous girl noticed it, and for a day or two was herself somewhat disturbed. But soon she grew used to this state of affairs too. So passed a month, during the whole course of which I suffered in silence. My feelings were marked by an unaccountable power of standing a strain, if I may so express it; my character is distinguished by an extreme capacity for endurance, so that the outbreak, the sudden manifestation of feeling only comes at the last extremity. It must be remembered that all this time Katya and I did not exchange more than half a dozen words; but little by little I noticed from certain elusive signs that it was not due to forgetfulness nor indifference on her part, but to intentional avoidance, as though she had inwardly vowed to keep me at a certain distance. But I could not sleep at night, and by day could not conceal my emotion even from Madame Leotard. My love for Katya approached the abnormal. One day I stealthily took her handkerchief, another time the ribbon that she plaited in her hair, and spent whole nights kissing it and bathing it in my tears. At first Katya's indifference wounded and mortified me, but then everything grew misty and I could not have given myself an account of my own feelings. In this way new impressions gradually crowded out the old, and memories of my sorrowful past lost their morbid power and were replaced by new life.

I remember I used sometimes to wake up at night, get out of bed, and go on tiptoe to the little princess in the dim light of our nightlight. I would gaze for hours at Katya sleeping; sometimes I would sit on her bed, bend down to her face and feel her hot breath on my cheeks. Softly, trembling with fear, I would kiss her little hands, her shoulders, hair, and feet if her foot peeped out from under the quilt. Little by little I began to notice—for I never took my eyes off Katya all that month—that Katya was growing more pensive from day to day; she had begun to lose the evenness of her temper: sometimes one would not hear her noise all day, while another time there would be such an uproar as never before. She became irritable, exacting, grew crimson and angry very often, and was even guilty of little cruelties in her behaviour to me. At one time she would suddenly refuse to have dinner with me, to sit beside me, as though she felt aversion for me; or she would go off to her mother's apartments and stay there for whole days together, knowing perhaps that I was pining in misery without her. Then she would suddenly begin staring for an hour at a stretch, so that I did not know what to do with myself from overwhelming confusion, turned red and pale by turns, and yet did not dare to get up and go out of the room. Twice Katya complained of feeling feverish, though she had never been known to feel ill before. All of a sudden one morning a new arrangement was made; at Katya's urgent desire she moved down-

stairs to the apartments of her mother, who was ready to die
with alarm when Katya complained of being feverish. I must
observe that Katya's mother was by no means pleased with me,
and put down the change in Katya, which she, too, observed,
to the influence of my morose disposition, as she expressed it,
on her daughter's character. She would have parted us long
before, but put off doing so for a time, knowing that she would
have to face a serious dispute with the prince, who, though he
gave way to her in nearly everything, sometimes became un-
yielding and immovably obstinate. She understood her husband
thoroughly.

I was overwhelmed by Katya's removal, and spent a whole
week in anguish of spirit. I was in desperate misery, racking
my brains to discover the cause of Katya's dislike. My heart
was torn with grief and indignation, and a sense of injustice
began to rise up in my wounded heart. A certain pride began
to stir within me, and when I met Katya at the hour when we
were taken out for a walk, I looked at her with such independence, such gravity, so differently from ever before, that even
she was struck by it. Of course this change continued only by
fits and starts, and my heart ached more and more afterwards,
and I grew weaker, and more faint-hearted than ever. At last
one morning, to my intense astonishment and joyful confusion, the little princess came back upstairs. At first she
threw herself on Madame Leotard's neck with a wild laugh
and announced that she had come back to live with us again,
then she nodded to me, asked to be excused lessons that morning, and spent the whole morning frolicking and racing about.
I had never seen her livelier and merrier. But towards evening
she grew quiet and dreamy, and again a sort of sadness seemed
to overshadow her charming little face. When her mother came
in in the evening to have a look at her, I saw that Katya made
an unnatural effort to seem gay. But after her mother had
gone she suddenly burst into tears. I was much impressed.
Katya noticed my attention and went out of the room. In short,
she was working up to some sudden crisis. Her mother was
consulting doctors, and every day sent for Madame Leotard to
question her minutely about Katya, and told her to watch over
all her actions. Only I had a foreboding of the truth, and my
heart beat with hope.

In short, my little romance was reaching its *dénouement*.
The third day after Katya's return to our floor, I noticed that
she was looking at me all the morning with a wonderful light

in her eyes, with a long persistent gaze. . . . Several times I met that gaze, and each time we both blushed and cast down our eyes as though we were ashamed. At last the little princess burst out laughing and walked away. It struck three, and we had to dress to go out.

"Your shoe's untied," she said to me, "let me tie it."

I was bending down to tie it up myself, turning as red as a cherry, at Katya's having at last spoken to me.

"Let me do it," she said impatiently, and she laughed. She bent down on the spot, took my foot by force, set it on her knee and tied the lace. I was breathless; I did not know what to do from a sort of sweet terror. When she had finished tying the shoe, she stood up and scrutinised me from head to foot.

"Your neck is too open," she said, touching the bare skin of my neck with her little finger. "There, let me wrap it up."

I did not oppose her. She untied my neckerchief and retied it in her own fashion.

"Or you may get a cough," she said, with a sly smile, flashing her black, shining eyes upon me.

I was beside myself, I did not know what was happening to me and what was happening to Katya. But, thank goodness, our walk was soon over or I should not have been able to restrain myself, and should have rushed to kiss her in the street. As we went up the stairs, however, I succeeded in stealthily kissing her on the shoulder. She noticed it, started, but said nothing. In the evening she was dressed up and taken downstairs. Her mother had visitors. But there was a strange commotion in the house that evening.

Katya had a nervous attack. Her mother was beside herself with alarm. The doctor came and did not know what to say. Of course it was all put down to Katya's age, but I thought otherwise. Next morning Katya made her appearance the same as ever, rosy and in good spirits, full of inexhaustible health, but of whims and caprices such as she had never had before.

In the first place, all that morning she disregarded Madame Leotard altogether. Then she suddenly wanted to go and see her old aunt. Contrary to her usual practice, the old lady, who could not endure her niece, was in continual conflict with her, and did not care to see her, on this occasion for some reason consented to see her. At first everything went well, and for the first hour they got on harmoniously. At first the little rogue asked her aunt's forgiveness for all her misdeeds, for her noisy play, for her shouting and disturbing her aunt. The old lady solemnly and with tears in her eyes forgave her. But the mischievous girl would go too far. She took it into her head to tell her aunt about pranks which were so far only in the stage of schemes and projects. Katya affected to be very meek and penitent, and to be very sorry for her sins; in short, the old fanatic was highly delighted, and her vanity was greatly flattered at the prospect of dominating Katya, the treasure and idol of the whole house, who could make even her mother gratify her whims. And so the naughty chit confessed in the first place that she had intended to pin a visiting card on her aunt's dress; then that she had planned to hide Falstaff under her bed; and then to break her spectacles, to carry off all her aunt's books, and put French novels from her mother's room in place of them, and to throw bits of flock all over the floor; then to hide a pack of cards in her aunt's pocket, and so on. In fact, she told her aunt of prank after prank each worse than the last. The old lady was beside herself, she turned pale and then red with anger. At last Katya could not keep it up any longer, she burst out laughing and ran away from her aunt. The old lady promptly sent for the child's mother. There was a fearful to-do, and the princess spent a couple of hours imploring her aunt with tears in her eyes to forgive Katya, to allow her not to be punished, and to take into consideration that the child was ill. At first the old lady would listen to nothing; she declared that next day she should leave the house, and was only softened when the princess promised that she would only put off punishment till her daughter was well again, and then would satisfy the just indignation of the old lady. Katya, however, received a stern reprimand. She was taken downstairs to her mother.

But the rogue positively tore herself away after dinner. Making my way downstairs, I met her on the staircase. She opened the door and called Falstaff. I instantly guessed that she was plotting a terrible vengeance. The fact was that her old aunt had no more irreconcilable enemy than Falstaff. He was not friendly with anyone, he liked no one, but he was proud, haughty, and conceited in the extreme. He did not like anyone, but unmistakably insisted on being treated with due respect by all. Everyone felt it for him indeed, mixed with a not uncalled-for terror. But all at once with the arrival of the old lady everything was changed; Falstaff was cruelly insulted, in other words he was definitely forbidden to go upstairs.

At first Falstaff was frantic with resentment, and spent the whole day scratching at the door at the bottom of the stairs that led to the upper storey; but he soon guessed the cause of his banishment, and the first Sunday that the old lady went out to church, Falstaff dashed at the poor lady, barking shrilly. It was with difficulty that they rescued her from the furious vengeance of the offended dog, for he had been banished by the orders of the old princess, who declared that she could not endure the sight of him. From that time forward Falstaff was sternly forbidden to go upstairs, and when the old lady came downstairs he was chased into the farthest room. The sternest injunctions were laid upon the servants. But the revengeful brute found means on three occasions to get upstairs As soon as he reached the top he ran through the whole chain of apartments till he came to the old princess's bedroom. Nothing could restrain him. Fortunately the old lady's door was always closed, and Falstaff confined himself to howling horribly before it till the servants ran up and chased him downstairs. During the whole time of the terrible bulldog's visit, the old lady screamed as though she were being devoured by him, and each time became really ill from terror. She had several times sent an ultimatum to the princess, and even came to the point of saying that either she or Falstaff must leave the house; but Katya's mother would not consent to part with Falstaff.

The princess was not fond of many people and, after her children, Falstaff was dearer to her than anyone in the world, and the reason was this. One day, six years before, the prince had come back from a walk bringing with him a sick and muddy puppy of the most pitiful appearance, though he was a bulldog of the purest breed. The prince had somehow saved him from death. But as this new-comer was extremely rude and unmannerly in his behaviour, he was at the instance of the princess banished to the backyard and put on a cord. The prince did not oppose this.

Two years later, when all the family were staying at a summer villa, little Sasha, Katya's younger brother, fell into the Neva. His mother uttered a shriek, and her first impulse was to fling herself into the water after her son. She was with difficulty kept back from certain death. Meanwhile the child was being rapidly carried away by the current, and only his clothes kept him afloat. They began hurriedly unmooring a boat, but to save him would have been a miracle. All at once a huge, gigantic bulldog leapt into the water across the path of the drowning child, caught him in his teeth, and swam triumphantly with him to the bank. The princess flew to kiss the wet and muddy dog. But Falstaff, who at that time bore the prosaic and plebian name of Frix, could not endure caresses from anyone, and responded to the lady's kisses and embraces by biting her shoulder. The princess suffered all her life from the wound, but her gratitude was unbounded. Falstaff was taken into the inner apartments, cleansed, washed, and decorated with a silver collar of fine workmanship. He was installed in the princess's study on a magnificent bearskin, and soon the princess was able to stroke him without risk of immediate punishment. She was horrified when she learned that her favourite was called Frix, and immediately looked out for a new name as ancient as possible. But such names as Hector, Cerberus, etc., were too hackneyed; a name was sought which would be perfectly suitable for the pet of the family. At last the prince proposed calling the dog Falstaff, on the ground of his preternatural voracity. The name was accepted with enthusiasm, and the bulldog was always called that. Falstaff behaved well. Like a regular Englishman, he was taciturn, morose, and never attacked anyone till he was touched; he only insisted that his place on the bearskin should be regarded as sacred, and that he should be shown fitting respect in general. Sometimes he seemed to have something like an attack of hysterics, as though he were overcome by the spleen, and at such moments Falstaff remembered with bitterness that his foe, his irreconcilable foe, who had encroached upon his rights, was still unpunished. Then he made his way stealthily to the staircase that led to the upper storey, and finding the door, as usual, closed, lay down somewhere not far from it, hid in a corner, and craftily waited till someone should be careless and leave the door open. Sometimes the revengeful beast would lie in wait for three days. But strict orders had been given to keep watch over the door, and for three months Falstaff had not got upstairs.

"Falstaff! Falstaff!" cried Katya, opening the door and coaxingly beckoning the dog to come to us on the stairs. At that very time Falstaff, with an instinctive feeling that the door would be opened, was preparing to leap across his Rubicon, but Katya's summons seemed to him so impossible that for some time he resolutely refused to believe his ears. He was as sly as a cat, and not to show that he noticed the heedless opening of the door, went up to the window, laid his powerful paws on the window-sill and began gazing at the building opposite— behaved, in fact, like a man quite uninterested who has gone out for a walk and stopped for a minute to admire the fine architecture of a neighbouring building. Meanwhile his heart was throbbing and swooning in voluptuous expectation. What was his amazement, his joy, his frantic joy, when the door was flung wide open before him, and not only that, but he was called, invited, besought to go upstairs and wreak his just vengeance. Whining with delight, he showed his teeth, and terrible, triumphant, darted upstairs like an arrow. His impetus was so great that a chair that happened to be in his way was sent flying and overturned seven feet away. Falstaff flew like a cannon-ball. Madame Leotard uttered a shriek of horror. But Falstaff had already dashed to the forbidden door, was beating upon it with both paws, but could not open it, and howled like a lost soul. He was answered by a fearful scream from the old maid within. But a whole legion of enemies was flocking from all quarters, the whole household was moving upstairs, and Falstaff, the ferocious Falstaff, with a muzzle deftly popped over his jaws, with all his four limbs tied up, was ingloriously withdrawn from the field of battle and led downstairs with a noose round him.

An envoy was sent to his mistress.

On this occasion the princess was in no mood for forgiving and showing mercy; but whom could she punish? She guessed at once, in a flash; her eyes fell upon Katya. . . . That was it: Katya stood pale and trembling with fear. It was only now that she realised, poor child, the results of her mischief. Suspicion might fall upon the servants, on innocent people, and Katya was already preparing to tell the whole truth.

"Are you responsible?" her mother asked sternly.

I saw Katya's deadly pallor and, stepping forward, I pronounced in a resolute voice—

"It was I let Falstaff in . . . by accident," I added, for all my courage vanished before the princess's threatening eyes.

"Madame Leotard, give her an exemplary punishment!" said the princess, and she walked out of the room.

I glanced at Katya: she stood as though thunder-struck; her hands hung down at her sides; her little blanched face was looking down.

The only punishment that was made use of for the prince's children was being shut up in an empty room. To stay for two hours in an empty room was nothing. But when a child is put there by force against its will and told that it is deprived of freedom, the punishment is considerable. As a rule, Katya and her brother were shut up for two hours. In view of the enormity of my offence, I was shut up for four. Faint with delight I entered my black hole. I thought about Katya. I knew that I had won her. But instead of being there four hours, I was there till four o'clock in the morning. This is how it happened.

Two hours after I had been put in confinement, Madame Leotard learned that her daughter had arrived from Moscow, had been taken ill and wanted to see her. Madame Leotard went off, forgetting me. The maid who looked after us probably took for granted that I had been released. Katya was sent for downstairs, and obliged to stay with her mother till eleven o'clock in the evening. When she came back she was very much surprised that I was not in bed. The maid undressed her and put her to bed, but Katya had her reasons for not inquiring about me. She got into bed expecting me to come, knowing for a fact that I had been shut up for four hours, and expecting me to be brought by our nurse. But Nastya forgot me entirely, the more readily as I always undressed myself. And so I was left to spend the night in prison.

At four o'clock in the night I heard someone knocking and trying to break in. I was aleep, lying anyhow on the floor. When I awoke, I cried out with terror, but at once recognised Katya's voice which rang out above all the rest, then the voice of Madame Leotard, then of the frightened Nastya, then of the housekeeper. At last the door was opened, and Madame Leotard hugged me with tears in her eyes, begging me to forgive her for having forgotten me. I flung myself on her neck in tears. I was shivering with cold, and all my bones ached from lying on the bare floor. I looked for Katya, but she had run into our bedroom, leapt into bed, and when I went in she was already asleep—or pretending to be. She had accidentally fallen asleep while waiting for me in the evening, and had slept on till four o'clock in the morning. When she woke, she had made a fuss, a regular uproar in fact, wakened Madame Leotard, who had returned, our nurse, all the maids, and released me.

In the morning the whole household knew of my adventure; even the princess said that I had been treated too severely. As for the prince, I saw him that day, for the first time, moved to anger. He came upstairs at ten o'clock in the morning in great excitement.

"Upon my word," he began to Madame Leotard, "what are you about? What a way to treat the poor child. It's barbarous.

simply barbarous! Savage! A delicate, sick child, such a dreamy, timid little girl, so imaginative, and you shut her in a dark room all night! Why, it is ruining her! Don't you know her story? It's barbarous, it's inhuman, I tell you, madam! And how is such a punishment possible? Who invented, who could have invented such a punishment?''

Poor Madame Leotard, with tears in her eyes, began in confusion explaining how it had all happened, how she had forgotten me, how her daughter had arrived; but that the punishment in itself was good if it did not last too long, and that Jean Jacques Rousseau indeed said something of the sort.

"Jean Jacques Rousseau, madam! But Jean Jacques could not have said that. Jean Jacques is no authority. Jean Jacques Rousseau should not have dared to talk of education, he had no right to do so. Jean Jacques Rousseau abandoned his own children, madam! Jean Jacques was a bad man, madam!''

"Jean Jacques Rousseau! Jean Jacques a bad man! Prince! Prince! What are you saying?''

And Madame Leotard flared up.

Madame Leotard was a splendid woman, and above all things disliked hurting anyone's feelings; but touch one of her favourites, trouble the classic shades of Corneille, or Racine, insult Voltaire, call Jean Jacques Rousseau a bad man, call him a barbarian and—good heavens! Tears came into Madame Leotard's eyes, and the old lady trembled with excitement.

"You are forgetting yourself, prince!'' she said at last, beside herself with agitation.

The prince pulled himself up at once and begged her pardon, then came up to me, kissed me with great feeling, made the sign of the cross over me, and left the room.

"Pauvre prince!'' said Madame Leotard growing sentimental in her turn. Then we sat down to the schoolroom table.

But Katya was very inattentive at her lessons. Before going in to dinner she came up to me, looking flushed, with a laugh on her lips, stood facing me, seized me by the shoulders and said hurriedly as though ashamed:

"Well? You were shut up for a long time for me, weren't you? After dinner let us go and play in the drawing-room.''

Someone passed by, and Katya instantly turned away from me.

In the dusk of evening we went down together to the big drawing-room, hand in hand. Katya was much moved and breathless with excitement. I was happy and joyful as I had never been before.

"Would you like a game of ball?" she said. "Stand here."

She set me in one corner of the room, but instead of walking away and throwing the ball to me, she stopped three steps from me, glanced at me, flushed crimson and sank on the sofa, hiding her face in both hands. I made a movement towards her; she thought that I meant to go away.

"Don't go, Nyetochka, stay with me," she said. "I shall be all right in a minute."

But in a flash she had jumped up from her place, and flushed and in tears flung herself on my neck. Her cheeks were wet, her lips were swollen like cherries, her curls were in disorder. She kissed me as though she were frantic, she kissed my face, eyes, lips, neck and hands, she sobbed as though she were in hysterics; I hugged her tight and we embraced each other sweetly, joyfully, like friends, like lovers who had met after a long separation. Katya's heart beat so violently that I could hear every throb.

But we heard a voice in the next room. Katya was called to go to her mother. She kissed me for the last time, quietly, silently, warmly, and flew from me at Nastya's call. I ran upstairs as though I had risen from the dead, flung myself on the sofa, hid my face in the pillow and sobbed with rapture. My heart was thumping as though it would burst my chest. I don't know how I existed until the night. At last it struck eleven and I went to bed. Katya did not come back till twelve; she smiled at me from a distance but did not say a word. Nastya began undressing her slowly as though on purpose.

"Make haste, make haste, Nastya," Katya muttered.

"What's the matter with you, princess? Have you been running upstairs that your heart beats so? . . ." Nastya inquired.

"Oh, dear, how tiresome you are, Nastya! Make haste, make haste!" And Katya stamped on the floor in her vexation.

"Ah, what a little heart!" said Nastya, kissing the little foot from which she was taking off the shoe.

At last everything was done, Katya got into bed and Nastya went out of the room. Instantly Katya jumped out of bed and flew to me. I cried out as she came to me.

"Get into my bed, sleep with me!" she said, pulling me out of bed. A minute later I was in her bed. We embraced and hugged each other eagerly. Katya kissed and kissed me.

"Ah, I remember how you kissed me in the night," she said, flushing as red as a poppy.

I sobbed.

"Nyetochka!" whispered Katya through her tears, "my angel, I have loved you for so long, for so long! Do you know since when?"

"Since when?"

"Ever since father told me to beg your pardon that time when you stood up for your father, Nyetochka . . . my little for—lorn one," she said, showering kisses on me again. She was crying and laughing together.

"Oh, Katya!"

"Oh, what—oh, what?"

"Why have we waited so long . . . so long . . ." and I could not go on. We hugged each other and said nothing for three minutes.

"Listen, what did you think of me?" asked Katya.

"Oh, what a lot I thought about you, Katya. I have been thinking about you all the time, I thought about you day and night."

"And at night you talked about me."

"Really?"

"You cried ever so many times."

"I say, why were you so proud all the time?"

"I was stupid, you know, Nyetochka. It comes upon me, and then it's all over with me. I was angry with you."

"What for?"

"Because I was horrid. First, because you were better than I was; and then because father loves you more than me! And father is a kind man, Nyetochka, isn't he?"

"Oh, yes," I said, thinking with tears of the prince.

"He's a good man," said Katya gravely. "But what am I to do with him? He's always so. . . . Well, then I asked your forgiveness, and I almost cried, and that made me cross again."

"And I saw, I saw that you wanted to cry."

"Well, hold your tongue, you little silly, you're a cry-baby yourself," Katya exclaimed, putting her hand over my mouth. "Listen. I very much wanted to like you, and then all at once began to want to hate you; and I did hate you so, I did hate you so! . . ."

"What for?"

"Oh, because I was cross with you. I don't know what for! And then I saw that you couldn't live without me, and I thought, 'I'll torment her, the horrid thing!' "

"Oh, Katya!"

"My darling!" said Katya, kissing my hand. "Then I wouldn't speak to you, I wouldn't for anything. But do you remember how I stroked Falstaff?"

"Ah, you fearless girl!"

"Wasn't I fri-ight-ened!" Katya drawled. "Do you know why I went up to him?"

"Why?"

"Why, you were looking at me. When I saw that you were looking . . . Ah, come what may, I would go up to him. I gave you a fright, didn't I? Were you afraid for me?"

"Horribly!"

"I saw. And how glad I was that Falstaff went away! Goodness, how frightened I was afterwards when he had gone, the mo-on-ster!"

And the little princess broke into an hysterical laugh; then she raised her feverish head and looked intently at me. Tears glistened like little pearls on her long eyelashes.

"Why, what is there in you that I should have grown so fond of you? Ah, you poor little thing with your flaxen hair; you silly little thing, such a cry-baby, with your little blue eyes; my little or-phan girl!"

And Katya bent down to give me countless kisses again. A few drops of her tears fell on my cheeks. She was deeply moved.

"How I loved you, but still I kept thinking, 'No, no! I won't tell her.' And you know how obstinate I was! What was I afraid of, why was I ashamed of you? See how happy we are now!"

"Katya! How it hurt me!" I said in a frenzy of joy. "It broke my heart!"

"Yes, Nyetochka, listen. . . . Yes, listen: who gave you your name Nyetochka?"

"Mother."

"You must tell me about your mother."

"Everything, everything," I answered rapturously.

"And where have you put those two handkerchiefs of mine with lace on them? And why did you carry off my ribbon? Ah, you shameless girl! I know all about it."

I laughed and blushed till the tears came.

" 'No,' I thought, 'I will torment her, let her wait.' And at other times I thought, 'I don't like her a bit, I can't bear her.' And you are always such a meek little thing, my little lamb! And how frightened I was that you would think me stupid. You are clever, Nyetochka, you are very clever, aren't you?"

"What do you mean, Katya?" I answered, almost offended.

"No, you are clever," said Katya, gravely and resolutely. "I know that. Only I got up one morning and felt awfully fond of you. I had been dreaming of you all night. I thought I would ask mother to let me live downstairs. 'I don't want to like her, I don't want to!' And the next night I woke up and thought, 'If only she would come as she did last night!' And you did come! Ah, how I pretended to be asleep. . . . Ah, what shameless creatures we are, Nyetochka?"

"But why did you want not to like me?"

"I don't know. But what nonsense I am talking, I liked you all the time, I always liked you. It was only afterwards I could not bear you; I thought, 'I will kiss her one day, or else I will pinch her to death.' There's one for you, you silly!" •

And the little princess pinched me.

"And do you remember my tying up your shoe?"

"Yes, I remember."

"I remember. Were you pleased? I looked at you. 'What a sweet darling,' I thought. 'If I tie up her shoe, what will she think?' But I was happy too. And do you know, really I wanted to kiss you . . . but I didn't kiss you. And then it seemed so funny, so funny! And when we were out on our walk together, all the way I kept wanting to laugh. I couldn't look at you it was so funny. And how glad I was that you went into the black hole for me."

The empty room was called the "black hole".

"And were you frightened?"

"Horribly frightened."

"I wasn't so glad at your saying you did it, but I was glad that you were ready to be punished for me! I thought, 'She is crying now, but how I love her! To-morrow how I will kiss her, how I will kiss her!' And I wasn't sorry, I really wasn't sorry for you, though I did cry."

"But I didn't cry, I was glad!"

"You didn't cry? Ah, you wicked girl!" cried Katya, fastening her little lips upon me.

"Katya, Katya! Oh, dear! how lovely you are!"

"Yes, am I not? Well, now you can do what you like to me. My tyrant, pinch me. Please pinch me! My darling, pinch me!"

"You silly!"

"Well, what next?"

"Idiot!"

"And what next?"

"Why, kiss me."

And we kissed each other, cried, laughed, and our lips were swollen with kissing.

"Nyetochka! To begin with, you are always to sleep with me. Are you fond of kissing? And we will kiss each other. Then I won't have you be so depressed. Why were you so depressed? You'll tell me, won't you?"

"I will tell you everything, but I am not sad now, but happy!"

"No, you are to have rosy cheeks like mine. Oh, if to-morrow would only come quickly! Are you sleepy, Nyetochka?"

"No."

"Well, then let's talk."

And we chattered away for another two hours. Goodness knows what we didn't talk about. To begin with, the little princess unfolded all her plans for the future, and explained the present position of affairs; and so I learned that she loved her father more than anyone, almost more than me. Then we both decided that Madame Leotard was a splendid woman, and that she was not at all strict. Then we settled what we would do the next day, and the day after, and, in fact, planned out our lives for the next twenty years. Katya decided that we should live in this way: one day she would give me orders and I should obey, and the next day it should be the other way round, I should command and she would obey unquestioningly, and so we should both give orders equally; and that if either disobeyed on purpose we would first quarrel just for appearances and then make haste to be reconciled. In short, an infinity of happiness lay before us. At last we were tired out with prattling, I could not keep my eyes open. Katya laughed at me and called me sleepy-head, but she fell asleep before I did. In the morning we woke up at the same moment, hurriedly kissed because someone was coming in, and I only just had time to scurry into my bed.

All day we did not know what to do for joy. We were continually hiding and running away from everyone, dreading other people's eyes more than anything. At last I began telling her my story. Katya was distressed to tears by what I told her.

"You wicked, wicked girl! Why didn't you tell me all this before? I should have loved you so. And did the boys in the street hurt you when they hit you?"

"Yes, I was so afraid of them."

"Oh, the wretches! Do you know, Nyetochka, I saw a boy beating another in the street. To-morrow I'll steal Falstaff's whip, and if I meet one like that, I'll give him such a beating!"

Her eyes were flashing with indignation.

We were frightened when anyone came in. We were afraid of being caught kissing each other. And we kissed each other that day at least a hundred times. So that day passed and the next. I was afraid that I should die of rapture, I was breathless with joy. But our happiness did not last long.

Madame Leotard had to report all the little princess's doings. She watched us for three days, and during those three days she gathered a great deal to relate. At last she went down to Katya's mother and told her all that she had observed—that we both seemed in a sort of frenzy; that for the last three days we had been inseparable; that we were continually kissing, crying and laughing like lunatics, and that like lunatics we babbled incessantly; that there had been nothing like this before, that she did not know to what to attribute it, but she fancied that the little princess was passing through some nervous crisis; and finally that she believed that it would be better for us to see each other more seldom.

"I have thought so for a long time," answered the princess. "I knew that queer little orphan would give us trouble. The things I have been told about her, about her life in the past! Awful, really awful! She has an unmistakable influence over Katya. You say that Katya is very fond of her?"

"Absolutely devoted."

The princess crimsoned with annoyance. She was already jealous of her daughter's feeling for me.

"It's not natural," she said. "At first they seemed to avoid each other, and I must confess I was glad of it. Though she is only a little girl, I would not answer for anything. You understand me? She has absorbed her bringing up, her habits and perhaps principles from infancy, and I don't understand what the prince sees in her. A thousand times I have suggested sending her to a boarding-school.''

Madame Leotard attempted to defend me, but the princess had already determined to separate us. Katya was sent for at once, and on arriving downstairs was informed that she would not see me again till the following Sunday—that is, for just a week.

I learned all this late in the evening and was horror-stricken; I thought of Katya, and it seemed to me that she would not be able to bear our separation. I was frantic with misery and grief and was taken ill in the night; in the morning the prince came to see me and whispered to me words of hope. The prince did his utmost, but all was in vain, the princess would not alter her intention. Little by little I was reduced to despair, I could hardly breathe for misery.

On the morning of the third day Nastya brought me a note from Katya. Katya wrote a fearful scrawl in pencil:

"I love you. I am sitting with mamma and thinking all the time how I can escape to you. But I shall escape, I have said so, and so I don't cry. Write and tell me how you love me. And I was hugging you in my dreams all night, and was very miserable, Nyetochka. I am sending you some sweets. Farewell.''

I answered in the same style. I spent the day crying over Katya's letter. Madame Leotard worried me with her caresses. In the evening she went to the prince and told him I should certainly be ill for the third time if I did not see Katya, and that she regretted having told the princess. I questioned Nastya about Katya. She told me that Katya was not crying but was very pale.

In the morning Nastya whispered to me:

"Go down to his Excellency's study. Go down by the staircase on the right.''

My whole being revived with a presentiment. Breathless with expectation, I ran down and opened the study door. She was not there. Suddenly Katya clutched me from behind and kissed me warmly. Laughter, tears. . . . In a flash Katya tore herself from my arms, clambered on her father, leapt on his shoulders like a squirrel, but losing her balance, sprang off on to the sofa. The prince fell on the sofa after her. Katya was shedding tears of joy.

"Father, what a good man you are!''

"You madcaps! What has happened to you? What's this

friendship? What's this love?"

"Be quiet, father, you know nothing about it."

And we rushed into each other's arms again.

I began looking at her more closely. She had grown thinner in three days. The red had begun to fade from her little face, and pallor was stealing into its place. I shed tears of grief.

At last Nastya knocked, a signal that Katya had been missed and was being asked for. Katya turned deathly pale.

"That's enough, children. We'll meet every day. Good-bye, and may God bless you," said the prince.

He was touched as he looked at us; but his words did not come true. In the evening the news came from Moscow that little Sasha had fallen ill and was almost on the point of death. The princess decided to set off next day. This happened so suddenly that I knew nothing about it till the moment of saying good-bye to Katya. The prince himself had insisted on our being allowed to say good-bye, and the princess had only reluctantly consented. Katya looked shattered. I ran downstairs hardly knowing what I was doing, and threw myself on her neck. The travelling coach was already at the door. Katya uttered a shriek when she saw me, and sank unconscious. I flew to kiss her. The princess began trying to restore her. At last she came to herself and hugged me again.

"Good-bye, Nyetochka," she said to me suddenly, laughing, with an indescribable expression on her face. "Don't mind me; it's nothing; I am not ill. I shall come back in a month, then we will not part again."

"That's enough," said the princess calmly. "Let us start."

But Katya came back once more. She squeezed me convulsively in her arms.

"My life," she succeeded in whispering, hugging me. "Good-bye till we meet again."

We kissed each other for the last time and Katya vanished—for a long, long time. Eight years passed before we met again.

•   •   •   •   •

I have purposely described so minutely this episode of my childhood, Katya's first appearance in my life. But our story is inseparable. Her romance was my romance. It was as though it were fated that I should meet her; that she should find me. And I could not deny myself the pleasure of going back once more in memory into my childhood. . . . Now my story will go more quickly. My life passed all at once into a dead calm, and I seemed only to wake up again when I had reached my sixteenth year. . . .

But a few words of what became of me on the departure of the prince's family to Moscow.

I was left with Madame Leotard.

A fortnight later a messenger arrived with the news that their return to Petersburg was postponed indefinitely. As for family reasons Madame Leotard could not go to Moscow, her duties in the prince's household were at an end; but she remained in the same family and entered the house of Alexandra Mihalovna, the princess's elder daughter.

I have said nothing yet about Alexandra Mihalovna, and indeed I had only seen her once. She was the daughter of the princess by her first husband. The origin and family of the princess was somewhat obscure. Her first husband was a contractor. When the princess married a second time she did not know what to do with her elder daughter. She could not hope that she would make a brilliant marriage. Her dowry was only a moderate one; at last, four years before, they had succeeded in marrying her to a wealthy man of a very decent grade in the service. Alexandra Mihalovna passed into a different circle and saw a different world around her. The princess used to visit her twice a year; the prince, her step-father, visited her once a week with Katya. But of late the princess had not liked letting Katya go to see her sister, and the prince took her on the sly. Katya adored her sister, but they were a great contrast in character. Alexandra Mihalovna was a woman of twenty-two, quiet, soft and loving; it was as though some secret sorrow, some hidden heartache had cast a shade of austerity on her lovely features. Gravity and austerity seemed out of keeping with the angelic candour of her face, it was like mourning on a child. One could not look at her without feeling greatly attracted. She was pale and was said to be inclined to be consumptive when I saw her for the first time. She led a very solitary life, and did not like receiving many guests or paying visits; she was like a nun. She had no children. I remember she came to see Madame Leotard, and coming up to me, kissed me with much feeling. She was accompanied by a lean, rather elderly man. Tears came into his eyes as he looked at me. This was the violinist B. Alexandra Mihalovna put her arms round me and asked whether I would like to live with her and be her daughter. Looking into her face, I recognised my Katya's sister, and hugged her with a dull pain in my heart which set my whole chest aching . . . as though someone had once more pronounced over me the word "orphan". Then Alexandra Mihalovna showed me a letter from the prince. In it were a few lines addressed to me, and I read them with smothered sobs. The prince sent his blessing and wished me long life and happiness, and begged me to love his other daughter. Katya wrote me a few lines too. She wrote to me that she would not now leave her mother.

And so that evening I passed into another family, into another house, to new people, for a second time tearing my heart away from all that had become so dear, that by now had become like my own. I arrived exhausted and lacerated by mental suffering. . . . Now a new story begins.

CHAPTER VI

MY new life was as calm and unruffled as though I had been living among hermits. . . . I lived more than eight years with my new guardians, and I remember only very few occasions in which there were evening parties, dinners, or gatherings of friends and relations. With the exception of two or three people who came from time to time, the musician B., who was the friend of the family, and the people who came to see Alexandra Mihalovna's husband, almost always on business, no one came to see us. Alexandra Mihalovna's husband was always occupied with business and the duties of his office, and could only with difficulty contrive to get even a little free time, and that was divided between his family and social life. The necessity of maintaining important connections which it was impossible to neglect led him to show himself fairly frequently in society. People talked on all hands of his boundless ambition; but as he enjoyed the reputation of a businesslike and serious man, as he had a very prominent post, and as happiness and success seemed to dog his path, public opinion by no means denied its approval. It went beyond that, in fact. People always felt a special liking for him which they never felt for his wife. Alexandra Mihalovna lived in complete isolation; but she seemed to be glad of it. Her gentle character seemed created for seclusion.

She was devoted to me with her whole heart, and loved me as though I had been her own child; and with the tears not yet dry from parting with Katya, with a still aching heart, I threw myself eagerly into the motherly arms of my kind benefactress. From that time forward my warm love for her has been uninterrupted. To me she was mother, sister, friend, she replaced all the world for me and cherished my youth. Moreover, I soon noticed by instinct, by intuition, that her lot was by no means so rosy as might be imagined at first sight from her quiet and apparently serene life, from the show of freedom, from the unclouded brightness of the smile which so often lighted up her face; and so every day of my development made clear to me something new in the life of my benefactress, something which my heart slowly and painfully surmised, and together with this sorrowful knowledge my devotion to her grew greater and greater.

She was of a timid disposition and weak will. Looking at the candid and serene features of her face, one would never have supposed that any agitation could trouble her upright heart. It was unthinkable that she could dislike anyone; compassion in her always got the upper hand even of repulsion—and yet there were few friends she was devoted to, and she lived in almost complete solitude. . . . She was passionate and impressionable by temperament, but at the same time she seemed afraid of her own impressionability, as though she were continually guarding her heart, not allowing it to forget itself even in dreams. Sometimes even at her sunniest moments I noticed tears in her eyes as though a sudden painful memory of something rankling in her conscience had flamed up in her soul, as though something were keeping hostile watch on her happiness and seeking to trouble it. And it seemed as though the happier she were, the calmer and serener the moment of her life, the nearer was this depression, the more likely to appear the sudden melancholy, the tears, as though some sudden crisis came over her. I don't remember one calm month in all the eight years. Her husband appeared to be very fond of her; she adored him. But at the first glance it seemed as though there were something unuttered between them. There was some secret in her life; at least I began to suspect it from the first moment. . . .

Alexandra Mihalovna's husband made a forbidding impression on me from the first. This impression arose in childhood and was never effaced. In appearance he was a tall, thin man, who seemed intentionally to conceal the look in his eyes behind green spectacles. He was dry and uncommunicative, and even *tête-à-tête* with his wife seemed unable to find anything to talk about. He was obviously oppressed by society. He took no notice of me, and every time when we all three met in Alexandra Mihalovna's drawing-room for tea I felt ill at ease in his presence. I would glance stealthily at Alexandra Mihalovna, and notice with pain that she seemed to be hesitating over every movement she made, turning pale if she fancied her husband was becoming particularly cross and severe, or suddenly flushing as though she heard or divined some hint in something her husband said. I felt that she was oppressed in his presence, and yet it seemed as though she could not live without him for a minute. I was struck by her extraordinary attentiveness to him, to every word he uttered, to every movement he made; as though her whole soul longed to please him in some way, as though she felt that she did not succeed in doing what he desired. She seemed to be entreating his approbation; the slightest smile on his face, half a word of kindness—and she was happy; as though she had been at the first stage of still timorous, still hopeless love. She waited on her husband as though he were dangerously ill. When he went off into his study after pressing the hand of Alexandra Mihalovna, at whom he always looked, as I fancied, with a compassion that weighed upon her, she was completely changed. Her movements, her talk, instantly became more light-hearted, and more free. But a sort of embarrassment remained for a long time after every interview with her husband. She began at once recalling every word as though weighing every sentence he had uttered. Frequently she turned to me with the question: had she heard right? Was that the expression Pyotr Alexandrovitch had used? as though looking for some other meaning in what he had said; and it was perhaps not for another hour that she quite regained her spirits, as though convinced that he was quite satisfied with her, and that she had no need to worry herself. Then she would suddenly become sweet, gay, and joyful; would kiss me, laugh with me, or go to the piano and improvise on it for an hour or two. But not infrequently her joy would be suddenly interrupted; she would begin to shed tears, and when I looked at her in agitation, in trouble and in anxiety, she would at once assure me in a whisper, as though afraid of being overheard, that her tears meant nothing, that she was happy, and that I must not worry about her. It would sometimes happen when her husband was away that she would suddenly begin to be agitated, would begin inquiring about him, would show anxiety, would send to find out what he was doing, would find out from the maid why the carriage was ordered and where he meant to drive, would inquire whether he were ill, in good spirits or depressed, what he said, and so on. It seemed as though she did not dare to speak to him herself about his business and pursuits. When he gave her some advice or asked her some question, she listened to him as quietly and was as overawed as though she were his slave. She very much liked him to praise something of hers, anything, a book or her needlework. She seemed flattered by this, and seemed to be made happy by it at once. But her joy was boundless when he chanced (which happened very rarely) to fondle one of their two tiny children. Her face was transformed, and beamed with happiness. And at such moments she sometimes let herself be *too much* carried away by joy in her husband's presence. She would be so emboldened as suddenly, without any invitation from him, to suggest, of course timidly and with a trembling voice, that he should listen to some new piece of music she had just received, or would give his opinion about some book, or even that he would let her read him a page or two of some author who had made a special impression upon her that day. Sometimes her husband would graciously fall in with her wishes and even smile condescendingly at her, as people smile at a spoilt child whom they do not want to check in some strange whim for fear of prematurely troubling its simplicity. But, I don't know why, I was revolted to the depths of my being by those smiles, that supercilious condescension, that inequality between them. I said nothing. I restrained myself and only watched them diligently with childish curiosity, but with prematurely harsh criticism. Another time I would notice that he suddenly seemed to pull himself up, seemed to recollect himself, as though he suddenly, painfully, and against his will were reminded of something disagreeable, awful, inevitable; instantly the condescending smile would vanish from his face, and his eyes would fasten on his nervously fluttered wife with a look of compassion which made me shudder, which, as I now realise, would have made me wretched if it had been turned upon me. At the same minute the joy vanished from Alexandra Mihalovna's face. The music or the reading was interrupted. She turned white, but controlled herself and was silent. There followed unpleasant moments, moments of anguish which sometimes lasted a long time. At last the husband put an end to them. He would get up from his seat, as though with an effort suppressing his emotion and vexation, and pacing two or three times up and down the room in gloomy silence would press his wife's hand, sigh deeply, and in undisguised perturbation would utter a few disconnected words in which the desire to comfort his wife was evident, and would go out of the room; while Alexandra Mihalovna would burst into tears, or would sink into a terrible prolonged melancholy. Often he blessed her and made the sign of the cross over her as though she were a child saying good-night to him, and she received his blessing with reverence and gratitude. But I cannot forget certain evenings in the house (two or three only, during those eight years) when Alexandra Mihalovna seemed suddenly transformed. An anger, an indignation, was reflected in her usually gentle face, instead of her invariable self-abasement and reverence for her husband. Sometimes the storm would be gathering for a whole hour; the husband would become more silent, more austere and more surly than usual. At last the poor woman's sore heart could bear no more. In a voice breaking with emotion she would begin talking, at first jerkily, disconnectedly, with hints and bitter pauses; then as though unable to endure her anguish she would suddenly break into tears and sobs, and then would follow an outburst of indignation, of reproaches, of complaints, of despair, as though she were passing through a nervous crisis. And then it was worth seeing with what patience the husband bore it, with what sympathy he bent down to comfort her, kissed her hands, and even at last began weeping with her; then she would seem to recollect herself, her conscience would seem to cry out and convict her of crime. Her husband's tears would have a shattering effect on her and, wringing her hands in despair, with convulsive sobs she would fall at his feet and beg the forgiveness that was instantly vouchsafed her. But the agonies of her conscience, the tears and the entreaties for forgiveness went on a long time, and she would be still more timid, still more tremulous in his presence for whole months. I could comprehend nothing of these reproaches and upbraidings; I was sent out of the room on these occasions and always very awkwardly. But they could not keep their secret from me entirely. I watched, I noticed, I divined, and from the very beginning a vague suspicion took shape in me that there was some mystery in all this, that these sudden outbreaks of an exasperated heart were not simply a nervous crisis; that there was some reason for the husband's always being sullen, that there was some reason for his double-edged compassion for his poor sick wife, that there was some reason for her everlasting timidity and trepidation before him, and this meek, strange love which she did not even dare to display in her husband's presence, that there was some reason for her isolation, her nun-like seclusion, that sudden flush and deathly pallor on her face in the presence of her husband.

But since such scenes with her husband were very rare, since life was very monotonous and I saw her from so close at hand, since indeed I was developing and growing very rapidly and much that was new was beginning to stir unconsciously in me, distracting me from my observations, I grew accustomed at last to the life, and to the habits and characters surrounding me. I could not, of course, help wondering at times as I looked at Alexandra Mihalovna, but my doubts so far reached no solution. I loved her warmly, respected her sadness, and so was afraid of troubling her over-sensitive heart by my curiosity. She understood me, and how many times she was ready to thank me for my devotion! Sometimes, noticing my anxiety, she would smile through her tears and make a joke herself at her frequent weeping, then suddenly she would begin telling me that she was very contented, very happy, that everyone was so kind to her, that everyone she had known had been so fond of her, that she was very much distressed that Pyotr Alexandrovitch was always so worried about her, about her peace of mind, while she was on the contrary so happy, so happy! . . . And then she would embrace me with such deep feeling, her face would be lighted up with such love, that my heart, if I may say so, ached with sympathy for her.

Her features were never effaced from my memory. They were regular, and their thinness and pallor only accentuated the severe charm of her beauty. Her thick black hair, combed smoothly down, framed her cheeks in sharp severe shadow; but that seemed to make more sweetly striking the contrast of her soft gaze, her large childishly clear blue eyes, which reflected at times so much simplicity, timidity, as it were defencelessness, as though fearful over every sensation, over every impulse of the heart—over the momentary gladness and over the frequent quiet sorrow. But at some happy unruffled moments there was so much that was serene and bright as day, so much goodness and tranquillity in the glance that penetrated to the heart The eyes, blue as the heavens, shone with such love and gazed so sweetly, and in them was reflected so deep a feeling of sympathy for everything that was noble, for everything that asked for love, that besought compassion—that the whole soul surrendered to her, was involuntarily drawn to her, and seemed to catch from her the same serenity, the same calm of spirit and peacemaking and love. So sometimes one gazes up at the blue sky and feels that one is ready to spend whole hours in secret contemplation, and that the soul is growing more free and calm, as though the vast vault of heaven were reflected in it as in a still sheet of water. When—and this happened often—exaltation sent the colour rushing to her face and her bosom heaved with emotion, then her eyes flashed like lightning and seemed to give forth sparks, as though her whole soul, which had chastely guarded the pure flame of beauty now inspiring her, had passed into them. At such moments she was as though inspired. And in this sudden rush of inspiration, in the transition from a mood of shrinking gentleness to lofty spiritual exaltation, to pure stern enthusiasm, there was at the same time so much that was naïve, so much that was childishly impulsive, so much childlike faith, that I believe an artist would have given half his life to portray such a moment of lofty ecstasy and to put that inspired face upon canvas.

From my first days in that house I noticed that she was positively delighted to have me in her solitude. She had only one child then, and had only been twelve months a mother. But I was quite like a daughter to her, and she was incapable of making any distinction between me and her own children. With what warmth she set about my education! She was in such a hurry at first that Madame Leotard could not help smiling as she looked at her. Indeed we set about everything at once, so that we could not understand each other. For instance, she undertook to teach me many things at once, but so many that it ended in more excitement, more heat, and more loving impatience on her part than in real benefit to me. At first she was disappointed at finding herself so incapable, but after a good laugh we started again from the beginning, though Alexandra Mihalovna, in spite of her first failure, still boldly declared herself opposed to Madame Leotard's system. They kept up a laughing argument, but my new instructress was absolutely opposed to every system, declaring that we should find the true method as we went along, that it was useless to stuff my head with dry information, and that success depended on understanding my instincts and on arousing my interest—and she was right, for she was triumphantly successful. To begin with, from the first the parts of pupil and teacher entirely disappeared. We studied like two friends, and sometimes it seemed as though I were teaching Alexandra Mihalovna, all unconscious of the subtlety of the method. So, too, arguments often sprung up between us, and I exerted myself to the utmost to prove that the thing was as I saw it, and imperceptibly Alexandra Mihalovna led me into the right way. But in the end when we reached the truth we were pursuing, I would guess how it was, would detect Alexandra Mihalovna's strategy, and pondering over all her efforts with me, sometimes whole hours sacrificed for my benefit, I fell on her neck and embraced her after every lesson. My sensibility touched and perplexed her. She began inquiring with interest about my past, wishing to hear it from me; and every time I told her anything, she grew more tender and more earnest with me, more earnest because through my unhappy childhood I aroused in her not only compassion, but a feeling as it were of respect. After I had told her about myself we usually fell into long conversations in which she explained my past experiences to me, so that I seemed really to live through them again and learnt a great deal that was new. Madame Leotard often thought such talk too serious and, seeing the tears I could not restrain, thought them quite unsuitable. I thought the very opposite, for after such *lessons* I felt as light-hearted and glad as though there had been nothing unhappy in my life. Moreover, I felt too grateful to Alexandra Mihalovna for making me love her more and more every day. Madame Leotard had no idea that all that had hitherto surged up from my soul fitfully with premature violence was gradually in this way being smoothed out and brought into tuneful harmony. She did not know that my childish, lacerated heart had suffered such agonising pain that it was unjust in its exasperation and resented its sufferings, not understanding whence they came.

The day began by our meeting in the nursery beside her baby; we woke him, washed and dressed him, fed him, played with him and taught him to talk. At last we left the baby and sat down to work. We studied a great deal, but they were strange lessons. There was everything in them, but nothing definite. We read, discussed our impressions, put aside the book and went to music, and whole hours flew by unnoticed. In the evenings B., who was a friend of Alexandra Mihalovna's, would come, and Madame Leotard would come too; often a very lively heated conversation would begin, about art, about life (which we in our little circle knew only by hearsay), about reality, about ideals, about the past and the future, and we would sit up till after midnight. I listened intently, grew enthusiastic with the others, laughed or was touched, and it was at this time that I learned in full detail everything concerning my father and my early childhood. Meanwhile I was growing up; teachers were engaged for me from whom I should have learned nothing but for Alexandra Mihalovna. With my geography teacher I should have simply gone blind hunting for towns and rivers on the map. With Alexandra Mihalovna we set off on such voyages, stayed in such countries, saw such wonders, spent such delightful, such fantastic hours; and so great was the ardour of both of us that the books she had read were not enough for us, we were obliged to have recourse to new ones. Soon I was equal to teaching my geography teacher, though I must do him the justice to say he kept to the end his superiority in exact knowledge of the degrees of latitude and longitude in which any town was situated, and the thousands, hundreds and even tens of inhabitants living in it. Our teacher of history was paid his fees regularly also, but when he went away Alexandra Mihalovna and I learnt history in our own way; we took up our books and were often reading them till far into the night, or rather Alexandra Mihalovna read, for she exercised some censorship. I never felt so enthusiastic as I did after this reading. We were both excited as though we had been ourselves the heroes. Of course we read more between the lines than in the words themselves; moreover, Alexandra Mihalovna was splendid at describing things, so that it seemed that all we read about had happened in her presence. It may perhaps have been absurd that we should have been so excited and sat up beyond midnight, I a child and she a stricken heart weighed down by the burden of life! I knew that she found, as it were, a rest from life beside me. I remember that at times I pondered strangely, looking at her. I was divining much before I had begun to live, I had already divined much in life.

At last I was thirteen. Meanwhile Alexandra Mihalovna's health grew worse and worse. She had become more irritable, her attacks of hopeless melancholy were more severe. Her husband's visits began to be more frequent, and he used to sit with her, as before, of course, gloomy, austere and almost silent, for longer and longer periods. I became more intensely absorbed in her lot.

I was growing out of childhood, a great number of new impressions, observations, enthusiasms, conjectures were taking shape in me. Certainly, the secret of this family began to worry me more and more. There were moments when it seemed to me that I understood something of that secret. At other times I would relapse into indifference, into apathy, even into annoyance, and forgot my curiosity as I found no answer to any question. At times—and this happened more and more frequently—I experienced a strange craving to be alone and to think, to do nothing but think. My present stage was like the time when I was living with my parents and when, before I had made friends with my father, I spent a whole year, thinking, imagining, looking out from my corner into God's world, so that at last I became like a wild creature, lost among the fantastic phantoms I had myself created. The difference was that now there was more impatience, more wretchedness, more new unconscious impulses, more thirst for movement, for thrills, so that I could not concentrate myself on one thing as in the past. On her side Alexandra Mihalovna seemed to hold herself more aloof from me. At that age I could hardly be her friend. I was not a child, I asked too many questions, and at times looked at her so that she was obliged to drop her eyes before me. These were strange moments. I could not bear to see her tears, and often tears rose into my own eyes as I looked at her. I flung myself on her neck and kissed her warmly. What answer could she make me? I felt that I was burdensome to her. But at other times—and they were sad and terrible times—she would convulsively embrace me as though in despair, as though seeking my sympathy, as though she were unable to endure her isolation, as though I understood her, as though we were suffering together. But yet the secret remained between us, that was unmistakable, and I began at such moments myself to feel aloof from her. I felt ill at ease with her. Moreover, there was little now we had in common, nothing but music. But the doctors began to forbid her music. And books were a greater difficulty than anything, she did not know how to read with me. We should, of course, have stopped at the first page; every word might have been a hint, every insignificant phrase an enigma. We both avoided warm, sincere conversation *tête-à-tête*.

And it was at this time that fate suddenly and unexpectedly gave a new turn to my life in a very strange way. My attention, my feelings, my heart, my brain were all at once sud-

denly turned with intense energy amounting almost to
enthusiasm into another, quite unexpected channel and,
without realising the fact, I was carried along into a new
world. I had no time to turn round, to look about me, to
think things over; I might be going to ruin, I felt that indeed;
but the temptation was too great for my fear, and I took my
chance shutting my eyes. And for a long time I was diverted
from the real life which was beginning to weigh upon me,
and from which I had so eagerly and so uselessly sought an
escape. This was what it was, and this is how it happened.

There were three doors leading out of the dining-room—
one leading to the sitting-room, another to my room and the
nursery, and the third to the library. From the library there
was another way out, only separated from my room by a study
in which Pyotr Alexandrovitch's assistant, his copyist, who was
at the same time his secretary and his agent, was installed. The
key of the bookcases and of the library was kept in his room.
After dinner one day, when he was not in the house, I found
the key on the floor. I was seized with curiosity, and arming
myself with my find I went into the library. It was rather a
large, very light room, furnished with eight large bookcases
filled with books. There were a great number of books, most
of which had come to Pyotr Alexandrovitch by inheritance.
The rest of the books had been added by Alexandra Mihalovna,
who was continually buying them. Great circumspection had
been exercised hitherto in giving me. books to read, so that I
readily guessed that a great deal was forbidden me, and that
many things were a secret from me. That was why I opened
the first bookcase and took out the first book with irresistible
curiosity, with a rush of terror and joy and of a peculiar un-
definable feeling. The bookcase was full of novels. I took one
of them, shut the bookcase and carried the book off to my room
with as strange a sensation, with as much throbbing and flutter-
ing of my heart, as though I foresaw that a great transforma-
tion would take place in my life. Going into my room, I locked
myself in and opened the book. But I could not read it, my
mind was full of another preoccupation; I had first to plan
securely and finally my access to the library in such a way
that no one would know, and that I should retain the possibility
of getting any book at any time. And so I postponed my enjoyment to a more convenient moment; I took the book back, but
hid the key in my room. I hid it, and that was the first evil
action in my life. I awaited the results; they were extremely

317

satisfactory: Pyotr Alexandrovitch's secretary, after looking for the key the whole evening and part of the night, searching on the floor with a candle, decided in the morning to send for a locksmith, who from the bunch of keys he had brought with him made a new one to fit. So the matter ended, and no one heard anything more about the loss of the key. I was so cautious that I did not go into the library till a week later, when I felt perfectly secure from all suspicion. At first I chose a moment when the secretary was not at home; afterwards I took to going into the library from the dining-room, for Pyotr Alexandrovitch's secretary merely kept the key in his pocket, and never entered into closer relations with the books, and therefore did not even go into the room in which they were kept.

I began reading greedily, and soon I was entirely absorbed in reading. All my new cravings, all my recent yearnings, all the still vague impulses of my adolescence, which had surged up with such restless violence in my soul, prematurely stimulated by my too early development—all this was suddenly turned aside into a new channel that unexpectedly presented itself, as though fully satisfied by its new food, as though it had found its true path. Soon my heart and my head were so enchanted, soon my imagination was developing so widely, that I seemed to forget the whole world which had hitherto surrounded me. It seemed as though fate itself had stopped me on the threshold of a new life, into which I longed to plunge, and about which I spent my days and nights conjecturing; and before letting me step into the unknown path, had led me up on to a height, showing me the future in a magic panorama, in dazzling and alluring perspective. I was destined to live through that future by getting to know it first in books, to live through it in dreams, in hopes, in passionate impulses, in the voluptuous emotion of a youthful spirit. I began reading indiscriminately the first book that came into my hands, but fate watched over me; what I had learned and experienced so far was so noble, so austere, that no evil unclean page could attract me. I was guarded by my childish instinct, my youth, my past. It was now that awakened intelligence suddenly, as it were, lighted up my whole past life. Indeed almost every page I read seemed to me as though it were already familiar, as though all these passions, all this life presented to me in such unexpected forms, in such enchanting pictures, was already familiar to me. And how could I help being carried away to the point of forgetting the present, of almost becoming estranged from reality, when in every book I read I found embodied the laws of the same destiny, the same spirit of adventure which dominates the life of man, yet is derived from some chief law of human life which is the condition of safety, preservation and happiness? This law which I suspected I strove my utmost to divine, with every instinct awakened in me almost by a feeling of self-preservation. It was as though I had been forewarned, as though someone were prompting me. It was as though something were stirring prophetically in my heart. And every day hope grew stronger and stronger in my breast, though at the same time my longings, too, grew stronger for that future, for that life which impressed me in what I had read each day with all the power of art, with all the fascination of poetry. But as I have said already, my imagination dominated my impatience, and I was, in fact, bold only in my dreams, while in reality I was instinctively timid of the future. And therefore, as though by previous compact with myself, I unconsciously decided to be satisfied, for the time being, with the world of imagination, the world of dreams, in which I was the sole sovereign, in which there was nothing but fascination, nothing but delights; and unhappiness itself, if it were admitted, played a passive part, a transitory part, essential for the sake of contrast and for the sudden turn of destiny that was to give a happy ending to the rapturous romances in my brain. That is how I interpret now my state of mind at that time.

And such a life, a life of the imagination, a life absolutely estranged from everything surrounding me, actually lasted for three whole years!

This life was my secret, and at the end of three years I did not know whether to be afraid of its suddenly being discovered or not. All that I had lived through in those three years was too precious, too close to me. I was myself too closely reflected in all my imaginings, so much so that I might have been confused and frightened if any eye, no matter whose, had carelessly peeped into my soul. Moreover we all, the whole household, led such an isolated life, so remote from society, in such monastic stillness, that each one of us must have become self-concentrated and have developed a craving for seclusion. That was what happened to me. Nothing about me was changed during those three years, everything remained as before. Dreary monotony reigned as before among us, which, I believe, if I had not been distracted by my secret hidden life, would have been an agony to my soul and would have driven me into some unknown and perilous path to escape from that spiritless and dreary circle, a path that might, perhaps, have led to my ruin. Madame Leotard had grown older, and was almost always shut up in her room; the children were still too little; B. was always the same; and Alexandra Mihalovna's husband was as austere, as unapproachable and as self-absorbed as ever. Between him and his wife there still persisted the same mysterious relation, which had begun to take a more and more grim and sinister aspect to my imagination. I felt more and more alarmed for Alexandra Mihalovna. Her joyless, colourless life was visibly wasting away before my eyes. Her health was growing weaker almost day by day. Despair, it seemed, had entered into her soul at last. She was obviously weighed down by something unknown, indefinite, of which she could not herself give an account—of something awful, though it was to her unintelligible; and she took it as an inevitable cross laid upon her life as a punishment. Her heart grew embittered at last in this mute anguish; even her intelligence took a different direction, dark and melancholy. One thing I observed struck me particularly: it seemed to me that, as I grew older, she held herself more aloof from me, so much so that her reserve with me took the form indeed of a sort of impatient annoyance. It even seemed to me, at some moments, that she did not like me; it seemed as though I were in her way. I have mentioned that I had purposely taken to holding myself aloof from her, and once apart from her I seemed as though I had caught the secretiveness of her character. That was how it was that all I passed through in those three years, all that was taking shape in my soul, in my dreams, in the knowledge I acquired, in my hopes and in my passionate transports—all was stubbornly kept to myself. Having once put up a screen between us we never came together again, though it seemed to me that I loved her more every day. I cannot recall without tears how devoted she was to me, and how deeply she felt in her heart the obligation to lavish upon me all the treasures of her love, and to keep her vow—to be a mother to me. It is true that her own sorrow often distracted her from me; for long intervals she seemed to forget me, the more readily as I tried not to remind her of my existence; so that my sixteenth year arrived and no one seemed aware of it. But in her moments of lucidity, when she took a clearer view of what was going on around her, Alexandra Mihalovna seemed suddenly to be troubled about me; she would impatiently send for me from my room, would shower questions upon me about my lessons and my pursuits, as it were testing me, examining me, would not part from me for days together, would divine all my yearnings, all my desires, evidently thinking anxiously of my age, of my present and my future, and with inexhaustible love, with a sort of reverence, making ready to come to my help. But she was too much out of touch with me, and hence sometimes set to work too naïvely, so that I could too easily understand and see through it. It happened, for instance, when I was sixteen that, after looking through my books and questioning me as to what I was reading, she seemed suddenly to take fright at finding that I had not yet got beyond the childish books suitable for a girl of twelve. I guessed what she was feeling, and watched her attentively. For a whole fortnight she seemed to be preparing me, trying me, trying to find out how far I was developed, and how much I needed. At last she made up her mind to begin, and Walter Scott's *Ivanhoe*, which I had already perused at least three times, made its appearance on our table At first with timid expectation she kept watch on my impressions, seemed to be weighing them, as though she were apprehensive of them. At last this strained attitude between us, of which I was only too well aware, vanished; we both grew excited, and I felt so happy, so overjoyed that I could be open with her! By the time we finished the novel, she was delighted with me. Every observation I made during our reading was true, every impression was correct. In her eyes my development had made strides already. Impressed by this, delighted with me, she was gladly intending to undertake my education once more—she did not want to part from me again; but this was not in her power. Fate soon parted us, and prevented us from being close friends again. The first attack of illness, the first attack of her everlasting depression was enough to do this; and then followed again estrangements, reserves, mistrustfulness, and perhaps even exasperation.

Yet even at such periods there were moments when we were carried away. Reading, a few sympathetic words passing between us, music, and we forgot ourselves, spoke freely, spoke sometimes too freely, and afterwards felt ill at ease with each other. When we thought it over, we looked at each other as though we were frightened, with suspicious curiosity and with mistrustfulness. Each of us had a line up to which our intimacy could go, but which we did not dare to overstep even if we had wished.

One day in the evening, just as it was getting dusk, I was reading inattentively in Alexandra Mihalovna's study. She was sitting at the piano, improvising variations on an Italian air which was a favourite of hers. When she passed at last to the tune itself, I was so carried away by the music that I began timidly in a low voice to hum the tune to myself. Soon completely carried away, I got up and went to the piano; as though she saw what I wanted, Alexandra Mihalovna began playing the accompaniment and lovingly followed every note of my voice. She seemed struck by its richness. I had never sung in her presence before, and indeed I scarcely knew my powers myself. Now we were both stirred. I raised my voice more and more; I was roused to energy, to passion, intensified by Alexandra Mihalovna's delighted wonder which I perceived in every touch of her accompaniment. At last the singing ended so successfully, with such fire and power, that she seized my hands in delight and looked at me joyfully.

"Anneta! But you have got a beautiful voice," she cried. "My goodness, how is it that I haven't noticed it?"

"I have only just noticed it myself," I answered, beside myself with joy.

"God bless you, my sweet, precious child! You must thank Him for this gift. Who knows . . . Oh, my God, my God!"

She was so touched by this surprise, in such a state of delight, that she did not know what to say to me, how to make enough of me. It was a moment of openness, mutual sympathy and close intimacy such as we had not had for a long while. Within an hour it seemed as though the house were keeping holiday. B. was sent for at once. While we were waiting for him to come we opened some other music-books at random which I knew better, and began a new air. This time I was shaking with nervousness. I did not want to spoil the first impression by failure. But soon my voice grew steadier and encouraged me. I was myself more and more astonished at its strength, and this second trial dispelled all doubts. In her impatient delight Alexandra Mihalovna sent for her children and their nurse; and at last, completely carried away, went to her husband and summoned him from his study, which she would hardly have dared to dream of doing at other times. Pyotr Alexandrovitch received the news graciously, congratulated me, and was the first to declare that I ought to have singing lessons. Alexandra

Mihalovna, as delighted and grateful as though something wonderful had been done for her, flew to kiss his hand. At last B. arrived. The old man was delighted. He was very fond of me. He talked of my father and of the past, and when I had sung before him two or three times, with a grave and anxious air, even with a certain mysteriousness in his tone, pronounced that I certainly had a voice and perhaps talent, and that it was out of the question to leave me untrained. Then, as though on second thoughts, Alexandra Mihalovna and he decided that it was risky to praise me too much at first; and I noticed how they exchanged glances and plotted together on the sly, so that their whole conspiracy against me was exceedingly naïve and awkward. I was laughing to myself all the evening, seeing how they tried to restrain themselves later on when I had sung again, and how they even went out of their way to remark on my defects. But they did not keep it up for long, and B. was the first to betray himself, growing sentimental again in his delight. I had never suspected that he was so fond of me. We had the warmest, the most affectionate conversation all the evening. B. told us of the lives of some celebrated singers and musicians, speaking with the enthusiasm of an artist, with reverence, with emotion. Then after touching upon my father, he passed to me, to my childhood, to Prince X., to his family, of whom I had heard so little since my parting from them. But Alexandra Mihalovna did not know much about them herself. B. knew more than the rest of us, for he had paid more than one visit to Moscow; but at that point the conversation took a somewhat mysterious turn that was a puzzle to me, and several circumstances, particularly affecting Prince X., were unintelligible to me. Alexandra Mihalovna spoke of Katya; but B. could tell us nothing particular about her, and seemed as though intentionally desirous of saying nothing about her. That struck me. Far from having forgotten Katya, far from having lost my old feeling for her, I did not even dream that Katya could have changed. The effect of separation and of the long years lived apart, in the course of which we had sent each other no news, and of the difference of bringing-up and of the difference of our characters, escaped my notice. Katya was, in fact, never absent from my thoughts. She seemed to be still living with me; in my dreams particularly, in my romancings, and in my imagined adventures, we always went hand in hand. While I imagined myself the heroine of every story I read, I immediately put beside me my friend Katya and immediately made the novel into two, of which one, of course, was my creation, though I cribbed unsparingly from my favourite authors. At last it was settled in our family council that a teacher of singing should be engaged for me. B. recommended someone very well known, one of the best. Next day an Italian called D. arrived; after hearing me, he confirmed his friend B.'s opinion, but declared that it would be far better for me to go to him for lessons, together with his other pupils, that emulation, imitation, and the various resources which would be at my disposal there would assist the development of my voice. Alexandra Mihalovna gave her consent, and from that time forth I used to go three times a week, at eight o'clock in the morning, to the Conservatoire.

Now I will describe a strange adventure which had a very great influence upon me, and with an abrupt transition began a new stage in my development. I had just reached my sixteenth year, and with it an incomprehensible apathy all at once came over my soul; I was sunk in an insufferable, miserable stagnation, incomprehensible to myself. All my dreams, all my yearnings seemed suddenly numb, even my dreaminess vanished as though from impotence. A cold indifference replaced the former ardour of my inexperienced heart. Even my gift, greeted with such enthusiasm by all whom I loved, lost its interest for me, and I callously neglected it. Nothing interested me, so much so that I felt even for Alexandra Mihalovna a cold indifference; for which I blamed myself, since I could not help recognising it. My apathy was interrupted from time to time by unaccountable melancholy and sudden tears. I sought solitude. At this strange moment a strange adventure shook my soul to its depths and transformed the dead calm into a real tempest. My heart was bitterly wounded. This was how it happened.

CHAPTER VII

I WENT into the library (it is a moment that I shall always remember) and took a novel of Walter Scott's, *St. Ronan's Well*, the only one of his novels I had not read. I remember that a poignant, indefinite misery made my heart ache as though with foreboding of trouble. I wanted to cry. There was a bright light in the room from the slanting rays of the setting sun which was streaming in at the high windows on to the parquetted floor; it was still; there was not a soul in the adjoining rooms. Pyotr Alexandrovitch was not at home, while Alexandra Mihalovna was in bed ill. I was actually crying, and, opening the second part of the book, was aimlessly turning over its pages, trying to discover some meaning in the disconnected phrases that flitted before my eyes. I was, as it were, trying my fortune, as people do, by opening a book at random. There are moments when all the intellectual and spiritual faculties, morbidly overstrained as it were, suddenly flare up in a bright flame of consciousness; and at such an instant the troubled soul, as though languishing with a foreboding of the future, with a foretaste of it, has something like prophetic vision. And your whole being so longs for life, so begs for life; and aflame with the most burning, blindest hope, your heart seems to summon the future with all its mystery, with all its uncertainty, even with its storms and upheavals, if only it brings life. Such was that moment.

I remember that I had just taken the book to open it at random again, and, reading the first page that presented itself, to divine the future from it. But as I opened it I noticed a piece of notepaper, covered with writing, folded into four and pressed as flat as though it had been laid in the book years ago and forgotten in it. With extreme curiosity I began examining my find; it was a letter with no address on it, signed with the two capital letters S. O. My interest was redoubled; I opened the paper, which almost stuck together, and from long lying between the pages left a clear imprint upon them. The folds of the letter were worn and frayed; one could see that it had at one time been read and re-read, and kept as a precious treasure. The ink had turned blue and faded—it had been written so long ago! A few words caught my eye by chance, and my heart began beating with expectation. In confusion I turned the letter over and over in my hands, as though purposely postponing the moment of reading. I took the letter to the light: yes! tears had dried, had dropped on those lines; the stain remained on the paper; here and there whole letters had been washed away by tears. Whose tears were they? At last, breathless with suspense, I read half of the first page, and a cry of astonishment broke from me. I shut the bookcase, put the book back in its case, and hiding the letter under my shawl ran to my room, locked myself in, and began reading the letter again from the beginning. But my heart was thumping so that the words and letters danced and flitted before my eyes. For a long while I could make out nothing. In the letter there was a discovery, the beginning of a mystery; it struck me like a flash of lightning, for I learned to whom it was written. I knew that I was committing almost a crime in reading the letter; but the moment was too strong for me! The letter was to Alexandra Mihalovna. This was the letter; I will reproduce it here. I vaguely understood what was in it, and long after was haunted by conjectures and painful surmises. My heart was stirred and troubled for a long time, almost for ever, for much was called forth by this letter. I had truly divined the future.

It was a farewell letter, the last, and terrible. As I read it I felt a painful tightening of the heart, as though I had myself lost everything, as though everything had been taken from me for ever, even my dreams and my hopes, as though nothing more were left me but a life no longer wanted. Who was he, the writer of this letter? What was his life like afterwards? There were so many hints in the letter, so many facts, that one could not make a mistake; so many riddles, too, that one could not but be lost in conjectures. But I was scarcely mistaken; besides, the style of the letter, which implied so much, implied the whole character of the tie through which two hearts had been broken. The feelings, the thoughts of the writer were laid bare. They were of too special a character and, as I have said already, implied too much. But here is the letter; I am copying it word for word.

"You will not forget me, you have said it—I believe it and all my life henceforth is in those words of yours. We must part, our hour has struck! I have known this for a long while, my gentle, my sad beauty, but only now I understand it. Through all *our* time, through all the time that you have loved me, my heart has yearned and ached over our love, and—would you believe it?—my heart is easier now! I knew long ago that this would be the end, and that this was destined from the first! It is fate! Let me tell you, Alexandra: we are not *equals;* I always felt that, *always!* I was not worthy of you, and I, I alone ought to bear the punishment for the happiness I have known! Tell me, what was I beside you till the time when you came to know me? My God! here two years have passed and I seem to have been unconscious of it till now; to this day I cannot grasp that *you* have loved *me!* I don't understand how we came to that point, how it began. Do you remember what I was compared with you? Was I worthy of you? In what did I excel, in what way was I particularly distinguished?

Till I knew you, I was coarse and common, I looked sullen and dejected. I desired no other life, did not dream of it, I did not invite it and did not want to invite it. Everything in me was somehow crushed, and I knew nothing in the world of more importance than my regular daily work. My only care was the morrow; and I was indifferent even to that. In the past, it was long ago, I had a dream of something like this, and I gave way to day-dreams like a fool. But a long, long time had passed since then, and I had begun living in solitude, calmly, gloomily, I actually did not feel the cold that froze my heart. And it slept. I knew and made up my mind that no other sun would ever rise for me, and believed it and did not repine at anything because I knew that so it was *bound to be*. When you crossed my path, I did not understand that I could dare to raise my eyes to you. I was like a slave beside you. There was no tremor, no ache in my heart when I was by you, it told me nothing; it was unmoved. My soul did not recognise yours, though it found new light beside its fair sister soul. I know that; I felt it dimly. That I could feel, since the light of God's day is shed on the lowest blade of grass and warms and cherishes it even as the gorgeous flower beside which it meekly grows. When I learned all—do you remember?—after that evening, after those words, which stirred my soul to its depth, I was dazed, shattered, everything in me was troubled, and—do you know?—I was so overwhelmed, and had so little faith in myself, that I did not understand you! I have never spoken to you of that. You knew nothing of that; I was not in the past the same as you have found me. If I had been able, if I had dared to speak, I should have confessed it to you all long ago. But I was silent, and I am telling you everything now that you may know the man you are leaving, the man from whom you are parting! Do you know how I understood you at first? Passion caught me like fire, flowed in my veins like poison; it confused all my thoughts and feelings, I was intoxicated, I was as though possessed, and responded to your pure *compassionate* love not as equal to equal, not as one worthy of your pure love, but without understanding, heartlessly. I did not recognise what you were. I responded to you as to one who in my eyes had *forgotten herself to my level,* and not one who wanted to raise me to hers. Do you know of what I suspected you, what is meant by those words, *forgotten herself to my level?* But no, I will not insult you with my confession; only one thing I will tell you: you have been cruelly mistaken in me! I could never rise to your level, never. I could only contemplate you in boundless love without ever coming near you. My passion, exalted by you, was not love, I was afraid of love; I dared not love you; love implies reciprocity, equality, and I was not worthy of them. . . . I don't know how it was with me! Ah! how can I tell you that, how can I make myself understood? . . . I did not believe it at first. . . . Oh! do you remember when my first excitement had subsided, when I could see things clearer, when nothing was left but a pure feeling purged of all that was gross, my first emotion was one of wonder, confusion, alarm, and—do you remember —how all at once I fell sobbing at your feet? Do you remember how, troubled and frightened, you kept asking with tears: what was I feeling? I said nothing, I could not answer you, but my heart was rent; my happiness weighed upon me like an unbearable burden, and my sobs seemed to whisper to me: 'Why is this? How have I deserved it? How am I deserving of bliss? My sister, my sister!' Oh! how many times—you did not know it—how many times I have in secret kissed your dress, in secret because I knew I was not worthy of you—and I could hardly breathe at such times, and my heart beat slowly, as though it meant to stop and swoon for ever. When I took your hand I turned pale and trembled all over; you confounded me by the purity of your soul. Ah, I cannot tell you all that has been accumulating in my heart and craving utterance! Do you know that at times your compassionate, everlasting tenderness was a burden and a torture to me? When you kissed me (it happened once and I shall never forget it), there was a mist before my eyes, and my whole spirit swooned in one instant. Why did I not die at that moment at your feet? Will you understand what I am trying to say? I want to tell you *everything* and I tell you this: yes, you love me very much, you have loved me as a sister loves a brother; you have loved me as your own creation, because you have raised my heart from the dead, awakened my mind from its slumber, and have instilled sweet hope into my breast. I could not, I dared not, I have not till now called you my sister, because I could not be your brother, because we were not equal, because you are mistaken in me!

"But, you see, I am writing all the while of myself; in this moment of fearful misery, I am thinking only of myself, though I know that you are worrying about me. Oh, do not worry about me, my dear one! If you only knew how humiliated I am in my own eyes! It has all been discovered, what a fuss there has been! You will be an outcast on my account. Contempt, jeers will be showered upon you, because I am so low in their eyes! Oh, how greatly I am to blame for being unworthy of you! If only I had had consequence, personal value in their eyes, if I had inspired more respect in them, they would have forgiven you; but I am low, I am insignificant, I am absurd, and nothing is lower than to be absurd. *Who* is it that is making a fuss? Because *they* have begun to make a fuss I have lost heart; I have always been weak. Do you know the state I am in now: I am laughing at myself, and it seems to me that they are right, because I am absurd and hateful even to myself. I feel that; I hate even my face, my figure, all my habits, all my ignoble ways; I have always hated them. Oh, forgive me my crude despair. You have taught me yourself to tell you everything. I have ruined you, I have brought anger and contempt upon you because I was below you.

"And this thought, too, tortures me; it is hammering at my brain the whole time, and poisons and lacerates my heart. And I keep fancying that you have not loved the man you thought you found in me, that you were deceived in me. That is what hurts, that is what tortures me, and will torture me to death if I do not go out of my mind!

"Farewell, farewell! Now when all has been discovered, after their outcry and their tittle-tattle (I have heard them), when I have been humiliated, degraded in my own eyes, made ashamed of myself, ashamed even of you for your choice, when I have cursed myself, now I must run away and disappear for the sake of your peace. They insist on it, and so you will never see me again, never! It must be so, it is fated. Too much has been given me; fate has blundered, now she will correct her mistake and take it all away again. We came together, learnt to know each other, and now we are parting till we meet again. When will that be, where will that be? Oh, tell me, my own, where shall we meet again? Where am I to find you, how am I to know you, will you know me then? My whole soul is full of you. Oh, why is it, why should this happen to us? Why are we parting? Teach me—I don't understand, I shall never understand it—teach me how to tear my life in two, how to tear my heart out of my bosom and to live without it. Ah, when I think that I shall never see you again, never, never! . . .

"My God, what an uproar they have made! How afraid I feel for you now! I have only just met your husband; we are both unworthy of him, though we have neither of us sinned against him. He knows all; he sees us, he understands it all, and even beforehand everything was as clear as day to him. He has championed you heroically, he will save you, he will protect you from this tittle-tattle and uproar; his love and respect for you are boundless; he is your saviour, while I am running away! . . . I rushed up to him, I wanted to kiss his hand! . . . He told me that I must go at once. It is settled! I am told that he has quarrelled with them, with everyone on your account; they are all against you. They blame him for weakness and laxity. My God! What are they not saying about you! They don't know, they *cannot understand,* they are *incapable* of it. Forgive them, forgive them, my poor darling, as I forgive them; and they have taken from me more than from you!

"I am beside myself, I don't know what I am writing to you. Of what did I talk to you last night at parting? I have forgotten it all. I was distracted, you were crying. . . . Forgive me those tears! I am so weak, so faint-hearted!

"There was something else I wanted to tell you. . . . Oh, if only I could once more bathe your hands in tears, as I am bathing this letter now! If I could be once more at your feet! If only *they* knew how noble was your feeling! But they are blind; their hearts are proud and haughty; they do not see it and will never see it. They have no eyes to see! They will not believe that you are innocent even according to their standards, not though everything on earth should swear it. As though they could understand! How can they fling a stone at you? Whose hand will throw the first? Oh, they will feel no shame, they will fling thousands of stones. They will fling them boldly, for they know how to do it. They will all throw them at once, and will say that they are without sin and will take the sin on themselves. Oh, if they knew what they are doing! If only one could tell them everything without concealment, so that they might see, might hear, might understand and be convinced! But no, they are not so spiteful. . . . I am in despair now, I am perhaps unjust to them. I am perhaps frightening you with my terror. Don't be afraid, don't be afraid of them, my own! They will understand you; one at least understands you already: have hope—it is your husband.

"Good-bye, good-bye. *I will not thank you.* Good-bye for ever.

"S. O."

My confusion was so great that for a long time I did not know what was happening to me. I was shaken and terrified. Reality had fallen upon me unawares in the midst of the easy life of dreams on which I had lived for three years. I felt with horror that there was a great secret in my hands, and that that secret was binding my whole existence. . . . How? I did not know that yet myself. I felt that from that moment a new future was beginning for me. I had now, not of my own choice, become too close a participator in the life and relations of the people who had hitherto made up the whole world surrounding me, and I was afraid for myself. How should I enter their life, I, unbidden, I, a stranger to them? What should I bring them? How would these fetters which had so suddenly riveted me to another person's secret be loosened? How could I tell? Perhaps my new part would be painful both for me and for them. I could not be silent, I could not refuse the part, and lock what I had learned in my heart for ever. But how would it be, and what would become of me? What was I to do? And what was it that I had found out, indeed? Thousands of questions, still vague and confused, rose up before me, and were already an unbearable weight upon my heart. I felt utterly lost.

Then, I remember, came another phase with new strange impressions I had not experienced before; I felt as though something were loosened in my bosom, as though my old misery had suddenly fallen off my heart and something new had begun to fill it, something such as I did not know yet whether to grieve or rejoice at. The moment was like that when a man leaves his home for ever, and a life hitherto calm and unruffled, for a far unknown journey, and for the last time looks round him, inwardly taking leave of his past, and at the same time feels a bitterness at heart from a mournful foreboding of the unknown future, perhaps gloomy and hostile, which awaits him on his new path. At last convulsive sobs broke from my bosom, and relieved my heart with hysterical weeping. I wanted to see someone, to hear someone, to hold someone tight, tight. I could not remain alone, I did not want solitude now; I flew to Alexandra Mihalovna and spent the whole evening with her. We were alone. I asked her not to play, and refused to sing in spite of her asking me. Everything seemed irksome to me, and I could not settle to anything. I believe we both shed tears. I only remember that I quite frightened her. She besought me to be calm, not to be agitated. She watched me in alarm, telling me that I was ill and that I did not take care of myself. At last, utterly exhausted and shattered, I left her; I was as though in delirium, I went to bed in a fever.

Several days passed before I could recover myself and consider my position more clearly. At this time Alexandra Mihalovna and I were living in complete isolation. Pyotr Alexandrovitch was not in Petersburg. He had gone to Moscow on business, and spent three weeks there. Though the separation was so short, Alexandra Mihalovna sank into terrible depression. At times she grew more serene, but she shut herself up alone, so that even my society must have been a burden to her. Moreover, I tried to be alone myself. My brain was working with feverish activity; I was like one possessed. At times hours of long agonisingly disconnected reverie came upon me; it was as though I were dreaming that someone was laughing at me on the sly, as though something had taken possession of me that poisoned and confounded every thought. I could not shake off the distressing images that were continually appearing before me and giving me no peace. I was haunted by pictures of prolonged hopeless suffering, martyrdom, sacrifice endured submissively, unrepiningly and fruitlessly. It seemed to me that he for whom the sacrifice was made scorned it and laughed at it. It seemed to me that I had seen a criminal forgiving the sins of the righteous, and my heart was torn! At the same time I longed to be rid of my suspicion; I cursed it, I hated myself because all my convictions were not convictions but simply intuitions, because I could not justify my impressions to myself.

Then I went over in my mind those phrases, those last shrieks of terrible farewell. I pictured that man—*not her equal;* I tried to grasp all the agonising meaning of those words, "not her equal". That despairing farewell made an agonising impression upon me: "I am absurd and am myself ashamed of your choice." What did that mean? What people were these? What were they grieving over? What were they miserable about? What had they lost? Mastering myself with an effort, I read again with strained attention the letter which was so full of heart-rending despair, though its meaning was so strange, so difficult for me to understand. But the letter fell from my hands, and my heart was more and more overcome by violent emotion. All this was bound to end in some way, but I did not see the way out, or was afraid of it.

I was almost seriously ill when the carriage rumbled one day

into the courtyard bringing Pyotr Alexandrovitch, who had
returned from Moscow. Alexandra Mihalovna flew to meet her
husband with a cry of joy, but I stood as though rooted to the
spot. I remember that I was struck myself by my own sudden
emotion. I could not control myself, and rushed to my room.
I did not understand why I was so suddenly alarmed, but I was
frightened at this alarm. A quarter of an hour later I was
summoned and given a letter from Prince X. In the drawing-
room I found a stranger whom Pyotr Alexandrovitch had
brought with him from Moscow, and, from some words which
I caught, I learned that he was to stay with us for a long time.
He was Prince X.'s agent, who had come to Petersburg about
some very important business of the family which Pyotr
Alexandrovitch had been looking after for some time. He gave
me a letter from Prince X., and told me that the young princess
wanted to write to me also, and had assured him to the last
moment that the letter would be ready, but had sent him away
empty-handed, begging him to tell me that it was absolutely
no use for her to write to me, that one could write nothing in
a letter, that she had spoilt five sheets of paper and had torn
them all up, that to begin writing to each other we should have
to make friends over again. Then she charged him to tell me
that she would soon be seeing me. The unknown gentleman
answered to my impatient questions that the news of our meeting soon was quite correct, and that the whole family was
preparing to visit Petersburg shortly. I did not know what to
do for joy at this information; I hastened to my room, locked
myself in, and dissolved into tears as I opened the prince's
letter. The prince promised me that I should soon see him and
Katya, and with deep feeling congratulated me on my talent;
finally he gave me his blessing and best wishes for the future,
which he promised to provide for. I wept as I read this letter,
but with those tears of joy was mingled such an insufferable
sadness that I remember I was alarmed at myself, I did not
know what was happening to me.

Several days passed. The newcomer used now to be working
every morning, and often in the evening till after midnight, in
the room next to mine, where Pyotr Alexandrovitch's secretary
used to be. Often this gentleman and Pyotr Alexandrovitch
shut themselves into the latter's study and worked together.
One day Alexandra Mihalovna told me to go into her husband's
study and ask him whether he would come and have tea with
us. Finding no one in the study, and expecting Pyotr

Alexandrovitch to come back shortly, I remained waiting for him. His portrait was hanging on the wall. I remember that I shuddered as I looked at the portrait, and with an excitement I could not myself understand I began scrutinising it intently. It was hung rather high up; moreover, it was beginning to get dark, and to see it better, I pushed a chair up and stood on it. I wanted to detect something, as though I hoped to find the solution of my doubts; and I remember what struck me first of all was the eyes in the portrait. It struck me at once that I had never seen the eyes of this man before, he always kept them hidden behind spectacles.

Even in my childhood I had disliked the way he looked at people, through some strange unaccountable prejudice, but now that prejudice seemed to be justified. My imagination was worked up. It suddenly seemed to me as though the eyes of the portrait in confusion turned away from my searching inquisitorial gaze, that they were trying to avoid it, that there was lying and duplicity in those eyes; it seemed to me that I had guessed right, and I cannot explain the secret joy that stirred in me at having guessed right. A faint cry broke from me. At that moment I heard a rustle behind me. I looked round; Pyotr Alexandrovitch was standing behind me, staring at me. I fancied that he reddened. I turned hot all over, and jumped down from the chair.

"What are you doing here?" he asked in a stern voice. "Why are you here?"

I did not know what to answer. Recovering myself a little, I gave him Alexandra Mihalovna's message after a fashion. I don't know what answer he made me, I don't remember how I got out of the room, but when I reached Alexandra Mihalovna I had completely forgotten the answer for which she was waiting, and said at a venture that he was coming.

"But what is the matter with you, Nyetochka?" she asked. "You are crimson; look at yourself! What's the matter with you?"

"I don't know . . . I have been running quickly . . ." I answered.

"What did Pyotr Alexandrovitch say to you?" she interrupted, troubled.

I did not answer. At that moment Pyotr Alexandrovitch's steps were heard, and I immediately walked out of the room. I waited for two full hours in great perturbation. At last I was summoned to Alexandra Mihalovna. I found her silent and preoccupied. As I went in she bent a rapid, searching glance upon me, but at once dropped her eyes. I fancied that some embarrassment was reflected in her face. I soon noticed that she was in low spirits; she spoke little, did not look at me at all, and in reply to B.'s anxious inquiries said she had a headache. Pyotr Alexandrovitch was more talkative than usual, but he talked only to B.

Alexandra Mihalovna went absent-mindedly to the piano.

"Sing something," said B., turning to me.

"Yes, Anneta, sing your new song," Alexandra Mihalovna chimed in, as though catching at the idea.

I glanced at her; she looked at me in uneasy suspense.

But I could not control myself. Instead of going to the piano and singing something, I was overcome with confusion, and in my embarrassment could not even think how to excuse myself; at last annoyance got the upper hand, and I refused point-blank.

"Why don't you want to sing?" said Alexandra Mihalovna, with a significant glance at me and a fleeting one at her husband.

Those two glances drove me out of all patience. I got up from the table in complete confusion; no longer concealing it, but shaking with a feeling of impatience and annoyance, I repeated with heat that I did not want to, I could not, that I was not well. As I said this I looked them all in the face, but God knows how I longed at that moment to be in my own room and to hide myself from them all.

B. was surprised, Alexandra Mihalovna was visibly distressed and did not say a word. But Pyotr Alexandrovitch suddenly got up from his chair and said that he had forgotten some work; and evidently vexed that he had wasted valuable time, went hurriedly out of the room, saying that he would perhaps look in later, but at the same time, in case he did not, he shook hands with B. by way of good-bye.

"What's the matter with you?" B. asked. "You look really ill."

"Yes, I am unwell, very unwell," I answered impatiently.

"Yes, you certainly are pale, and just now you were so flushed," observed Alexandra Mihalovna, and she 'suddenly checked herself.

"Do stop!" I said, going straight up to her and looking her in the face. The poor thing could not face my eyes, she dropped hers as though she were guilty, and a faint flush

335

suffused her pale cheeks. I took her hand and kissed it. Alexandra Mihalovna looked at me, with a show of naïve pleasure.

"Forgive me for having been such an ill-tempered, naughty child to-day," I said with feeling; "but I really am ill. Let me go, and don't be angry."

"We are all children," she said with a timid smile. "And indeed I am a child too, and worse, much worse than you," she added in my ear. "Good-night, be well. Only for God's sake don't be cross with me."

"What for?" I asked, I was so struck by this naïve entreaty.

"What for?" she repeated, greatly confused, and even frightened at herself. "What for? Why, you see what I am like, Nyetochka. What did I say to you? Good-night! You are cleverer than I am. . . . And I am worse than a child."

"Come, that's enough," I answered, much moved, and not knowing what to say to her. Kissing her once more, I went hurriedly out of the room.

I felt horribly vexed and sad. Moreover, I was furious with myself, feeling that I was not on my guard and did not know how to behave. I was ashamed to the point of tears, and fell asleep in the depths of depression. When I woke up in the morning my first thought was that the whole previous evening was a pure creation of the imagination, a mirage, that we had only been mystifying each other, that we had been in a nervous flutter, had made a regular adventure out of a trifle, and that it was all due to inexperience and our not being used to receiving external impressions. I felt that the letter was to blame for it all, that it was disturbing me too much, and that my imagination was overwrought, and I made up my mind for the future that I had better not think about anything. Settling all my trouble with such exceptional ease, and fully convinced that I could as easily act as I had resolved, I felt calmer, and set off to my singing lesson in quite a cheerful mood. The morning air completely cleared away my head-ache. I was very fond of my morning walks to my lessons. It was so enjoyable going through the town, which was already by nine o'clock full of life, and was busily beginning its daily round. We usually went by the liveliest and busiest streets. And I delighted in this background for the beginning of my artistic life, the contrast between this petty everyday life, these trivial but living cares, and the art which was awaiting me two paces away from this life, on the third storey of a huge house crowded from top to bottom with inhabitants who, as it seemed to me, had nothing whatever to do with any art. These busy cross passers-by, among whom I moved with my music-book under my arm; old Natalya who escorted me and always unconsciously set me trying to solve the riddle of what she was thinking about—then my teacher, a queer fellow, half Italian and half French, at moments a genuine enthusiast, far more often a pedant and most of all a money-grubber—all this intertained me, and made me laugh or ponder. Moreover, I loved music with timid but passionate hope, built castles in the air, fashioned for myself the most marvellous future, and often as I came back was fired by my own imaginings. In fact, at those hours I was almost happy.

I had just such a moment that day, when at ten o'clock I was coming home from my lesson. I had forgotten everything, and I remember I was absorbed in some joyful dream. But all at once, as I was going upstairs, I started as though I were scalded. I heard above me the voice of Pyotr Alexandrovitch, who at that moment was coming downstairs. The unpleasant feeling that came over me was so intense, the memory of yesterday's incident impressed me so disagreeably, that I could not conceal my discomfort. I made a slight bow to him, but my face was probably expressive at the moment, for he stopped short, facing me in surprise. Noticing his movement, I flushed crimson and went hurriedly upstairs; he muttered something after me and went his way. I was ready to cry with vexation, and could not understand what it was that had happened. I was not myself all the morning, and did not know what course to take in order to make an end of it and be rid of it all as quickly as possible. A thousand times I vowed to myself to be more sensible, and a thousand times I was overwhelmed with dread of what I might do. I felt that I hated Alexandra Mihalovna's husband, and yet at the same time I was in despair over my own behaviour. Continual agitation made me quite unwell on this occasion, and I was utterly unable to control myself. I felt vexed with everyone; I sat in my room all the morning and did not even go to Alexandra Mihalovna. She came to see me. She almost cried out when she glanced at me. I was so pale that I was frightened myself when I looked in the looking-glass. Alexandra Mihalovna stayed a whole hour with me, looking after me as though I were a little child.

337

But her attention made me so depressed, her kindness weighed upon me so, it was such an agony to look at her, that at last I asked her to leave me alone. She went away in great anxiety about me. At last my misery found a vent in tears and hysterics. Towards evening I felt better. . . .

Better, because I made up my mind to go to her. I made up my mind to fall on my knees before her, to give her the letter she had lost, and to tell her about everything; to tell her about all the agonies I had endured, all my doubts; to embrace her with the boundless love that glowed in my heart, for her, my martyr; to tell her that I was her child, her friend, that my heart was open to her, that she must look into it and see the ardent, steadfast feeling for her in it. My God! I knew, I felt, that I was the last to whom she could open her heart, but it seemed to me that that made the salvation more certain, and would make the effect of my words more powerful . . . Though vaguely and obscurely, I did understand her sufferings, and my heart boiled with indignation at the thought that she might blush before me, before my judgment. . . . Poor darling, my poor darling, as though you were the sinner! That's what I should say to her, weeping at her feet. My sense of justice was revolted, I was furious. I don't know what I should have done, but I only came to my senses afterwards when an unexpected incident saved me and her from disaster, by checking me at my first step. Then I was horrified. Could her tortured heart have risen to hope again? I should have killed her at one blow!

This is what happened. I was on my way to her study and only two rooms from it, when Pyotr Alexandrovitch came in by a side door and, not noticing me, went on before me. He, too, was going to see her. I stood stock-still; he was the last person I wanted to meet at such a moment. I wanted to get away, but curiosity kept me rooted to the spot.

He stood for a minute before the looking-glass, arranged his hair, and to my intense astonishment I suddenly heard him begin humming a tune. Instantly an obscure far-away incident of my childhood rose to my memory. To understand the strange sensation I felt at that moment, I will describe the incident. It was an incident that made a profound impression upon me in the first year of my living in that house, although only now its significance became clear, for only now, only at this moment, I realised what was the origin of my unaccountable aversion for the man! I have already mentioned that even in those days I always felt ill at ease with him. I have already described the

338

depressing effect on me of his frowning anxious air, and the expression of his face so frequently melancholy and dejected; how unhappy I was after the hours we spent together at Alexandra Mihalovna's tea-table, and what agonising misery rent my heart on the two or three occasions when it was my lot to witness the gloomy, sinister scenes which I have referred to already. It happened that I came upon him then just as I had done now—in the same room, at the same time, when he, like me, was going to see Alexandra Mihalovna. I had been overcome with purely childish shyness of meeting him alone, and so hid in a corner as though I had done something wrong, praying to fate that he might not notice me. Just as now he had stopped before the looking-glass, and I shuddered with a vague unchildlike feeling. It seemed to me as though he were making up his face. Anyway, I had clearly seen a smile on his face before he went to the looking-glass; I saw him laughing, as I had never seen him before, for (I remember that it was this that had struck me most of all) he never laughed in the presence of Alexandra Mihalovna. But as soon as he looked in the looking-glass his face was completely transformed. The smile disappeared as though at the word of command, and his lips were twisted by some bitter feeling, which seemed to spring from the heart spontaneously against his will, a feeling which it seemed beyond human power to disguise in spite of the most magnanimous efforts, a paroxysm of pain brought lines into his forehead and seemed to weigh upon his brow. His eyes were darkly concealed behind spectacles—in short, he seemed as though at a given signal to be changed into a different man. I remember that I, as a little child, shuddered with fear from dread of understanding what I had seen, and from that time an uncomfortable, disagreeable impression was stored away in my heart for ever. After looking at himself for a minute in the looking-glass, he, with bent head and bowed figure, looking as he always did before Alexandra Mihalovna, went on tiptoe to her study. This was the incident that had struck me in the past.

Now, just as then, he stopped before the same looking-glass and thought that he was alone. Just as then I, with a hostile, unpleasant feeling, found myself alone with him; but when I heard that singing (singing from him, from whom it was so impossible to expect anything of the kind!), which struck me as so unexpected that I stood as though rooted to the spot, when at that very instant I was reminded of the almost exactly similar moment of my childhood, I cannot describe the malignant feeling that went through my heart. All my nerves quivered, and in response to this luckless song I went off into such a peal of laughter that the poor singer, uttering a cry, stepped two paces back from the looking-glass and, pale as death, as though ignominiously caught in the act, looked at me, beside himself with alarm, wonder and fury. His expression affected me nervously. I replied to it with a nervous hysterical laugh right in his face, I walked by him laughing and, still laughing, went in to Alexandra Mihalovna. I knew that he was standing behind the curtains over the door, that he was perhaps hesitating whether to come in or not, that he was rooted to the spot by rage and cowardice, and with a nervous defiant impatience I wanted to see what he would do. I was ready to bet that he would not come in, and I was right. He did not come in till half an hour later. Alexandra Mihalovna looked at me for a long time in the utmost perplexity. But her inquiries as to what was the matter with me were fruitless. I could not answer, I was gasping for breath. At last she understood that I was in hysterics, and looked after me anxiously. When I had recovered I took her hands and began kissing them. Only then I grasped the position, and only then the thought occurred to me that I should have been the death of her if it had not been for the encounter with her husband. I looked at her as one risen from the dead.

Pyotr Alexandrovitch walked in. I took a furtive glance at him; he looked as though nothing had passed between us, that is, he was gloomy and austere as usual. But from his pale face and the faintly twitching corners of his mouth I guessed that he could hardly conceal his perturbation. He greeted Alexandra Mihalovna coldly and sat down in his place without a word. His hand trembled as he took his cup of tea. I expected an explosion, and I was overcome by an exaggerated terror. I should have liked to retreat, but could not bring myself to leave Alexandra Mihalovna. At the sight of her husband, she, too, had a foreboding of trouble. At last, what I was expecting with such terror happened.

In the midst of a profound silence I raised my eyes and met Pyotr Alexandrovitch's spectacles turned straight upon me. This was so unexpected that I started, almost cried out, and dropped my eyes. Alexandra Mihalovna noticed my perturbation.

"What's the matter with you? What are you blushing at?" I heard Pyotr Alexandrovitch's harsh voice.

I was silent; my heart was thumping so that I could not answer a word.

"What is she blushing at? Why is she always blushing?" he asked, addressing Alexandra Mihalovna and rudely pointing towards me.

I could hardly breathe for indignation. I flung an imploring glance at Alexandra Mihalovna. She understood me. Her pale cheeks flushed.

"Anneta," she said to me in a firm voice, such as I should never have expected from her, "go to your own room, I'll come to you in a minute; we will spend the evening together. . . ."

"I asked you a question, did you hear me or not?" Pyotr Alexandrovitch interrupted, raising his voice still higher, and seeming not to hear what his wife had said. "Why do you blush when you meet me? Answer!"

"Because you make her blush and me too," answered Alexandra Mihalovna in a breaking voice.

I looked with surprise at Alexandra Mihalovna. The heat of her retort was quite incomprehensible to me for the first moment.

"*I* make you blush—*I?*" answered Pyotr Alexandrovitch, emphasising the word *I,* and apparently roused to fury too. "*You* have blushed for *me?* Do you mean to tell me *I* can make *you* blush for *me?* It's for *you* to blush, not for me, don't you think?"

This phrase, uttered with such callous biting sarcasm, was so intelligible to me that I gave a cry of horror and rushed to Alexandra Mihalovna. Surprise, pain, reproach and horror were all depicted on her face, which began to turn deathly pale. Clasping my hands with a look of entreaty, I glanced at Pyotr Alexandrovitch. It seemed as though he himself thought he had gone too far; but the fury that had wrung that phrase out of him had not passed. Noticing my mute prayer, he was confused, however. My gesture betrayed clearly that I knew a great deal of what had hitherto been a secret between them, and that I quite understood his words.

"Anneta, go to your room," Alexandra Mihalovna repeated in a weak but firm voice, getting up from her chair. "I want to speak to Pyotr Alexandrovitch . . ."

She was calm on the surface; but that calm made me more frightened than any excitement would have done. I behaved as though I did not hear what she said, and remained stock-still. I strained every nerve to read in her face what was passing in her soul at that instant. It seemed to me that she had under-

341

stood neither my gesture nor my exclamation.

"See what you have done, miss!" said Pyotr Alexandrovitch, taking my hand and pointing to his wife.

My God! I have never seen such despair as I read now on that crushed, deathly-looking face. He took me by the hand and led me out of the room. I took one last look at them. Alexandra Mihalovna was standing with her elbows on the mantelpiece, holding her head tight in both hands. Her whole attitude was expressive of unbearable torture. I seized Pyotr Alexandrovitch's hand and squeezed it warmly.

"For God's sake, for God's sake," I brought out in a breaking voice, "spare her!"

"Don't be afraid, don't be afraid," he said, looking at me strangely; "it's nothing, it's nerves. Go along, go along."

Going into my room, I threw myself on the sofa and hid my face in my hands. For three whole hours I remained in that attitude, and I passed through a perfect hell during those hours. At last I could bear it no longer, and sent to inquire whether I could go to Alexandra Mihalovna. Madame Leotard came with an answer. Pyotr Alexandrovitch sent to say that the attack was over, that there was no need for anxiety, but that Alexandra Mihalovna must have rest. I did not go to bed till three o'clock in the morning, but walked up and down the room thinking. My position was more perplexing than ever, but I somehow felt calmer, perhaps because I felt myself more to blame than anyone. I went to bed looking forward impatiently to the next day.

But next day, to my grievous surprise, I found an unaccountable coldness in Alexandra Mihalovna. At first I fancied that it was painful to her pure and noble heart to be with me after the scene of the day before with her husband, of which I had been the involuntary witness. I knew that the childlike creature was capable of blushing at the sight of me, and begging my forgiveness for the unlucky scene's having wounded me the day before. But I soon noticed in her another anxiety and an annoyance, which showed itself very awkwardly; at one time she would answer me coldly and dryly, then a peculiar significance could be detected in her words, then she would suddenly become very tender with me as though repenting the harshness which she could not feel in her heart, and there was a note of reproach in her affectionate and gentle words. At last I asked her directly what was the matter, and whether she had anything to say to me. She was a little taken aback at my rapid question, but at once raising her large clear eyes and looking at me with a tender smile, she said—

"It's nothing, Nyetochka; only do you know, when you asked me so quickly I was rather taken aback. That was because you asked me so quickly. . . . I assure you. But listen—tell me the truth, my child—have you got anything on your mind which would have made you as confused if you had been asked about it so quickly and unexpectedly?"

"No," I answered, looking at her with clear eyes.

"Well, that is good to hear! If you only knew, my dear, how grateful I am to you for that good answer. Not that I could suspect you of anything bad—never. I could not forgive myself the thought of such a thing. But listen; I took you as a child, and now you are seventeen. You see for yourself: I am ill, I am like a child myself, I have to be looked after. I cannot fully take the place of a mother to you, although there was more than enough love in my heart for that. If I am troubled by anxiety now it is, of course, not your fault, but mine. Forgive me for the question, and for my having perhaps involuntarily failed in keeping the promises I made to you and my father when I took you into my house. This worries me very much, and has often worried me, my dear."

I embraced her and shed tears.

"Oh, I thank you; I thank you for everything," I said, bathing her hands with my tears. "Don't talk to me like that, don't break my heart. You have been more than a mother to me, yes; may God bless you and the prince for all you have both done for a poor, desolate child!"

"Hush, Nyetochka, hush! Hug me instead; that's right, hold me tight! Do you know, I believe, I don't know why, that it is the last time you will embrace me."

"No, no," I said, sobbing like a child; "no, that cannot be. You will be happy. . . . You have many days before you. Believe me, we shall be happy."

"Thank you, thank you for loving me so much. I have not many friends about me now; they have all abandoned me!"

"Who have abandoned you? Who are they?"

"There used to be other people round me; you don't know, Nyetochka. They have all left me. They have all faded away as though they were ghosts. And I have been waiting for them, waiting for them all my life. God be with them. Look, Nyetochka, you see it is late autumn, soon the snow will be

343

here; with the first snow I shall die—but I do not regret it. Farewell."

Her face was pale and thin, an ominous patch of red glowed on each cheek, her lips quivered and were parched by fever.

She went up to the piano and struck a few chords; at that instant a string snapped with a clang and died away in a long jarring sound . . .

"Do you hear, Nyetochka, do you hear?" she said all at once in a sort of inspired voice, pointing to the piano. "That string was strained too much, to the breaking point, it could bear no more and has perished. Do you hear how plaintively the sound is dying away?"

She spoke with difficulty. Mute spiritual pain was reflected in her face, her eyes filled with tears.

"Come, Nyetochka, enough of that, my dear. Fetch the children."

I brought them in. She seemed to find repose as she looked at them, and sent them away an hour later.

"You will not forsake them when I am dead, Nyetochka? Will you?" she said in a whisper, as though afraid someone might overhear us.

"Hush, you are killing me!" was all I could say to her in answer.

"I was joking," she said with a smile, after a brief pause. "And you believed me. You know, I talk all sorts of nonsense sometimes. I am like a child now, you must forgive me everything."

Then she looked at me timidly, as though afraid to say something. I waited.

"Mind you don't alarm him," she said at last, dropping her eyes, with a faint flush in her cheeks, and in so low a voice that I could hardly catch her words.

"Whom?" I asked, with surprise.

"My husband. You might perhaps tell him what I have said."

"What for, what for?" I repeated, more and more surprised.

"Well, perhaps you wouldn't tell him, how can I say!" she answered, trying to glance shyly at me, though the same simple-hearted smile was shining on her lips, and the colour was mounting more and more into her face. "Enough of that; I am still joking, you know."

My heart ached more and more.

344

"Only you will love them when I am dead, won't you?" she added gravely, and again, as it seemed, with a mysterious air. "You will love them as if they were your own. Won't you? Remember, I always looked on you as my own, and made no difference between you and the children."

"Yes, yes," I answered, not knowing what I was saying, and breathless with tears and confusion.

A hot kiss scalded my hand before I had time to snatch it away. I was tongue-tied with amazement.

What is the matter with her? What is she thinking? What happened between them yesterday? was the thought that floated through my mind.

A minute later she began to complain of being tired.

"I have been ill a long time, but I did not want to frighten you two. You both love me—don't you . . . ? Good-bye for now, Nyetochka; leave me, but be sure to come in the evening. You will, won't you?"

I promised to; but I was glad to get away, I could not have borne any more.

"Poor darling, poor darling! What suspicion are you taking with you to the grave?" I exclaimed to myself, sobbing. "What new trouble is poisoning and gnawing your heart, though you scarcely dare to breathe a word of it? My God! This long suffering which I understand now through and through, this life without a ray of sunshine, this timid love that asks for nothing! And even now, now, almost on her death-bed, when her heart is torn in two with pain, she is afraid, like a criminal, to utter the faintest murmur, the slightest complaint—and imagining, inventing a new sorrow, she has already submitted to it, is already resigned to it . . ."

Towards the evening, in the twilight, I took advantage of the absence of Ovrov (the man who had come from Moscow) to go into the library and, unlocking a bookcase, began rummaging among the bookshelves to choose something to read aloud to Alexandra Mihalovna. I wanted to distract her mind from gloomy thoughts, and to choose something gay and light . . . I was a long time, absent-mindedly choosing. It got darker, and my depression grew with the darkness. I found in my hands the same book again, with the page turned down on which even now I saw the imprint of the letter, which had never left my bosom since that day—the secret with which my existence seemed, as it were, to have been broken and to have begun anew, and with which so much that was cold, unknown, mysterious, forbidding and now so ominously menacing in the distance had come upon me . . . What will happen to me? I wondered: the corner in which I had been so snug and comfortable would be empty. The pure clean spirit which had guarded my youth would leave me. What was before me? I was standing in a reverie over my past, now so dear to my heart, as it were striving to gaze into the future, into the unknown that menaced me . . . I recall that minute as though I were living it again; it cut so sharply into my memory.

I was holding the letter and the open book in my hands, my face was wet with tears. All at once I started with dismay; I heard the sound of a familiar voice. At the same time I felt that the letter was torn out of my hands. I shrieked and looked round; Pyotr Alexandrovitch was standing before me. He seized me by the arm and held me firmly; with his right hand he raised the letter to the light and tried to decipher the first lines . . . I cried out, and would have faced death rather than leave the letter in his hands. From his triumphant smile I saw that he had succeeded in making out the first lines. I lost my head . . .

A moment later I had dashed at him, hardly knowing what I was doing, and snatched the letter from him. All this happened so quickly that I had not time to realise how I had got the letter again. But seeing that he meant to snatch it out of my hand again, I made haste to thrust it into my bosom and step back three or four paces.

For half a minute we stared at each other in silence. I was still trembling with terror, pale. With quivering lips that turned blue with rage, he broke the silence.

"That's enough!" he said in a voice weak with excitement. "You surely don't wish me to use force; give me back the letter of your own accord."

Only now I realised what had happened and I was breathless with resentment, shame, and indignation at this coarse brutality. Hot tears rolled down my burning cheeks. I was shaking all over with excitement, and was for some time incapable of uttering a word.

"Did you hear?" he said, advancing two paces towards me.

"Leave me alone, leave me alone!" I cried, moving away from him. "Your behaviour is low, ungentlemanly. You are forgetting yourself! Let me go! . . ."

"What? What's the meaning of this? And you dare to

take up that tone to me . . . after what you've . . . Give it me, I tell you!''

He took another step towards me, but glancing at me saw such determination in my eyes that he stopped, as though hesitating.

"Very good!" he said dryly at last, as though he had reached a decision, though he could still scarcely control himself. "That will do later, but first . . ."

Here he looked round him.

"You . . . Who let you into the library? How is it that this bookcase is open? Where did you get the key?''

"I am not going to answer you," I said. "I can't talk to you. Let me go, let me go.''

I went towards the door.

"Excuse me," he said, holding me by the arm. "You are not going away like that.''

I tore my arm away from him without a word, and again made a movement towards the door.

"Very well. But I really cannot allow you to receive letters from your lovers in my house. . . .''

I cried out with horror, and looked at him frantically. . . .

"And so . . .''

"Stop!" I cried. "How can you? How could you say it to me? My God! My God! . . .''

"What? What? Are you threatening me too?''

But as I gazed at him, I was pale and overwhelmed with despair. The scene between us had reached a degree of exasperation I could not understand. My eyes besought him not to prolong it. I was ready to forgive the outrage if only he would stop. He looked at me intently, and visibly hesitated.

"Don't drive me to extremes," I whispered in horror.

"No, I must get to the bottom of it,'' he said at last, as though considering. "I must confess the look in your eyes almost made me hesitate," he added with a strange smile. "But unluckily, the fact speaks for itself. I succeeded in reading the first words of your letter. It's a love letter. You won't persuade me it isn't! No, dismiss that idea from your mind! And that I could doubt it for a moment only proves that I must add to your excellent qualities your abilities as an expert liar, and therefore I repeat . . .''

As he talked, his face was more and more distorted with anger. He turned white, his lips were drawn and twitching, so that he could hardly articulate the last words. It was getting

347

dark. I stood defenceless, alone, facing a man who was capable of insulting a woman. All appearances were against me too; I was tortured with shame, distracted, and could not understand this man's fury. Beside myself with terror, I rushed out of the room without answering him, and only came to myself as I stood on the threshold of Alexandra Mihalovna's study. At that instant I heard his footsteps; I was just about to go in when I stopped short as though thunderstruck.

"What will happen to her?" was the thought that flashed through my mind. "That letter! . . . No; better anything in the world than that last blow to her," and I was rushing back. But it was too late; he was standing beside me.

"Let us go where you like, only not here, not here!" I whispered, clutching at his arm. "Spare her! I will go back to the library or . . . where you like! You will kill her!"

"It is you who are killing her," he said, pushing me away.

Every hope vanished. I felt that to bring the whole scene before Alexandra Mihalovna was just what he wanted.

"For God's sake," I said, doing my utmost to hold him back. But at that instant the curtain was raised, and Alexandra Mihalovna stood facing us. She looked at us in surprise. Her face was paler than usual. She could hardly stand on her feet. It was evident that it had cost her a great effort to get as far as us when she heard our voices.

"Who is here? What are you talking about here?" she asked, looking at us in the utmost amazement.

There was a silence that lasted several moments, and she turned as white as a sheet. I flew to her, held her tight in my arms, and drew her back into her room. Pyotr Alexandrovitch walked in after me. I hid my face on her bosom and clasped her more and more tightly in my arms, half dead with suspense.

"What is it, Nyetochka, what's happened to you both?" Alexandra Mihalovna asked a second time.

"Ask her, you defended her so warmly yesterday," said Pyotr Alexandrovitch, sinking heavily into an arm-chair.

I held her more tightly in my embrace.

"But, my goodness, what is the meaning of it?" said Alexandra Mihalovna in great alarm. "You are so irritated, and she is frightened and crying. Anneta, tell me all that has happened."

"No, allow me first," said Pyotr Alexandrovitch, coming up to us, taking me by the arm, and pulling me away from Alexandra Mihalovna. "Stand here," he said, putting me in

348

the middle of the room. "I wish to judge you before her who has been a mother to you. And don't worry yourself, sit down," he added, motioning Alexandra Mihalovna to an easy-chair. "It grieves me that I cannot spare you this unpleasant scene; but it must be so."

"Good heavens! What is coming?" said Alexandra Mihalovna, in great distress, gazing alternately at me and her husband. I wrung my hands, feeling that the fatal moment was at hand. I expected no mercy from him now.

"In short," Pyotr Alexandrovitch went on, "I want you to judge between us. You always (and I can't understand why, it is one of your whims), you always—yesterday, for instance—thought and said . . . but I don't know how to say it, I blush at the suggestion. . . . In short, you defended her, you attacked me, you charged me with *undue* severity; you even hinted at *another feeling*, suggesting that that provoked me to *undue* severity; you . . . but I do not understand why, I cannot help my confusion, and the colour that flushes my face at the thought of your suppositions; and so I cannot speak of them directly, openly before her. . . . In fact you . . ."

"Oh, you won't do that! No, you won't say that!" cried Alexandra Mihalovna in great agitation, hot with shame. "No, spare her. It was all my fault, it was my idea! I have no suspicions now. Forgive me for them, forgive me. I am ill, you must forgive me, only do not speak of it to her, don't. . . . Anneta," she said, coming up to me, "Anneta, go out of the room, make haste, make haste! He was joking; it is all my fault; it is a tactless joke. . . ."

"In short, you were jealous of her on my account," said Pyotr Alexandrovitch, ruthlessly flinging those words in the face of her agonised suspense.

She gave a shriek, turned pale and leaned against her chair for support, hardly able to stand on her feet.

"God forgive you," she said at last in a faint voice. "Forgive me for him, Nyetochka, forgive me; it was all my fault, I was ill, I . . ."

"But this is tyrannical, shameless, vile!" I cried in a frenzy, understanding it all at last, understanding why he wanted to discredit me in his wife's eyes. "It's below contempt; you . . ."

"Anneta!" cried Alexandra Mihalovna, clutching my hands in horror.

"It's a farce, a farce, and nothing else!" said Pyotr

349

Alexandrovitch, coming up to us in indescribable excitement. "It's a farce, I tell you," he went on, looking intently with a malignant smile at his wife. "And the only one deceived by the farce is—you. Believe me, *we*," he brought out breathlessly, pointing at me, "are not at all afraid of discussing such matters; believe me, that we are not so maidenly as to be offended, to blush and to cover our ears, when we are talked to about such subjects. You must excuse me, I express myself plainly, simply, coarsely perhaps, but—it is necessary. Are you so sure, madam, of this . . . young person's correctness of behaviour?"

"My God! What is the matter with you? You are forgetting yourself!" said Alexandra Mihalovna, numb and half dead with horror.

"Not so loud, please," Pyotr Alexandrovitch interrupted her contemptuously. "I don't like it. This is a simple matter, plain, vulgar in the extreme. I am asking you about her behaviour. Do you know . . ."

But I did not let him finish, and seizing him by the arm, I forcibly drew him away. Another minute—and everything might have been lost.

"Don't speak of the letter," I said quickly, in a whisper. "You will kill her on the spot. Censure of me will be censure of her too. She cannot judge me, for I know all. . . . Do you understand? I know *all!*"

He looked at me intently with wild curiosity, was confused; the blood rushed to his face.

"I know *all, all!*" I repeated.

He was still hesitating. A question was trembling on his lips. I forestalled him.

"This is what happened," I said aloud hurriedly, addressing Alexandra Mihalovna, who was looking at us with timid and anxious amazement. "It was all my fault. I have been deceiving you for the last four years. I carried off the key of the library, and have for four years been secretly reading the books in it. Pyotr Alexandrovitch caught me reading a book which . . . could not, should not have been in my hands. In his anxiety over me, he has exaggerated the danger! . . . But I do not justify myself," I added quickly, noticing a sarcastic smile on his lips. "It is all my fault. The temptation was too great for me, and having once done wrong, I was ashamed to confess what I had done. . . . That's all, almost all that has passed between us."

"Oho, how smart," Pyotr Alexandrovitch whispered beside me.

Alexandra Mihalovna listened to me intently; but there was an unmistakable shade of mistrustfulness on her face. She kept looking first at me, then at her husband. A silence followed. I could hardly breathe. She let her head fall on her bosom and hid her face in her hands, considering and evidently weighing every word I had uttered. At last she raised her head and looked at me intently.

"Nyetochka, my child," she said, "I know you cannot lie. Was this everything that happened, absolutely all?"

"Yes, all," I answered.

"Was that all?" she asked, addressing her husband.

"Yes," he answered with an effort, "all!"

I heaved a sigh.

"On your word of honour, Nyetochka?"

"Yes," I answered without faltering.

But I could not refrain from glancing at Pyotr Alexandrovitch. He laughed as he heard my answer. I flushed hotly, and my confusion did not escape poor Alexandra Mihalovna. There was a look of overwhelming agonising misery in her face.

"That's enough," she said mournfully. "I believe you. I cannot but believe you."

"I think such a confession is sufficient," said Pyotr Alexandrovitch. "You have heard! What would you have me think?"

Alexandra Mihalovna made no answer. The scene became more and more unbearable.

"I will look through all the books to-morrow," Pyotr Alexandrovitch went on. "I don't know what else there was there; but . . ."

"But what book was she reading?" asked Alexandra Mihalovna.

"What book? Answer," he said, addressing me. "You can *explain things* better than I can," he said, with a hidden irony.

I was confused, and could not say a word. Alexandra Mihalovna blushed and dropped her eyes. A long pause followed Pyotr Alexandrovitch walked up and down the room in vexation.

"I don't know what has passed between you," Alexandra Mihalovna began at last, timidly articulating each word; "but if *that* was *all*," she went on, trying to put a special significance into her voice, though she was embarrassed by her husband's

351

fixed stare and trying not to look at him, "if that was *all*, I don't know what we all have to be so unhappy and despairing about. I am most to blame, I alone, and it troubles me very much. I have neglected her education, and I ought to answer for it all. She must forgive me, and I cannot and dare not blame her. But, again, what is there to be so desperate about? The danger is over. Look at her," she went on, speaking with more and more feeling, and casting a searching glance at her husband, "look at her, has her indiscretion left any trace on her? Do you suppose I don't know her, my child, my darling daughter? Don't I know that her heart is pure and noble, that in that pretty little head," she went on, drawing me towards her and fondling me, "there is clear, candid intelligence and a conscience that fears deceit. . . . Enough of this, my dear! Let us drop it! Surely something else is underlying our distress; perhaps it was only a passing shadow of antagonism. But we will drive it away by love, by good-will, and let us put away our perplexities. Perhaps there is a good deal that has not been spoken out between us, and I blame myself most. I was first reserved with you, I was the first to be suspicious—goodness knows of what, and my sick brain is to blame for it. . . . But since we have been open to some extent, you must both forgive me because . . . because indeed there was no great sin in what I suspected. . . ."

As she said this she glanced shyly, with a flush on her cheek, at her husband, and anxiously awaited his words. As he heard her a sarcastic smile came on to his lips. He left off walking about and stopped directly facing her, with his hands behind his back. He seemed to be scrutinising her confusion, watched it, revelled in it; feeling his eyes fixed upon her, she was overwhelmed with confusion. He waited a moment as though he expected something more. At last he cut short the uncomfortable scene by a soft, prolonged, malignant laugh.

"I am sorry for you, poor woman!" he said at last gravely and bitterly, leaving off smiling. "You have taken up an attitude which you cannot keep up. What did you want? You wanted to incite me to answer, to rouse me by fresh suspicions, or rather by the old suspicion which you have failed to conceal in your words. The implication of your words, that there is no need to be angry with her, that she is good even after reading immoral books, the morality of which—I am saying what I think—seems already to have borne fruits, that you will answer for her yourself; wasn't that it? Well, in explaining that, you hint at something else; you imagine that my suspiciousness and my persecution arise from some other feeling. You even hinted to me yesterday—please do not stop me, I like to speak straight out—you even hinted yesterday that in some people (I remember that you observed that such people were most frequently steady, severe, straightforward, clever, strong, and God knows what other qualities you did not bestow on them in your generosity), that in some people, I repeat, love (and God knows why you imagined such a thing) cannot show itself except harshly, hotly, sternly, often in the form of suspicions and persecutions. I don't quite remember whether that was just what you said yesterday . . . please don't stop me. I know your protégée well: she can hear all, all, I repeat for the hundredth time, all. You are deceived. But I do not know why it pleases you to insist on my being just such a man. God knows why you want to dress me up like a tomfool. It is out of the question, at my age, to be in love with this young girl; moreover, let me tell you, madam, *I know my duty*, and however generously you may excuse me, I shall say as before, that *crime will always remain crime, that sin will always be sin, shameful, abominable, dishonourable, to whatever height of grandeur you raise the vicious feeling!* But enough, enough, and let me hear no more of these abominations!"

Alexandra Mihalovna was crying. "Well, let me endure this, let this be for me!" she said at last, sobbing and embracing me. "My suspicions may have been shameful, you may jeer so harshly at them; but you, my poor child, why are you condemned to hear such insults? and I cannot defend you! I am speechless! My God! I cannot be silent, sir, I can't endure it. . . . Your behaviour is insane."

"Hush, hush," I whispered, trying to calm her excitement, afraid that her cruel reproaches would put him out of patience. I was still trembling with fear for her.

"But, blind woman!" he shouted, "you do not know, you do not see."

He stopped for a moment.

"Away from her!" he said, addressing me and tearing my hand out of the hands of Alexandra Mihalovna. "I will not allow you to touch my wife; you pollute her, you insult her by your presence. But . . . but what forces me to be silent when it is necessary, when it is essential to speak?" he shouted, stamping. "And I will speak, I will tell you everything. I don't know what you *know*, madam, and with what you tried

353

to threaten me, and I don't care to know. Listen!" he went on, addressing Alexandra Mihalovna. "Listen . . ."

"Be silent!" I cried, darting forward. "Hold your tongue, not a word!"

"Listen! . . ."

"Hold your tongue in the name of . . ."

"In the name of what, madam?" he interrupted, with a rapid and piercing glance into my eyes. "In the name of what?" Let me tell you I pulled out of her hands a letter from a lover! So that's what's going on in our house! That's what's going on at your side! That's what you have not noticed, not seen!"

I could hardly stand. Alexandra Mihalovna turned white as death.

"It cannot be," she whispered in a voice hardly audible.

"I have seen the letter, madam; it has been in my hands; I have read the first lines and I am not mistaken: the letter was from a lover. She snatched it out of my hands. It is in her possession now—it is clear, it is so, there is no doubt of it; and if you still doubt it, look at her and then try and hope for a shadow of doubt."

"Nyetochka!" cried Alexandra Mihalovna, rushing at me. "But no, don't speak, don't speak! I don't understand what it was, how it was. . . . My God! My God!"

And she sobbed, hiding her face in her hands.

"But no, it cannot be," she cried again. "You are mistaken. I know . . . I know what it means," she said, looking intently at her husband. "You . . . I . . . could not . . . you are not deceiving me, Nyetochka, you cannot deceive me. Tell me all, all without reserve. He has made a mistake? Yes, he has made a mistake, hasn't he? He has seen something else, he was blind! Yes, wasn't he, wasn't he? Why did you not tell me all about it, Nyetochka, my child, my own child?"

"Answer, make haste, make haste!" I heard Pyotr Alexandrovitch's voice above my head. "Answer: did I or did I not see the letter in your hand?"

"Yes!" I answered, breathless with emotion.

"Is that letter from your lover?"

"Yes!" I answered.

"With whom you are now carrying on an intrigue?"

"Yes, yes, yes!" I said, hardly knowing what I was doing by now, and answering yes to every question, simply to put an end to our agony.

354

"You hear her. Well, what do you say now? Believe me, you kind, too confiding heart," he added, taking his wife's hand; "believe me and distrust all that your sick imagination has created. You see now, what this . . . young person is. I only wanted to show how impossible your suspicions were. I noticed all this long ago, and am glad that at last I have unmasked her before you. It was disagreeable to me to see her beside you, in your arms, at the same table with us, in my house, in fact, I was revolted by your blindness. That was the reason and the only reason that I observed her, watched her; my attention attracted your notice, and starting from God knows what suspicion, God only knows what you have deduced from it. But now the position is clear, every doubt is at an end, and to-morrow, madam, to-morrow you will leave my house," he concluded, addressing me.

"Stop!" cried Alexandra Mihalovna, getting up from her chair. "I don't believe in all this scene. Don't look at me so dreadfully, don't laugh at me. I want to judge you now. Anneta, my child, come to me, give me your hand, so. We are all sinners!" she said in a voice that quivered with tears, and she looked meekly at her husband. "And which of us can refuse anyone's hand? Give me your hand, Anneta, my dear child; I am no worthier, no better than you; you cannot injure me by your presence, for I too, I *too* am a *sinner*."

"Madam!" yelled Pyotr Alexandrovitch in amazement. "Madam! Restrain yourself! Do not forget yourself! . . ."

"I am not forgetting anything. Do not interrupt me, but let me have my say. You saw a letter in her hand, you even read it, you say, and she . . . has admitted that this letter is from the man she loves. But does that show that she is a criminal? Does that justify your treating her like this, insulting her like this before your wife? Yes, sir, before your wife? Have you gone into this affair? Do you know how it has happened?"

"The only thing is for me to run and beg her pardon. Is that what you want?" cried Pyotr Alexandrovitch. "It puts me out of all patience listening to you! Think what you are talking about. Do you know what you are talking about? Do you know what and whom you are defending? Why, I see through it all. . . ."

"And you don't see the very first thing because anger and pride prevent your seeing. You don't see what I am defending and what I mean. I am not defending vice. But have you considered—and you will see clearly if you do consider—have

355

you considered that perhaps she is as innocent as a child? Yes, I am not defending vice! I will make haste and explain myself, if that will be pleasant to you. Yes; if she had been a wife, a mother, and had forgotten her duties, oh, then I would have agreed with you. . . . You see I have made a reservation. Notice that and don't reproach me. But what if she has received this letter thinking no harm? What if in her inexperience she has been carried away by her feelings and had no one to hold her back? If I am more to blame than anyone because I did not watch over her heart? If this letter is the first? If you have insulted her fragrant maidenly feelings with your coarse suspicions? What if you have sullied her imagination with your cynical talk about the letter? If you did not see the chaste maidenly shame which was shining on her face, pure as innocence, which I see now, which I saw when distracted, harassed, not knowing what to say and torn with anguish, she answered yes to all your inhuman questions? Yes, yes! Yes, it is inhuman; it is cruel. I don't know you; I shall never forgive you this, never!"

"Yes, have mercy on me, have mercy on me!" I cried, holding her in my arms. "Spare me, trust me, do not repulse me. . . ."

I fell on my knees before her.

"What if I had not been beside her," she went on breathlessly, "and if you had frightened her with your words, and if the poor child had been herself persuaded that she was guilty, if you had confounded her conscience and soul and shattered the peace of her heart? My God! You mean to turn her out of the house! But do you know who are treated like that? You know that if you turn her out of the house, you are turning us out together, both of us. Do you hear me, sir?"

Her eyes flashed; her bosom heaved; her feverish excitement reached a climax. . . .

"Yes, I've heard enough, madam!" Pyotr Alexandrovitch shouted at last. "Enough of this! I know that there are Platonic passions, and to my sorrow I know it, madam, do you hear? To my sorrow. But I cannot put up with gilded vice, madam! I do not understand it. Away with tawdry trappings! And if you feel guilty, if you are conscious of some wrong-doing on your part (it is not for me to remind you of it, madam), if you, in fact, like the idea of leaving my house . . . there is nothing left for me to say, but that you made a mistake in not carrying out your design when it was the fitting moment.

If you have forgotten how many years ago, I will help you. . . ."

I glanced at Alexandra Mihalovna, she was leaning on me and clutching convulsively at me, helpless with inward agony, half closing her eyes in intense misery. Another minute and she would have been ready to drop.

"Oh, for God's sake, if only this once, spare her! Don't say the last word," I cried, flinging myself on my knees before Pyotr Alexandrovitch, and forgetting that I was betraying myself; but it was too late. A faint scream greeted my words, and the poor woman fell senseless on the floor.

"It is all over! You have killed her," I said. "Call the servants, save her! I will wait for you in your study. I must speak to you; I will tell you all. . . ."

"But what? But what?"

"Afterwards!"

The fainting and hysterics lasted two hours. The whole household was alarmed. The doctor shook his head dubiously. Two hours later I went into Pyotr Alexandrovitch's study. He had only just come back from his wife, and was walking up and down the room, pale and distracted, biting his nails till they bled. I had never seen him in such a state.

"What do you want to say to me?" he said in a harsh coarse voice. "You wanted to say something?"

"Here is the letter you found in my possession. Do you recognise it?"

"Yes."

"Take it."

He took the letter and raised it to the light. I watched him attentively. A few minutes later, he turned quickly to the fourth page and read the signature. I saw the blood rush to his head.

"What's this?" he asked me, petrified with amazement.

"It's three years ago that I found that letter in a book. I guessed that it was forgotten, I read it and learned everything. From that time forth it has been in my possession because I had no one to whom to give it. I could not give it to her. Could I to you? But you must have known the contents of this letter, and all the sorrowful story in it. . . . What your pretending is for, I don't know. That is for the present dark to me. I cannot yet see clearly into your dark soul. You wanted to keep up your superiority over her, and have done so. But for what object? To triumph over a phantom, over a

357

sick woman's unhinged imagination, to prove to her that she has erred and you are more sinless than she! And you have attained your aim, for this suspicion of hers is the fixed idea of a failing brain, perhaps, the last plaint of a heart broken against the injustice of men's verdict, with which you were at one. 'What does it matter if you have fallen in love with her?' That is what she said, that is what she wanted to show you. Your vanity, your jealous egoism have been merciless. Good-bye! No need to explain! But mind, I know you, I see through you. Don't forget that!"

I went to my own room, scarcely knowing what was happening to me. At the door I was stopped by Ovrov, Pyotr Alexandrovich's secretary.

"I should like to have a word with you," he said with a respectful bow.

I looked at him, scarcely understanding what he said to me.

"Afterwards. Excuse me, I am not well," I answered at last, passing him.

"To-morrow then," he said, bowing with an ambiguous smile.

But perhaps that was my fancy. All this seemed to flit before my eyes.

Q5